Love in the New Millennium

Foreword by Eileen Myles

Translated from the Chinese by
Annelise Finegan Wasmoen

Yale UNIVERSITY PRESS | NEW HAVEN AND LONDON

A MARGELLOS
WORLD REPUBLIC OF LETTERS BOOK

Can Xue

Love
in the New
Millennium

The Margellos World Republic of Letters is dedicated to
making literary works from around the globe available in English
through translation. It brings to the English-speaking world the work
of leading poets, novelists, essayists, philosophers, and playwrights
from Europe, Latin America, Africa, Asia, and the Middle East to
stimulate international discourse and creative exchange.

Yale University Press books may be purchased in quantity for educational,
business, or promotional use. For information, please e-mail sales.press@yale
.edu (U.S. office) or sales@yaleup.co.uk (U.K. office).

Set in Scala and Joanna types by
Tseng Information Systems, Inc., Durham, North Carolina.

Printed in the United States of America.

Library of Congress Control Number: 2018938630
ISBN 978-0-300-22431-3 (hardcover : alk. paper)

A catalogue record for this book is available from the British Library.

This paper meets the requirements of ANSI/NISO Z39.48-1992
(Permanence of Paper).

10 9 8 7 6 5 4 3 2 1

BOOKS BY CAN XUE IN ENGLISH TRANSLATION

Love in the New Millennium

Frontier

Vertical Motion: Stories

The Last Lover

Five Spice Street

Blue Light in the Sky and Other Stories

The Embroidered Shoes: Stories

Old Floating Cloud: Two Novellas

Dialogues in Paradise

Contents

Foreword

INSIDE CAN XUE
Eileen Myles

"Have you always treated the whole world as your home, Fourth Uncle?"
"Not the whole world—I'm always wandering nearby."

Books have lighting I think. And I speak as a dedicated and conflicted reader lured hopelessly from the page by television and the entire history of film available *now* on various sites—yet some books drop me nicely in the middle—right in between the modes of reading and watching, to live alongside me in the dilemma.

Can Xue's *Love in the New Millennium* is lit a lot like Tarkovsky's *Solaris*. The astronaut wanders through the weeds and trees of his dacha before he heads off on his voyage. Yet he is already gone. We are leaving the earth but *that* is the earth. This crazy nostalgic light. I mean it's not exactly that. Maybe it's that light of uncanniness that follows our departure from the movie theater during the day, maybe *that's* the version of lighting or reality that Can Xue's book shares with film. I also think of Fellini's *Satyricon* and the ancient mode of storytelling in which a character begins to speak and the film darts swiftly after them down the rabbit hole of the story. In Can Xue's *Love* all the characters are connected to each other. There's no one story I can tell. And they are laughing about it too. At their own inconstancy, their changeability.

At the outset, you meet Cuilan, a widow, so you think it's about her. No . . . but it's way more about her lover Wei Bo. Wei Bo appears at her door to say that something has come up and he can't keep their date. Weeks pass and he never returns. Cuilan treks off mournfully to her ancestral home. Her relatives (who have all become mysteriously mangled and wizened since the last time she saw them) are hardly welcoming. Then they begin speaking about Wei Bo. Which feels inside out, but the world already is. The countryside is destroyed. In the relatives' house there's an ambient estranged type of hearing that's become commonplace here. People chattering out the window, there's a banging upstairs even if there isn't an upstairs. At night her relatives are in a tree fighting and laughing and one falls, hits the ground with a thud. She goes out to investigate and everything goes silent at once. Next day (while practically pushing her out the door) her cousin offers this, "Our daytime and nighttime are two completely different days. If you always lived here and never left you'd be able to sense this. It's too bad you won't have the chance."

Cuilan goes home and is soon walking down the city streets, empty-hearted, when Mr. You, a creep (who later turns marvelous), steps up. He's been interested in her for a while, and seeing her dejected state he happily calls out: "Can this candidate enter the field now?" As well as being a relentless pursuer of women, Mr. You deals in rare antiques, especially these very wonderful ancient vases which morph into cavernous spaces—a metonym it seems to me for a vagina, which might just be the shape of this world. Time and again the narrative tips us off to the fact that reality is intrinsically female. Women *are* connected, women have friends. When he discovers a pair of women, A Liang and Xiao Lan, hiding in a cabinet in his shop (just having a conversation) we learn the salient fact about Mr. You's antique artifacts, which is that they are all alive. That is this antiquarian's secret. And the broadest interpretation of his lust.

> Mr. You . . . asked, staring into her face, "In your opinion, does this vase signify nobility?"
>
> "Of course. I can tell that it's dark and deep inside. Listen, doves' wings fluttering!"
>
> She placed the mouth of the vase to her ear. . . .
>
> "The vases . . . fit doves in them. The vase appears small when it's actually vast inside—vast to an extent we cannot imagine, so we need an appraiser of treasures like you to measure it."

Is it praise of his knowledge or is it flirtation. Soon we are back out on the street. We're thinking of Wei Bo again who incidentally is married. Xiao Yuan is Wei Bo's ex-wife. Their children are grown, their love is depleted. Yet they are friends, even admire each other. In regards love everyone here is immensely practical and ready to go. Xiao Yuan is a teacher who is obsessed with timepieces that she takes with her on her enigmatic trips. Lying on her bunk on a train she announces aloud, "I like to travel. Making a journey is the same as clinging to one place. If you settle down in your hometown, it feels instead as though you are drifting along." Later the young man listening from the bunk overhead rolls over, falling dead on the floor. There's a loud sound followed by some bureaucratic fuss and finally there's nothing left but a bad smell. On the same voyage Xiao Yuan meets an old man who makes cricket sounds so well he makes her laugh. And then he explains that he has become a timepiece himself. She feels his wrist and it is indeed a clock. All his life he has wanted someone to hear his heart and Xiao Yuan does and it is indeed keeping time. They joke about the inevitability of death.

> "I've always wanted to make someone hear my heartbeat, and now I've succeeded. I'm so glad, knowing that you heard."
> Yet his expression was not glad. He seemed to be waiting for something, gloomily.
> "The time is two-ten and twenty seconds," he said.
> "Correct. She's coming over," Xiao Yuan said.
> "Who?"
> "That thing that has an appointment with you."
> "Ah yes, she's coming!" He began to laugh.

Xiao Yuan's journey takes her to a county town (Nest) for a new teaching job and also to get closer to Dr. Liu, though in a few days she begins wondering if it would be "more real" if the "central role" were played instead by one of her fellows, Teacher Zhong.

I mean, sure, Dr. Liu *is* a little unavailable, but there's a sense here too that everyone is just singing a song, waving a hand, and having a next thought about how else the drama of their life might unfold. There's always time for that.

Also ages change fluidly. Because everyone's preparing for dying. A janitor, who had fallen to the floor outside Dr. Liu's office and curled into a ball, explains, "I want to go for a walk inside the ancient city walls, otherwise I cannot close my eyes in death." It seems like an old man's final wish, simple enough, yet the word "inside" has a shifting purpose here. Dr. Liu wonders whether Old Man Yu (who he is learning from) actually came from "inside." Is this related to the boundless world inside a vase. Is it like the inside of a house perpetually penetrated by outside? Isn't prison inside. Here in Dr. Liu's office it indicates perhaps a spiritual rightness, in reference to healing, but it also expresses the versatility of nature and how aptly technology may pierce it. We grow accustomed to the warm philosophical thoughts of Dr. Liu: "He believed needles entering the body were sounding the universe. No need to fear the divide of mountains and rivers—the distance would vanish in an instant. Many years of practice led him to believe this more and more deeply."

Dr. Liu explains his own confirmed bachelorhood as the result of trying to see everything dimensionally, and if you looked at marriage that way you'd never enter. Though it seems that right about now he will. At her new job Xiao Yuan discovers that the children she teaches know everything already about the Gobi Desert. Why is she going on, her students ask the other teachers. Children, especially in Nest, are the most magical beings of all. They throw seeds wildly on the ground and grow rapturous gardens because they know how to wait. Adults are busily making rules against owning mice and a small boy quietly goes about making a home for each one of his. Little Rose, one of Xiao Yuan's students, wanders off into the forest at night and her teacher follows to protect her, getting herself lost. The child is okay. All the children are fine. Teacher Zhong (the one Xiao Yuan's considered falling in love with) advises her to relax with the children and "join a collective absentmindedness. Just think, it would be excellent communication!"

Back in the city Cuilan is moving with a group of mostly middle-aged women (Long Sixiang, Jin Zhu, A Si) who all worked together for a long time at a cotton mill, but today they are sex workers. Cuilan is teetering. Her friends hook up with men at a spa, a few of the lucky ones wind up living with their lovers at the Mandarin Ducks Suites. The spa, by the way, is where Cuilan met Wei Bo. She didn't like him. She thought he was a jerk.

From the Mandarin Ducks Suites you can see the prison where Wei Bo has mysteriously begun living. Though sometimes you can't see the prison. And you don't necessarily go there because of a *crime*. Perhaps the most interesting thing about the prison is the huge tree behind it that resembles the one behind Cuilan's ancestral home. Is it the same place. Few know what crimes they are in there for. Trying to get the picture, Wei Bo asks his fellows, "Then what sort of people should stay in prison?" "People like us, more dead than alive, always indecisive. We ought to stay here. I think Lao Lu stays here more for us than for himself."

The "real" time of the book is unusual. Everyone seems to be outside their life, on a day off, in prison, or on a trip—forever. Yet people eagerly clamor—everywhere they go—in the city streets at night in order to collectively compose the immense play of social reality.

To talk, perhaps? There is no small talk, no phatic. It's emphatic all the time.

In *Love in the New Millennium* everyone is a wit, especially children, and everyone has thought deeply about things. The surface is deep. To speak in operatic utterances is the norm. They have great names: Mr. You, Fourth Uncle, Little Rose, a vagrant is named Long Hair. A cabdriver arrives at exactly the right moment to hiss at his passenger: "Your problem is written on your face. The answer is inside my taxi. Get in the car."

Part of the difficulty of reading *Love* is I couldn't stop tweeting passages. To be a reader was to become a trailer, or to become an actor too. It's irresistible, the way one enters this laughable shifting no time that everyone inside is talking about like the weather. It's also very boring, as a plotless book is. A circling nonbuilding narrative gets tiring. What's the pleasure, then? *Humor* and *surprise*. It's a frankly poetic existence. Plus my reader's sense of awe grew continually at the endless refillability of the thing. The book is a vase, it's a form.

It's just that light I mean, which is plot, endless circling pink streams of never-ending plot. Or no plot. Wei Bo "thought of his own life, a tangle of string." This guy who does not know what he's doing is the through-line. There's a matter-of-fact instrumentality about self in this book. One is as wry about existence as existence seems to be about the humans that occupy it and eagerly fill the pages of its novels.

I first heard about Can Xue's work in the aughts, and on the advice of another wonderful novelist, Laurie Weeks (*Zipper Mouth*), I picked up a copy of Can Xue's *Dialogues in Paradise*—the stories in it were accompanied by a single memoir, in which the writer, a married woman with kids, described writing by hand in notebooks after dinner, after a day of exhausting labor working alongside her husband tailoring clothes. The memoir made manifest the distinct experience of growing up during the Cultural Revolution when people entirely ill-prepared for hard physical labor discovered suddenly that that had become their lot. Can Xue told about living an impoverished childhood in the countryside with an inventive and ebullient father and a grandmother who explained to the author the magical fairy tales of the earth. This same grandmother starved to death, though we're told it may've been for the best. She was sixty. In both books one is confronted by the fact that bodily hardship and labor can produce surreal conditions similar to the Rimbaudian "disorganization of the senses" that my own writing world tried to manifest in our poetry and fiction. Can Xue's work proposes most astonishingly to me that starvation and suffering also get you high, visionary and even playful. Work, astonishingly hard work, is part of this writer's kit.

The factory, that cotton mill that we hear so much about in this present book, the back-breaking place that women escaped from to become unlikely yet considerably happier middle-aged whores, is the unforgettable setting for the book's final moments.

A Si, the youngest of the group (and herself an ex of Wei Bo), climbs a tree and breaks into the now bankrupt and abandoned factory. Going up its damaged staircases she finds an old man, Hong Sheng, gleefully poring over a ledger. He was once the receptionist at the factory. He greets A Si like this.

> "I lost my job. I built this loft to live in myself. I want to record the history of the cotton mill. Did you know this factory has a hundred-and-fifty-year history?" A Si watched his face with its tree-bark skin while she shook her head.
>
> "I've written almost up to your generation. You, and Long Sixiang, Jin Zhu, Xiao Yan . . . I gave you the name 'lovebirds.' You are the lovebirds who flew away from this hell. Even though I've grown old, I'm excited every time I hear news about Miss Si. You are the pride of the cotton mill workers."
>
> He pulled a large notebook out of the desk drawer, paged through it for a few seconds, then shut it again with a thwack. The path of his thoughts seemed to be broken off, as he started in again from a different point. . . .
>
> "Miss Si, you belong to the earliest group to jump into the sea of business. I've already recorded some of your deeds. The spinning mill will vanish from this earth, but history cannot disappear. This hellish workshop cultivated outstanding women like you. It's truly a human miracle. You lovebird, now you fly higher and higher. You will not fall so easily, will you?"

That Can Xue, a female novelist, is placing these words in the mouth of a derelict male historian is so upending. In such a momentary and provisional space as a book, this book! It's Mr. You all over again and his vases—all the serious men in Can Xue's world are eagerly studying womankind. This time he's a classicist, in his way, at work.

It's a lovely, very cinematic moment that gets undone swiftly. Such arcades are made for smashing. Four patrolling bureaucrats with helmets and sticks barge in, charging both of them with wrongdoing. And almost at once their ludicrous presence and their accusations start magically taking the building down. And the skin on the historian's face begins to peel. It's falling away like a mask, like bark. It is all simply a bad and wondrous dream. Or a movie.

"Were you and this person trying to reverse the verdict of history?"

A Si didn't answer, because she honestly didn't know.

"Huh, even if he's hiding in hell," they go, "I'll catch him. He actually dares to construct historical incidents! Look at these rotten boards." These "cops" are so obviously on the wrong side of things. They are not inside at all.

A Si took a final look at the cotton mill and felt empty. She remembered what Hong Sheng had said and understood what he meant in speaking the word "history." Wasn't history an event that repeated unforgettably in the mind?

Then she does what anyone would. She goes to a café and calls her friends on her cell. The scene shifts from epic to pop. The girlfriends are laughing together at A Si's crazy story about Uncle Hong's history project. Their lightheartedness suggests they might even be a little bit ashamed to be written up as sex workers now. The undoing of the manuscript for them is a delight. "It turns out this is also history. Fortunately it's been destroyed!" In the coffee shop a strange tall girl waiting on them looks like she's in high school. Now she's part of it too! Her name is Silver, a perfectly good name for someone young who's actually old.

"I am that history," she said to A Si, a thread of a bitter smile on her face.

"What history?" A Si asked her.

"The history of the cotton mill. Don't believe my outer appearance, I am thirty-five years old. I also used to be at the cotton mill. One day I suddenly thought and saw clearly, and I became history. Isn't history thinking and seeing clearly? Don't the two of you agree?" She stuck the candle to the table. No one answered her question. . . .

"Silver, you've left your suffering behind, how wonderful," A Si said.

Then they all walk to the river. Of course. We are still in the inarguable logic of dreams. Silver explains to the others that she is also a prostitute. We're in another kind of inside. Silver simply says, "I prefer to follow my heart and do as I please." They are all standing on the riverbank and there are couples in the water loudly fighting. Because there is always a sound and then another.

Fortunately the boom mike is right *here*.

> "Why are these people standing in the river? I sense they are unwell."
>
> "They don't have our good fortune, they haven't become history yet. It takes suffering and waiting."

People loved that line when I put it on Twitter. And there's just a little bit more:

> "You are saying your history, Silver. I am listening," A Si said gently.

Acknowledgments

I would like first to thank this book's translator, Annelise Finegan Wasmoen. Her magnificent literary talent and her childlike and pure sense of humor renew the artistic performance of Can Xue's fiction. While reading this English version I have myself been deeply moved.

I would also like to thank this book's publisher, John Donatich. I believe that his passion for literature and profound insights, and his support from the beginning to today, has brought great courage to my life of literature. Especially in a world where the influence of literature is becoming weaker and weaker.

I think of this book as the fruit born of the love between Eastern and Western cultures, its images pushing forward a wholly new type of human self and mechanism of freedom.

Can Xue

With gratitude to Can Xue and to everyone at Yale University Press.

As always this translation would never have happened without the editorial eye of Nikolaus, who understands.

AFW

Love in the New Millennium

ONE

Cuilan and Wei Bo

The widow Niu Cuilan rose before the sky was light to wash, comb her hair, and dress because today her lover Wei Bo would probably come to see her. Cuilan was thirty-five years old, in what she believed to be a woman's best time of life. Her husband had died eight years earlier. Wei Bo was forty-eight. He worked in a soap factory, although he was well-educated for an unskilled worker.

Cuilan and Wei Bo had met a year before at a hot spring spa that offered sex among its services. Cuilan had gone to bathe in the hot springs. After she finished soaking she climbed out languidly, went to the changing room to put on her clothing, and got ready to go home. It was still early. The customers appeared and disappeared like ghosts in the steam. Some of them bumped her elbows suggestively. Cuilan, filled with destructive rage, spat on the ground after them. That was when she caught sight of Wei Bo, furtive and louche in a plum-colored workout shirt. She knew at once what he had come here for and snickered, saying to herself, What's he thinking, wearing workout clothes to a place like this?

As they brushed shoulders in the narrow hallway (he was heading toward the "special services" area), Cuilan shoved Wei Bo viciously with her elbow, so hard that he shouted and stuck close to the wall.

Who could have known that the man on his way to the prostitutes would become Cuilan's lover? Wei Bo later told her that he had gone to the spa that day for its sex services, but when he left, his mind was not emptied, as it usually was, of all desire. Instead he felt distracted. He quickly realized the cause. He went to the reception hall to find out Cuilan's contact information, asking around until he made his way to her apartment. The two experts went right to bed and had a good time, leaving their bodies covered in sweat.

Wei Bo had a family. He also had a few illicit sources of "gray income" that let him escape to places like the hot spring spa every now and then. He was fairly potent, in that regard, and skillful. At first Cuilan had been satisfied with her new life. She discarded the other partners she'd had and cheerfully enjoyed this new passion. As for Wei Bo himself, she could not claim to be infatuated, but she felt that having this one lover was enough. She was particular about the quality of her sex life. Wei Bo usually came to see her two or three times a month.

Over time, Cuilan came to see Wei Bo as her underground husband. She was an independent woman who thought it only right to have an underground husband. Wasn't this what life was all about? It was only right to have some happiness. His full name was Wei Siqiang, or Wei Four Powers, a vulgar name. Since he acted mature for his age, everyone had started calling him Uncle Wei, or Wei Bo, when he turned thirty. Cuilan especially liked to call him Wei Bo.

Cuilan hurried through breakfast, tidied the apartment's two bedrooms and living room until they were completely clean, then retouched her eyeliner in the mirror. She felt a little nervy today, for no apparent reason, and jumped with alarm whenever she heard the sound of steps in the hallway, believing her lover had arrived. Every time it was her neighbors passing, and not him. She was disappointed by her loss of dignity. Cuilan had never thought that she was the kind of woman to simper or ingratiate herself with men. She walked over to the refrigerator and opened it, took out a few mangoes, washed them, peeled the skins, and ate. Her hands and face were soiled, ruining her tasteful makeup. Still irritated, she didn't touch up the makeup. She wanted Wei Bo to see the real Cuilan.

It was almost noon when someone cautiously knocked four times on the door. It was him. Cuilan's mind filled with suspicion because she had not heard Wei Bo's footsteps. Was he trying to play a trick on her? She looked at the man, remembering the hellish suffering of her morning, and was suddenly all out of ideas.

"Cuilan, I came to tell you that I have to go right away. Something important at home."

His face had a look of genuine honesty.

"You might have called," Cuilan said apprehensively.

"Called?" He seemed surprised. "Would calling be right? That's no way to treat you. Aren't we a couple? I love you."

4

He had to go as soon as he finished saying this, and so he did.

As though in a dream Cuilan sat for a long time motionless at the table. Her emotions had been strained to a high pitch since early morning. Her behavior was inexplicable. She remembered how she had looked at herself in the mirror repeatedly, rapidly changed the way she was wearing her hair, twice, and even wiped off her makeup. Now, though, all that waiting had brought was this man's two-minute layover. He had seemed restless, so much so that he failed to look at her face even once. Something important must have happened at home. Cuilan tried not to guess what it was. She never went looking for trouble. Oh, today she really was down on her luck. A whole day off wasted, and tomorrow she would have to go back to the gauges and meters factory where she was a warehouse clerk.

The next day Cuilan worked overtime at the factory and came home late, so she went to a small noodle shop called Heaven on Earth instead of making dinner. The restaurant was on a street near her home. Since it was already late, only two or three customers were there when she entered, and they soon got up to leave. She sat by herself in a corner, which suited her. Before long her peace was shattered.

The glass door of the noodle shop was kicked open with a bang. A slick, over-dressed dandy, a man Cuilan recognized as one of the city's antiques appraisers, followed. She had never seen him behave so rudely. The man, whose surname was You, greeted Cuilan and sat down opposite her. She eyed the street through the window. She didn't want to talk, because she was tired and not in a very good mood.

"Have you been to the spa recently? They've added a premium service called a fish bath where a school of little fish nibble the dirt off of your body. A very original way to relax."

Mr. You showed two rows of snow-white teeth as he talked. Cuilan thought he looked like a wolfhound. She snorted without answering, thinking he was trying to provoke her.

"Someone you know was in the pool with me yesterday."

At this moment Cuilan's mushroom and vegetable noodles arrived. She buried her face in her food.

"Aren't you interested in what I was going to tell you?" Mr. You watched her attentively.

"No, not at all!"

Cuilan stood as she answered and went to pay her bill at the counter. She heard Mr. You's plaintive sigh behind her, but with an effort she kept from looking at him, even though she was curious. Mr. You might be staring at her at this very moment. She felt a pain in her back as though she were being stabbed by needles.

Niu Cuilan resolved to get her life back on the right track. What she called the right track was the relatively calm existence she'd enjoyed before taking a regular lover. There had been a few other flings, but ending things was as easy as saying so afterward. She had never believed herself to be the type of person who can't make a clean break. The affair with Wei Bo was good enough, but it was nothing she could eat. People still have to eat, and they have to seek out other pleasures. Besides, nothing had happened. There had never been anything between them. A brief affair between lovers, as temporary as the dew, was best. Two months had passed since that day off without Wei Bo reappearing. Cuilan noticed her calmness. She was so calm it surprised her.

The work at the instrument factory was monotonous and untaxing, as hardly needs saying. Her relationships with her coworkers were neither warm nor cold. Cuilan's sole amusement was bathing in the hot springs, but the city's only spa was also a brothel. Her distaste was not strong enough to repulse her, so she decided to go back on a Sunday. She thought it would be all right as long as she didn't run into Mr. You.

That Saturday night she had a dream. She saw herself swimming the breaststroke in the hot spring pool when she caught hold of someone's foot. She stood up, frightened, and looked into the surrounding mists, seeing someone in the bamboo plants on the other side who called to her, "Niu Cuilan! Niu Cuilan!"

She dashed into the changing room, put on her clothes, glanced at her watch, and saw that it was two in the morning. She couldn't remember why she had come to the hot springs at this hour. She passed through the reception hall to the entrance, but the door was shut and locked. Terror struck her heart. She dripped with cold sweat. At this instant, the silhouette of a man appeared. To her surprise, it was Wei Bo. Cuilan forced a smile that was not a smile and said, "Are you here to get your fill? Good! Who can help me open the front door?"

Wei Bo said he would find someone, then changed direction and went into the main building. Cuilan sat down in a lounge chair beside the walkway. She waited a long time without seeing anyone and almost fell asleep. Then, suddenly, someone shot an arm around her waist from behind, holding her in place. Cuilan saw a plum-colored workout shirt swaying in front of her eyes. She struggled for her life, shouting "Help!" At this moment she woke up.

She almost cancelled her plan to go to the spa because of this bizarre dream, but, after delaying until nine, she went anyway.

There weren't many customers on the women's side of the hot spring pool, just three women who lay on their backs like corpses floating on the surface of the water. For a moment Cuilan thought one of them actually was a corpse. The woman lay motionless, her stomach distended, protruding. Cuilan kept from screaming with difficulty. Before long, though, she heard their loud voices, and realized all three women knew each other. Cuilan felt relieved. She sat down and leaned against the side of the pool, half-closing her eyes in enjoyment. The pool was well-designed, with running water, a thick layer of fine sand spread at the bottom, and beautiful scholartrees planted beside it.

Cuilan's whole body relaxed as she listened to the women. At first she didn't understand, then, gradually, she made out the main features of their conversation. They were talking about a prostitute who was leaving to get married. The three women worked at a cotton mill where they did heavy labor. They envied the young woman, who had worked at the same factory before becoming a prostitute, then spent only four years at the spa before retiring. They had heard that a group of men were helping her buy real estate in an apartment complex.

Cuilan fell asleep listening to them talk. All of a sudden she was startled awake by the two syllables *Wei Bo*. Raising her eyes, she saw the three women just getting out of the water and moving toward the changing room. Cuilan wondered, Could they be talking about Wei Bo? Had Wei Bo helped the young woman from the cotton mill buy an apartment? Was Wei Bo capable of this? She vaguely remembered hearing him say he had another job, one that was profitable. At the time she'd thought he was trying to show off and nothing more. "Gray income" was everywhere now. Cuilan didn't need Wei Bo's money. There was no financial relationship between them.

A feeling of dejection overcame her. She was here to rest, but instead she heard news about Wei Bo. Last night's strange dream had been the same. It was as though the entire spa belonged to him. More people began to fill the pool. Cuilan gloomily climbed onto the edge.

When she reached the main entrance she carefully studied the door, trying to remember her dream. She looked it up and down, feeling that this was not the door in the dream. Someone spoke behind her.

"I am certain the emotion is real. None of the others believe in this kind of thing."

It was one of the women from the cotton mill, the one who'd lain in the pool with her stomach swelling like a drum.

Cuilan smiled at her, as if they knew each other.

"My name is Long Sixiang. I've seen you here a few times, you're Niu Cuilan. Do you come here looking for sympathy, like those of us who work at the mill? My two friends and I have been coming here a lot recently. We want to work in the 'special services,' but everyone thinks we're too old. We all know Wei Bo, he gets people to like him. We've heard him talk about you."

"What did he say about me?"

"He says you're a virtuous woman. My friends and I are the fair maiden type, too, but we don't want to be. We realized too late that we'd rather be fallen women. Now no one will take us on because we're old."

"I want to be fallen, too!" The words escaped Cuilan's lips. "It's too bad, I'm also too old."

"I know what you mean. All the women Wei Bo falls for are like this. He insists that you're virtuous, but I never believe what he says. Besides, would a virtuous woman come to a place like this?"

Long Sixiang, whose name Sixiang meant "homesick," rolled her eyes as she spoke, as if she were trying to suppress some repulsive memory. Cuilan didn't think she was very attractive, but had to admit that the talkative woman's way of speaking made her somehow charming.

"So you and Wei Bo have an arrangement, too?" Cuilan asked, in a joking manner.

"No," Long Sixiang shook her head sadly. "I want to, but he only thinks of Miss Si. An old cow prefers young seedlings. I heard he's gone into debt for her."

They walked a way together and then parted. Cuilan found in Long Sixiang a woman much to her own taste. She planned to stay in contact with her if she could.

Returning home, Cuilan became increasingly confused. Why had Wei Bo's ghost been troubling her for the past two days? Hadn't she accepted what had happened to their relationship? A worker at a soap factory had been involved with her, for a time, but now their affinity was at an end, leaving each to seek his or her own pleasure. That was just how it was. She hadn't even thought of Wei Bo before going to the hot springs. She was only anxious about seeing Mr. You from the antiques shop there. It was clear, then, that Wei Bo was no longer in her heart. Yet he would not let her be, whether in dreams or broad daylight. From what Long Sixiang had said, Wei Bo was popular with women and must be skilled in dealing with them.

When Cuilan was newly widowed a number of men pursued her. She thought of herself as selfish for not wanting to sacrifice anything for these men, so she remained unmarried. Living alone for so long, even if she was not entirely free to do whatever she wanted, had not done her any harm. Wei Bo was a little better than other men, of course, but not to the extent that she wanted to hang herself on his tree. She didn't need to lean on anyone. What was the matter with the women who worked at the cotton mill? They all wanted to be prostitutes, and they all liked Wei Bo. It seemed Wei Bo was no ordinary person. Cuilan's thoughts wound back and forth, always revolving around him.

With these thoughts heavy on her mind, she ate dinner, washed the dishes, and saw that it was already dark outside. A few children ran back and forth across the window of her apartment. The vendors selling wontons in the market cried their wares. The streetlights in front of the dormitory where she lived began to turn on; a group of people gathered in their dim light. They sat there every day, although they never played mahjong or chatted with each other. Over the years Cuilan had thought that they came outside to sit at the side of the road because they felt lonely staying at home. They faced Cuilan's window. She had never minded before, treating them like so many wooden posts. Today, for some reason, she did not want them to see her, so she closed the window and went to sit in the bedroom at the back.

There was nothing to do in the bedroom, after she sorted her purse, but it was too early to go to sleep. Her gaze was drawn to the picture of a beautiful woman on the wall, a close-up of a film actress she liked. She had sensed the woman on the wall watching her, even turning her face toward her. Yet when she looked at the photograph directly, this was not the case.

When Cuilan was almost asleep she was still thinking, Did Mr. You know every detail of her life?

Wei Bo had not stolen away to Cuilan's place for some time. He happened to meet one of her ex-boyfriends at a party. The boyfriend somehow knew Wei Bo's secret, coming right up to him and talking about Cuilan. He said she was "the epitome of evil and extremely violent." She was a woman who opened her eyes when she saw money. He warned Wei Bo that it would be dangerous to continue the relationship. Wei Bo was shocked and refused to believe him. Then Cuilan's ex-boyfriend pulled out a dirty, wrinkled letter and showed it to him. The handwriting on the paper belonged to Cuilan. She ordered this man to transfer 20,000 yuan to her bank account, to serve as "a fee for the loss of my youth." Menacing threats followed.

Wei Bo read the letter through and studied it over once again. There could be no mistake, Cuilan had written it. His heart contracted. He dripped with cold sweat.

"Is this why you broke things off with her?" he asked.

"No, I didn't want to break up with her. I sent her the money, intending to continue the relationship. What did she do? She sent criminals who threatened to kill me."

Wei Bo discovered that as the man told his story his expression grew distracted, and he even smiled sweetly from time to time. He didn't seem embarrassed at all. Wei Bo suspected that he was mentally ill. He suddenly grabbed both of Wei Bo's hands and said eagerly, "Do you think there's still hope for me? You can judge objectively. Tell me, do I still have hope? I have another 20,000 yuan ready, and I'll send it to her if there's any hope."

The man's hands felt ice-cold and sticky. Wei Bo tried to withdraw his hands but couldn't free them. He, too, became nervy. He answered vaguely, "I don't know. How would I know? You'll know best. A distant relative of mine, a nephew, murdered someone because he was in love. It was meaningless. Don't you think so? Being in love is wonderful. How many times in a person's life can such a beautiful thing happen? Hmm?"

His answer disappointed Cuilan's ex-boyfriend. He indignantly let go of Wei Bo's hands.

The party was at a coworker's home, and no one noticed their conversation among the general noise. Wei Bo wanted to move to another seat, so he stood up and went to the bathroom. When he came back the ex-boyfriend was nowhere to be seen. Wei Bo sighed with relief and sat back down. When he raised his head he saw an uninvited guest push open the door of the room. It was Mr. You from the antiques shop. Wei Bo recognized him, although they didn't know each other well. Mr. You walked straight up to Wei Bo and sat down at his side. As soon as he opened his mouth Wei Bo was startled, because he spoke as if he were a close friend.

"Love has been an unlucky pursuit recently. There's a feeling of having reached the ends of the earth. I believe you know this from experience. Ah, women, the world is endlessly happy because of them. Don't you think so?"

The fragrance wafting from Mr. You's body made Wei Bo lightheaded.

"Where are the women? I can never find them! Look how many enchanting ladies there are in this room, but when the party ends, they vanish. Sometimes I wake up in the middle of the night and look out the window. From where I live on the third floor I can see an army of women passing by, marching from the west to the east. Each of them walks in an alluring way. Ms. Niu Cuilan is one of them."

Mr. You began to laugh, showing his beastly white teeth. Wei Bo creased his brow in disgust.

He couldn't stand this freakish, dandified man anymore. He said goodbye to the host. As he stood up to leave Mr. You hung his head and looked completely dejected.

Wei Bo broke up with Cuilan after this party. Sometimes he felt the way he had chosen to break things off was extremely tactful. Sometimes he thought he had behaved despicably. In either case there was one thing Wei Bo could not figure out: was he really separated from her or not? He had a vague feeling that the question was not so simple; Cuilan was not the sort of woman he could break up with just because he felt like it. Wei Bo had known this from their first meeting, and it was the reason he was trying to break up with her. He tried to examine his own heart. Wei Bo believed himself to be unusual. He always liked to play at this game of examination.

Wei Bo's relationship with his wife was a type of superficial indifference, a kind of gentlemen's agreement in which each side had secrets, although both were careful to keep the family peace. Their two sons lived away from home, so the family only reunited when they brought their wives and children to visit on holidays. In Wei Bo's view, his wife also needed to be examined. He was not examining her, naturally, but rather his own views about her. She was a middle school teacher, well-educated, who spoke indirectly enough to make her meaning impossible to follow. They had fallen in love at first sight at a very young age and tied the knot, with a passion that lasted seven or eight years. Later on their relationship cooled by degrees, as they grew estranged, probably because they knew each other too well.

Wei Bo discovered, although he was not sure when exactly, that he was popular with women. In any group of women, from the young to the mature, a few would respond to him. Wei Bo was sensitive and circumspect, so he eventually began having affairs with them. His conduct was well-concealed and had never been exposed so far.

Niu Cuilan was his fourth lover, give or take. She excited him, although he was not sure what specifically he liked about her, when he thought about it. He had gone to the hot springs that day to see his young mistress and discovered new prey instead. He was caught unawares—it made his head spin. What happened afterward proved that the new romance was extraordinary, in that he abandoned his younger lover to the back of his mind for an entire month. While he was involved with Cuilan, he would say to himself, Oh, Wei Bo, can't you stop your head from spinning? Your life is already a mess! Without knowing why, he kept trying to escape and go back to his old way of life.

Wei Bo sat at home balancing his accounts (he did the accounting for both jobs at once). He worked away for a while, then stopped and stared into space for a while, recalling his relationship with Cuilan and its shameful end. He was the one who had behaved shamefully; his baseness was original. Her ex-boyfriend had confused him, of course, but he was not why Wei Bo decided to break things off with Cuilan. Wei Bo was not gullible enough to think he understood the relationship between that man and Cuilan. Had he wanted to separate from Cuilan because they knew each other too well (the same as with his wife)? That was not the whole of it. On further thought, the most likely reason was that hedonism had gotten the better of him. Wei Bo was afraid of being hurt. Once he had actually fainted when he cut his arm. He was a coward, soft at heart, apt to be spoiled by the female sex.

When Wei Bo finally finished his accounts night was falling. He reheated leftovers from lunch, ate them, and cleaned the kitchen. He saw a silhouette looking in at the window.

"Who is it?" Wei Bo asked, lowering his voice.

"It's me, Mr. You from the antiques shop. Quick, open the door. It's urgent!"

Mr. You came in with a flustered expression, pulled over a chair, and sat down without waiting for an invitation.

"Your wife isn't home?"

"She's not here. What is it?" Wei Bo felt his heart pounding.

"Wei Bo, are you still in a relationship with Ms. Niu Cuilan? I know you don't want to answer. I need to tell you that Cuilan is working as a prostitute at the spa. A good friend of hers, my lover, told me personally. Cuilan said she wanted to learn sex techniques there."

Wei Bo saw him show his beastly white teeth and felt involuntary disgust.

"My wife will be home soon," he said.

Mr. You glared at Wei Bo and walked to the door, then turned back and screamed, "The world is in chaos! The world is in chaos! Women are vanishing off the face of the earth! When you go outside at night all you can see are black crows!"

He left. The room was as quiet as if he had never been there.

Wei Bo sank into deep thought. Who was this Mr. You? Why was Mr. You sinking his teeth into him? Wei Bo had to admit that Mr. You had brought him shattering news. Of course, he could have been lying. One thing was clear: Mr. You knew about Wei Bo and Cuilan's affair, was keeping an eye on him, and would not let go. Was he another of Cuilan's lovers?

Wei Bo had seen this man just yesterday. He was on his way home after work and not far from the factory entrance when he saw a sturdy middle-aged woman knock a man to the ground and trample him. Then the woman left. Wei Bo walked over to look at the man, who turned out to be Mr. You. Mr. You picked up his broken glasses from the ground, looked right and left, then slowly, trembling, put them on and got to his feet. He obviously couldn't have recognized Wei Bo through the shattered lenses. He peered nervously around and clapped the dirt from his jacket and trousers before sneaking into a nearby haircutter's. Wei Bo, curious, hid outside the door to eavesdrop. He heard Mr. You and the owner flirting inside, both of them laughing loudly.

As Wei Bo recalled the incident, the shadow over his heart grew thicker. Could something significant be taking place in secret, without him knowing? Since he had been left in the dark, if he did nothing, wasn't that the same as if nothing had happened? Should he care about what might be happening in secret, even if it was directly related to him? Wei Bo, lost in the shadows, did not know what to do. He went outside to get some air.

The living quarters of the soap factory were old-fashioned single-story buildings in long rows, with an enormous scholartree at each family's entrance, and a stone table and stone benches underneath the tree. Wei Bo was fond of the structure of these buildings. He strolled beneath the scholartrees with his hands clasped behind his back, the cordial summer breeze adding a slightly sentimental air that made him think all at once of his lover Cuilan. Had she really left her job and gone to work at the hot springs as a prostitute? Wasn't it a little too late for her to make this decision? Wei Bo knew that none of Cuilan's decisions was related to him directly. He understood her too well. He didn't think there was anything wrong with being a whore, but this was Cuilan, not anyone else. The fact (supposing it was a fact) perplexed him. The Cuilan he remembered seemed to have many faces. He didn't understand her well enough, maybe even less than Mr. You did.

Once, when he and Cuilan had woken up in the middle of the night, he'd experienced something unusual. He got out of bed and went to get a drink, pouring hot water from the thermos in the dining room, and then sitting as he waited for the water to cool before drinking it. He suddenly heard a man's voice coming from the shadows in a corner of the room, a voice that seemed ambiguous, almost like a dialect. Wei Bo stood and went over to look at the large cabinet in the corner.

Sure enough, there was an elegant middle-aged man standing behind the cabinet. He made a sign with his hand, motioning to Wei Bo not to be alarmed.

"I'm her friend," he said quietly. "I often sneak into her home and hide here. You might think it's strange, but it's something I need to do. Please don't be angry. Cuilan is a diamond in this filthy city."

He stood on tiptoe, exaggeratedly snuck to the door, opened it, and left. Wei Bo stared, stunned. He suspected he was dreaming. Then he heard Cuilan in the room with him.

"That's the Insomniac!"

"How does he get in?" Wei Bo asked stupidly.

"I gave him a key, of course!"

"Didn't you think I'd be angry?"

"The Insomniac wanders around the city all night. Shouldn't we show people like him mercy?"

A dark flame shone in Cuilan's eyes; there were two dark circles under her eyes. Wei Bo fell silent.

The two of them talked late into the night. Their conversation focused on the distant years of childhood. The city had looked different then. In memory they went back to the symbolic places, agreeing as they went that once the sky was light they would revisit those old places to see how they had changed.

Remembering up to this point, Wei Bo sat down on a stone bench. He saw a figure moving toward his house. He only recognized his wife as she neared him. She was very late coming home.

To cast off her entanglement with Wei Bo, Cuilan used her saved vacation days to go to the countryside. A cousin on her father's side lived to the east, alone with his wife, since none of their children lived nearby. Their house stood beside a half-acre paddy field and a vegetable plot where they raised chickens and ducks while passing quiet days.

Cuilan stepped off the long-distance bus and walked along the cobblestone path. She had to go about three kilometers on foot to reach her cousin's house. This place was also Cuilan's ancestral home, which she had visited twice before. It was very dear to her, even though her cousin was the only family there now. Yet, without knowing why, she found the landscape before her eyes to be unfamiliar. She didn't recognize anything except for the cobblestone path. Where had the two low hills along the side of the road gone, for instance? The weeping willows and ancient camphor, the deteriorating village under the trees, were nowhere to be seen. Along both sides of the road, uncultivated land and wild grass filled the view. At one point the gigantic forms of two starving dogs appeared, tearing straight toward her, then, jerking abruptly around when they reached her, they ran until they were out of sight. She was so frightened she broke into a cold sweat. She vaguely sensed, without any reason to, that her cousin and his wife were no longer on this earth, and that something strange would happen to her on this journey.

When she finally saw the small, familiar mudbrick building with the half-collapsed wall, she was exhausted. By her own calculation, she had walked at least five kilometers. An oddly shaped camphor tree shrouded the house like an evil dragon. Cuilan finally had a sense of familiarity.

"Niu Yiqing! Niu Yiqing!" she shouted, ignoring everything else.

First she heard the old-fashioned wooden door opening, then after a pause her cousin and his wife slowly emerged from the house and stood under the low eaves. Cuilan thought they looked unusually small, both black as coal, their features indistinct. She could not see them clearly. She speculated that the evil dragon-like camphor might have absorbed the vitality from their bodies. She raised her head and saw that against the sky the leaves of the tall tree were actually the color of black ink, with a metallic gleam.

"Come in, come in and sit down." Her cousin-in-law's voice sounded like a cicada.

Of the tile-roofed house's five original rooms, two had caved in, with three remaining intact. One served as the dining room, and two as bedrooms. All of the rooms were small and dark. Her cousin's wife limped away to busy herself in the kitchen at the back. Her leg had been crushed when a production team was building the reservoir. Cuilan's cousin sat silently smoking his tobacco, as if he had already forgotten Cuilan. She eyed the familiar dining room. It looked the same as before, but she felt something had changed. She mulled briefly, then remembered that, the last time she had been here, a large framed picture that was supposed to be of her cousin's deceased father had hung on the wall. Cuilan thought that the elderly man looked like her. Now the wall was bare.

"Oh, Yiqing, you've managed your life well," she could not help saying.

Before her cousin had time to answer, his wife carried poached eggs to the table. Cuilan glanced over and saw that there were four eggs. Warm memories made her nostalgic, and she wept as she ate. When she finished eating, she wiped her tears with tissues she had brought, turned to her cousin, and asked him, "Why haven't you retired?"

"It isn't time yet," he answered quickly. "My wishes can be fulfilled here in our hometown."

When her cousin spoke, his wife made a sound like a cicada. Cuilan wasn't sure whether she was laughing, but could tell that she was showing her approval. She sensed how the woman's heart brimmed with delight. Cuilan handed her a gift box, which she accepted before limping to the inner room.

"What do you do every day?" Cuilan asked, lowering her voice.

"I analyze the composition of the soil. Every day I manipulate the earth and the crops, and gradually I figure out the soil's quality. I also pay attention to the atmosphere. My wife is even more enthusiastic than I am. Sometimes, instead of sleeping, she takes a little stool outside and sits on the ridges between the fields all night."

He stopped speaking when his wife appeared.

He pointed at her and asked, "Cuilan, don't you think she looks like a cicada? She imitates a cicada every day!"

Cuilan laughed cheerily, although she was inwardly startled, thinking, Life is so wonderful in the countryside after all! Watching the small, dark-skinned woman in front of her, she remembered what her cousin's wife had looked like many years before. She had been a plump, healthy farmer's wife, and not short or dark! Had the injury to her leg caused such a great change? Still, the transformation was not all for the worse. Cuilan sensed that the woman's body possessed an extraordinary spiritual power. There are not many people in this world who can train their voices to sound like cicadas. Cuilan exclaimed, "The air in the city is filthy compared to our hometown!"

"But my true ideal is in the city," her cousin quickly said.

That evening they burned a large bundle of mugwort to keep away the mosquitoes. Cuilan sat in the lingering smoke as though her body were in a celestial paradise. She regretted not returning home more often. She stood on the rice threshing floor in the moonlight, looking off into the distance. At the furthest visible point she saw dark red fireballs tumbling, rolling back and forth, mysterious and entrancing. She asked her cousin what they were.

"It's someone burning grass on the deserted land. He's trying to make signals."

"Who is he signaling?"

"Probably no one. People are all like this now in the countryside."

"Lovely."

"But he's a murderer. They kill people, then they feel lonely, so they burn grass on the wilderness as a way to communicate. When I see him in the daytime, he lowers his eyes out of fear."

It was too quiet. Cuilan could not fall asleep for a long time. Finally she dozed, but was soon woken by people talking outside.

"We can burn grass, too. First cut it up fine, let it dry in the sun, then light it on fire. It's not hard. That's the way Wei Bo does it."

Her cousin placed stronger emphasis on the two syllables of the name *Wei Bo*.

Cuilan jumped up, since this was the first time she had heard Wei Bo's name since coming to the countryside. It was fantastic. How did her cousin know Wei Bo? She cracked the wooden door open and saw her cousin and his wife sitting in the thick bower of the tall camphor tree, their four legs swaying. Her cousin's wife made a sound like a cicada now and then as her cousin continued, "There will be a south wind tomorrow afternoon. Once it blows, the entire wilderness will be burned away. We're not murderers, we don't have to lower our eyes in front of other people."

Cuilan heard two muffled thuds. It was the two of them crashing down from the tree. They began to groan loudly. Cuilan hurried over to them.

"Why pull the bench away? Why pull it away?" her cousin's wife asked.

Cuilan was startled—they must be shatterproof. She would be dead if she fell from such a height.

She was scared to raise them. If they had broken bones, they shouldn't be moved. She had to make sure first.

As she examined the couple, they struggled one after the other from the ground to their feet. It was truly a miracle.

Her cousin's wife staggered ahead into the house. Her cousin stood in the same place, turning to look left and right. Cuilan swept the surroundings with her eyes, discovering nothing unusual. Her cousin struck his lighter and raised the flame aloft. A number of seconds passed before he extinguished the lighter and put it away.

"Who are you signaling?"

"No one." He started to laugh.

"Does anyone come visit you here in the quiet countryside?" Cuilan drummed up the courage to ask.

"Aha, you're trying to pry into my background, aren't you? I'm sorry, Cuilan, I will keep my secrets. Life here is full of taboos. I know you want to ask why my wife and I sit in the tree. This is why: we want to get a little further away from the earth's clamor, to become calmer, so that we can make certain decisions."

"The earth's clamor?" Cuilan asked, blinking.

"Yes, you must have heard it. Isn't that what woke you up?"

"I woke up because you were talking so loudly."

"That's only what you think. You were awake before then."

Cuilan fell silent. She reflected for a moment, then asked, "Cousin, could I come live in the countryside? Maybe I could build another house over there."

"No, Cuilan, you couldn't. It's too late. Can people do whatever they want to?"

As he spoke the sky was already growing light. Cuilan wondered how it could be daybreak when she had not slept yet. She saw her cousin squinting and staring ahead, so she looked, too, and saw through the mist the red fireballs rolling along. Was it really Wei Bo?

When they went back into the house, her cousin said something disconnected, "From each according to his ability, to each according to his needs."

His wife placed a big pot of congee and two smaller plates of pickled vegetables on the table, then sat down on a stool and cried. Her husband said, "She's reminded of her youth." He bent over and stroked her back to console her. She gradually grew quieter and went to sit at the dining table. Then, suddenly, she made the cicada sound twice, so loud and clear Cuilan was startled.

Breakfast took a long time because the couple kept putting down their chopsticks to go look out at the door. Cuilan went with them, but she saw nothing other than the balls of fire in the distance. Later the fireballs disappeared, too.

"Outsiders are always coming here to burn the grass on the deserted land.

They buy and sell the land, then there's no sign of them again. I can understand their impatience."

Her cousin said this with a smile. Cuilan stared at his face, seasoned as it was with time, thinking, He's enchanted with his life! Then she felt ashamed.

During the day the couple went to work in the field, while Cuilan sat under the camphor tree worrying about her own problems.

The countryside was so bleak and so tranquil! Maybe something was wrong with her ears, as she could not hear the clamor of the earth her cousin mentioned. This made her ashamed. There was another thing she couldn't figure out: there used to be a village to the east of her cousin's house. Cuilan's parents had lived in the village, and Cuilan had gone there when she was younger. Ten years ago when she visited her cousin its old houses still stood. Where had the village gone? She planned to wait and ask her cousin. The thick maple grove beside the tile-roofed houses that were connected by passageways into a larger complex floated up in her mind. She looked to the east, where there was no grove of maples, nor the former houses, only wasteland.

An idea suddenly occurred to her: what if she and Wei Bo were to live here, like her cousin and his wife? Oh, what a pity, her cousin said it was impossible, it was too late. He must have his reasons. Besides, Wei Bo had responsibilities. What about Mr. You? In the countryside, far from the city, Cuilan's affections began to change. She no longer found You loathsome. Maybe his slickness, his dandyism, was an image. Everyone wears a mask. Like Cuilan herself, for instance, whom others might see as a professional whore—there was no telling.

Cuilan had made no arrangements for what would happen after her death. She was only thirty-five. When she happened to think about dying, she comforted herself by saying it was no use to be afraid. She would ask a neighbor or colleague to send her to the crematorium and throw away the ashes of her bones and that would be that. However, at this moment a rush of longing poured into her heart, a yearning to die here, in the future. Why she longed for this she could not say. She had not anticipated this emotion. Looking out from the shadow of the tree into the golden sunlight all around, she thought the scene must be what doomsday would look like. She found it touching. She had been touched constantly during her stay of now a little more than a day in the countryside. Yet in ordinary life she was not easily moved.

Cuilan didn't believe Wei Bo had come across her cousin by chance. She and Wei Bo must truly be connected by fate. She often thought at dusk of the ancient destiny of love. Last year when she bumped into Wei Bo at the spa was, naturally, a meeting he had planned in advance.

At dusk Cuilan finished making dinner and waited for her cousin and his wife to come back to eat. She burned mugwort inside and outside to fumigate the building until it reeked. Then she continued to wait, but they did not return. The moon had risen, and a ball of fire reappeared in the distance. This time the fireball stood there, not moving, changing from red to black, and again from black to red, not at all like someone burning grass on the wasteland. Cuilan wondered, if it was Wei Bo, would he grace the little house with his presence this evening?

She could not eat for the cares weighing on her mind, so she went outside. For kilometers around there were no people or even dogs. She could only walk in the direction of the fireball, but she was afraid of losing her way. Hadn't she nearly gotten lost on the way here? That was in broad daylight. Anxious or not, she did not stop.

After walking for a while she heard someone calling her name. Who? Not her cousin, not Wei Bo. Once she answered, the man no longer called for her. Cuilan grew scared and began to walk back. She sensed someone following her. Without daring to look, she picked up her pace and flew all the way back to the darkened house, where she bolted the door shut.

"Cuilan, Cuilan! It's your Fourth Uncle!" the man outside said impatiently.

Cuilan looked out of the window, but saw no human figure.

"I have something to tell you. Wei Bo and I sleep together every night," said the ghost of the man dead for many years.

"Wei Bo? What did he tell you?" Cuilan asked, her voice trembling.

"Nothing important, just that he will not abandon you."

Fourth Uncle was silent after saying these words. Cuilan saw the air outside flooded with a pale green color and a tiny flame floating along. She didn't dare to turn on the light and panted quietly in the dark instead. Suddenly she began to doubt whether her cousin and his wife were alive. How could living persons fall from so high in a tree without getting hurt? Hadn't she vaguely felt when she arrived that the couple were not of this world anymore? Was there some basis to this? Cuilan's body would not stop shaking, although, despite her fear, she was inwardly excited, and yearning for a certain turn in events.

Cuilan waited for a long time, but nothing happened. Suddenly her mental process began expanding. She resolutely opened the front door and stepped under the ancient camphor. She spread her arms, leaning her entire body against the rough bark of the trunk, her mind at ease.

In the distance tiny silhouettes appeared, like Lilliputians in the moonlight. It was her cousin, his wife, and another man. Cuilan's heart pounded wildly. Could he be Wei Bo?

They slowly walked closer. Unfortunately it was not Wei Bo, but an older man in ragged clothing.

"You're late coming back!" Cuilan said reprovingly.

"A little late. This is our family's benefactor. He ran into some trouble, so we helped him take care of the problem, and now everything's fine. Do you recognize him, Cuilan?" her cousin said.

Cuilan looked at the man's face, seeing in the dim light the eyes gleaming green like a cat's. She burst out, "Oh, are you Fourth Uncle?"

"No, girl, I'm not a member of your family. I'm a tinker," he answered quickly.

They all went into the house together, but the stranger soon went out again. Cuilan asked her cousin where the man was going. Her cousin said up into the tree.

"He carries sadness in his heart. Sitting in the camphor tree lessens the pain."

Her second night in the countryside Cuilan fell asleep like the dead, before she was once again awakened by noises. It was the tinker talking loudly with a woman in what sounded like a romantic tone. Cuilan got up because she couldn't go back to sleep. Nor could she resist pushing the wooden door slightly open to look around outside. She was badly frightened by the spectacle she saw. The man and woman held knives glittering like snow in their hands and appeared to be about to duel. Cuilan hurriedly shut the door, retreated, and quietly called her cousin, "Yiqing! Yiqing!"

Her cousin coughed in the inner room. After a while he finally, slowly asked, "What is it, Cuilan?"

He emerged without turning on the light. In the dark he asked Cuilan whether she wanted to get a better view of the scene outside. As he was speaking he opened the wooden door.

The man and woman had turned into silver statues that stood in front of the building, in the same posture, still holding the knives in their hands. Their bodies flickered with snow-white flashes of electricity.

"This is what they became in the end," her cousin said with disappointment and shut the door.

"Who is he really?"

"He really used to be a tinker. Then he went missing. Everyone said he ran away into the mountains with a woman. Many years later my wife and I came across him in broad daylight. He said he'd escaped from the mountains." Her cousin glanced through the crack in the door, then turned and said to Cuilan, "Ha! One after another up the tree! Like two monkeys! Ha ha!"

He rubbed his hands in amusement. Then he bolted the door.

"Why not invite them in?" Cuilan asked, not understanding.

"It's easy to say invite them in! Do you know how high their temperatures are? He'd be manageable on his own, but once the woman comes they turn into branding irons! Let them stay up in the tree. The tree cannot die."

In the rear room her cousin-in-law made the sad, shrill sound of the cicada. The hairs on Cuilan's body stood on end.

Her cousin returned to the inner room. His wife finally grew peaceful.

"Cuilan, it's time to rest now. You have to go back home tomorrow," her cousin said loudly.

"Why are you driving me away?"

"We're not driving you away. It's because Wei Bo will be at your home tomorrow."

"Where did you see Wei Bo?"

"At Fourth Uncle's. Don't ask questions, it's time to rest now. Do you want Wei Bo to go there for nothing? He really is a good person."

Everything became peaceful, and Cuilan felt the urge to sleep. Yet she strained her ears as hard as she could trying to hear the two people in the tree. Their voices were audible, but for all that she couldn't tell what they were saying, because the old camphor tree echoed their sound with a metallic drone, *weng weng*. To Cuilan it sounded like a plane circling overhead. Before entering a dream, she thought, a little enviously, They must be so happy. In her dream, she heard the couple outside referring to her as "the orphan." When she heard these two syllables, *or—phan,* her tears rolled down in waves, soaking the pillow. Her dreamscape was passionate, with two silvery forms always floating around her. She saw milkvetch all around, honeybees everywhere, to her right the houses of the disappearing village, and the maple leaves burning like fire. Her cousin and his wife stood at the door of the old house looking like two dwarves.

When Cuilan woke up her cousin's wife had already put breakfast on the table. They both seemed to be in lively spirits. Cuilan searched outside for a while, but the things that happened the night before had left no trace. Her cousin came outside, too, and said, "Our daytime and nighttime are two completely different days. If you always lived here and never left you'd be able to sense this. It's too bad you won't have the chance."

After breakfast Cuilan left. Her cousin and his wife stood under the camphor tree following her departure with their eyes.

When Cuilan walked beyond the paddy field and turned to look back, she discovered that the house and camphor tree had both vanished from the earth. The cobblestone path underfoot was comforting. She reflected that the tree with its metallic leaves reaching to the sky, the mugwort's thick fragrance, the silver-white human statues, and the tumbling balls of fire could never be forgotten.

A person fortunate enough to have a hometown like this one didn't need to be afraid of losing the way.

Cuilan returned. The next day Wei Bo really did come to her home.

She was cleaning at the time, straddling the windowsill to wipe the glass with a rag. Her body filled with energy as she smelled the fresh, clean air spreading through the rooms. Wei Bo entered without greeting her. He came in, picked up the mop, and started cleaning the floor.

"Did you go to my family's home to burn grass on the deserted land?" Cuilan asked him in a whisper.

"Uh-huh."

"Then you've known my cousin for a long time?"

"Your hometown is beautiful."

"Why did you come back here?"

"I didn't come on purpose. The city is so cramped, where else could I go?"

They made potatoes with beef and ate a good meal.

Cuilan asked Wei Bo whether he had met her Fourth Uncle.

"He has no home of his own, but he has one unique skill: digging holes in the ground. He carries the tools on his back wherever he wanders. Once the site is chosen, whether in the wasteland or on a rock, he only needs two hours to make a place to hide."

"Did you stay in a hole with him?"

"Yes. We could hear each other's breathing. Your Fourth Uncle brings people peace. There are many people like him in your family."

Wei Bo talked about some other things. As he spoke his eyes narrowed, then he bent over the dining table and began to snore. Cuilan said to herself, These past few days must have been such a strain on him!

She moved him with some effort into her bed. She looked at her lover, in an excited but also gloomy mood. She thought of the enormous ghastly camphor tree. Was it secretly sheltering her? What sort of protection was this?

When Wei Bo woke up they had great sex, much better than the first time. Even so, Cuilan seemed to be almost in a trance. Mr. You from the antiques shop, that slick, overdressed man, appeared before her eyes. She wondered, What was the relationship between Mr. You and Wei Bo? Were they as close as brothers? She snickered.

"Are you thinking of another lover?" Wei Bo asked, watching her attentively.

"No. There's someone pursuing me, but just looking at him makes me sick."

"There's nothing wrong with that. All of us have things about us that make other people sick."

It was already after midnight, but Wei Bo put on his clothes and said he needed to go home. Cuilan looked at him, wanting to say something that she did not say. What came out was something she never expected to say.

"Oh, Wei Bo, how did I come across you in such a remote place? I smoked out the mosquitoes with bundles of mugwort, until the fumes smoked you out. Sometimes I think that place must not be my hometown, because I don't understand anything about it. When I see you, you float on the horizon, pushing the flaming red wheel. You must have suffered?"

She could not continue; she stared straight ahead.

"I didn't suffer. Could I suffer when you were there? The wheel was scorching and hard to push, but the air in the countryside stimulates my every pore! Then there are the caves, with advantages you could never imagine!"

He quietly shut the door and left.

Cuilan heard the shout coming from her own mouth, "Mr. You! Mr. You!"

Once she came to her senses she was frightened. She tried her best to visualize Wei Bo and Fourth Uncle hiding in the caves. What sort of caves were they? The next time she would not be content unless she found them and saw what they were actually like. Why hadn't she thought of speaking face-to-face with her Fourth Uncle when he called to her from the window?

After returning from the countryside, Cuilan went to the hot springs on her days off out of boredom.

Business at the spa was light, especially in the women's baths, where she soaked alone as a few multicolored, narrow-bodied fish moved through the water, producing a bizarre hallucination, as though she were in some foreign land. In her drowsy state she heard someone calling her, furtively, "Cuilan! Cuilan! How could you forget me . . ."

She opened her eyes with an effort and stood, sweeping her eyes in a circle. The whole bathing area was like a desolate, abandoned woman. She heard the faint sound of weeping, a young woman weeping, sometimes stopping, sometimes continuing.

"Who's playing tricks?" she yelled spitefully.

Who was the ghost? No one. She went to the changing room in a rage.

By the time she came out of the changing room, she still had not seen a single person. She finally heard the sound of laughter when she went to the reception desk in the lobby. Oh, it was Long Sixiang and her friend! The women were heavily made-up, aggressively perfumed, and had obviously left their manual labor at the cotton mill to become whores. Cuilan thought the women were a little old to be prostitutes, but their confidence was out of all proportion. They were flirting with a man who stood with his back to Cuilan. Then he turned around, and it was Mr. You.

"Long Sixiang is my lover," he told Cuilan in an oily voice. "Not a one- or two-year affair—we've known each other more than twenty years. The job she's doing now brings out my old affection for her."

He and Long Sixiang fell together onto the long sofa with their arms around each other's shoulders. The second woman, not wanting to be left out, squeezed onto the sofa, and Mr. You embraced one with each arm.

Cuilan walked quickly toward the exit, taking advantage of the disturbance. She heard Mr. You scream frantically behind her, "Where are you going, Ms. Niu Cuilan? I have something to say to you!"

He chased Cuilan and caught up with her at the door. Seeing his purple, swollen face and agitated look, she said, "How strange. What do you want to talk to me for?"

"It's something important," he said, a little embarrassed, and lowered his head.

Cuilan caught the smell of perfume and wrinkled her brow. As if guided by a spirit she said, "In that case, let's go to the teahouse across the street and sit down for a bit."

"Oh, thank you!"

They sat down in the small tearoom. Mr. You appeared uneasy, craning his neck to look around, and heaving sighs. Cuilan, impatient, demanded, "Do you actually have something to say? If not, then I'm leaving!"

Mr. You seemed to be startled from a dream and motioned with a hand for her to sit back down.

"It will take a long time to explain, Ms. Niu Cuilan! Many years ago I made an arrangement with your parents. You don't know about our agreement, but some people in your hometown do. After your parents passed away I couldn't bring it up without seeming unkind. But you're a single woman now. There would be nothing improper if I were to court you, would there?"

"Go ahead and try!" Cuilan sputtered.

"Wait, I wasn't saying I want to make demands. What I meant was, you have that hometown in your background, and that's why I'm interested in you."

"Please, say something about my hometown."

"Oh, it's hard to tell everything at once. What can I say? I've been to many out-of-the-way places without seeing a village transform so quickly . . . It's an ordinary little farmhouse, of course, with enormous water vats and the stone mortar for crushing rice in the outer room, and grounds outside the building for drying rice in the sun. If you go there once, you lose the measure of yourself in everyday life."

Cuilan felt, as Mr. You began to speak about her hometown, that his oily, dandyish look was disappearing. He became more like a civilized man whose mind was disturbed. One of Cuilan's former lovers had been highly educated, too, but he was not disturbed in the way Mr. You was. Cuilan found one thing hard to understand: how could her parents think she and Mr. You were a match? Cuilan believed herself to be a plain, unaffected, practical person, as were her parents. They were as far in temperament from Mr. You as the distance between the sky and the ground. The affairs of the world are hard to understand. It was this very man, flighty as he was, who took an interest in her rustic, dreary hometown.

"My hometown seems to have made an impression on you," Cuilan said, teasing him.

Mr. You looked at her, his face suddenly overcast. Then he sat there not saying a word, from time to time with a savage expression, as if he had changed into a different man.

They parted unpleasantly.

Cuilan found this incident both strange and frightening. She made up her mind to avoid Mr. You when she saw him. He might be deranged. The thought also occurred to her, Long Sixiang is apparently his lover, but what do they have in common? Then there were her parents, who would never have engaged her to a man who was mentally ill. Reviewing these questions, Cuilan felt that she might be worrying too much.

Now she had doubts about going to the hot springs. She might run into people like Mr. You or Long Sixiang and get entangled in a bad way. Still, she was an unmarried woman, with no way to pass the time. Dull days arrived. To lighten the boredom, she even learned to embroider, and her handiwork was of the highest quality. In her loneliness she suddenly felt the misery of old age approaching. Her lovers from the past came and called to her from outside, while she sat inside unmoved.

One night, during a violent storm, Cuilan was listening to the sound of the rain when all at once she remembered the disconnected words her cousin had said: *From each according to his ability, to each according to his needs.* She felt her comprehension of the sentence's meaning in a visceral way. She believed people should be able to live in this manner, whether in the countryside or in the city.

She had not realized Wei Bo's views were similar to hers. Their relationship resumed.

Cuilan asked Wei Bo, "What year were you first in contact with my family?"

Wei Bo rolled his eyes back and thought for a long time before finally answering, "It's hard to say exactly. My impression is that I've always known your cousin and your Fourth Uncle, but wasn't in contact with them. Cuilan, tell me, if I'm shut away in prison someday, will you still remember me?"

"Of course I'll remember you. You won't be sent to prison, will you?"

"You're wrong. I think I've broken the law."

Cuilan did not question Wei Bo. She thought she should not. She was no longer the Cuilan she had been.

Before long Wei Bo did go to prison.

That day he and Cuilan were sitting in the park when the police suddenly arrived. Wei Bo continued speaking with her as he stood and walked toward them. He put out both hands to let them handcuff him.

"What are you doing? Why?" Cuilan raved, losing control of her emotions.

"He belongs to a criminal organization," a young policeman said.

Then they took Wei Bo away. He looked cheerful and optimistic, as though putting down a stone that had weighed on his mind.

Cuilan sobbed when she got home. She was once again alone. Before this disaster, she had planned on a long-term relationship with Wei Bo. She could visit him in prison sometimes, of course. She sensed that her partner had an unfathomable quality, something she could not articulate. Something to do with the smell of wormwood?

"Oh, Wei Bo," she thought, "why be with me, if you wanted to join criminals? Why waste time with me when I can't satisfy you?"

Her eyes hazy with tears, she began, to her surprise, to feel her crying was artificial, and the tears stopped.

As soon as she stopped crying, she thought of Mr. You. Which part of her was that slick, overdressed man attracted to? In her former life, she had disliked men like him and felt nauseated at the sight of them. Remembering Mr. You now, she felt curious and titillated. Apparently her nature had changed since her return from the countryside.

She wanted to provoke Mr. You, to make him spit out the secrets hidden in his heart. She wanted to clarify things: did Mr. You have any connection to her deceased parents? If so, why had she never met him before? If not, how was he able to describe her parents and her hometown so vividly?

Cuilan thought up to this point, sat down, and dialed Long Sixiang's cell phone.

"Long Sixiang, where are you?" she asked.

"Where else would I be? With a client, someone you know."

"Is it Mr. You?"

"Yes, I'll have him come to the phone."

"Ms. Cuilan, control your grief." She heard Mr. You's sticky voice. "After all, there are so many alternatives in life. Have you considered me, for example?"

"I was just considering you."

"Good, sparks may be struck between us."

Cuilan pondered Mr. You's words for a long time after she hung up the phone. He talked like her father. Cuilan had always believed that she had a dark history, and now this man had emerged out of this secret side of her history. An unclassifiable man.

Cuilan's father had been a silent man. Her impression of her father was always vague, and she couldn't peer into his mind. Her relationship with her father was sometimes good and sometimes bad. Yet even at the times when it was closest, Cuilan continued to feel that she and her father both kept themselves wrapped up tightly, doing all they could to show the other an image. She realized this when she was very young, thinking then that it might be because she and her father were both unhappy with themselves and wanted to be a different kind of person. As she got older, though, she came to look at it from another perspective. Her current view was that people created images to fool other people because the truth was too frightening, too difficult for them to accept. Apparently she and her father had a similar way of thinking, a similar temperament. Cuilan inferred from this that the impression she made on other people was probably vague, too. For example, the woman who was the head of Cuilan's workshop often stood off to the side and stared at her for a long time, without saying a word. Cuilan had never heard any evaluation of her work from her supervisor. Was no evaluation her evaluation? Cuilan didn't care what other people thought of her, but this kind of vagueness made her feel a little nervous. What if someday a poisonous snake slithered out from a dark thicket?

She thought once more of her father. What if Mr. You were the poisonous snake? Hadn't her father made an arrangement with him? The arrangement was itself ridiculous, because her father knew on a fundamental level that he couldn't dictate Cuilan's life. She had not sought his consent for her eventual marriage. The day she announced her news, her father hadn't said anything. Of course, he wasn't fond of talking.

She approved of Long Sixiang's carefree lifestyle as a woman who never quit what she started and concealed nothing, unlike Cuilan. Could this part of Long Sixiang's nature be what attracted Mr. You? At this thought, she decided that You did have a certain elite quality. Ha ha, as soon as Wei Bo went to prison, had her heart altered?

Two weeks later Cuilan went to visit Wei Bo at the detention center on the outskirts of the city.

The detention center's management was very kind. An older man had her wait in the reception room. He said to her, "How old are you? Thirty-five? What a pity. The earlier you break things off with him the better. He's incurable, and has been for a long time. How many children do you have? None? Then cut him off right away!"

He walked away indignant.

The reception room was empty, with a narrow bed placed in the precise center, but no chairs or tables. The white cover and quilt spread on the bed were untidy, as though someone had just slept there. Not wanting to sit on the bed, Cuilan stood rigidly, despite her inner agitation.

After a short while Wei Bo entered. His evasive manner reminded Cuilan of the first time she saw him at the spa. Wei Bo embraced Cuilan, falling with her onto the bed, madly groping at her body. She couldn't stand this and violently pushed him away, shouting, "You're mad!"

Wei Bo was stupefied, then a shrewd expression appeared on his face as he said, "I've thought of you day and night here on the inside. Why not seize the chance? Damn it, the old guy's coming back."

Cuilan turned around and saw the elderly man entering with a woman behind him. She heard the woman say sharply, "The dregs of society. I get faint just looking. Let's go."

So they left as soon as they entered and shut the door.

"Such a good opportunity!" Wei Bo said mournfully, "Why don't you want to?"

"I feel nauseated."

"You're too picky."

Cuilan gave Wei Bo the reading material and food that she'd brought. Wei Bo flipped through the issue of *Popular Cinema*, his eyes shiny like a rat's. Cuilan, sore at heart, reflected, "Prison really does change a man!" She thought this Wei Bo really did seem like he belonged in a criminal organization.

"When do you expect your verdict?" Cuilan asked him.

"Don't plan on it. Once you enter these doors, you have to resign yourself to living inside. Impatience is a dead end."

"But you didn't commit a crime, did you?"

"Of course I didn't. This is my fate."

Wei Bo lowered his eyes and wrung his hands with a slightly absentminded look.

"Go on back, since you don't want to do anything. It's awkward just standing here talking. I'm worried someone will take advantage and add to my crimes."

Wei Bo finished speaking, embraced Cuilan tightly, then pushed her away. He urged her to go. She left in confusion.

As Cuilan walked along the paved road through the outskirts of the city, the cool wind cleared her head a bit. She came to a stop and turned to look back at the detention center. Strangely, there was a tree reaching to the sky behind the two-story building. Even its shape resembled the tree at the door of her cousin's house, and its thick leaves were black, too, glimmering with metallic light in the sun. This association filled her heart with dread. Her legs went limp all of a sudden, and she sank into the weeds at the side of the road. Wei Bo's disappointed face weighed on her heart. Was she putting on an act? If he really were to lose his freedom, didn't the way she had just treated him prove she did not love him?

Her mood was much gloomier than when she had arrived. Her whole body felt weak. She was still about three kilometers from the bus stop, although the walk had not been a strain in the morning. Now everything had changed, and the return road was harder for her. Every part of her body hurt. Her gums were swelling. She couldn't sit in the weeds for too long because there might be scorpions or poisonous snakes. She dragged herself back to the road and made her way forward with slow steps. She was on the verge of nervous collapse after walking a short way. Suddenly she heard a creaking sound behind her. It was an old man pulling a two-wheeled cart toward her.

"Want to get on? Eight kuai," he said in a muffled voice.

Cuilan thanked him repeatedly and sat in the cart.

The detention center never vanished from her field of vision, nor did the enormous tree. The cart had traveled quite far and turned twice, yet she still saw the building. It was so clear even the sheets drying in the sun could be seen distinctly. She thought something was not right. The old man kept moving forward without rushing or slowing down. Cuilan smelled the sweat spreading through his undershirt. This man reminded her of her father. Her father had rescued her from danger on several occasions. Her teeth still hurt, and the cart was uncomfortable. The worst was that she kept seeing the building and that tree. Could she not leave this magic circle? The thought made her even more confused.

She was sure they hadn't taken the wrong way, since there was only the one paved road. Why hadn't they reached the station after an hour and a half? The detention center was no longer visible, but now the scenery along the road was unfamiliar. There were a few low, bare hills she had not seen on the way here. She began to feel nervous.

"Old man, are we almost there?"

"Yes. But we'd better rest here for a bit. My niece's house is on the right."

The old man put down the cart while he was still speaking, burrowed into the thick brush at the side of the road, and was soon out of sight. Cuilan stood on the bed of the cart to scan ahead. There was no bus stop in view, or even the tall buildings of the city. At the furthest point she could see, the asphalt vanished in a haze.

Cuilan jumped down from the cart and walked to the foot of one of the hills. There was not a single tree on it, only a few weeds and in the growths of wild grass two untended graves. Cuilan's thoughts returned to the detention center. It depressed her. The man she cared for had become a savage. Was this good or bad for her? Turning into a savage was probably best for Wei Bo. Otherwise the long nights on the inside would be hard to endure. She didn't know why she wasn't anxious to go home, to the empty apartment that had lost its appeal. She decided to stay here and go climbing, since she didn't need to go to work the next day. Once Cuilan made this plan, her teeth no longer hurt, and her body regained strength.

She climbed halfway up the hill and soon approached the graves. Only then did she see the man sitting in the weeds on top of a grave mound. He turned his face to her, and she recognized her Fourth Uncle.

"Have you always treated the whole world as your home, Fourth Uncle?"

"Not the whole world—I'm always wandering nearby."

Fourth Uncle's voice sounded as though he were speaking into a microphone. It was ugly to see his legs, with ulcers showing below the rolled pant cuffs, propped on the grave. Cuilan thought his whole body must have rotted from constantly getting in and out of damp, moldy places.

"Then you know about Wei Bo's problems?"

"What problems could Wei Bo have? He's not a simple man. Go home, the sky's getting dark. You should make long-term plans, my girl."

He got down from the grave mound and walked to the other side of the hill. Cuilan wanted to follow him, but he stopped, turned around, and glowered at her, his eyes gleaming green like a lynx's in the dim light. Cuilan, frightened, had to go back down the slope.

The sky was dark when she reached the bottom of the hill. She practically groped her way back to the road. She heard shrill cries coming from the direction of the detention center, scream after scream, as if the people there were being tortured. Cuilan concentrated, listening carefully, trying to distinguish Wei Bo's voice, but could not. Her suffering as she stood there was like a torrent through her heart. Someone in the dark spoke to her, in a voice that was strangely familiar.

"This kind of thing happens every day. Don't take it to heart."

It turned out to be Long Sixiang. She was sitting in the two-wheeled cart Cuilan had ridden before.

"Long Sixiang, what are you doing?"

"I'm this man's mistress—I mean the owner of the cart. Don't think he's an ordinary man just because he pulls a cart. None of the people I know are ordinary. Take this one: I suspect him of being a wealthy landowner. He spends money like flowing water. I can't deal with him by myself, Cuilan. You and I can do this job together!" Her voice grew louder and louder.

Cuilan, controlling her panic, repeated, "I haven't decided yet, I'm still thinking it over! Even if I start this kind of work, it would be alone, not with anyone else."

Long Sixiang snorted and said nothing for a long time.

The old man who had been pulling the cart came toward them, muttering curses and reeking of liquor.

"You lazy whore, are you trying to rip me off? Bah!"

He stamped his feet and raised an arm to hit Long Sixiang. From her higher position she pounced at him, holding him tightly as they fell together into the grass alongside the road.

Cuilan heard them rolling back and forth on the ground for a long time, without seeming to get tired. Eventually she decided to go to the bus station on foot. She was walking away when Long Sixiang called, "Stop! You can't go!"

She stopped, astonished.

Long Sixiang rushed over, grabbed her arm, and said, grinding her teeth, "Trying to run? Trying to pretend you're innocent? It's useless!"

She ordered Cuilan to sit in the cart with her.

The old man pulled both of them along, guiding the cart into the weeds at the side of the road. Cuilan couldn't tell whether there was a path under her and was too tired to care. She leaned against Long Sixiang's shoulder, noticed that she smelled of pine, and dozed surrounded by the scent. In her hazy state she heard Long Sixiang fiddling with a lighter as she smoked. Long Sixiang was so composed. She must be a dependable woman, someone who was sure of herself. Halfway between dreaming and waking Cuilan suddenly realized that she had known Long Sixiang a long time before. She had seen her many times at the home of an acquaintance whose name she could not remember. Long Sixiang had been a pretty wife whose eyes curved like the crescent moon when she laughed. By the time Cuilan had met her again she was a haggard mill laborer and growing old.

They came alongside a long row of two-story buildings.

"These are the 'mandarin ducks suites' for newlyweds. Lao Yong and I reserved the fifth suite down."

Long Sixiang embraced Cuilan as they went inside, her voice becoming more sexual.

"But I don't want to play this three-person game," Cuilan said in a low voice.

"Damn you!" Long Sixiang shoved Cuilan to the right.

She was pushed into the central room. Long Sixiang locked her inside and went around to the rear room with Lao Yong. Cuilan heard him singing a dirty tune.

At least the room had a tiny lamp. Cuilan could distinguish the items of furniture in the room, all constructed out of solid, unpolished wood that filled the air with a fresh scent. Several large cabinets with birds and flowers carved on the doors were placed against the walls. Cuilan sat at the table listening. She heard the man and woman going upstairs from the back of the building. They seemed extremely heavy, shaking the stairs with each step until they seemed ready to collapse. The horrible part was that she could still hear the shrill sound of weeping coming from the direction of the detention center, even clearer now than when she first heard it on the road. For a moment she could even distinguish Wei Bo's voice—slightly hoarse at first, hesitating, then erupting in an explosion of hysteria. She could not help the tears that flowed down her face.

Someone outside knocked violently on the door, wailing, *wa wa*. It was a woman whose voice seemed familiar. Cuilan told her the door was locked from outside. The crying stopped, then the woman opened the door with a single kick. Cuilan was startled by her strength.

It was Long Sixiang's colleague from the mill, the other one who'd become a prostitute. In the dim light, her face appeared younger than before, so much so that she looked enchanting. It might have been the effect of her makeup.

"He used to be my client, but Long Sixiang snatched him away!"

She pointed to the ceiling. Cuilan noticed that footsteps were still audible above, with every step seeming likely to break through the floorboards. "What are they doing?" she asked, panicking.

"Fighting, of course! What else would they be doing? Long Sixiang won't give up until she's squeezed everything out of her client! Why are you standing there like an idiot? These armchairs are so comfortable. Come over here and talk with me."

She sat in the shadow of the large cabinets. Cuilan went over and sat down beside her. She drew one of Cuilan's hands to her, holding it tight, her whole body shaking.

"What's your name?"

"Jin Zhu, the Gold Pearl."

"Are you cold?"

"No. I'm nervous. Something terrifying is happening upstairs. If things go badly between men and women, it ends in murder. Our job is extremely dangerous."

"If you're so afraid, just wash your hands of it."

"You really are stupid. It's the risk that makes it interesting. Do you know what life was like for Long Sixiang and me at the cotton mill?"

Jin Zhu's eyes had not left the ceiling for a moment as she talked. Dust was falling from the ceiling in the shadows to the left. They could hear the people above jumping up and down. Guessing at the spectacle overhead, Cuilan felt her sadness gradually changing into curiosity, and her nerves relaxed. Jin Zhu grasped her hand firmly, although she fidgeted uneasily. They were sitting in the dark, so Cuilan could not see the expression on Jin Zhu's face.

"Have you ever been on the floor of the cotton mill? It hardly needs saying—it's like being sealed in a cement mixer! When I started vomiting blood, I told Long Sixiang, 'I'll never get away, I'll die at the mill.' And so she and I escaped. Just think: neither of us is young, we have no skills, our health is not very good . . . What work could we do? Long Sixiang had the idea to work as prostitutes, but people didn't want us because we were too old. She doesn't give up, though, and she figured out a way. Then we got a footing in this business. Eventually we came to love it. Can you imagine that? We get more energetic the more we work. We have our own network of clients, the income isn't bad . . . But she, she doesn't know her place, she has great ambitions!"

This last comment was full of admiration. Cuilan wondered, What was Jin Zhu's actual relationship to Long Sixiang?

"What do you think of my body now?" she asked Cuilan abruptly.

"It's great, nothing like the women who work at the mill."

"Good! I wanted to hear you say it. My past life is as far away from the present as heaven is from hell!"

"Is Long Sixiang trying to get money from the old man Yong?" Cuilan asked.

"What? Don't be vulgar. Would it take so much effort to get a little money? This is love, I tell you! Who could cheat the two of us? We can only be conquered by love, the genuine article. First I fell in love with old Yong; now she's taken him. But I'm not jealous of her. Why? Because her passion is greater than mine. Damn it, let's not talk about that. When I think about how I left the factory, that sea of sorrow, I'm so happy I jump for joy, even when I'm just walking down the street. Long Sixiang and I, our backs are straight now, we know what we are capable of, and we can also love!"

Jin Zhu's mood suddenly changed. Her gaze dropped from the ceiling. She let go of Cuilan and held her head in both hands.

"What's the matter?" Cuilan asked.

"They've gone." Her voice was miserable. "They came down so quickly and went far away . . . Is love really so short-lived?"

"What makes you say that?"

"Oh, the cotton, the flying cotton! Do you know how much cotton Long Sixiang and I have in our lungs? The whole twenty years . . . the loose cotton forming pellets that stick to the lobes. It was unlikely we'd live this long. I've always hoped that one of us, whether me or Sixiang, would be happy."

"Is Lao Yong really a wealthy landowner?"

"To us he's rich. We're tricking him into falling into our hands."

Cuilan remembered Wei Bo and asked Jin Zhu whether she knew there was a detention center nearby, with many criminals locked away inside.

"Of course I know. Aren't these the Mandarin Ducks Suites? Crimes are unavoidable when men and women mix together. That's why there's a jail."

"Your powers of association are impressive."

"I'm in a pessimistic mood. I killed someone. Should I turn myself in? I cannot forget what the man I killed looked like as he struggled for life."

Cuilan patted Jin Zhu on the back and asked whether she had loved him.

"Yes. I'm an idiot. Can you help me open the door?"

When Cuilan opened the door, she saw a pair of sweethearts embracing each other on their way past. From the back the man looked like Wei Bo. She went outside to get a better look, but a gust of sand and dust blew in her face, obscuring them from her view. Inside the room, Jin Zhu cried out in despair, "My lungs! I'm going to suffocate."

Cuilan returned to the armchair and patted her gently on the back.

After Jin Zhu caught her breath, she asked Cuilan whether she heard footsteps upstairs. Cuilan listened carefully, then said she did not hear them.

"Those two, they appear and disappear like ghosts, and now they're back upstairs. This love has no future, but I hope Long Sixiang will find happiness."

"You are truly good," Cuilan said sincerely.

"Don't talk nonsense, I'm no good. A few times I've almost murdered Sixiang. She and I compete in love and jealousy. I hope she will be happy, because I won't concede—why can't we find happiness?"

Cuilan hadn't heard movement upstairs this whole time. She thought Jin Zhu might be hallucinating.

Jin Zhu pulled her into the chair with a sweaty hand and said, "People only come here for one thing. You and Sixiang had your reasons, but why did I come here? I'm a little confused, I've forgotten what I came here to do. I ran and ran, got into a cart, then ended up here. On the cart I felt as free as a little bird. Didn't I escape from the cement mixer? Don't I have my own life? Why am I so pessimistic? I know this illness will flare up again. My lungs, oh!" She let out a heart-rending cry.

"Jin Zhu, Jin Zhu, don't be sad. You will find your own happiness."

Cuilan felt stranded after saying these words. She thought, What am I talking all this nonsense about? Jin Zhu didn't answer, but she stopped shouting.

They were silent in the dark for a long time. Cuilan almost fell asleep leaning into the armchair. She hazily reached out a hand toward the woman in the other seat, where she felt an empty space, and was startled back awake.

"Jin Zhu! Where are you?"

"I'm outside. Quick, come here!"

Cuilan felt her way outside and stood in front of the door with Jin Zhu. It was quiet, without a single person there. The moon had already risen to the middle of the sky. Cuilan had never seen such a big moon, as large as a sink basin. She pinched her thigh hard to make sure she wasn't dreaming. To the right, the long row of honeymoon suites stretched into the distance like a black dragon.

"There's a side door. We can go to the back of the building and get upstairs from there. We'll make a surprise attack on Lao Yong and Sixiang."

Jin Zhu seemed enthusiastic, but Cuilan hesitated, not wanting to move from where she stood. Jin Zhu kept talking. "Lao Yong is a cement merchant. He intentionally produces inferior cement and got rich from this scheme. One-third of the new buildings in our city were built with cement he supplied. I was planning to overcharge him and make a bundle, but I never thought things would go wrong so quickly. Long Sixiang has been a good influence on him. Are you coming? Otherwise I'll go upstairs by myself."

Cuilan couldn't resist the temptation to follow her.

As they went upstairs, one in front, one behind, the narrow staircase seemed about to collapse. Cuilan let out a scream and broke out in a cold sweat—she had launched into the air. Luckily Jin Zhu caught the back of her clothing with an iron grip and pulled her back onto the staircase.

"Damn it!" Jin Zhu said, gritting her teeth.

The upper floor had a sloping roof and was lit with a tiny lamp. There was a narrow bed in the center of the room, reminding Cuilan of the room in the detention center. The quilts were folded neatly on the bed.

"They aren't here," Cuilan said.

"Don't be misled by surface appearances." Jin Zhu busily opened the cabinets and closets, using a flashlight to look under the bed.

Cuilan stood baffled in the dim light, when suddenly she felt someone tugging at her hem. Bowing her head she saw a snow-white arm reaching out of a large wooden trunk next to her. Oh, it was them! They were only wearing scant underthings, the man below, the woman on top, stuck tight to each other.

Jin Zhu came over and stood with Cuilan next to the wooden trunk watching them.

"There's nothing I can do." Long Sixiang's voice was plaintive. "Oh, Jin Zhu, you got away from the den of demons! If only at the beginning . . ."

"Don't talk about 'at the beginning'! You're like a puppet! I won't let you beat a retreat. Why can't we have good lives?" Jin Zhu's voice grew calmer, then turned to admonition: "Sixiang, have you forgotten everything we planned? You have to struggle; I won't let you be lazy. Look at our sister here next to you, she's so strong. Her lover is in jail, but she's not discouraged. You should be ashamed. Listen to yourself, when Lao Yong is there beside you. Lao Yong! Lao Yong! Are you listening?"

"I'm listening," the man said in a low voice.

"She's a priceless treasure," Jin Zhu said. She pushed Cuilan along with her, and in a moment the two of them were downstairs.

They stood under the enormous moon.

"Why is my heart so empty?" Jin Zhu said softly.

"It's because you love Lao Yong, too," Cuilan said.

"Maybe. We should go back to the city."

Cuilan and Jin Zhu walked back into the city. It was full daylight when Jin Zhu said she was going back to the hot springs and said goodbye to Cuilan at the side of the road. Cuilan watched as she left, discovering Jin Zhu was full of life and showed no sign of having stayed up through the night, even less of being ill. Jin Zhu had just left her when she saw Mr. You sticking his head out of the door of a McDonald's. She waved and Mr. You came over.

"What are you doing?" Cuilan asked him, smiling.

"I was waiting for you, Ms. Cuilan. Can this candidate enter the field now?"

"Why don't you go after Jin Zhu?"

"Jin Zhu is pursuing someone else with so much enthusiasm that I can't cut in now."

He was the same overdressed dandy. Even his fingernails were trimmed in a womanly curve. He invited Cuilan to the coffee shop across the street.

Cuilan didn't drink coffee, but she was starving and ate two egg sandwiches in a row. She noticed Mr. You's lack of attention and his distracted expression. Could he be waiting for another woman?

"If you have nothing important to say, I'll say goodbye," she said, standing.

"No, don't!" He gestured to her, in alarm, to sit down. "Please, tell me, what is Wei Bo's actual situation?"

"Oh, don't ask, it's awful! I still don't understand how people can be locked up like that. What's even more frightening is the place doesn't feel solid, it's like you—like you're in a land of illusion! I think he's already given up hope."

Cuilan's face turned pale when she finished. Her vision blurred, and she had a sensation of drowning. She heard Mr. You's flustered voice. "Cuilan! Cuilan! What's wrong?"

Cuilan leaned against the table for several seconds, recovering her sight by degrees.

"I'm fine," she said weakly.

"Drink a little tea," Mr. You said solicitously.

She watched his back as he poured out the tea, thinking that he looked like the species of flat fish in the hot spring pools. There were not many soft-spoken men like him in the city.

When they finished drinking their tea, Mr. You wanted to see her back home. Cuilan thought he might want to sleep with her.

He didn't try going to bed with her, but only sat at the table looking at her blankly.

"A long time ago I thought of taking walks near your home sometimes, but you were too proud," he said, a smile on his face that was not a smile. "We received a batch of Longquan celadon vases at the antiques shop. I'm afraid to stay above the shop at night."

Cuilan couldn't help starting to laugh.

"Don't laugh." His face reddened. "Let me tell you, this job means dealing with specters. People who do this kind of work are bound to have short lives. I'm hopeless. You see, I've never had a family, because I always think I'll be dead soon."

"You're too pessimistic. You seem in good health."

"That's only looking at the surface. I've lived in the underworld for a long time, seeing life above ground as if separated from it by a layer of glass, without understanding it. But I'm not willing to give up. People like me are the type whose 'desires are never fulfilled, like the snake that swallowed an elephant.' At night I roam through the empty, deserted ancient cities, using up all of my inner energy. Let's not talk about me, though, let's talk about Wei Bo. Tell me, is he in a bad state? Could you misunderstand his situation? I've learned indirectly about Wei Bo's nature, and I don't think he would put himself in a bad place."

"Ha ha, I'm happy to hear you say that!"

"I came to your home to make you happy. You were the idol of my youth. Wei Bo's situation is normal. They won't let him out right away, of course. Why didn't you take the opportunity?"

"What?" Cuilan howled.

She thought he was referring to when she had not slept with Wei Bo at the detention center.

"I mean that with someone like him you should dig to the root, investigate the scope of his activities, so that you can take the initiative."

"Oh, so that's what you meant. Mr. You, let me ask you, why are you so interested in women? Do you think they're a different organism?"

"Ha ha, that's exactly what I think, you've guessed it! Women are mysterious and unfathomable. Take Miss Long Sixiang: I've known her many years, but I've never been able to guess what she intends to do. This is enchantment. In those years her eyes burned. I would meet her at the entrance to the cotton mill. There was no talk of physical needs then. Just eating a meal together meant intimacy."

Mr. You stood and got ready to go home as he was speaking, but Cuilan hoped he would say more about himself and Long Sixiang.

"What a pity you didn't stay on good terms with her."

"What's there to pity? Didn't I tell you that I always think I'll be dead soon?"

He swam outside like one of the fish in the hot springs and left.

Cuilan finally felt like she had returned home. She was back at her own one-person apartment. How long had she been away? One day, one night. Yesterday's feelings of despair vanished, she didn't know how, and an inner emotional world vastly unlike what had come before appeared. She still hadn't made up her mind whether to risk going deeper into this world, but one thing was certain: she could not return to her former, unconcerned life. Think of how senseless she had been, believing Mr. You wanted to take advantage of her! He, and Long Sixiang, and Jin Zhu—what kind of people were they? Then there was the most critical question: what kind of person was Wei Bo? What was his relationship to Miss Si from the cotton mill? When Cuilan thought of this side of things, everything went dim before her eyes. Perhaps it was a world she would never comprehend, never grasp. Why did she have to think about things that had so little to do with her? She clenched her teeth and decided to focus only on what was in her heart.

Cuilan entered a dreamland. Everything in the dream moved her, without reason: gray streets, gray buildings on both sides of the street, gray pedestrians and trees on the sidewalks, a flock of gray pigeons in the sky, a gray station wagon driving down the middle of the road, a girl stretching half of her body outside of the gray car, wearing a gray hat to block the sun . . . Cuilan came to the road that went down the embankment along the river, where she saw Wei Bo walking toward her. Wei Bo asked her whether she would go with him to the soap factory. She nodded over and over, feeling lighthearted. Wei Bo pointed to the river and said the soap factory was underneath it. He dove into the water every day to go to work. Cuilan found this comical and laughed aloud. Then her laughter woke her and she said, "You are a superb actor!"

She looked at the clock on the wall. It was midnight. There was a racket outside, a few people shouting in unison, "The Red Sailboat! The Red Sailboat! Business is booming!" There was a café for lovers nearby called the Red Sailboat. She had happened to go there once or twice, and thought the place was shady because of the heavily tattooed men who passed through it. She stood up and went to look out the window, but everything appeared still. No one was there. She looked again and saw one person standing at the mailbox. She waited patiently, even though the noise had stopped. All of a sudden, the man by the mailbox raised a small rectangular box, probably a tape recorder. The noise came from inside it. He had several tattoos and was built like a pylon. Cuilan, frightened, quickly turned off the light and retreated to the bed. She tried to return to her dream, but could no longer go back. She shut her eyes, but the din outside her window continued, causing continual, bizarre associations in her mind. She decided she would go to the café at sunrise to see what was going on there. She remembered the picture of the boat with red sails that covered an entire wall.

Even when Cuilan tried to concentrate, she made small errors in her work. She made them several days in a row. The head of the workshop wanted to speak with her.

Cuilan sat in the office fidgeting uneasily, calculating whether she should go work as an attendant at the hot springs after being put on a "retained post with suspended salary." She knew that the spa was hiring.

The head of the workshop came in without a hint of reproach in her expression. On the contrary, she chatted with Cuilan seemingly at random. Cuilan was on guard, thinking there must be a hidden trap in the words of this middle-aged, but attractive, woman.

"When I was younger I worked as a warehouse clerk, too. Just like you, I didn't like this work—a boring job. Yes, I can understand what's upsetting you."

"What will my discipline be?"

"Discipline?" she asked in reply, her eyes widening until they looked like copper bells. "Don't misunderstand, Cuilan, we can hardly sympathize with you enough. How could we discipline you?"

"But I made mistakes in my work and should receive the usual punishment."

"Who doesn't make mistakes when she's young? Cuilan, I know there are some men who wish you ill, who are waiting to see you brought low, but I will make sure they fail. When you go back, nothing should weigh on your mind. Hold your head proudly, as an upright person!"

The head of the workshop massaged Cuilan's shoulders with her fleshy hands, as if communicating a sexual suggestion. Cuilan stared at her in astonishment.

The workshop head let go and said, as if nothing had happened, "I won't note it in your record."

Cuilan exited the factory gates and boarded the public bus back to her home. On the bus ride she pondered the meaning of her supervisor's words, sensing that something unforeseen would happen to her. She was a little unsettled, a little excited, and a little eager. After all, she was tired of her work at the instrument factory. The monotonous pattern every day, the familiar faces, suddenly filled her with aversion.

That evening she received a phone call from the head of the workshop telling her to take two weeks off, with full pay. Cuilan doubted her ears and asked three times to be sure, each time with an affirmative reply. Yet she felt no reassurance.

"Cuilan, I'll tell you a secret: the man in the antiques shop is my benefactor. I know you don't love him, but that doesn't keep him from loving you." Her voice sounded peculiar.

"He doesn't love me at all," Cuilan said.

"Doesn't love you? Don't joke around."

The head of the workshop seemed angry when she hung up the phone. Cuilan stared blankly at the picture of a film star on her wall. Her mind in its turmoil couldn't judge what happened right in front of her. Everything seemed to be turned upside down. She had unexpectedly been given two weeks' vacation through Mr. You's influence. Her supervisor believed Mr. You cared for Cuilan. To repay him, because he was her benefactor, she had given Cuilan a holiday instead of punishing her. What was the matter? Had the world gone mad?

Now that Cuilan had two weeks of freedom, she ought to visit Wei Bo, who was, after all, the only person in the world dear to her. Yet once she thought of the awkwardness of the last time, once she thought of having to go to that place again, she hesitated. She believed she loved Wei Bo, but she was not used to the way he was behaving. He seemed to have turned into a different person, vulgar and coarse, like an animal, as soon as he entered the detention center.

If loving someone meant loving through all, could she love this animal? She thought again of Miss Si at the cotton mill. Was Wei Bo like this with her? The more closely she had thought about such things, the more she had despised herself. Someone knocked on the door.

It was her ex-boyfriend Xiao He.

"I'm not here to get involved. I came to share some information." He smiled placatingly. "They're transferring Wei Bo to the detention center at Pear Mountain. I saw them on the road. Wei Bo looked unstable. You can call to confirm. The number is 228153."

Cuilan let him into the apartment. She had no way of knowing whether he was lying.

Xiao He rudely sat down at the table. Cuilan knew his wretched appearance was an act, and it did not move her.

"Pear Mountain is cold and deserted, with wolves howling in the wilderness."

"I received the money you sent," Cuilan said, "altogether 20,000 yuan."

"I'm so glad. I have to go now. Write down the phone number: 228153."

"Don't fill your head with random numbers, it's not good for your health. Is it the same Pear Mountain where I went with you?"

"Exactly, the same place."

He left, a breath of the wilderness lingering where he had sat.

Many years earlier Cuilan and Xiao He had roamed the city, strolling through the markets, going to snack shops and teahouses, meeting friends in small restaurants. There had been more cheerfulness than anxiety in her youth. Her relationship with Xiao He lasted a year. Toward the end of autumn they took a bus to Pear Mountain.

Pear Mountain was covered with scattered stones, without any trees. They stood at the foot of the mountain watching the summit merge into the mist and clouds. Xiao He said there were wolves, so they circled the base of the mountain, too scared to climb it. The strange thing was the absence of villages or cottages near the mountain, which rose abruptly from the ground. There was only a stretch of wilderness to the west.

Without venturing a word they walked on, two people with vacant minds. Cuilan was intrigued by the narrow, winding footpath. It was unclear who had blazed this trail ringing the mountain, not too close or too far.

The sun would soon set behind the mountain. A chill fall wind started to gust. They went hand-in-hand along the road home. Cuilan kept turning back to look at Pear Mountain, but the peak stayed immersed in the clouds. She asked Xiao He, "Why is that path there?"

"I've been thinking about the path, too. Pear Mountain must have drawn many people here. Just now, when we were walking, I felt I had reached the center of the earth. Even though I'm a traffic cop—isn't my work ridiculous? Damn it."

After that Cuilan never went back to Pear Mountain, and she soon forgot the place completely.

While Xiao He held the memory firmly.

Now Cuilan longed for someone to come talk with her about Pear Mountain. Should she dial the phone number? Xiao He might be deceiving her. She had never been able to understand this policeman with his mind full of stratagems. This trait had been what attracted her to him. Afterward she summed up her experience: doing what he said was more often than not the best option.

"Hello, is this the Number 3 Detention Center?"

"Why are you calling in the middle of the night? I'm on duty, what is it?"

"Has Wei Siqiang been brought there for questioning?"

"There is someone by that name here. Why are you looking for him? Oh, I know, you're Cuilan!"

"How do you know my name?"

"I'm not the only one. Everyone in the detention center knows you! Wei Siqiang wrote a song about you and sings it at the top of his voice. He's been punished for it a number of times." The man speaking became excited.

Cuilan hung up the phone, her face burning. She stood and paced back and forth in a haze of confusion. She hated Wei Bo so much she ground her teeth. Even when she was a child she had not liked being in public. Well, now she was newsworthy. She didn't mind that those people would think she was a whore, but she couldn't stand being notorious.

She didn't have to go to work tomorrow, and she couldn't go back to sleep, so she went for a stroll outside.

In the deep of night the city appeared to be dead. The streetlights failed to illuminate its dark places. Suddenly Cuilan sensed some object churning in the depths of the shadows. She heard these rolling things make a sound, *hu hu hu*. She thought the sound was melancholy, also pleasant, reminding her of how she felt sitting in the honeymoon suite talking with Jin Zhu. She wondered, What kind of person is Jin Zhu? It was as if she had different expectations from life than Cuilan. What kind of expectations? The two women who'd escaped from the mill and made their way in the world seemed already to have experienced many changes. Cuilan admired them, but knew she could not be like them. What category did she belong to? "Calling it 'not one type or the other' would fit pretty well," she said aloud, to herself.

Someone in the shadows below a high-rise called to her, "Sister," three times, then walked out of the shadows. It was a tall, martial young man.

"Who are you?"

"I'm the man who answered your phone call."

"Then you're not at Pear Mountain? Are you guys trying to fool me?"

Cuilan glared at him in fury, wanting to slap him in the face.

"I'm off today, so I'm not there. But Wei Bo really is at Pear Mountain. I'm a good friend of Xiao He. He and I talked about you and Wei Bo, and he told me to help you."

"Go to hell. Drop dead!"

She indignantly turned to go back, regretting having gone out in the middle of the night.

"My name is Yuan Hei, Black Yuan. I'm a guard at the Number 3 Detention Center. Don't be angry, what I told you about Wei Bo is true. I never lie."

He followed behind stubbornly.

Cuilan reached her building and climbed to the second floor. He followed her upstairs.

"Please come in!" Cuilan opened the door wide.

He turned bashful, saying, "Would that be appropriate?"

Cuilan was about to close the door when he squeezed into the room.

He wouldn't sit down and just stood in the middle of the room twisting his hands. The boy looked honest enough. Cuilan didn't know why he had come.

"Cuilan, my name is Yuan Hei."

"You said that already."

"Wei Bo told me you weren't satisfied with the location the detention center provided for your rendezvous. The matter has already been reported to the higher authorities and will be improved in the future."

"Will Wei Bo always be kept under investigation?"

"I don't know, but you should make long-term plans."

"Does he want to stay on the inside?"

"I haven't asked him. You can ask him yourself next time." He paused and changed the topic. "Cuilan, Xiao He is a trustworthy man. There aren't many like him left."

"What do you mean? That we should be a couple like before? But you're helping Wei Bo by passing information. What's the matter? My mind is in chaos."

"No, no, that's not what I meant!" He was so anxious she could see his face turning red in the lamplight. "I was saying that Xiao He is an admirable man. From now on I will try to be like him. Do you think there's hope for me?"

"I can't judge. My mind is in chaos," Cuilan said dejectedly.

"I have to go back. Goodbye!"

For a long time after turning off the lights, Cuilan thought about what had just happened. When had she parted ways with Xiao He? She couldn't remember. In fact, even when the physical relationship was over, it seemed as though they had not broken up completely. They were in touch once or twice a year. He was usually the one who contacted her, but she didn't mind, because he always made her curious, amused her—she wanted to hear what he had to say. Sometimes she imagined Xiao He as a spider endlessly spinning out threads of aimless clues. Tonight, right after Xiao He went away, she had dredged the hallway a few times with her hands to see whether he left behind cobwebs. She had thought at first that he must be jealous of Wei Bo, but now understood this was not the case. This proved Xiao He did not love her anymore, although he continued to focus his attention on her, and she did not know what he had in mind.

Thoughts are clearest before dawn. Cuilan visualized the narrow, winding trail beneath Pear Mountain, then all at once recalled a sight she had forgotten all these years—the lynxes appearing and disappearing among the loose stones on the mountainside, a number of them . . . and she had smelled food and cooking fires. That was to say, the mountain was alive. She had wanted to climb the mountain, but Xiao He held her back, saying, "There are things you can study for twenty, thirty years and still not understand." He wanted to go back home, urgently, so she abandoned her plan.

"Xiao He, Xiao He, you cunning man." She quietly rehearsed these words, then noticed the windowpane growing lighter by degrees.

She slept soundly in the sunlight.

At the foot of the building, a young man squatted in a clump of rouge-flower, smoking. It was Yuan Hei from the detention center. Yuan Hei had been through such difficulties on account of love that he had almost tried to kill himself. He was the first of Miss Si's lovers, Miss Si from the cotton mill whose name meant "silk." Now he had fallen in love with a forty-three-year-old jailer and was again facing the prospect of abandonment.

Xiao He had planned the previous night's events to enlighten Yuan Hei. Xiao He couldn't have actually said in which regard he wanted to enlighten him. Wasn't Yuan Hei doing well enough? Once they started drinking, though, once they started talking, Xiao He could not help boasting and told him about his scheme.

Cuilan slept heavily among the traces of these clues.

TWO

Wei Bo and A Si's Past Affair

The relationship between Wei Bo and A Si was partly public, in that everyone except Wei Bo's wife knew about it. His wife might have known, too, but without caring. She had her own entanglements. Among all of Wei Bo's affairs, only the one with Miss Si was not a secret.

Wei Bo first saw A Si and fell head over heels for her when he held a part-time job at the same cotton mill. He tailed the young woman around the factory grounds for days on end. A Si, discovering early on that she was being followed, sized up Wei Bo from a distance. Over the following days she felt waves of emotion rise and fall and lost sleep at night. Then one day she walked straight up to Wei Bo and said, "How much will you pay to keep me?"

Wei Bo blinked and thought for a while before answering honestly, "I'm not a wealthy man, but I will do my best to help you."

A Si promptly drew her arm through his, and they made a show of leaving the factory together.

Getting a job at the hot springs as a sex worker was A Si's own idea. At first Wei Bo tried to object, but after he went to see her workroom at the factory a few times he did not say a thing.

Wei Bo threw himself into various jobs, hoping to rescue Miss Si as soon as possible. After two years he realized A Si was not disgusted by her new job. She was calm, managed her work with composure, and no longer showed any of the feelings of anxiety from when she'd worked at the cotton mill. Being young and pretty, she earned enough to plan for buying herself a unit in an apartment complex.

What attracted Wei Bo was the lively look in A Si's eyes. He had never met a young woman as lovely and clever as she was. He felt that her every glance held at least two meanings, making him, a grown man, lose track of his tangled thoughts. He could never make up his mind when he was with her. A Si was very candid with him and never talked in circles. Wei Bo knew she had at least two other boyfriends.

Speaking in general, sex workers rarely fall in love with their clients because the transaction is monetary. Miss Si, it seemed, lacked a head for business and time after time had romantic affairs with hers. Even when other people pointed out her mistake, she didn't think it was one.

"I can't see how what I'm doing is wrong," she said to Wei Bo. "What's so great about business? Is life just for doing business? People are judged by whether they're good at it. I'm not, of course, but I don't fault other people, either."

She said this all with a radiant smile that Wei Bo found incredibly touching.

"What I regret most is not leaving the cotton mill sooner." She added, "This job is much better than that one. I'll have more control over my work after you and my other friends help me buy a place. Some people tell me I should stop working, and sometimes I want to stop. But what will I do if I'm not working? I'd be too lonely. I'd rather keep my life the way it is. I'm sort of fond of taking risks."

One time A Si was abused by someone in the criminal underworld who covered her face in bruises and cut off a chunk of her hair so that she had to shave all of it and wear a hat. Wei Bo sat in her cozy two-room apartment, watching her with the scene of when he had first met her flickering across his mind, as though he were in a dreamworld. She was still beautiful, of course, even though she had experienced so much of life already. He suddenly heard her say, "I'm the kind of person who would die for love. Why do I keep misjudging people?"

"You don't misjudge people, you only follow what your heart tells you to do. The other person changes his mind. It's a common thing," Wei Bo answered her calmly.

"You're too good, Wei Bo. I love you." Her panda bear eyes (the result of violence) glittered.

"I love you too, A Si."

That day they talked about many things together. They discovered that they had as much in common as twins.

Wei Bo only had to think of A Si for a vague ache to appear somewhere in the area of his heart. *Ah, the ages that pass like the flowers! Ah, an abyss too deep to see the bottom! Ah, the perilous future! Ah, the endless turmoil and confused wandering! Ah* . . . These were the exclamations of wonder his heart made at the way A Si lived. He sometimes felt depressed from constantly worrying about her. The strange thing was that he rarely thought about whether A Si actually loved him or not. Maybe he had decided from the start that this question was meaningless. She was too lovely. Her body was as tender as a tropical fish. Wei Bo felt as though he had been given a gift he didn't deserve, which left him no room for debate.

"A Si, A Si, I love you . . ." he repeated in a murmur.

"Wei Bo, I love you too!" she answered, gasping. "What if there were no men like Wei Bo in the world? What a loss!"

Wei Bo saw more than once the quietly smoldering black torch in A Si's eyes. He understood this young woman's internal energy, as well as the capacity for danger to which it led. Many people knew she worked in this apartment complex as a prostitute. She might suddenly disappear any day.

A Si was talented in addition to being beautiful, gifted at managing her life, vivacious, and considerate. Wei Bo couldn't stand to see her meet misfortune.

One time Wei Bo bumped into Long Sixiang at A Si's apartment complex. Long Sixiang rushed over and took his arm, her face filled with envy.

"Wei Bo, Wei Bo, you're so charming. Miss Si has feelings for you. You must seize the opportunity! So far as I know, none of her lovers has lasted more than a year. You've had several."

"I love her one day at a time. On the day I don't love her, I'll leave her."

"There's also Cuilan. Have you forgotten her? I think you and Cuilan are a better match."

"It's possible, but Cuilan wouldn't stay with me for long."

"Hmm, do you really still believe in everlasting love? Isn't that nonsense?"

"I'm sorry, Sixiang, I've said the wrong thing again."

Long Sixiang indignantly let go of his arm and moved a little further away.

Wei Bo's whole face burned. He felt like a rotten egg. He had made up his mind so many times not to go to A Si's apartment. He didn't know why he had to come when she called on the phone. She was also lonely. It was hard for a woman like her to find a lover who was her equal. Wei Bo excused himself for coming here time after time.

The apartment complex was called the Camellia Apartments, a name Wei Bo thought extremely fitting for Miss Si's home. Wasn't she a deep red camellia? They had looked for a place together, and Wei Bo was there the day she moved into it. While several of her "brothers" had a drink together, Wei Bo, his head full of camellias, watched A Si's cheeks flush crimson. As it turned out the place was not as suitable as its name suggested. Before long Wei Bo discovered A Si was being watched.

"I've known for a while," A Si said with a composed smile. "People like me are always exposed under a spotlight. There's nothing to talk about. So what?"

"You're very brave."

"How could I not be? Ever since leaving the cotton mill, I feel like I could adapt to anything. It wouldn't matter if I lived in a den of wolves."

The curtains in her room were always pulled shut with an opening left at the side. She liked to stand there and steal a look outdoors. Whenever Wei Bo saw her standing at the window he couldn't help sighing over and over. A Si would start to laugh, saying he "did not understand the mindset of the poor." Wei Bo asked her what she meant by "the poor." She answered that the poor were those without privacy. She said that the poor knew how to enjoy themselves, too; she had mastered the subtleties of this. Wei Bo thought A Si extraordinary, to hold this sophistication in her bosom at such a young age.

Miss Si was finally arrested for unlicensed prostitution and taken away "to be educated." Wei Bo learned from another prostitute that when A Si was questioned by the judicial officials she often seemed absentminded and had to be reprimanded many times for giving answers that did not fit the questions. She was sentenced to hauling sand, very hard labor. Wei Bo and another of her "brothers" spent a large sum of money to buy her out again.

"They keep saying I'm fallen, but I don't think I am. It's only prejudice, it's the rigid laws," she said to Wei Bo.

Wei Bo just smiled bitterly. They both knew the informant was the old man downstairs, but A Si did not hold a grudge against him. On the contrary, she said the old man wasn't really so old, that he was all alone without a woman for a companion, and that he needed pity. "Not that I want him to keep informing on me, of course. I'm not fit to go to prison. I might start having hallucinations about never being able to leave, which would be like returning to the workroom at the cotton mill. When they were questioning me, all I could hear was the *bang bang bang* of the machines. They think I'm resisting, but I'm not doing it on purpose."

Every time Wei Bo recalled these words, he would realize again what kind of memories the factory had left her, and at the same time be shocked at her resilience. Without having met Miss Si, Wei Bo could never have imagined someone in her situation being so undisturbed. He sensed that the young woman was able to think deeply and thoroughly about what happened to her and was in this respect more experienced than himself.

Wei Bo wanted to go back to the cotton mill with A Si so they could find the wooden bench where they'd sat the first time they talked. Although A Si was reluctant, she finally agreed to go.

Choosing a day when the mill was closed, they snuck onto the factory grounds and looked here and there with welling emotions. They sat down on the wooden bench with the *yulan* magnolia behind them. Wei Bo suggested on a whim that they go look at the workroom, saying he had seen the door was left open. A Si hesitated, but agreed.

Wei Bo would forever regret what happened next: A Si fell fainting among the machines and cut her head open. He gathered her in his arms, ran from the factory, and hailed a taxi to take them to the emergency room. The wound from the machine tool was so deep he was convinced A Si was dying.

Later it turned out to be a false alarm. The doctor said the wound was deep, to be sure, but somehow not a serious injury. The doctor also said A Si's health was exceptional. If it had been someone else, the injury might have been grave. Wei Bo wondered, not understanding what the doctor's words meant. He stood in the corridor outside the observation room berating himself, repentant to the point of madness.

After only two days of observation, the doctor said A Si could leave the hospital. How was this possible? Such a large wound, which had not been sutured or treated for inflammation, and just like that . . . discharged? Wei Bo tried asking for more information, but the doctor waved him off and told them to leave.

"A Si, will you be all right?" Wei Bo's voice shook.

"Oh, Wei Bo, you think too little of me! I wanted to fall against the machines and get hurt, so of course I'm sure of my recovery. You don't need to worry."

As she was speaking A Si moved the white sheet aside and got out of bed. Wei Bo saw the deep cavity on her head, and cold sweat oozed down his back.

She bent over to tie her shoelaces like a normal person, then picked up her bag and said she wanted to go home. Wei Bo hurried to support her.

A Si sat in the car with the side of her head that was not injured toward Wei Bo, looking at him from time to time with a foolish smile. Wei Bo couldn't guess why she was so happy.

"Does it hurt?"

"What does it matter? I could stand the pain even if it were ten times worse."

Once they got back to A Si's home at the Camellia Apartments, Wei Bo asked her why she had wanted to hurt herself. She answered that she could not stand the hallucination she was having.

He kept her company for three unforgettable days. No one disturbed them. He was like her husband.

A Si made a large white flower out of gauze to cover her wound. She was still weak from the loss of blood. She leaned on Wei Bo's shoulder and told him quietly about how when they were on the workroom floor of the cotton mill she suddenly felt as though she belonged there, that she would always belong to that place. Then the accident followed. When she had worked there, young men hid in the holly trees at the factory entrance waiting for her shift to end. She remembered it as her golden age. She was not sad to have left that life, though, because one must mature. Why would she injure herself? Wei Bo exhausted his mind without figuring out why. A Si was too strange. If she thought she would always belong there, then going back was simply going back. She also thought that she could never go back, that staying at the cotton mill was a dead end, just like it was for her good friend (that girl who died in the workroom, who sat down feebly, and it was over). No, A Si wasn't like a horse that always grazes in the same place.

After dinner they sat nestling on the balcony, watching the sky grow darker by degrees. There was someone in the flower garden across the way watching them with binoculars. A Si said it was the Informant.

"This is what I like best," A Si whispered in Wei Bo's ear. "Isn't it like judgment day? Look, he stood up—ha, he squatted back down. He's next to the acacia tree, the lover's tree. Give me a kiss—no, on this side. Oh, terrific! I love that old man. Don't you believe me?"

After a while, she continued, "I've never even spoken to him! He always hides from me. I want to tell him not to feel any regret . . . Wei Bo, you have to go to work tomorrow, but I can't be without you! What can he see, now that it's dark?"

On the walk home Wei Bo cried the whole way. The expanse of darkness in his mind made him feel like he was looking out over an abyss.

When he reached home, his wife didn't seem to notice anything out of the ordinary. Wei Bo ordered himself not to go to A Si, at least for a short time. He hoped he would be able to do this.

As it turned out, he didn't go to her place for a long time. He became a little bit . . . how could one put it? A little bit decadent. Many things inside him were in the gradual process of dying. He turned into a work machine. Beyond his original job, he took on all kinds of part-time work, including a job transporting corpses at the hospital. The work of moving corpses brought him a certain comfort. He harbored a gentle state of mind as he thought of these bodies that had stopped breathing, as he carefully arranged them.

When the door closed behind him, A Si thought, What a sensible man! If souls are reincarnated, could the two of them have been the same person at an earlier time?

She picked up her cosmetics case and began to do her makeup, applying a thick layer of powder to her pallid face. Now, with the large white flower of gauze on her head, Miss Si looked a little like a Japanese geisha.

She walked back and forth across the room, ghostly. She heard the clock on the wall strike nine.

Someone knocked on the door.

"Who is it?"

"It's me, your neighbor."

The Informant entered. He was not as old as he usually appeared to be and even looked energetic in the mild lamplight. His eyes latched onto Miss Si's body like hooks. He was muttering something ambiguous. A Si leaned closer and heard that he was asking her to take off the large white flower on her head. He wanted to see the wound.

A Si removed the white flower and leaned her head toward him.

She heard the elderly man make a strange cry and run from the apartment. She laughed coldly and went across to close the door. She wondered, What had the old man seen? If she saw him tomorrow she would have to ask. Shortly before A Si's father passed away he had told her to find a friend of his, but without telling her how to get in contact. Could this strange elderly man be her father's close friend?

She sank into melancholy recollections. Oh, that winter, the sky full of snow-flakes! Her father struggling to breathe, her mother weeping at the bedside, A Si suctioning the phlegm for her father with a tube. Even now she could hear her panicking voice, "Father, do you feel a little better?"

Her father pointed with one finger to something outside the window and repeated, "Si . . . Si . . ."

She never understood, from beginning to end, what her father wanted. She was so upset she wept along with her mother, their arms around each other.

Her father had not died then, but lasted another year before passing. It was a hellish time. Every evening, as the sun fell behind the mountains, the paroxysms started. The demons surged in feverishly with the night, yet her father was tenacious. She wished he would die, to ease his pain, but he refused to go. That year was A Si's greatest trial, her soft heart hardening in the wake of each of those terrifying fits.

In his final moments her father left her with a smile. He was pleased with his daughter.

She and her mother took her father's ashes and buried them a little here and a little there around the courtyard. Not long after the courtyard was flattened by bulldozers.

A Si felt the wound on her head with her hand. The cut was a little swollen, though not painful. Why had she wanted to throw herself against the machines? She didn't know. Maybe she wanted to find out what material made up her body. That year her father had already made this experiment. She remembered that as she threw herself against that ice-cold object she had repeated to herself, "I have to, I have to . . ." Afterward she felt guilty toward Wei Bo. Inwardly she called herself "a woman who ruins other people's lives."

Since she had left the cotton mill, the scope of her activities had expanded. She dug into the city's crevices, avidly absorbing the nourishment of life. She knew innately which places would be nourishing. Naturally, rejection was the best teacher. Nothing could make her mature more quickly than running against walls and being rebuffed. She thought she even wanted to be rebuffed. So she had thrown herself against the machine tool. Ha, that was why! Couldn't she say she was becoming more intelligent?

In her memories A Si walked through the gloomy shadows cast by the small town's single-story buildings. Her mother was the most enlightened mother in the world. She and A Si parted ways when the daughter was seventeen and found a job as a spinner at the cotton mill. A Si's mother said she was going to the countryside to visit relatives and would be away for a long time.

"I haven't been to see them since I married your father. I heard they've all moved into Dongting Lake, putting up thatched-roofed sheds where the water is shallow and raising ducks for a living. What would that be like? I have to see in person to know for sure."

Her mother's face flushed as she spoke these words. Her eyes showed her yearning for a life of freedom. A Si sensed vaguely that this time they were separating never to meet again. She wanted to cry, but instead she began to laugh foolishly. Her mother laughed along with her, then she said, "Come to join me soon."

After she left she never contacted A Si again. A Si thought about how she was so much like her mother. Thinking of these events now, she was grateful to her parents. She had gone to the lake region when she happened to pass by it on her way somewhere else. She had seen the thatched huts, but they were crooked and leaned in all directions. There couldn't possibly be anyone living in them. The huts where people lived seemed to have been gone for many years. An old fisherman told her, "In those days it was as lively here as when the theater is in town."

Before falling asleep A Si heard an ancient voice singing a love song in the flower garden out front. It sounded like the downstairs Informant. The ardent, ringing voice accompanied A Si's somber, extended dream. In the dream A Si said to the hidden singer, "Where I live the winter thunder is rolling in and those leaning shacks are everywhere I look. Can you sing about this scene?" She was actually standing beside Dongting Lake, the lake of caves, with the wind from the lake blowing so hard she could not keep her footing. She said to herself softly, "Such a good dream, I don't want to wake up."

She woke up at noon the next day.

She saw her lover from when she worked at the cotton mill, the Trailblazer, sitting on the windowsill. The curtains were open. Golden sunlight filled the whole room.

"I heard you were injured and hurried over. Your door was unlocked and opened with one push. What's the matter with it? I saw an old man messing with the lock. Was he playing a trick on you?"

"That old man is a friend of mine," A Si said, disappointed.

"Once I heard about your injury, all the affection I had for you came back to life. Do you still remember those times we spent in the factory park? You're not badly hurt?"

A Si dully observed the Trailblazer's handsome face and felt the same seduction as before. Yet this temptation seemed to be separated from her by a membrane, such that at this moment it no longer touched her. He had so much life in him! Had he come to test her? A Si lowered her head and started giggling.

The Trailblazer pounced on her. A Si snatched a pair of scissors from the table and stabbed the man in the arm.

"You're really extreme." He retreated through the door, saying, "A Si, I love you even more!"

"Love, what's love? My door is unlocked. You can visit any time."

After he left, her neighbor the Informant stuck his head in at the door.

"Couldn't you wear a shower cap?" he implored.

"I can't. The cut needs air. What did you see in it?"

"I saw—an abyss!"

He slammed the door shut in despair.

A Si lay in the bathtub, listening silently to the noise in the hallway, with an intuition that the Trailblazer had not gone yet. Maybe he was talking with the old man. Years ago, he was the one who had altered her stifled life and helped her through difficulties. Now she repaid his kindness with revenge. The old man was the kind of person who interested her. He had seen an abyss in her wound that horrified him. Was he her father's friend?

A Si dressed slowly and deliberately. Her movements in the sunlight seemed to her almost unreal. She heard the sound of cloth tearing. It must be him binding his wound—the indomitable Trailblazer.

Many years earlier Wei Bo and Long Sixiang had a brief affair. Long Sixiang was still a young woman and bashful around men. Without knowing how it happened, she fell in love with him, bewildered, convinced that Wei Bo was a suitable man to take as a lover. Wei Bo did not fall in love with her at first, although he soon recognized her distinctive charm. She was the uninhibited type of woman, with more vigor than normal people, and so exuberant it was hard to believe. For long afterward Wei Bo's blood surged when he thought of her. Then she married. He consciously distanced himself from her. After she was married she didn't seek him out either, so he believed she had found happiness. She left him with glorious memories.

Many years later, when Wei Bo ran into this former lover at the hot springs, the shock was enormous. He saw the vivacious young Sixiang now middle-aged, her beauty faded and face wrinkled. She had lost her family and was all alone.

"Oh, Wei Bo, I'm not good enough for you now, but I'm still searching for what will make me happy."

When she said the word *hap—py* she bared her teeth, showing a wide gap between the front two.

Wei Bo's heart tensed and shrank. He grasped both of her hands tight. She abruptly pushed him away and burst into laughter.

"You big idiot! You're like a brother to me now. You have to help me! My friend Jin Zhu and I waited too long to leave the cotton mill. But I believe there's no too late, only too lazy. Don't you think so? When there's enough will, it's never too late."

"Well said! Well said!" Wei Bo's commendation was loud and sincere.

This was when he finally noticed Jin Zhu, a dark, thin, middle-aged laborer who appeared to be ill, standing behind Long Sixiang. Jin Zhu walked over to him in a poised way and took his arm. The two women, one on each side, were all but hanging off of Wei Bo. Then the three of them went to the reception room together and fell onto the sofa.

That same day Wei Bo helped the women find jobs as sex workers at the spa.

The two women fell in love with Wei Bo at the same time, although it wasn't a sexual attraction.

After Long Sixiang learned about Wei Bo's relationship with Miss Si, she went through a period of jealousy during which she did all she could to slander A Si, leaving Wei Bo very unhappy. Long Sixiang's unconventional way of attacking A Si also puzzled him. For example, she talked about A Si having a secret lover. This lover was a powerful man who could help A Si leave her current situation to lead an upper-class life. A Si's nature, however, was difficult to change. She preferred to be a prostitute, to struggle bitterly on the lowest level of society.

Why? Because she was the kind of woman whom nothing could satisfy. That lover would not relinquish her and waited, suffering, for her to change her mind. Another time Long Sixiang said A Si had an unmentionable disease that prevented her from getting pregnant. Lacking that ability, she had "vowed to enjoy the pleasures of sex to the fullest." When Long Sixiang attacked A Si in this furtive manner, while appearing so excited, Wei Bo vaguely felt that her words had multiple meanings. Could she possibly be praising A Si to enflame Wei Bo? Long Sixiang gossiped about these things so much that Wei Bo was no longer angry. He gradually learned how to listen attentively for the information she gave him.

Wei Bo sat in Long Sixiang's small room with advertisements featuring handsome men pasted all over the walls and said to her, "You're concerned for A Si, aren't you? You don't need to worry."

Long Sixiang's tears fell as she said gently, "Hush, this doesn't need saying!"

Wei Bo stroked Long Sixiang's hair, which was black as a crow's wing, and sighed with many emotions. He knew the life in front of her was the same as A Si's, filled with hardship and uncertainty. From the bottom of his heart he prayed for Long Sixiang to have good luck, to keep her health.

"Wei Bo, I'm going to take you somewhere," she whispered in his ear.

"Where?"

"To hell. Do you dare? I'm talking about the little house where A Si's mother lives on the outskirts of the city. Are you interested?"

"Of course I'm interested. I've never heard A Si mention her mother. Does she even know where she lives? It's crazy!"

"It is crazy. She doesn't know where her mother lives, but I do."

So the two of them went to where A Si's mother lived.

What a place it was! A low single mudbrick room surrounded on all sides by pigsties belonging to her relatives. Sitting in her room they could hear the pigs' constant squealing, plaintive, as though they were being starved by their owners. The elderly woman wore a patterned scarf the way peasant women do, her manner also like a woman from the countryside. Wei Bo was surprised that in broad daylight she had pulled the curtains tight, concealing the inside of the room. A television set placed on a worn, crooked table was playing a pornographic film with the sound turned down low. When they came in, the old woman might have been watching it. She didn't turn off the TV when they sat down. Wei Bo watched for a moment, but, finding the film too stimulating, he promptly turned his eyes away. The moans still reached his ears.

"Mother, this is A Si's friend, I've brought him to you," Long Sixiang said, hugging her.

"Who are you?" she asked.

Wei Bo felt a pair of panther's eyes staring at him. His heart pounded and raced.

"I work at a soap factory and part-time at a few other jobs . . . I, I'm a good friend of your daughter. We've known each other for . . ."

"Who are you really?" she interrupted impatiently. "Was it you who took me to the hospital twenty-eight years ago? Why do you look so familiar?"

"Answer Mother honestly," Long Sixiang said quietly in Wei Bo's ear.

"It could be, Mother." Wei Bo grew calmer. "I might have done something like that. I know that your daughter A Si is very distinctive."

"Don't flatter, it's no use. You don't seem to be a complete disaster, like A Si has always been. Sixiang, who's she fooling around with now?"

"The largest opium dealer in the South China region. He's an addict who's been to prison twice."

"Huh, can messing around with a man like that end well?"

A sudden burst of squealing outside made their hair stand on end. The three were silent. For a while none of them opened their mouths. There were only the lewd sounds coming from the couple (two women) on the TV. The atmosphere in the room was very strange.

"Mother," Long Sixiang spoke first, "has the old pig keeper gone out?"

"Oh, he went to market. Two of the pigs are going to customers who've arranged to buy them. He left first thing this morning. He didn't feed the pigs and won't let me help him. He's a killer!"

Long Sixiang told Wei Bo in a lowered voice that the swineherd, a very handsome old man, was the boyfriend of A Si's mother. "If I were in her place, I'd be in love with him, too!" She abruptly raised her voice. "You shouldn't think being a pig keeper is a bad job. Every field has its high achievers," she added.

A Si's mother watched Long Sixiang, nodding as she spoke, as though immersed in memories.

"Winter was so cold that year! The pigs almost froze to death, but we had no money. The doors and windows of the pigsties were shattered by the wind. The troughs turned to ice. I'd never seen such a snowstorm."

After these few sentences she stopped, growing irritated.

"How can he still be wandering around outside? Damn that guy! I'll kill him! I'm easily provoked . . . Hey, soap factory drudge, you've seen that the women in our family can get upset easily! I suggest you settle down as soon as possible. Humph."

Long Sixiang saw that things were going poorly and hauled Wei Bo outside.

They walked back and forth among the pigsties. Wei Bo covered his ears with both hands, but the shrieks still turned his face white. He felt as if he were the pig being slaughtered.

Long Sixiang, meanwhile, was as calm as if she did not hear them.

"Do you understand everything now?" she asked.

Wei Bo did not understand at all. What sort of woman was A Si's mother? Why had Long Sixiang wanted him to come here? His sole impression was that the old woman had a cruel temper.

"No, Sixiang, I don't understand."

"Good!" Long Sixiang clapped her hands. "Your not understanding *is* understanding!"

With her first clap the pigs went mad, their cries rising straight to the heavens. Two spotted pigs burst out of the pen and tore toward them. Wei Bo rushed to push Long Sixiang away, shielding her. He heard A Si's mother in the distance stomping her feet and cursing.

After the two possessed pigs rushed past, they turned around and dashed back toward them. Wei Bo dragged Long Sixiang against the earthen wall of the building—there were even more pigs inside.

The spotted pigs finally disappeared from sight. Wei Bo, who was dripping with sweat, asked Long Sixiang, "Will we make it back alive?"

"What are you talking about, Wei Bo? You're shameless!"

He saw her eyes shining with boundless excitement.

They walked for at least half an hour before leaving the pigsties behind and coming to the main road.

Long Sixiang grew listless and complained to Wei Bo as they walked. She said she'd been disappointed in love recently and sometimes thought she couldn't go on living.

"I wish I were A Si's mother!" she suddenly cried.

Then she dragged on Wei Bo's arm, forcing him to pull her slowly along as she told him her sorrows. Her words were ambiguous. Wei Bo couldn't tell what she was saying, aside from constantly bringing up A Si, which unsettled him.

The bus to the hot springs arrived. Wei Bo helped Long Sixiang onto the bus, supporting her by the arm into a seat. She fell asleep propped against the back of the seat. When the bus reached their stop, Wei Bo had to carry her off in his arms and walk her to her little room at the spa. Standing out front, she finally woke up and found her keys in the little purse she was carrying. She reproached Wei Bo: "Why are you here?"

"I was seeing you back."

"Ha, I'd forgotten. You really can't come in, because A Si's in the room next door. She's doing business with her new customer, and there's only a partition between the rooms. You can hear everything. I'm afraid you won't be able to stand it!"

"Then I'll go."

"Come back! I'll call A Si to come out! A Si! A Si!"

A small gate to the side creaked as A Si's pale face appeared. She looked like she hadn't slept enough. The gauze flower on her head was kneaded into wrinkles.

Wei Bo remembered the wound on her head, shivered involuntarily, and could not speak. The greatest question in his mind was, Why did A Si still come to the spa to meet her clients when she had her own apartment? Then Long Sixiang pushed him to the side, telling him, "All right, all right, you've seen her. You should go. A Si's busy."

He left unwillingly. Long Sixiang saw him to the entrance of the spa and asked about his reaction to seeing A Si. He asked her why A Si came here to meet her clients.

"Maybe it's to avoid someone. A Si is very clever. She often meets customers here. Don't think of her as injured. It doesn't seem to affect her business. I hear her calling me. Go back home, quick!"

Wei Bo felt abandoned by these two women. He was an outsider who couldn't enter their world. Hadn't A Si stared at him with indifferent eyes? That proved she and he were not on the same path. Wei Bo was suddenly exhausted, mentally and physically. He blindly busied himself here and there, but what was he looking for? Didn't the two women's behavior toward him show he was extraneous? His mind a stretch of hollowness, his steps slowed—he should go home.

Without knowing how it happened, Wei Bo did not go home, but to a small bar instead.

He ordered rice wine because he rarely drank. One man sat at the other end of the bar, the brim of his hat lowered so that his face couldn't be seen. He had ordered Five Grain liquor, so he was probably well-off. They drank their own drinks and ate their own food.

After finishing two cups of rice wine and a plate of celery with pork liver, Wei Bo felt his spirits lift. Through the door he could see that it was already dusk. He thought, Should I go home right away?

"Home is always here, but if you miss a liaison it will never happen," the man opposite said, raising his hat.

He turned out to be Mr. You from the antiques shop.

"I know you went to the pigsties with Long Sixiang. No, don't misunderstand me. I'm not in love with A Si. Sixiang is the one I love, that woman warrior."

He continued, "I've been drinking here all day with the old pig keeper. We trust each other. There's something I can't figure out, though. A Si's mother took over the pig keeper, but she's unfaithful, which makes things painful for him. Why?"

Wei Bo was a little surprised at Mr. You treating him as if he were a friend. It might have been Long Sixiang's influence.

"I can't understand why," Wei Bo said. "From my observations of A Si's mother, maybe this is true love. The pig keeper must feel that she loves him. She's a very special mother. My time at her home was unforgettable."

They talked about a few irrelevant things. Wei Bo saw the moon had already risen. As his mood mellowed, he finally wanted to go home.

Returning home, he saw his wife eating alone. The food was delectable, and she ate with an appetite. She asked Wei Bo whether he had eaten. He said he had eaten at a friend's.

When Wei Bo came out of the shower, Xiao Yuan had also finished eating.

"Wei Bo," she began, "I've known for a long time that you had affairs. I have too, but I don't want to lose you or this home." Her expression showed her perplexity.

"Then don't throw them away," Wei Bo answered tensely.

"I saw that young woman. The strange thing is that I wasn't jealous. I even admired her. Can you tell me how that's possible? I do admire A Si, but I couldn't live the way she does. Of course, you can't either, though I think you two would be a good match."

"That's ridiculous. I'm not with her anymore. She doesn't belong to me."

Wei Bo sat at home thinking back over what had happened during the day. Feelings of remorse assaulted him. Why couldn't he answer when A Si's mother asked him who he was? Like a fool he referred to his occupation, which naturally proved nothing, so the old woman had stormed and raged, and now she looked down on him. His words were spilled water and could not be taken back. Today was the day he regretted the most of any since he was born. He thought his performance had been especially bad. He could not face A Si again.

In the middle of the night, he woke up again and lay in the dark pondering. He thought his relationship with A Si must be the greatest failure of his life. He was a rotten sort of man. He also thought of Cuilan, whom he had met not long before. This woman was obviously more significant, more capable, than himself. Now that his relationship with A Si had fallen into dishonor, he should draw from the teachings of experience and treat a woman like Cuilan well. Recently he had been seeing the same familiar place in his dreams, a place similar to the pigsties he had visited that day. Sometimes he was there alone, sometimes he was walking back and forth with Cuilan. He didn't know what he was looking for there, only, in short, that he was looking for something. Cuilan seemed to know what he was looking for while not wanting to help him look. She mocked him, saying he could not see the road under his feet. Could the thing he was looking for be underfoot? When he lowered his head, he couldn't even see his feet. Wei Bo recalled what Cuilan said in the dream with a vague premonition: maybe he had reached a turning point in his life; maybe from today forward he would not be so awful. Yet Wei Bo was Wei Bo. What could he change into?

"How can I change into anything?"

His voice was so loud he woke up Xiao Yuan in the adjoining room.

"People can change themselves into forms they could never imagine in dreams," she responded from that direction.

In the dark Wei Bo's face burned. He changed his clothes with quiet motions and went outside to the main road. A man followed behind him, chattering.

"There are night wanderers like us everywhere in the city. Look over that way, there's a light shining in a window on the ninth floor. Who is she waiting for? It must be for people like us. Where are you going? You're a reckless one, you want to go into the dark . . . Come with me!"

He shoved Wei Bo into an alleyway alongside a theater where gamblers gathered throughout the year.

Wei Bo obediently let the man drag him along. In any case he could not see in the darkness.

They went down many flights of stairs together before reaching level ground. Wei Bo heard the man say, "Sit down." He and Wei Bo sat on the same bench. Someone lit a candle and walked toward them with an agitated look. Wei Bo thought the face above the candle looked like an uncle, his father's younger brother. The man stood in front of Wei Bo, reached out a hand, and pressed down on his head. The agony in Wei Bo's mind lifted.

"Go back often to see your hometown," he told Wei Bo. "People shouldn't forget their roots."

A gust of wind blew past, extinguishing the candle in his hand.

Wei Bo was submerged by the dark again. He sat for a while with the sensation of emptiness around him. He reached out a hand to feel to the side without touching the person who had sat down with him. Wei Bo wondered if the other two had stealthily left. Figuring that he wouldn't be able to find the way back, he lay down on the bench. Soon he heard a woman's whimpering, not too far away, and a hoarse male voice at her side consoling her. The man repeated the same thing, "A Si, A Si, we'll fly far, far away . . ."

The woman was not Wei Bo's girlfriend A Si. How many A Si's were there in this city? He had been startled to hear that person tell him to go back often to see his hometown. He'd used to have an ancestral home. When his father was alive, he took Wei Bo back every year. His father had a strange habit, which was that every time before they boarded the train he covered Wei Bo's eyes with an eyeshade and made him pretend to be blind. He threatened Wei Bo, saying that if he removed the eyeshade they would not reach their hometown. Young Wei Bo obediently let his eyes be covered and sat motionless on the train—he wanted so much to go to their hometown. Not until they reached the home of his uncle, his father's older brother, was Wei Bo finally allowed to take off the eyeshade. The train ran along for a day and a night, little Wei Bo so lonesome he couldn't stand it. He asked his father over and over whether their hometown was in the north or in the south. Each time his father said it was in the south. Then why was the large courtyard where his uncle's family lived always so cold? The south should be warm. The walls enclosing the courtyard were as tall as two adults. The courtyard was so enormous that it took half an hour to walk from one end to the other. Wild grass even taller than Wei Bo grew everywhere, drowning the path beneath. The old building had two stories with many, many rooms, which Wei Bo could never count exactly because of the peculiar structure of the ancient architecture. One time he actually got lost inside those empty rooms and corridors. He walked and walked, but whenever he thought he had found the entrance to the stairs, he was hemmed in again by the unfamiliar passages. This went on until nightfall. He was almost losing hope when his aunt finally found him and led him to the kitchen below to eat dinner. He had returned three times altogether before he turned ten years old. He had countless questions regarding the location of his ancestral home, the geography beyond the courtyard, and so on. His father was too impatient to answer him. Only two people, Wei Bo's uncle and aunt, lived in the family's ancestral home. The gate to the courtyard was always locked, and only the adults had the keys. Even though Wei Bo decided to investigate, he was not once able to do what he wanted. His uncle and aunt rarely spoke and never responded to Wei Bo's questions. The three adults' pastime was evening tea on the second-floor balcony. The balcony was large and meticulously clean, with rattan chairs placed all over. The evening wind blew gently as they drank black tea and watched the moon rise bit by bit. In Wei Bo's memory the moon was brighter than in the city and as big as the copper basin for handwashing. Was his hometown in the countryside then? That wasn't right, either. Sitting on the balcony Wei Bo could hear the faint sound of motor vehicles driving past in the distance and see the work lamps of a construction site. If his hometown were located in an urban area, how could there be this courtyard as large as the imperial palaces? The three adults only drank tea, looked at the moon, did not speak. Pot after pot of black tea brewed as they sat late into the night. Each time Wei Bo fell asleep in

Even so, an intuition told her that her mother was the kind of woman who did not collapse under pressure, who would never sink to ruin. She wondered, What's wrong with her living between the pigsties? As long as her mind was clear and clean it wouldn't matter. When A Si's father was ill for so many years, hadn't her mother survived and never left him? A Si grew happier at this thought. Her mother liked to cry, but out of loneliness, not weakness. Many years ago, once A Si, who'd gained a thorough understanding of her mother's nature, was separated from her, she'd felt to her surprise that a difficulty in her life had been resolved, as if a stone weighing on her mind had fallen to the ground. Now, years later, she received news of her mother's whereabouts. She did not need to go see her since, Long Sixiang hinted, her mother did not wish to see her. Indirect reports were enough for them to encourage one another.

"A Si, you're smiling. What's the good news?" the opium dealer asked in bed.

"My mother had someone bring me a message." A Si turned over to face him.

"Congratulations! Your mother must be an extreme woman."

"She's never hurt anyone."

"An admirable woman."

The opium dealer was suddenly restless and said he needed to catch the night train.

He put on his clothes, picked up his briefcase, reached out to open the door, thought for a moment, stood in place, turned back to look fixedly at A Si, and then said one syllable at a time, "I will be gone for three hundred days and nights. Can you withstand the trial?"

He finished and left.

A Si said loudly in the direction of the door, "Three hundred days and nights leading to the grave!"

She burrowed into his lingering warmth in the blankets and turned off the light. She supposed that from now on her mother would often send her messages. So many years had passed. How many times they had plotted out their lives together while looking at the little violet flowers in the fava bean fields on the hillside! Her mother had even suggested A Si join a troupe of acrobats. Her mother would travel with them to manage the apparatus and scrape together food. She said mother and daughter would see the world, looking after one another. In fact, her mother had known already that A Si was the kind of girl who didn't need looking after. As A Si remembered now, her mother had been examining her all along, analyzing her nature with complete precision. Could those long talks in the fava bean fields have formed A Si's character, without her being aware?

"A Si! A Si!" Wei Bo knocked gently at the door.

"Come in, the door isn't shut!" A Si responded in a loud voice.

He entered, repeating, "Don't turn on the light! Don't turn on the light! I'm so ashamed I'll go mad, A Si!"

Wei Bo hid in the shadow of a large cabinet, trying to reduce the size of his body as much as possible. A Si could picture how distressed he was when he said, "I shouldn't have come, I'm worthless."

"There's a stool next to you. You can sit down," A Si answered.

Wei Bo sat down, his heart trying to jump into his mouth.

"Look at me. I've come to you out of loneliness. It's despicable, and I'm always causing you trouble. All of a sudden I just had to come back."

"Don't blame yourself too much, Wei Bo. Sometimes it's better not to care about things. Like I do, for instance, though I'm not a good example. You couldn't stand my life. Oh, Wei Bo, you are a good person. Meeting you has been the greatest happiness of my life."

"I'll leave, A Si. You've given me strength. You always give me strength."

He came and then left. A Si felt the cut on her head. The wound was healing. It itched.

Back then, by the flower garden at the mill, Wei Bo had given her an impression of freshness, like roses early in the morning! She would use roses to describe Wei Bo. Whether they were together or apart, from beginning to end, Wei Bo was the rose in the dark places of her heart. The sky would soon be light. She knew the Informant had not gone to sleep. He was downstairs shining a flashlight at her window, one of his favorite things to do. A Si gathered the blankets in her arms under the influence of the simmering passion within the apartments. "Camellia Apartments, Camellia Apartments . . . ," she intoned. Waves of happiness engulfed her.

Long Sixiang came to see her at home the next day.

"Wei Bo's acting strange. I'm worried he's going to extremes," A Si said in a dejected tone of voice.

"Impossible, he's not that kind of person. Even if he did go to extremes, wouldn't that be an enterprise?" Long Sixiang said, her eyes widening.

"Sixiang! Sixiang! You really are like a sister to me . . ."

In her enthusiasm A Si kissed Long Sixiang on the cheek.

"I simply have to invite you to the West Pavilion for a drink!" she added.

Half an hour later, the two of them appeared at the West Pavilion bar.

They had just sat down when Mr. You came over.

"Ah, beautiful women! My good fortune. It's drizzling outside. Did you bring umbrellas? I'm here to shelter you under my umbrella. It's only right to protect precious royalty such as yourselves."

His expression was melancholy, the beautiful eyes in his pale face no longer twinkling. He seemed to be avoiding the women's glances. Long Sixiang deduced that he had gone the whole night without sleeping.

The lights were never turned on inside the West Pavilion, which was lit only with candles. Shadows swayed on the gray walls. In the spirit of drinking, the three people gradually turned into one person, not distinguishing you and me among themselves. Without knowing why, they all came to believe they had grown up together in a small courtyard with a raised calabash arbor. Seen from beneath the arbor, the sun seemed to rest on the tiled roof of the place where they all lived. Mr. You said, "A voice shouting into the wind, 'Come back, Little Phoenix! Come back . . .'"

Long Sixiang and A Si could not help weeping at Mr. You's story. They bent over the table and sobbed, *wu wu*. Long Sixiang said through her tears, "Dear You, how could I have fallen in love with someone like you?"

"It's because you and I are like parts of the same body. People who come from our little courtyard know each other by sight, throughout society . . . Do you both still remember the black snake? The one next to the well?"

"Of course I remember!" the women said at the same time and stopped crying. They stared at Mr. You, waiting for him to describe it.

Mr. You's mouth opened wider and wider, but no words tumbled out. His mind was a stretch of white space. He slapped himself in the head, stamped his feet in annoyance, poured himself a cup and drained it. Then, face flushed red, he shouted, "It's . . . It's . . . I've forgotten what it was!"

The fat bartender walked over, patted Mr. You on the shoulder, and said affably, "What else could it be? The woman who left, of course!"

"How did you know?" Mr. You seized the front of the bartender's shirt.

"Wei Bo told me. I know everything about your group and its affairs."

Mr. You released him and stared blankly at the dark windowpane.

When A Si heard him say "Wei Bo," a rush of warmth rose in her heart. She snatched the bartender's hand and kissed it. Tears obscuring her eyes, she looked at him and said, "Everything about you reminds me of my father!"

The bartender, pleased to hear this, hummed a tune as he walked, swaying, over to the counter.

The three companions walked, swaying, holding each other up, down the street. No one knew who first said they were going to find Wei Bo. They all remembered the words of the bartender at the West Pavilion, "Wei Bo is in prison undergoing reform."

A farm tractor emerged from the dark. The driver was a rough young man.

"Did Lao Yong send you? We want to use the tractor!" Long Sixiang said, her hands on her hips.

The young man didn't make a sound, so the three of them got onto the tractor and sat in the tow bed behind.

A Si shivered the entire ride. Long Sixiang leaned over eagerly, "Lao Yong sent the tractor. Can you believe it? He sits in his spider hole predicting what will happen like some supernatural spirit. When he and I were at the Mandarin Ducks Suites, I thought many times of us turning into one person. A Si, do you think I'm being foolish? You'll make it, we'll be at the prison in less than two hours . . . although I'm not sure, maybe Wei Bo doesn't want us to disturb him. He's being reformed. It must be pleasant. He'll be enjoying himself."

"He's always unhappy with himself." A Si squeezed Long Sixiang's hand. "I don't think it's strange that someone like him would go to prison on purpose. Are there any rats there?"

"Of course there are rats!" Mr. You said, "I can understand why A Si is Wei Bo's idol. He's a lucky man!"

The tractor did not head toward the prison on the outskirts of the city. When they woke from their naps, they discovered it was circling a low hill. The place was deserted and obscured in the dark so they couldn't tell whether there was a road; they couldn't see anything. All three sensed that they were going in circles. The young man sat holding the steering wheel straight.

"Oh, Lao Yong, you're full of tricks!" Long Sixiang cried, although it was unclear whether in fury or admiration. The chugging of the tractor, *tu tu tu*, drowned out her voice.

The wind blew violently. On the tractor A Si huddled into a ball, dust and grit striking her in the face, the oily smoke from the diesel choking her until she almost vomited. She heard Mr. You beside her say, "I want to get down. I'm going to jump, but don't tell Wei Bo, either of you . . . One, two, three! I'm jumping!"

A Si couldn't see whether he had jumped or not. She only knew Long Sixiang was no longer next to her. She felt as though she couldn't defend herself. The specter of death was approaching. Her last thought was that dying on the road to find Wei Bo would sound good as a cause of death.

Then the tractor overturned in a pond.

Without struggling, A Si easily swam to the shore. It was only when the wind blew the wet clothing against her body that she worried she might catch her death of cold. Someone handed her a bundle of clothing. Her teeth chattered, *ge ge*, and her whole body seemed to shake like a sieve. It took her a long time to manage to put on the clothing.

"Are you Lao Yong?" she asked.

"Who else would I be? This is all part of Long Sixiang's plan. A woman with fantastic, grand ideas! Yesterday she told me that being attached to me means being attached to death. You'll see, she'll be here soon to put things in motion. Nothing on heaven or earth frightens her."

"Is that why you love her?"

"Bah! Don't talk about loving, not loving. She's trash."

"How can I get home, uncle?"

"Ha, I'd forgotten that you'd want to go home. Do you see that light to the right up ahead? Just walk toward it. Don't be afraid."

A Si had not seen any light ahead to the right, but now that Lao Yong said it was there, there it was. She strode in the direction she imagined to be the right diagonal. Strangely enough, she went smoothly along level ground. She could still hear Lao Yong behind her saying, "Yes, that's it."

At daybreak Miss Si, wearing a bizarre outfit, reached the Camellia Apartments.

She was embarrassed and hoped no one had seen her.

The Informant stood at the main entrance to her unit. The elderly man was obviously waiting for her with a basket of chrysanthemums in his hands. He was actually wearing wrinkled formal wear.

As she went upstairs, he followed her, chattering.

"Why do you have to do illegal things? Your friend Sixiang's partner is being monitored. He's the subject of investigation for dealing in inferior steel. Oh, why do you get involved in their mists of collusion? Did you think your trip on the tractor was just to go for a spin? They're using you as a front to smuggle the inferior goods. I followed on a motor scooter, but couldn't catch up with you!"

"Interesting, these 'mists of collusion,' how literary. Aren't I the subject of investigation, too?"

A Si opened the door and invited him into the apartment. He insisted instead on standing at the entrance.

"Oh, Miss Si, how can you see yourself this way? It's not good. I've always thought . . . I won't lie to you, I've always thought you were one of the most important people in this apartment complex."

"Now that I have a big scar on my completely bald head, look—." She took off her hat to show him. "What do you think now? Do you still think I'm important?"

A Si sat down, the light in her eyes duller. Looking at the dirty straw hat in her hand, she began to remember what had happened during the night. Where had Long Sixiang and Mr. You gone? It seemed as though they were the only ones who could go down into hell. She could not remember how she had gotten home. There seemed to have been so many wheelbarrows on the road always pressing her to one side. She had fallen into the gutter once. Hadn't the three of them started out looking for Wei Bo? How had she clean forgotten this?

"The scar on your head doesn't affect your status in the apartment complex."
The old man placed the basket of flowers on her table and withdrew.

A Si was grateful to him because he was the only one in the apartment complex who showed any concern for her. As for his reporting her to authorities, that could be forgiven. For someone as publicized as she was, there would always be people who informed. She had just heard him say she was one of the most important people in the apartments. What did that mean? A Si thought of herself as important, of course, but she had never considered whether she was important to this community. She hadn't interacted with the other residents of the Camellia Apartments, except for this Informant. She had assumed the Camellia Apartments were a paradise of happiness because the few happy events in her life had taken place here. As this miniature world tolerated her happiness, it was essentially good. In comparison to the mill, that sealed boxcar, she could certainly call the Camellia Apartments a "paradise of happiness."

She walked out onto the balcony. She saw that the sun was out as well as a few bareheaded men just leaving the apartment complex. They were all wearing black suits, tall, thin, and seeming to lack confidence. A Si sighed again and again as she watched them closely. She began to recall the boys of her younger days who'd resembled these men. She hallucinated that time was flowing backward. So much had happened since then! She told herself, "A Si, don't forget the rose."

She made herself noodles, singing cheerfully as she watched them boil in the pot. It was a nursery rhyme, the one her father had sung, stopping and starting, the day before he passed. The lyrics were about the lonely life of a brown bear. When she was little she cried every time she sang it, especially when she got to the part about "its fur." She suddenly became conscious that she sang this song because Wei Bo had gone to prison. Wasn't he the bear?

A Si, in a grateful frame of mind, analyzed her good fortune while she ate her spinach noodles. The rays of sun in the air were so brilliant. Even in his gloomy prison cell Wei Bo could enjoy the sunshine. He had a special talent, which A Si had experienced, for building a beautiful world for himself. Under what cold moon, over what bleak desert was he wandering today? After all, hadn't he gone to prison in order to have a more searching life? Perhaps she'd never really understood Wei Bo. His nature had another side to it. What should she do to repay the warmth he'd given her? She thought back and forth, and felt the best thing to do was to forget Wei Bo. Only this would repay his goodness.

A Si buried Wei Bo in the abyss of her heart and did not think of him again.

When she woke up from a long dream, she started to think of the vigorous, frenetic opium dealer. Where was that guy who always came and went like a ghost? When he had been here, he'd wanted to take her to the border region. He wanted her to experience the pleasure of his death-wish adventures. A Si was not interested. She thought taking risks for money was meaningless. They often fought over this issue. The opium dealer would slam the door and leave after accusing A Si of having "narrow interests." Before too long he would be back through the door again. A Si thought he was as naive as a child. She felt that if someone was in the state of mind to seek out death, no one could prevent it. It saddened her, but she prayed that he would enjoy the moment of his death to the greatest extent possible. She repeatedly imagined the scene of him on the truck being shot by the border patrol. He was the kind of man who shows calculated bravery when it comes to himself. A Si found this quality of his captivating.

When Long Sixiang announced that she was taking her to meet someone, A Si's heart pounded and started to race. So many years had passed. Was this still necessary?

"No, not your mother, someone else. He's one of my customers. You already know him."

So A Si met a neighbor from her childhood, two years younger than she was, in the spa's dimly lit tearoom. He had grown into a handsome man. He claimed that he had never been able to forget A Si.

Once Long Sixiang left, the man's face became blurred. A Si sensed a deception.

"Are you really Xiao Qi?" she asked him.

"Don't you think I look like him?" he asked in return.

"I don't know. I think you look similar, but not the same. The expression on your face fluctuates too much. When I look at you from the left and from the right, I see completely different men. The light in here is too low. Move under this lamp. Aaah!" She let out a scream.

Long Sixiang appeared at her cry, and the man ran away.

"He's not Xiao Qi. He's a policeman. You should be afraid of him," A Si said, trembling.

Long Sixiang started to laugh, hugged A Si tight, and said soothingly, "Maybe. He's my customer, at any rate, and I can't be scared of my customers. With us, who's afraid of whom? After we take off our clothes I can tell him to go to hell! Do you want me to help you get revenge, A Si? Let me tell you, though, he really is very gentle."

"It's possible," A Si said, sinking into thought. "After working in this business for a while, we know that a person has many faces," she added.

"You're right." Sixiang looked at her admiringly and patted her on the shoulder. "He was the one who wanted to see you. He has a guilty conscience about you. He said he was your neighbor Xiao Qi. Is he Xiao Qi or isn't he?"

"Is he Xiao Qi or isn't he?" A Si repeated this irritating question like an echo.

"I think he is! Once he told me he'd turned into a black panther, then changed back again. Oh no! It's pouring outside, and he ran out into the rain. What a pity. He said that he changed into a panther out of terror. All day he would say, 'Let me turn into a panther, let me turn into a panther,' until he actually became one."

"How is that possible?" A Si muttered.

"Why couldn't it be? It's his character! Haven't you seen that yet? No wonder you don't love him, while he has always loved you."

In that tiny tearoom, listening to the sound of the rain striking the asphalt, the thoughts of the two women lingered on all of the dangerous situations through which they had passed. It was satisfying to savor past danger from a position of safety, and they were both eager to tell each other these fantastic stories. They basked in the warm, familiar affection of the conversation. Then Long Sixiang interrupted, "I don't think he's left. Do you want to see him?"

A Si again trembled uncontrollably. Long Sixiang left.

The policeman came back in and sat timidly in a corner of the tearoom.

"Why did you pretend that you'd cut off your hand that day in the interrogation room?"

The policeman hung his head at first, but raised it to sweep A Si with his eyes when he heard her question.

A Si saw the chill light in his eyes and couldn't stop the severe shaking.

"It was fear, of course. You're the kind of woman who makes me afraid. I've cut myself many times trying to test my ability to feel. You see—"

He pulled up the leg of his trousers, revealing his scars. She counted for a moment. There were six altogether, one lined up next to another. The leg was visibly thinner than his other one because of the cuts.

"When I saw you, I had the impulse to perform. I'm not fit for police work because I'm attracted to you whores. I've resigned, I lost my job. I wish you would change your opinion of me."

"So are you really Xiao Qi? You used to be as skinny as a monkey."

"I often ask myself that. If even you can't recognize me, it's clear that it will be hard for me to change back into myself. Yesterday I heard Sixiang mention you, and it upset me. I told her I had to see you and apologize face-to-face."

"What will you do for a living?"

"Oh, don't worry. I'm earning my way. I opened a sesame cake stand. I wear dark glasses when I serve shoppers. Business is good. I know the way people see things can't change in just a short time. At least the dark glasses don't get in the way."

"Don't lose heart." A Si grew calmer. "There is nothing to be afraid of. Just count to yourself—one, two, three!—to be brave. That's what I used to do."

"Thank you, A Si. Now the knot in my heart is untied. Remember, you have a friend at the sesame cake stand. You are welcome there any time."

Wei Bo, feeling downcast, had not contacted Cuilan for many days. He did go often to the alleyway next to the theater, even though he never ventured deeper inside. The quiet depths of the hutong with the buildings on both sides blocking the sky frightened him. There were several gaps on both sides of the concrete surface, with small patches of open ground in the breaches. He had spent that earlier night on one of these pieces of open ground until the street cleaners drove him back to the world above. He counted down more than a hundred stairs from the main road to this level. After the descent there was an empty flat space that functioned as an open market, with a few suspect-looking vendors all hawking cigarettes, though heaven knew what they were really selling. The backs of the buildings encircling this flat, empty space had no doors, only windows, and the single hutong opened onto it.

After his first visit Wei Bo felt deeply drawn to this place. He even thought of inviting Cuilan to come here with him. Concealed by the curtain of night, he would tell Cuilan in the dark about his former relationship with Miss Si and about how he loathed himself. Or he wouldn't talk about these things, but instead about his mysterious hometown and the connection between his hometown and Cuilan's. In fact, he didn't know what relationship there was between the two ancestral homes, but he had a vague feeling that in the alleyway's depths the solution to the riddle would flash into his mind. Of course, what was he thinking? He couldn't invite Cuilan here. Hadn't he planned to distance himself from her gradually?

There was a vendor with a straw hat who spoke with a Shanxi accent. He put an arm around Wei Bo's shoulders, blew the smoke of an inferior cigarette in his face, and said, "We have more fun over there. Aren't you coming? The spot is in the basement of that building. We call it the Valley of Forgetting. The women are all first rate. Some are tigers!"

Wei Bo pushed him away with force. He heard the man groan. He was ill, perhaps dying. He smoked cheap cigarettes, but dealt in the highest quality Red Pagoda Mountain brand.

The vendor slowly fell to his knees, his cigarettes spilling onto the ground. Instead of collapsing, he knelt, muttering. Wei Bo went over, gathered up the cigarettes, and placed them in the man's cloth bag. In the man's ambiguous words, Wei Bo could hear his fervent hope. What did he hope for? Wei Bo thought of his own life, a tangle of string, and became curious about the vendor. He spent all his time in this ominous den while filled with a beautiful longing!

"I'm saving up energy and wealth," the man offered.

"Why?"

"To have a glorious life. Sometimes I think I might as well go to prison. It would be better for contemplation. What do you think of my idea?"

"It's a good idea. How come I've never thought of it? You see, I'm too narrow-minded. My father was an outstanding man. I'm not a bit like him."

Wei Bo suddenly felt that in his distant childhood, at his father's old home, he had experienced a moment like this one. Put it this way: Wei Bo had forgotten his roots. His present melancholy was because of forgetting his roots. He had lost the enlightenment his father and the others had given him by pushing it to the back of his mind. He drifted through life without ambition. He had not, fundamentally, reflected on his life.

"You might not see me here tomorrow," the morose vendor said. "My name is Yuan Hei. I'm a guard, but soon I won't be. I want to be a criminal. What do you think?"

"Interesting." Wei Bo's answer was also morose.

All of a sudden the sky clouded over, and a cold wind gusted through the alleyway. Wei Bo said goodbye to Yuan Hei and left for home. At the stairs he turned back and saw that the vendor had lain down on a wooden chair. He seemed to feel neither the wind nor the rain. Wei Bo thought that the man's inner self must be strong.

Wei Bo climbed more than a hundred stairs to the sidewalk. The wind continued to blow down the avenue. It was about to rain. He didn't want to go home. The door of the theater was open, and there were still tickets for the performance of La Traviata. He bought a ticket and went inside.

He entered from an upstairs side door, feeling his way in the dark to a seat at the back. The stage lights were dimmed, with only a spotlight illuminating the Lady of the Camellias, who was, oddly, wearing a black skirt. Her arias were unbearable, sounding as she did like a woman from the countryside wailing at a funeral. Wei Bo wondered, Was this really La Traviata? The Lady of the Camellias always sang alone, her words incomprehensible. The other actors never appeared onstage. Wei Bo grew impatient listening. There was a couple in the row in front of him, the man embracing the woman and whispering sweet nothings the entire time.

The Lady of the Camellias finally finished singing. Once she stopped the stage was an expanse of blackness, as was the auditorium, where the doors and windows were all closed tight. Wei Bo wanted to leave, but could not move. Some members of the audience were skipping over the seats, stepping on him and cursing him for being "old and past his time." As they shoved him back and forth, a large man suddenly picked him up and placed him in the aisle. The people around Wei Bo started to cheer. Many were saying, "He's escaping! He's getting away! Ha ha . . ." Then an extremely small side door appeared in front of him. The audience members were bending over to squeeze through it. Wei Bo lined up at the back until it was his turn and wormed his way outside.

He stood on a street where he had never been before, the cold wind blowing so hard it made him sneeze. The audience dispersed rapidly, leaving him alone standing on the sidewalk debating which way he should go. He had no plans in mind. It appeared to be a business district, with no shops, and not a single pedestrian in sight. He had just decided to go to the left when he saw the Lady of the Camellias dressed in black emerging from the same small side door. Her face was coated with powder so that she looked like a ghost. Wei Bo felt a gust of ill wind strike him.

"Young man, let's walk together." The woman spoke naturally, taking his arm. Wei Bo saw the wrinkled hand of an elderly woman.

"I've sung *La Traviata* for forty years. What was your impression?"

"I—I'm confused—in the theater . . ."

"Correct, young man! Very good feedback. You respect my work!"

The old woman pulled him by the arm into the center of the road. There were no cars or pedestrians, which seemed to please her.

"I love strolling down the avenue just like this—without taking off my costume, looking like a ghost. As I walk along, I can see my husband who died."

"When you were singing onstage, I thought that you must have had a glorious life—to tell the truth, I've only realized this now. At the time I did not respond, I—my mind was full of chaotic thoughts. I was too impatient to listen to you. Now, though, as you and I walk along in the wind, I can recall your brilliant performance and fall right in love with you! It truly was a stirring performance."

Wei Bo felt he was about to weep. He struck himself on the forehead in contrition.

"Young man, did you see him?"

"Who?"

"My dead husband. He's there, turning things over in the trash can. He's persistent, he'll eat whatever's there. I think he will always be near me." A terrifying smile appeared on her face.

"Of course he will. You've had such a glorious life together. You're not like me, I'm a useless piece of trash, an empty shell. People like me should disappear from the earth."

"Please don't say things like that. People who give up on themselves don't deserve to be my audience."

They walked back and forth along the empty street, talking about performing. Once in a while, the elderly woman would ask, "Did you see him?" in an ardent tone of voice. Then Wei Bo would say he had seen him. He talked with her about his past life. A few times he found himself almost weeping, but he willed himself not to cry. Slowly, he stopped thinking he should give up on himself. The old woman led him to experience a different kind of life, and he leaped at the chance to try it.

"Where do you live?"

"Over on that side, in the fifteen-story building. It's been lovely to take a walk with you."

The actress walked in the direction of the tall building. A gust of wind lifted her black skirt, and Wei Bo saw her fly upward like a great bird, both feet leaving the ground. She alighted at the entrance to the building. The door opened itself, she all but flapped through it, then the door shut. The large black door with its pair of copper ring handles made a mournful impression. Before long her aria emerged through an upstairs window, although Wei Bo could not understand a word. Someone spoke to him. He turned around and saw the vendor who had been wearing a straw hat.

"Do you know who she is?" he asked.

"I don't know."

"The capital's most famous soprano, who suffers from a psychological mania. She's always lived in a sanatorium. Then our theater's manager invited her to come. She changed her stage name and stepped onstage to perform."

"How do you know what goes on backstage?"

"Because I'm her ex-husband."

Wei Bo only then looked carefully at the vendor, whom he discovered to be at least seventy, older than he had thought. He felt as though he understood something of the vendor's mental state.

"I can tell that you love each other," Wei Bo said.

"Naturally. Mania is a wonderful illness. Without falling to this level, we cannot know how deep our love is. Have you heard her sing onstage?"

"I have. A unique performance—at the time I could not react to it, and I only realized later that it was unforgettable. Your wife is an incredible genius."

"But genius does not suit romance."

74

"Maybe not. I was deeply moved. You will carry on, I have a premonition. How could you not love a woman like her? She's too beautiful."

"Yes, I am a worshiper of beauty, as well as a sacrificial victim. I'm willing to be sacrificed. You see, she's on the fifteenth floor, while I live in the miserable basement rooms I share with the prostitutes. First thing every morning I go out to sell cigarettes, and then return late at night. It's so noisy in our apartment there've even been murders over it. I've grown old and can't be as active as them anymore, so I stay outdoors as much as I can. Look, your friend is here to meet you."

Wei Bo turned to look and saw Mr. You. It turned out that without his knowing it they had walked to the street where the soap factory dormitories were. Turning his head again, he no longer saw the elderly man. Maybe he had gone to the public bathroom.

"He's a moneylender," Mr. You said. "He's responsible for two people's lives. There's a rumor that he became a moneylender because of that woman, then, after he went to prison, she threw off their marriage. Today he is greatly changed. Thirty years ago, he inspired awe in this city!"

"Do you envy him?" Wei Bo asked.

"Yes. There aren't many people like him left, the same way there aren't many Longquan celadon vases. He's an authentic product. He was nearly sentenced to death and even hauled off to the execution site before being sent back. When I was little I saw it with my own eyes. I went with some people to watch the excitement. I saw the others fall, but he was put back on the truck. Then, to our surprise, they released him into the street."

"How strange!"

"Yes, the events of that time cannot be understood. His former wife is the most impenetrable part. After she broke off with him she went mad and went to live in the finest sanatorium in the capital. When she grew older, I don't know why, she returned to her hometown to perform onstage. Some people say she's involved with the manager of the theater."

"Aren't you bitter?" Wei Bo took careful note of him.

"Why would I come here looking for you if I weren't bitter? Why haven't I been as fortunate as him? To my mind he's lived like an emperor."

"You're right, Mr. You. You see things extremely well. I met him in the small area underneath the theater. He has inner calm; the pathways of his mind are open. He's ill, of course, but which of us isn't? He's a brave man with a purpose in life."

"Are you going home, Wei Bo? It's good to have a home, but for me as impossible as paradise. I mean that it's too late for me. I have an appointment with the specters. Every night I must sleep among the ancient tombs, while you . . . every opportunity is yours."

Wei Bo, watching him, returned all of a sudden to thirty years earlier. At that time there had been a small bird always singing under the city's blazing sky. What did the man in front of him expect from him? Mr. You was politely waving goodbye, but he had been waiting here to meet Wei Bo, to talk with him about his mental distress. Wei Bo stared at his shadowy receding back, certain that he was no ordinary man. Mr. You knew everything. He could reenact the Lady of the Camellias' emotional life in his mind at any time. Wei Bo's youth, like that of many people, had its time of passion, but the Wei Bo of that time was a fool banished to the outside of life. Now he seemed to have grown a little more intelligent, although he was still bad at coping with life's difficulties. He remembered that Cuilan had once told him Mr. You was a distant relative of hers and presided over a secret in her life. She was desperate to know the secret, but didn't want to be associated with this painted and powdered man. Mr. You had said every opportunity was Wei Bo's, when he had already dedicated himself to an undertaking that had no affinity with everyday life. Had Mr. You been expressing his genuine feelings?

Wei Bo stood under the scholartree in front of his house and once again thought of Cuilan. This woman, her way of carrying herself and her manner, were so well-suited to what he wanted. Why couldn't he live with her outright? Wei Bo didn't know and only sensed that it would be dangerous. It would be possible to lose her completely. Not only because of her, but also because of the defects in his character. His innate shortcomings were obvious. Why would he be avoiding her otherwise? He had devils on his conscience.

His home was deserted. His wife Xiao Yuan was traveling for work. He had made a spiritual journey outside the home and returned. What had he accomplished? There was a photograph of his deceased father in a picture frame on the wall. His father looked at him calmly, as if he were about to place the piece of cloth in his hand over Wei Bo's eyes. Oh, what a father! At home, ordinarily, he hadn't responded to things emotionally. He had neither discussed his ancestral home with Wei Bo's mother, nor returned there with her. Even so, he was a kind husband and father. He had left the world too early. Wei Bo could remember him sitting in a large armchair with the setting sun illuminating him as his lips moved soundlessly a few times, and then as he closed his eyes with a tired expression. It seemed as though he were pleased with his life. The young Wei Bo had thought that a man who came from that enormous mansion might even be the master of his own life and death. When this idea occurred to him, a detail appeared in his mind: his aunt sat in a corner drinking water from a jade brush pot, saying to him, "This is called 'drinking ink.' This is education." Could his father have taught him, through imperceptible influence, how to live in his own way, and the skill of overcoming life's sorrows? Wei Bo did not know how the man on the wall had done this.

"I'm almost forty-eight years old," Wei Bo said to his father on the wall.

His father seemed to grin for a moment. Naturally it was an illusion. His father had seldom smiled. What would have happened if Wei Bo had rebelled on the train and torn off the eyeshade? His father knew he wouldn't. He understood his son so well that he knew curiosity came before everything else. He introduced his son to that ancient house while never letting him get a sense of the structure of its interior or its location. Wei Bo harbored a deep love and respect for his father precisely for these reasons.

Outside someone heaved a sigh. It sounded like Mr. You. Hadn't he said goodbye? He was difficult to fathom. Wei Bo opened the door, and Mr. You squeezed inside.

"I have nowhere to escape to," he said with a miserable face.

"I heard you and Cuilan are relatives." Wei Bo watched him attentively.

"No, you can't say we're relatives. Look, how can people like you and me not recognize each other, no matter where we meet? Her father and I, in those days—no, I won't drag out this idle conversation with you. Let me ask you, how would you evaluate your relationship with her? Don't you know? Damn it, you should be forging ahead."

Wei Bo started to laugh, Mr. You roared. After the laughter passed, Mr. You said seriously, "Now I really will go back. There's a batch of Song dynasty wares locked in my room. The underworld has an eye on it. Could tonight be my final end?"

"It's dangerous for people like you who casually reveal secrets," Wei Bo said.

"I am not casually revealing secrets. You're the only person I've told."

"So you see me as a relative?"

"Ha! What does being a relative matter? Wei Bo, do you really not understand, or are you just pretending not to?"

"I really don't understand."

"You fail me, too, like Sixiang and Cuilan. You can just be confused then. I don't want to tell you everything. As someone without hope, it's all the same to me."

This time he really left. Wei Bo followed him out and watched him turn the corner before vanishing at the end of the street.

Thinking of what Mr. You had said, Wei Bo felt that he had failed Cuilan and

Long Sixiang. He had not become the brave man he could have been, like the Lady of the Camellias' former husband, for instance, or even Mr. You. What did Wei Bo count for now? He was just a guy who went looking for small, meaningless advantages over other people. He was worth less than one of Long Sixiang's toes.

Suddenly exhausted, he threw together noodles for a meal and went to bed very early. He slept only a half hour or so before waking up again.

Mr. You was back outside calling to him. The sky was already dark.

In an irritated mood, Wei Bo opened the door and stepped out. Mr. You stood in front of him hanging his head, on which a large welt was swelling.

"You see, the lives of people in my line of business are in constant danger."

Wei Bo noticed the excitement in his voice and became excited in turn. He stayed quiet, wanting to hear Mr. You describe what had happened to him. At this moment he envied the antiques appraiser.

"Oh, there's nothing to say. It always happens this way. They come, push, hit, jostle, and spit. Then everything disappears except their smell hanging in the air, while you sink into despair."

"Why into despair?" Wei Bo asked naively.

"Because of love, and because of not wanting to let go of things."

"So that's what happens. And you wait for them every night?"

"You've finally figured something out. I always said you were in the know. There could be a label stuck on your head. You're the kind who's always loving different people and causing problems where there are none."

"Will you come inside for a rest?"

"No rest. Look, it's almost one a.m. This is when the groups of men usually come and shatter the display cases downstairs with sticks, *pa pa pa.*"

He left once again. Wei Bo thought he would probably wander like this through the night.

Wei Bo got into bed and turned off the light, his thoughts entering Mr. You's antiques shop. In the high-ceilinged hall, the jade wares glistened insidiously in the dark. When car headlights swept across them, one or two jumped, startled, making a brittle *ding ding dang dang* sound. How could someone preserve a kind of love for decades in an environment like this? Wei Bo felt as though he understood something of this love, but that was far from genuine understanding. Perhaps he understood nothing, and simply felt a similar tender emotion for this man? In the days of Wei Bo's emotional crisis, hadn't Mr. You brought him unexpected revelations again and again?

Wei Bo's wife Xiao Yuan returned. Her train always reached the station in the middle of the night, strangely enough!

"Xiao Yuan, was it you who took my pocket watch?" He lay motionless in sleep.

"Yes, Wei Bo. When I travel for work I always like to measure the time exactly. I have to bring at least three timepieces. During the day I also watch the sun constantly."

Xiao Yuan went to the door of the bedroom and held up the pocket watch for Wei Bo to see. In the dark the pocket watch shone in all directions as radiant as the sun. Wei Bo nearly tumbled out of bed.

"The pocket watch is here, I'll put it in the cabinet for you."

She went into the next room. Wei Bo saw that the door of the cabinet was not shut tight, and rays of light streamed from inside. He sat up, but then, thinking it over, went back to sleep. The new interest his wife Xiao Yuan had developed frightened him. How this world was suddenly flying forward!

In Wei Bo's memories, objects like pocket watches, safety pins, and old-fashioned magnifying glasses all belonged to a class of mysterious and supernatural things. Yet this was only his generalized notion, and not something he had divulged to Xiao Yuan. Before, in the old house, his uncle had let him see a magnifying glass in the study. His uncle placed the magnifying glass over an ancient book's bamboo paper and said, "Look." Wei Bo looked through the glass and saw a black eye, three-dimensional and slowly revolving. He was too surprised to speak. "Don't be afraid, you just need to get used to it. Relax, look at the right side, look over here. Good!" his uncle kindly guided him. Wei Bo observed for about five minutes. The eyeball was wherever he looked, with a sharp line between the crystalline lens and the gelatinous part.

He drummed up the courage to ask his uncle, "This isn't a magnifying glass, is it?"

"Of course it's a magnifying glass!" his uncle reproached him. "This is what a magnifying glass does, it makes things larger for your eyes—and enlarges eyes." As he finished saying this he locked the object in the desk. Afterward his uncle never mentioned it to Wei Bo again, and he even locked the study.

When Wei Bo called to mind the incident with the magnifying glass, he unexpectedly understood the meaning of the words "Go back often to see your hometown." This was the sentence the vagrant named Long Hair had said to him beside the theater. He could not find on a map his father's family home, his own family home, which was probably where all of this had originated. Recently Wei Bo had noticed more and more that everyone around him was longing for the past. The enormous power in memories of the past was permeating present-day life, eroding the judgment of every person, himself included. Wei Bo had heard long ago of the passing of his uncle and aunt. The ancient house must have been demolished long ago, too.

While eating breakfast, he asked Xiao Yuan, "Did you go to see *La Traviata* at the theater?"

"Yes, I've seen it three times. A remarkable woman!"

"Some people say she's a nervous wreck."

"What of it? We're all nervous wrecks."

Wei Bo once again sensed that Xiao Yuan was an extremely intelligent woman.

"I haven't been to the theater for over a year. When I went yesterday, it felt like there'd been a transformation. I can't say what exactly changed, but as I sat there, everything surprised me," Wei Bo said.

Xiao Yuan made a face at Wei Bo and lowered her head to examine the pocket watch on the table.

"Without warning, it can shine like the sun." Wei Bo pointed at the pocket watch.

Mr. You called to Wei Bo from outside, and Wei Bo hurried out.

After a night of misery Mr. You looked like a vampire. His shoelaces were untied, too, so he might trip and fall over at any moment.

"Wei Bo, Wei Bo, why haven't I been able to catch them?" he said and then walked on carelessly.

Wei Bo returned to the house and saw Xiao Yuan still staring at the pocket watch.

"This watch has lasted from when your father was young straight through to this moment. It's rare, isn't it? It has the quality of flowing water. Your father was fond of wandering around rivers and lakes," Xiao Yuan said.

"I didn't notice whether he was or not. He wasn't someone who showed his emotions."

"Haven't I said that when I travel for work I take at least three clocks?"

"You said that yesterday."

"I do that because when I'm away everything becomes so subtle. Sometimes it's as free as hovering in midair, going to the south, to the west . . . I don't like to be too free." As she spoke she picked up the watch, made a motion as if she were going to smash it on the floor, and then carefully placed it back in the cabinet.

"I've been to where the Lady of the Camellias lives in the capital."

"What?" Wei Bo panicked.

"It's true. She lives in a sanatorium—what kind of sanatorium is that? A garden full of decaying ancient trees with strange growths on the trunks and bizarrely shaped red leaves growing from the burls. There's a kind of bird I'd never seen before with a hook on its beak that perches on the burls and pecks away at them with a constant shrill cry. The Lady of the Camellias sat among the trees wearing a white cotton skirt. She appeared to be sleeping. As I walked quickly up to her I suddenly heard her say, 'I wake up because someone calls me. Is it our hometown's honored guest?' I introduced myself to her. She listened to me seriously and held my hand tight. She said she was waiting in the forest for her 'beloved,' but her hometown's guest arrived instead. Her eyes watched me without seeing me. She had penetrating vision—I could feel her gaze pass through my face to a faraway place. She said she wanted to sing and then began her song. How could that be called singing? It was random shrieking. After the burst of screaming she became silent, without any expression left on her face. She had forgotten I was there. She has a kind of power that leaves you staring open-mouthed. I don't know what the nature of her power is. I turned and ran from the sanatorium. I found a secluded place and wept for a while. This happened ten years ago."

"Was it really the Lady of the Camellias you saw?" Wei Bo asked.

"It's difficult to say. The face was unfamiliar but very beautiful. I think it was her. Who else could it have been? Although it might not have been the Lady of the Camellias, but just me taking her to be."

"This is too frightening."

"Is it? I'm very brave."

Xiao Yuan began to float in front of Wei Bo. Wei Bo rubbed his eyes, trying to make certain both her feet had not left the ground. For a moment the noise of bowls and chopsticks clattering against each other came from the kitchen sink.

THREE

Long Sixiang's Inner Quest

After Long Sixiang's infant stopped breathing, she fainted onto the wooden floor of the hospital.

She revived two days and two nights later. She discovered herself lying in the emergency room with a needle in her arm receiving an infusion. There was a spectral man with his back to her standing by the door.

She did not know how much time passed before she recognized him as her husband Xiao Wu.

"Xiao Wu, whatever you do, don't turn around and look at me," she said feebly.

He submissively slipped out of the room.

After having her son cremated Long Sixiang returned to her family, squeezing into a tiny storage room next to her parents' bedroom. She went back to work at the cotton mill. During the day and at night, her dead son clung to her like an evil spirit. Her cheeks sank inward. The expression in her eyes became that of the mentally ill. Over that stretch of time, her parents hid everything that might remind her of her son and no longer allowed their son-in-law into their home. It was not that they held this big fellow responsible, but rather that they knew Long Sixiang's mind. Their daughter was not ready to see their son-in-law, because on seeing him she would think of the infant, and soon after that she would lose her mind. All day long their daughter's face was ashen. It was a complete nervous breakdown.

Six months later, Long Sixiang made a decision. She would divorce Xiao Wu, and in this way finally bury her son in the depths of her memory. Xiao Wu did not agree. They were deadlocked for a time, until at last he had to consent. He thought he had been robbed and unlucky, to lose his wife and child at the same time.

No one dared face her in the workroom or the dining hall. The expression in her eyes frightened many of them away. To her colleagues, this young wife became a stranger.

Yet time can heal all wounds.

One day as Long Sixiang left the dining hall an unbelievably beautiful young woman was playing featherball on the flat cement surface. All the people surrounding her to watch were captivated. Long Sixiang was among them.

The nineteen-year-old woman stopped, walked over to Long Sixiang, and grabbed her hand, saying shyly, "Sixiang, I heard you're a much better player than I am."

"No, I'm not nearly as good as you."

"Sixiang is too modest. Can I come visit you this evening?"

"No, don't come. I don't have my own home, the room I live in is like a doghouse."

That night Long Sixiang finished dinner, sat blankly for a while, and had just thought of going to bed when A Si appeared at her window. Long Sixiang could hear her own heart race. She didn't want her parents to know what was going on, so she rushed out into the dark. A Si's ice-cold hand grasped hers. She was breathing rapidly and lowered her voice, "Oh, Sixiang, Sixiang, I've come so far, so far, to finally reach you here!"

"A Si, what are you saying?"

"I'm speaking from the heart."

"Your hands are so cold!"

"It's because my heart is weak. I won't live for long."

"Hush, don't say foolish things. I watched you kicking the featherball, so I know your heart is strong and healthy."

"That's an image, just like Sixiang's."

"For some reason hearing you say that makes me believe in myself."

"So, we'll both keep on living."

The two women walked back and forth, hand in hand, feeling overwrought, through the small, unlit hutong. For Long Sixiang, who had not communicated with anyone for so long, it was like someone had opened a gramophone. Strange thoughts and ideas rushed from her mouth. Without knowing why, she wanted to hug this young woman. She told A Si, and then they held each other close. As they embraced, a cat on the encircling wall yowled, sounding like the cry of an infant. A thought flashed across Long Sixiang's mind, Had her son returned? A Si told her that the flowers she was wearing in her hair were jasmine.

The next night, A Si came again. Long Sixiang had a feeling she would come and ran outside early to wait. A Si was gasping for breath from running.

"Sixiang, I'm changing shifts tomorrow, so I absolutely had to come today. Why? Because three men are pursuing me at the same time. They split up and block the way when I'm going to the dining hall or the dormitories. They won't leave me alone, but I can't make up my mind, so I came to ask your advice."

"Tell them to go to hell! There's an iron bar I keep behind my door that I can give you."

"Let them taste the iron rod? There's one of them I like a little bit, though."

"If you like him you should still make him taste the rod!"

Long Sixiang got the iron bar and gave it to A Si, following her with her eyes as she walked into the distance before going back inside the building. Recalling the scene that had just taken place, she had to laugh so hard she bent over at the waist.

"All right, good!" Long Sixiang's mother said, applauding. "My daughter's illness is gone. Truly heaven has eyes! Good people will have their good rewards."

It was already a year and a half since Long Sixiang's son had passed. Xiao Wu had married someone else. Long Sixiang was all alone. She loved her parents, but she secretly decided to move away from home. At the time this appeared to be impossible. There were no dormitory rooms for single women at the cotton mill, so for a worker like her to find a room was like trying to climb to heaven. She also knew her looks were gradually failing, on account of giving birth when she was older, the strenuous work, and that terrible misfortune. She looked in the mirror and saw her face like an autumn cucumber, sending chill spasms through her body.

Long Sixiang would not submit to age. She insisted she was still young and resolved to wait for her chance to begin a new life. Where was there opportunity? Her only technical skill was having worked as a spinner. She was sloppy with housework and would have struggled even if she were to marry and become a housewife. What's more, she wouldn't sell herself for a loveless marriage. What she wanted was a life with love in it. She was very confident in her sexuality.

After two more months passed, Long Sixiang's health recovered, and she was ready to pursue a man.

Her natural resources were limited to the ordinary workers at the cotton mill, all of whom she knew. There were only a few of a suitable age who were unmarried, but they had taken on the habits of the elderly and just wanted a home, not romance. She weighed each of them in turn before giving up and deciding to find another path for herself outside of the factory.

She then made two ventures among her parents' neighbors, both times without success. In ordinary people's eyes Long Sixiang was not only neither pretty nor young, but also poor. The only men who were willing to start a relationship with her were the failures—ones who were looking for a woman to take care of the housework for them, ones who were looking for someone to talk to as the long years passed. None of them was very interested in sex, and they were fairly bad at it. Long Sixiang's goal was to have a sex life with a man who was compatible with her.

After these setbacks, Long Sixiang set her brain in motion. She considered whether she could be a prostitute. It was not so easy: first, she would have to have her own room; second, there needed to be someone to introduce her to clients; and beyond this she needed to get on good terms with the police. For her these were all insurmountable obstacles. One of her colleagues was a divorcee named Jin Zhu. She and Long Sixiang got along well. Jin Zhu had health problems and suffered from tuberculosis, but she was always thinking about men. Long Sixiang could tell what she was yearning for and sometimes introduced her male friends to Jin Zhu. Even though they never discussed men when they were together, they understood each other's hunger and thirst.

Two more years passed, dark, unfair days when the two women were almost hopeless about their lives. It was at this same time that the city's sex industry began to flourish. At first it was furtive, then increasingly brazen. The women workers at the cotton mill, especially the ones who were young and good-looking, moved in succession to this line of work. Miss Si belonged to the first set to jump into the sea of enterprise.

Long Sixiang and Jin Zhu went almost every day they had off of work to visit the erotic venues. They had no money in their pockets and were just looking for work. The managers swept disdainful eyes across their bodies. No one wanted to recruit them.

"Oh, Jin Zhu, do you think we're too old?" Long Sixiang was dismayed.

"Oh, Sixiang, in my eyes you're more attractive than anyone else. We can't retreat, no matter what. I think this world still holds many new wonders for us!"

When Jin Zhu said this, Long Sixiang looked admiringly at her. In that face with its signs of tuberculosis she saw a young woman's purity that brought her to tears. Yet she kept from crying. She recalled the different pieces of news about the sex industry she had recently picked up: some women caught venereal diseases, some of which were incurable; a woman's corpse had been concealed in a certain place; a prostitute had murdered the johns she hated; and it went on and on. Long Sixiang and Jin Zhu understood that it was a high-risk venture and, to the minds of ordinary people, a line of work where "the gains were not worth the losses." Looking back on days when their lives were no better than death, did they have anything left to lose? Continuing to work at the cotton mill would end in early death, without a doubt, but they didn't know how to do anything else and were not interested in learning another trade. They were convinced they would die before they mastered it.

They went out together in the mornings and sauntered around the city for a while before heading into the sex districts. It was clear they had the same thing in mind and shared the same sense of urgency. For all their urgency, things never took a turn for the better. They thought of going to Miss Si for help, but she had become a big favorite and was so incredibly busy they couldn't even catch a glimpse of her.

The fate that loves to play tricks on people oppressed the two workers from the cotton mill for another four months. One day, unexpectedly, Long Sixiang saw Wei Bo at the hot springs, leading to an unforeseen turn for the better. Through the elaborate machinations of Wei Bo and A Si, they finally got the jobs they coveted at the spa and left the factory that had devoured their youths.

"I love you more than ever, Wei Bo. Good people should have good rewards. If you ever suffer from an incurable disease, I will rush to take care of you."

"How did you come up with such an unlucky analogy, Sixiang?"

"My thoughts are random when I'm this excited!"

Long Sixiang's clients were all older men without much money. Generally she was able to satisfy them, but sometimes unpleasant things happened. Once a guy with glasses, who overestimated his ability in bed, got what he wanted and then started making accusations, saying Long Sixiang was like an icy corpse and had no enthusiasm for her work. He called in the manager and demanded a refund. Long Sixiang could not check her rage. She knocked him through the door with a single kick. Her boss said "oh" in surprise and couldn't stop grinning.

"Miss Plum Blossom (Long Sixiang's professional name), have you studied martial arts?"

"Just a little bit."

In those days Jin Zhu and Long Sixiang, despite being sought like prey, were disappointed one time after another. Their lives lacked interest; there were too few good men. They were able to make each other understand, tacitly, what the standard for a good man was. They had waited patiently enough. Hadn't they already waited half their lives? Why would it matter to wait a little longer?

One day the farmer-entrepreneur Lao Yong burst into both of their lives. Lao Yong was probably past fifty and a fiend for drink. His enthusiasm for sex, both plain and colorful varieties, was high. Jin Zhu was the first to service him, and he soon captivated the tubercular woman. She thought of him as her sweetheart and would gladly have died for him.

"You should be more reserved," Long Sixiang reminded Jin Zhu.

Jin Zhu had no need for Long Sixiang's warnings because the fickle old man soon shifted his affection. His new prey was none other than Long Sixiang. He said she had more energy than Jin Zhu, plus her health was better.

Jin Zhu was disconsolate. She gnashed her teeth through the slow nights, brewing murderous schemes. She plotted to get rid of her two enemies and then kill herself. Yet somehow she never struck. Her hand failed to hold the knife, which fell to the ground every time she raised it. Time passed, and she gradually changed her mind. She loved the drunk, she wished him happiness, and now that her friend's body made him happy, she should "step down." She learned this way of rethinking the problem on her own, without instruction.

Jin Zhu quieted down. She had lost a lover, but Lao Yong had left her with glorious memories, enough to last her entire life. She knew she would not live long, which was reason to know when enough was enough. Besides, Lao Yong had landed on none other than her best friend. When he came looking for Long Sixiang, Jin Zhu could sometimes see him. He treated her as though they were still close and kissed her face every time. She slowly grew used to this pattern.

Even at dizzying moments of surging passion, Long Sixiang would never agree to Lao Yong's plea to "make a respectable woman out of you." Lao Yong's wife had passed away from illness years before, and his children were independent, so there were no obstacles to his bringing Long Sixiang home as his bride. She, though, did not want to be any man's wife and was even less willing to have children. She knew she would be finished if she experienced the nightmare of losing a child again. There was also no reason to marry if she wasn't going to have children. She didn't need a family, she only needed to pursue what made her happy. If she did want a family, hadn't Xiao Wu been a better match for her than the old man? Her foresight told her that the first day she and Lao Yong were married, the appeal of the relationship would be cut by more than half, and might even vanish. People do change. Even if Lao Yong did not, she would. So their present arrangement was ideal: Lao Yong in a state of suspension, worried she would go looking for other customers; Long Sixiang keeping a close watch on him, concerned he would seek his pleasures elsewhere. These things really had happened. They argued, then in the end took back their words and set things right—because they really did need each other.

Long Sixiang was full and lush like a fall chrysanthemum in bloom. She and Lao Yong went to the mountains together to see the autumn leaves and wildly caressed each other among the red foliage, ready to die in the other's arms in this setting.

Now it was Jin Zhu's turn to warn Long Sixiang. Still, she didn't say the things Long Sixiang had said to her, understanding that a woman who was Lao Yong's lover would not listen to meaningless advice.

"Sixiang, you should come home with me," Lao Yong said.

"You go back to your home, and I'll go back to mine, Lao Yong."

"You don't have a home. Your home belongs to the public."

"What's wrong with belonging to the public? I like it that way."

Her refusal made everything go black in front of Lao Yong's eyes.

They both continued to be tormented, and to torment each other, with that absurd hope of monopolizing the other party. The vigorous pair often wore themselves out, mentally and physically. Long Sixiang eventually had a number of new customers. For a middle-aged prostitute she had quite the reputation at the hot springs. The manager chuckled about her all the time and even wanted to have a try himself. Long Sixiang sensibly didn't let him take advantage. Lao Yong, unable to bundle Long Sixiang away, could only loaf around like a homeless dog. He would gnash his teeth out of hatred for her. He fell drunk onto the floor of the manager's office and covered the room with vomit.

"I'll take her back by force. I have money, a carload of cash," he raved.

"Your money's not worth shit! She would fight to the death," the manager said darkly.

"Who is she with today?"

"A thief. The kind who never leave their work behind. Even with a whore they manage to scoop up something. I'm very worried."

"It's strange that I've never had the impulse to kill her. I'm soft-hearted."

"You love her."

"Ridiculous. What's love to a whore?"

"Where are you going? It's two in the morning!"

"I'm going looking for death."

Lao Yong lay down in a filthy gutter where he was discovered the next day and sent to the hospital.

Long Sixiang rushed to the hospital room. He smiled at her shyly. She had never seen this expression on him.

"What were you doing in the gutter?" she asked him.

"I fought with someone. He pulls out a knife, I offer my chest to him, the knife goes in clean and comes out red . . . a satisfying end to this life."

"Coward. Don't you have money? Couldn't you have any woman at all?"

"Yes, I'm an old fool."

Not long after leaving the hospital Lao Yong rented a small villa at the Mandarin Ducks Suites and lived there, short-term, with Long Sixiang. It was a very strange residence. During the day hardly the shadow of a person appeared in the area surrounding the long row of villas. Despite this, in your room you could tell that your life was under observation. The ghostly feel of the well-lit suites was oppressive. The cries of unknown animals came from outside the windows. Long Sixiang could not get used to this place. It felt like being in a foreign country. Many times she and Lao Yong awakened from dreams, and she thought by mistake that they were refugees sleeping in a simple hostel beside the road on which they fled. She kept urging Lao Yong to leave right away. Lao Yong was tired of listening to her.

When Long Sixiang pressed Lao Yong to leave, he threw off her hands, walked in bare feet to the window, and pulled open the curtains, filling the room with spreading sunbeams, although the cries of the beasts outside became even more piercing. Long Sixiang felt her every strand of hair standing on end. When she was young she had heard her mother tell stories about the netherworld. Was this that kind of place? Had Lao Yong brought her here to provoke himself to kill her? Or was it the opposite, that living here would provoke her to kill him?

Someone brought food to them unobtrusively, so they didn't even have to go downstairs. Long Sixiang refused to go downstairs out of fear. For Lao Yong, it was because he'd quit drinking. He had a silly idea that if he stopped drinking Long Sixiang would return home with him. She made fun of his plan time and again, but he didn't dare go downstairs.

The result can be imagined. The life of imprisonment quickly turned them into enemies. She jumped from the windowsill and, miraculously, could still run away after the fall.

After Long Sixiang escaped from the Mandarin Ducks Suites, there was a short separation before she went back with Lao Yong. After that, they separated again and went back once again. Long Sixiang could not make sense of it. The small villas constructed in a deserted district on the far outskirts of the city held a surprising magical power over her, a bewitching that obviously had something to do with Lao Yong. Each time he proposed going to the Mandarin Ducks Suites, it brought out an irrepressible longing in her. What did she long for? She tried to understand, but could not make anything clear. Certainly she could not stay there very long with this man, either, because the urge to kill would rise, and she was afraid both of being killed by him and of killing him.

One time when they started quarreling Lao Yong sat inside the wooden chest (when Long Sixiang wondered why there was such a large chest in the room, Lao Yong told her it was the coffin he had prepared for himself), rolled his protruding eyes back in his head, and sighed at her, "Oh, Sixiang, I won't keep you in the dark. This place is where I was born. It was a low foothill back then. The people from our village dug out cellar-caves in a long row like these honeymoon suites. Then, one year, every young and middle-aged adult in the village went away to look for work. When they came back they discovered the village had been razed to the ground. The elderly and the children had gone to hide in the neighboring villages. We were actually pleased at the village being leveled flat. Everyone put up tents, reclaimed the land, and tilled the soil. Who could have foreseen the cholera outbreak? All of them died. Only four people left of the whole village. This was what came before the Mandarin Ducks Suites."

Long Sixiang sat on the bed listening, terrified in her bones. She sank into silence.

Gust after gust of wind blew outside with a metallic clattering sound. In the lamplight, the walls slowly shifted; in the dark gloom of a corner, two cleavers were sinisterly gleaming.

"Lao Yong, why don't you believe in me?" Long Sixiang said slowly.

"It's fate, Sixiang. Tell me, can you believe in me?"

"No." Long Sixiang began to smile. "You're right, it's fate. In fact, living in the caves would be so much better. You close to me, me close to you, listening to the sounds coming from the earth's core. People grow discontent, they flatten mountains into the ground and run madly all over like weasels."

"I miss those old cave dwellings. Our family's cave was dug so deep every time I went inside I felt like I wouldn't be able to find my way out again. At night we slept like the dead."

"I was sitting here thinking of the way your family lived, when my thoughts suddenly turned to my past life at the cotton mill. Inside that big, sealed box, I've also heard the rumbling sound coming from the earth's core."

As Long Sixiang spoke she heard an animal outside scratching at the door. Somehow, without the door opening, the animal got into the room. It was as large as a goat, but not a goat. It came in and stood motionless, with a very stubborn look.

"Can it hurt people?" Long Sixiang whispered to Lao Yong.

"What are you talking about? This is my father!" Lao Yong laughed, "Ha ha."

Lao Yong's laugh startled the wild animal, which fled, scurrying, and knocked the door so that it shook noisily. There appeared to be a pack of its kind in the corridor outside. They ran one after another down the stairs.

"Lao Yong, tell the truth: is there really an entire village of people buried beneath here?"

"Why would I fool you about something like this? Everyone around here knows about it."

Long Sixiang got down from the bed and went with Lao Yong into the large wooden chest to sleep.

She held him close, whispering in his ear, "In the future, when you die, will you sleep inside here?"

Lao Yong didn't answer. She was shivering; he was shivering. They both felt as though the piercing cold infected the other's body the tighter they held each other.

Long Sixiang loosened her embrace first, followed by Lao Yong.

"October 13th is the anniversary of my infant's death," she said.

"I want to drink Maotai liquor," Lao Yong said. "If I died I couldn't drink it."

"There's a bottle to your right. I put it there."

"I saw it there a while ago. I can't drink it, I'll die if I do. You really are a treacherous woman. Listen, all of the monkeys on the mountain are howling."

They talked, tired of talking, and finally dozed off to sleep. In her dream Long Sixiang fell into an ice cave. She saw Lao Yong and cried out to him for help. Lao Yong jumped down, not to save her, but instead to drag her with him down into the water. The water was so cold, she felt herself gradually dying . . .

Long Sixiang slept in the ice cave for a long time—for a week? She could faintly sense Lao Yong underwater, under her feet, at an even greater depth. She couldn't get herself out, so she could do nothing for him. An idea would occasionally ooze into her numbed mind, "Is this death?" She tried to struggle, but she was not nearly strong enough.

An object like a sword jabbed at her, stabbing her forehead. "Ouch!" she shouted, opening her eyes. It turned out to be the sunlight.

Lao Yong was nowhere to be seen, and the room was quiet. Those two cleavers still hung in the corner, but they had a fainter luster and were inconspicuous. "Who's there?" she demanded.

"Who? No one." Jin Zhu's muffled voice reached her.

"Oh, it's you! Jin Zhu, I'm dying."

"I would die in your place. What a pity Lao Yong won't agree."

"I'm sorry, Jin Zhu. No, I shouldn't say that. There's nothing to be sorry about."

Jin Zhu stepped from her hiding place, hauled Long Sixiang out of the wooden chest, and ordered her to shower and put on her makeup. Jin Zhu said it was already growing dark, and she wanted to go for a drive with her. The car she had rented was downstairs.

In the shower Long Sixiang, recalling the events of the past eight days, shivered in fits even though it wasn't cold. She asked herself whether all of this were what she had once wished for night and day. It must be, or why would she keep hurrying back to this place? It was only here that she genuinely knew how deep Lao Yong's foundations ran. He had said to her at the beginning, "I'm a drinker, and I work in the cement business."

Long Sixiang finished putting on her makeup and then went down the stairs and outside with Jin Zhu. The sun was sinking, and, at the same time, the entire complex appeared to sink. Even though she clutched Jin Zhu's arm, the fear of death had not fully retreated from her body.

The driver was a hunchback who spoke in an ugly and angry way.

The car drove away in a puff of smoke. Long Sixiang noticed blood-red lanterns hanging at the entrances to all the villas.

"I think where I'm staying is actually Lao Yong's home, not a place he rents. Why would he lie about it?" Long Sixiang said.

"Of course it's his home. He couldn't put it on the mountainside, so he would have to hide it where there are crowds of people." Jin Zhu was not a bit surprised by the topic.

While they talked the car reached the foot of a hill. The driver got out and was gone in an instant, in what direction they did not know. In front of them was a dark slope that had been shoveled flat. Jin Zhu waved an arm in the air and said to Long Sixiang, "This part is covered in cave dwellings." She asked Long Sixiang whether she wanted to see one of the caves.

"Are there people in the caves?" Long Sixiang began to tremble.

"People really do live in the caves, but they seal themselves into the back parts and never come out again. I found out about the caves by accident."

"It's hard to blame Lao Yong for being so vicious. He survived a catastrophe," Long Sixiang sighed.

Long Sixiang didn't want to stay in that murky place. She pushed Jin Zhu into the taxi, squeezed in herself, and slammed the door shut. She was going right back to the city.

They waited a long time for the hunchbacked driver, who arrived cursing and complaining to start the car.

"What a pity," Jin Zhu said, "aren't you even a little curious? A few days ago I stuck my ear against the earth wall and heard part of a conversation between Lao Yong and his elderly father. I think his father has almost turned into a mummy."

"Do you mean Lao Yong lives in the cave dwellings?"

"Yes. Everyone from the Mandarin Ducks Suites lives on two sides this way. Isn't it romantic?"

A herd of animals on the road blocked the car. There were too many to count. Long Sixiang could tell that they were the same kind of animal that had gotten upstairs. The driver clenched his teeth and stepped on the gas, charging ahead. Tragic screams of pain erupted all around them. It sounded like an infant crying. Long Sixiang fainted.

When she opened her eyes, Jin Zhu was placing a damp towel on her forehead. She found herself lying in her room at the Mandarin Ducks Suites.

"I carried you upstairs on my back. See how strong I am?" Jin Zhu beamed. "You have a fever. I asked the cousin to drive us here."

"Whose cousin?"

"The hunchback is Lao Yong's cousin and business partner. He and I are lovers."

"Oh, congratulations," Long Sixiang said gloomily.

"He's wonderful. I'm planning to marry him. It turns out he's ill, too, and won't live long. We want to spend what's left of our days together. Camel is a good person, don't look at the surface . . . See, he sent this soup. Drink some."

Long Sixiang felt much better after the bowl of chicken soup.

"Will you live here after you marry?"

"No, Camel and I plan to live in one of the caves. We've chosen the best one and renovated it. Yesterday evening I was actually going to give you a tour of my new house."

"You won't be afraid of living with the dead?"

"At first Camel wouldn't agree, but I persuaded him. What's wrong with the dead? Won't everyone die? I'm very fond of those caves, they're so warm inside. When he and I sleep there we have sweet dreams about being with people from our villages. There are canola flowers everywhere. Sixiang, Sixiang, don't be jealous of me. I'll take you there in a few days."

Long Sixiang rolled her eyes, at a loss, feeling her future to be a dismal expanse. Now Jin Zhu had found a home, a resting place of her own, while she . . . she was being sentimental, probably because she was ill. She regulated her emotions soon enough and began to be pleased at her friend's good fortune. She and Jin Zhu agreed to meet the next day to see Jin Zhu's new house. Long Sixiang also wanted to experience the cave because Lao Yong's memories were inside.

When Jin Zhu was about to leave, Long Sixiang anxiously grabbed her arm and repeated a warning, "Don't go and not come back, Jin Zhu! Love is wonderful, but not as steady as sisterly affection. Romance is a dangerous thing. I have a premonition that your cave hides a secret that can't be told. I don't know yet what the secret is, so you must be careful."

Long Sixiang finished speaking and let Jin Zhu go.

Jin Zhu discovered she had been furrowing her brow this whole time.

The hunchbacked man brought them to the cave dwelling, then turned the car around and drove away.

Once the two of them entered, holding each other, Long Sixiang smelled a thick, sour odor that might have been spreading from the coating on the walls. Although the light was low, she could tell that the room was newly renovated. They went into an inner room, then another even more interior room, and again into a third one. The third room had an open door through which they could see a fourth room even further inside, so they entered that room. Long Sixiang began to be frightened and stopped. Standing there eyeing the fourth room in the low light, she could distinguish on its wall a door, open a tiny fraction, that led to a fifth room. "Oh my," she said lightly. "Are you and Camel going to live in the belly of the mountain? But the mountain was leveled. What's that sound?"

"It's the pangolins, armored to cross the mountain. Now that there's no mountain, they still cross back and forth, those frenzied little animals. Sixiang, here's the sofa, sit down."

They sat down with their arms around each other like they had done in the old days. Long Sixiang's eyes did not leave the fifth room. She saw a long, thin silhouette enter through that door, then it went out (or went in) again. This incident gave her a sensation she had never felt before. Her anxiety gradually disappeared. Another short while passed, and then the lights went out, leaving only the feeble light from a sixth room shining through the door of the fifth.

A rumbling sound like someone pushing a millstone came from the sixth room. Long Sixiang had not heard the sound of manual milling for so long. It evoked in her thoughts of what had happened in remote ages. She stood there, touched by an inexpressible mystery. Jin Zhu pushed her, wanting her to go into the next room to see what was there.

As they walked to the door of the sixth room, the lamp there went dark.

The sound of hand-milling continued. A man was speaking.

"Jin Zhu, do you and your guest want to drink bone-powder tea? I'll have it ready in a moment. Yesterday there was a rainstorm. The bones were all drenched."

Long Sixiang felt a fluffy object close by her face. She screamed and ran back the way they had come, dragging Jin Zhu with her. They returned to the out-most room.

Seen outside through the glass door, the glittering stars in the distance and the lamplight blended into one, a landscape of inspiration. Long Sixiang remembered it as having been night, but what she saw at this moment was twilight. Someone nearby played "Butterfly Lovers" on the erhu, and while she listened she felt warm tears tumble down her face. She could still hear the rumble of the milling behind her. However, at the sight of the lovely scenery, the dread in her heart went away.

"Sixiang, I've found happiness," Jin Zhu said.

"I thought so, Jin Zhu! Ah, how could good fortune ever fall on us? I'm so happy I can't stand it, I'm going to cry. Look, in the sky, it's a leopard!"

She leaned on Jin Zhu's shoulder and wept.

"Now, now! Don't get sentimental. On rainy days, you can think of me. This cave is my place of rest. We've already been on such a long journey! If we were to keep walking straight inside, the cave has many rooms, many people pushing millstones. I've never counted all of the rooms. Sometimes I lose sleep thinking about what happened in the past. If I can quiet down, the sound of the millstones grinding helps me fall asleep, like a lullaby. Camel has prepared everything here on his own. At first he was only one of my clients, then we fell in love, and everything changed! Sixiang, look at that leopard, it's running into the Mandarin Ducks Suites! Such fine weather! What year did we leave the spinning factory, do you still remember? I'm too happy, even when I remember those terrifying days my heart overflows with happiness. Camel spent most of his life renovating this cave into a palace. One time he led me inside, further inside, crossing through one room after another. He said, 'We've walked through one quarter,' and asked me whether I wanted to go further. I was afraid, like you were just now, and retreated backward. Since then I've tried many times, but stopped after going into the outer rooms. There are beds on the floor of each room spread with soft, thin leaves of *xiangru*, very comfortable for sleeping. Do you want to sleep here tonight?"

While Long Sixiang listened closely to Jin Zhu's words, she continued to reflect on the architecture of the cave dwelling. For an instant, a light seemed to shine in her mind, but was immediately obscured. She evaluated her situation with caution and then told Jin Zhu in a lowered voice that she would sleep here, except that she should return to the Mandarin Ducks Suites to look for Lao Yong. She sensed that Lao Yong was feeling his way back and forth through those dark rooms, his mind filled with despair. Now that she was Lao Yong's lover, she would regret it her whole life if she disappointed him. She was grateful to Jin Zhu, because tonight Jin Zhu had helped her master a new kind of knowledge, one that would give her greater confidence in her life from this day forward.

She said farewell to Jin Zhu at the entrance to the cave before climbing into the hunchback's car.

She was sitting in the back seat napping when all of a sudden she heard Camel speak.

"How many tens of thousands of kilometers is the lifelong journey the women at the cotton mill fear making in the workroom? The structure of the cave I rebuilt is similar to your workroom, although the function is completely different."

"Camel, now I understand, Jin Zhu has truly found what makes her happy. Living with someone like you, she will never be depressed again."

The Mandarin Ducks Suites appeared ahead of them. It was decorated for a festival. Long Sixiang wanted to fly back as swiftly as an arrow. Camel turned on the car's interior light for several seconds, and Long Sixiang saw the wrinkles like ravines across his forehead. A certain expression of his gave Long Sixiang a familiar impression.

"Camel, is Lao Yong really your younger cousin?"

"No, he is my younger brother," he answered without showing emotion. "I told Jin Zhu he was my cousin because I was afraid she would look into things. Things that are embarrassing."

"What things? Can you tell me?"

"Of course I can, you're a strong and healthy woman. This is what happened: when I was twelve years old, my brother pushed me into a well because he wanted the pretty cleaver all to himself. The cleaver was for cutting firewood and forged by the best blacksmith from outside the village. The fall broke my spine, but I didn't drown. Don't you think that's strange?"

"Do you hate him?"

"No, I don't. Everyone felt sorry for him. For many years we feared he would be crushed under his drinking. Now he's with you, so we're all relieved. He's very fortunate."

"You are also fortunate, Camel."

"Yes, I am. Jin Zhu doesn't think of me as disabled, not at all. Sixiang, here you are. Take good care of yourself."

Long Sixiang got out of the car, walked into the building, went upstairs from the back, and sat on the bed. Lights swayed outside the window, lamps everywhere, and even a few spotlights. She thought as hard as she could, but couldn't remember what holiday today was. She had returned to this place again. She saw that the large wooden chest facing her was empty except for Lao Yong's old

T-shirt spread at the bottom. It was already the middle of the night. She embraced the idea that Lao Yong would appear at her side when she was not expecting or looking for him. After time passed, and he had not come, she found the idea almost comical. She went to the refrigerator, took out a box of milk, drank it, and ate some cookies.

She walked back and forth across the room, watching the light rays falling across the floorboards. She imagined herself as an elephant in the forest, with a rich inner life, a steady disposition, a female elephant. Later she tired of walking, fell onto the bed, and pretended to swim joyously in an ocean of light.

The next day, Lao Yong did not come. Long Sixiang wondered, Did he guess that I know the secret of his life? Was it a blow to him, and that's why he hasn't come?

At noon a child served her a delicious lunch. She grabbed the child as he attempted to slip from the room and ordered him to tell the truth, or else she wouldn't let him go.

"Are you asking about my grandfather? My grandfather went to the south on business and will be away more than a month. He said to bring you food every day if you hadn't left."

"Is he your biological grandfather?"

"No, he isn't. I bring food for all the guests here. Grandfather said you have emotional problems, so not to let the goats into your suite. I shooed away all the goats, but I don't understand how that makes sense."

Long Sixiang noticed the boy's serious look and thought that he was too old for his age. She let him go, absentmindedly motioning for him to leave. As calmly as a cat, he vanished.

She felt resentment toward Lao Yong.

She went downstairs to the entrance. It was quiet in all directions, with no trace of the previous night's holiday decorations. Where had all those colorful lights gone?

A girl came over from the villa on the right, lithe and graceful as she walked up to Long Sixiang.

"Are you waiting for your lover?" she asked, blinking her large eyes.

"Who would I be waiting for somewhere like this?" Long Sixiang answered, dejected.

"I saw him here waiting for you not long ago. While he waited, he kept saying you would be here soon, and refused to leave even for a moment. Where were you then?" She stared at Long Sixiang earnestly.

Long Sixiang could not answer her question. Finding the girl unbearable, she walked away and flagged a taxi that was driving past.

As she got into the taxi she heard the girl behind her shout, "He's back already, but now you're gone. It's ridiculous!"

Long Sixiang returned to her snail shell of a tiny room at the hot springs.

She had not kept track of how long she had been away, but in any case it had been a very long time.

The spa's manager was outside knocking. She put her head around the door to ask him what was the matter.

"Miss Plum Blossom, your going in for this line of business is the reason you haven't hung from a tree. Besides, there's Lao Yong's moral character, as you know without my saying. What wouldn't he dare to sell? He'd sell his own father to pay a debt."

As the manager was speaking, his eyes swept craftily across Long Sixiang's body.

"Boss, I'm at a dead end. What do you think I should do?"

Long Sixiang looked at him with tears in her eyes.

"Yes, what should you do?" The manager was now in low spirits, too. "Normally if our staff has issues like this with the customers, it ends badly. I share responsibility, I should have warned you earlier. Well, let me ask you: would you ever murder someone?"

"I've never tried it. It shouldn't be a problem."

"Good. At worst someone dies, and that happens often enough."

The manager left her doorway and walked down the path that led to the reception hall. Long Sixiang thought that from the back he looked terribly lonely, like a vagrant with no home to which to return. She savored what he had said for a long time. He had definitely not said Lao Yong was trying to kill her. Could he be hinting that she would kill Lao Yong? This was an old problem. Calling to mind what it had been like at the Mandarin Ducks Suites, she seemed to see herself standing on a precipice. Had she fallen to this point? Or was the manager exaggerating the facts? Even Jin Zhu thought Lao Yong gentle, though he sometimes lost his temper. No matter what, Long Sixiang couldn't connect him with the youth his brother had described. It seemed as though people could not be judged by appearance. Then what sort of person was she?

As the sky grew light she had an unusual dream. In the dream someone armed with a knife was chasing A Si, trying to kill her. Long Sixiang had not seen A Si for a long time and was astounded. How had A Si come to look like this? It was not only the way her beautiful face had grown ugly, but also that her expression was vulgar. As she ran past Long Sixiang, the attacker was about to catch her. Long Sixiang dashed forward, getting between A Si and her attacker.

The dagger pierced Long Sixiang's chest. She said gently, as if freed of a heavy burden, "It's me, I've murdered myself."

Her blood spurted out, a sticky mess. The attacker swayed before her eyes. He looked like her ex-husband Xiao Wu, with a horrifying expression in his eyes.

Someone was cautiously knocking on the door. It was her customer, a bashful middle-aged repairman.

Long Sixiang opened the door, and he entered.

"Miss Plum Blossom, I thought something had happened to you. Your boss said you'd gone back to your hometown."

"You can't trust what my boss says. He's always lying."

"Miss Plum Blossom, you see, I have a wife at home, but I'm always thinking of you. I try, but I can't keep myself from running here. Can you tell me whether I'm a bad person?"

"No good people come to this kind of place."

"I understand."

They coupled gloomily. The expression in the man's eyes was like the expression in the eyes of the attacker in the dream. Long Sixiang's body was satisfied. She asked the repairman, "You won't keep tormenting yourself, will you?"

"I imagine myself as a ghost after death."

After he left, Long Sixiang stayed in bed for a long, long time, listening to the sounds coming from the hot springs. There seemed to be many men and women playing in the water, their voices mixed together, often with an exaggerated scream. It was a scene of false animation.

FOUR

Wei Bo's Wife Xiao Yuan

Xiao Yuan had left her teaching post many years before. Her current job was somewhere between administration and operations. Concretely, that meant business trips to other regions made up her main responsibility.

Xiao Yuan met Dr. Liu while traveling for work. Dr. Liu, who had opened a Chinese medicine clinic in Nest County, was taking the train to the capital to purchase medical supplies when he met Xiao Yuan. They had both reserved lower bunks, face-to-face. Xiao Yuan hung a pocket watch at the head of the bed, put a small digital clock on the side table, and placed a radio next to the pillow. A digital timer on the radio glimmered.

Dr. Liu was handsome, with the expressionless look of the studious type. Once Xiao Yuan was settled in place she naturally took a good look at the face of this man about the same age as herself.

Dr. Liu bumped into her digital clock when he was pouring himself some hot water and apologized repeatedly. His voice was unpleasant. Xiao Yuan furrowed her brow.

Late at night, despite turning his face toward the partition between the sleeper cars, Dr. Liu was still made restless by Xiao Yuan's timepieces. He sensed an evil influence in the air emanating from the body of the woman opposite him, like an aura. The passengers in the upper and middle bunks on Dr. Liu's side slipped away one after the other. The upper and middle bunks on Xiao Yuan's side had been empty to start. This left them as the only two people in this enclosed area. Dr. Liu, exasperated, sat up with the thought of switching to another berth to get a good night's sleep. At this precise moment Xiao Yuan, fast asleep, turned over in her bunk.

"What are you doing?" she demanded.

"I . . . I was going to switch bunks . . ." Dr. Liu stammered.

"Can't you see it's two in the morning? Do you want to die? You'll be taken for a criminal and arrested! What a hick . . ." As she spoke she tapped the timer on the radio.

"Then I won't switch bunks. I'll lie down. Don't be angry."

"Who's angry? If you think this is strange, you haven't seen anything yet!" She covered her face with the blanket and giggled.

Dr. Liu glanced sideways at Xiao Yuan in the dark and saw her fiddling with the radio set. The radio was very unusual. At intervals it reported the time, but every time the same time: eleven p.m. Dr. Liu thought, Damn it, no hope of sleep tonight. To control his irritation, he imagined himself picking medicinal herbs in the mountains of Nest County. He was fond of an herb with the common name *qingmuxiang*, an extremely delicate plant with round, very lovable fruit. Because he loved the shape of the fruit, he often gave his patients this herb for pain relief. There was a cliff on the mountain with a cave slightly lower down where a good amount of *qingmuxiang* grew. Dr. Liu only gathered a bit at a time, reluctant to pick too much. He climbed the cliff mostly to survey the herb. Such a lovely wild plant—perhaps it grew there because that was a safe place for it to reveal its inexplicable stance of freedom? Dr. Liu's gaze returned from Xiao Yuan to the darkness over his bunk, his agitation growing calmer little by little. He had seen the *qingmuxiang* before leaving for the train station, spending an afternoon at the side of the cliff, and felt contented.

"Do you practice Chinese medicine?"

Xiao Yuan spoke so abruptly Dr. Liu started.

"That's strange, how did you know?"

"Your things all smell like herbal prescriptions. I can't stand Chinese medicine. It's all superstition, ghosts, and spirits. It doesn't kill people, but it doesn't cure disease, either."

"I don't purely practice Chinese medicine. I use the methods of Western medicine to treat people using traditional medicine."

"Hmm, that would be much better. Chinese herbal medicines are mystical, and people associate them with sex."

"Do you ever go to pharmacies that sell Chinese medicine?"

"Yes. Especially the well-known brands. I don't go to buy medicine, I like to stand at the counter and observe. I like to read medical books and can identify many of the traditional herbs."

"Before I got on the train I spent an afternoon in the mountains. Nest County's mountains have the finest medicinal herbs in the world. They've grown there generation after generation. Naturally they are not growing for people who are ill. Yet who can prove that they don't grow to treat illness?"

"You're very interesting. I share your point of view. Every object has secret purposes. What I mean is, life is in and of itself inspiring."

Dr. Liu noticed that when they were speaking the radio set stopped reporting the time.

"Do you control the sequence of the radio's time announcements?" he asked quietly.

"I'm controlling it with my thoughts." Her voice was, like his, in a whisper.

After reaching the capital, they stayed together at the home of Dr. Liu's younger sister. They both soon completed their work. Xiao Yuan wanted to go to Nest County, so they took the train back to Dr. Liu's home, which is to say, the train back to Dr. Liu's clinic. He lived above the dispensary on the second floor.

It was morning when they reached his home, where many of his patients were already waiting for him. He remained busy with his work until nightfall, Xiao Yuan at his side all along observing him and the Chinese medicines. Also the patients.

"You make me nervous. It takes all my strength not to be distracted," he said.

The next day first thing in the morning they went for a ramble on Nest Mountain and stayed the entire day. As they went back down the mountain to the clinic, Xiao Yuan sensed that the next time they met would be in the distant future, perhaps even worse: never to meet again. To avoid an emotional parting, she didn't return with Dr. Liu to the clinic, but said goodbye at a crossroads instead and went straight to the train station, a small, rundown station.

For a long, long time, when Xiao Yuan remembered Dr. Liu, she could not uncover her true feelings. Had those three days really been what people call a "romantic encounter"? She kept the train ticket and a small piece of rhinoceros horn Dr. Liu had given her. What could these objects prove? He had said to her as they sat on the mountainside, "I understand. You are time itself, time that no one can possess."

The radio in her bag answered him, "The time is eleven p.m."

They glanced at each other and both laughed out loud until tears flowed from their eyes, and the two, both strangely embarrassed, turned their faces away to look in different directions.

After their parting at the small county town, Xiao Yuan had never seen Dr. Liu again. She gradually became aware that he belonged to another world. Xiao Yuan vaguely sensed that world, even revered it, but after all it was not her world. He calmly wallowed along in that little town, in his own tiny kingdom, saying he was never satisfied, which meant he could always find things on which to expend himself. Also, his being alone verified what he said. He was handsome, warm by nature, but surprisingly unmarried.

Xiao Yuan thought of herself as a woman of taste. She had loved her husband Wei Bo, and the two were evenly matched. Did this Dr. Liu have good taste? This question flooded Xiao Yuan with waves of emotion so that she couldn't think clearly. Maybe Dr. Liu was the same type of person as the Lady of the Camellias, the difference lying only in one being demented and one being sane?

Afterward Xiao Yuan loved to travel for work even more because the atmosphere of her journeys made it easy to relive the scenes with Dr. Liu. Especially on days of heavy rain, when the drops struck the train car windows toward evening. So strange, she remembered that the two times she had taken the train with Dr. Liu were both sunny days.

She switched to an automatic timekeeping instrument. Every two hours a woman's voice inside it reported, "The time is now two p.m." Now that Dr. Liu had turned into a bottomless abyss, she stopped wanting to see him. She could not forget him, either, even if there hadn't been the rhinoceros horn. Who can forget the abyss of the heart?

Afterward Xiao Yuan got to know two other men and continued a physical relationship with one of them. Although she was fond of this man, she had never ridden the train with him. She would rather go to bed with him.

"I want to go to the capital with you and see *La Traviata* at the National Theater. When do you have time off? I'm going to turn into a dried fish in this city," Xiao Yuan's boyfriend said.

"I can't go to the capital with you. It's a depressing place," Xiao Yuan said, feeling downcast and looking out the window.

Flax (the boyfriend's nickname) thought, She was so passionate in bed just now! Although he suspected she had not reached real satisfaction. Was she the kind of woman who was difficult to satisfy? The first time they slept together, he was terrified by all the timepieces she had arranged beside the bed and couldn't get used to them for a long time. When he did, and not easily, adapt to the timepieces, he discovered that she lived in two places at the same time, and was sometimes almost as hard to predict as someone invisible. It saddened Flax, who was a very attentive man, not to be able to enter Xiao Yuan's spaces. He and Xiao Yuan had one thing in common: they both valued sensual pleasures. His greatest wish was to sit in the darkened National Theater and listen to *La Traviata* with her. He thought that after experiencing that atmosphere, their sex life would become satisfying. His idea was naive; Xiao Yuan said he was "too practical." She added, "Sex is a black hole. People can't understand all of its implications within a lifetime."

Flax felt overburdened every time he left Xiao Yuan. Sometimes he wanted to break things off with her, and he tried quite a few times, but without any effect.

"Once I sit on the train I become a different person," she said to him absentmindedly, "someone you wouldn't recognize. It's a matter of the body not being under its own control. When I am with you, I am sure of myself. I like this feeling."

Flax understood that Xiao Yuan was telling the truth and that he had to give up the idea, although unwillingly. Sometimes he even thought that her unpredictable nature was precisely what attracted him. Why turn over every stone lying at the bottom of the river? Besides, to do so was beyond him. Obviously he was greedy, but who can plumb one's own soul?

Xiao Yuan had said to Flax not long before, "You give me the sensation of a grove of trees. I pass through it. Feathery leaves everywhere whisk across my face, as if they are trying to say something to me. Then I say to myself, 'This is happiness.'"

"I don't think you're happy enough, though," Flax said.

Late at night when everything was quiet, Xiao Yuan took out the piece of rhinoceros horn to look at it. The keratinous material did not seem to be anything special. Why would Dr. Liu give her this object? Squinting, she turned it toward the light. She heard the racket of a tropical rainforest and far-off claps of thunder. She lost hold of the horn, which fell under the bed. By the time she arched her back like a cat to search for it with the flashlight, it was already crawling with ants.

In the abyss of her heart some object was churning. Her hands shook. She fixed her eyes on the rhinoceros horn again, but those minuscule living things had vanished, leaving no sign they had been there. She wrapped up the shattered pieces of horn, groans spilling from her throat. The groans were nothing like her ordinary voice, but instead like the groan of some unknown beast. The flaring of the hallucination soon passed.

Xiao Yuan asked herself, Is Dr. Liu tormenting me? Would this hopeless, one-sided longing last the rest of her life? Or was this an alternative type of happiness? The thought inspired Xiao Yuan. All of a sudden, she felt that she was very fortunate, extremely powerful—her sadness vanished entirely. Dr. Liu knew when to be content with his lot, and she should, too. Everything was in the past, but everything still remained with her. What she had first pursued turned out to be this ideal! Many events can only be understood after they happen! People cannot see what the murky future contains; instead they should be calm and seize hold of what lies before them in the present.

At midnight she heard a bell, *ding dong, ding dong,* silent and then striking. It was coming from that enormous timepiece in the sky. She was given precise information about the time. She was so fortunate. Surely few people in this city had her good fortune.

Xiao Yuan walked outside underneath the ancient scholartree. Not a single person was in sight, but she could sense a few of the workers from the soap factory strolling through the dormitory area. There was no moon, a peaceful night imbued with passion.

She found her husband Wei Bo sitting at the stone table under the scholartree.

"Oh, it's you! Why didn't I see you just now?" she cried out in surprise.

"I've been sitting here the whole time. It would be a pity to sleep on a night like this."

"True," Xiao Yuan sincerely agreed. "When I'm away on a business trip, there might be a night like this one once in a while, but it's most beautiful at the soap factory dormitories. So long as I'm willing, it seems, I can hear the voice of someone I know. They always pace around the edges. Sometimes, I also hear the tiny groans they make."

"I bought you a small desk clock. A new design, the kind with a calendar."

"Oh, you're so thoughtful, Wei Bo!"

"It's a light little thing, but hard to break."

They went back inside the building together to look at the small desk clock Wei Bo had purchased.

As soon as Wei Bo opened the packaging, the clock chimed, *ding dong, ding dong,* quite soft, not startling. Xiao Yuan was astounded: this was the same exact sound she had heard coming from overhead! Was it because someone was thinking about her, so that time also thought about her?

They watched the clock, a surge of emotion rising and falling.

"Today is New Year's Day."

"What?"

They returned to their own rooms.

Outside their windows, the workers began to talk. In the dark Xiao Yuan listened, carried away and filled with rapture, to voices that seemed to have been once familiar.

"It's her! It's her . . ."

"The Lady of the Camellias—turned into a stone pillar at the entrance of the theater."

"Let's circle again, for a different perspective."

"I'm so excited I can't breathe. Let's go this way, there are too many people on that side . . ."

Xiao Yuan, gently laughing, burrowed her face into her pillow. There were so many people swimming back and forth around her, it felt very good. Maybe Flax was among them. Where else would he be? She tried to sleep for a while, but the seething night kept her from closing her eyes. Weren't even the windowpanes making a cracking sound?

The next day at noon she was on the train northeast to Manchuria. On this trip the passenger in the facing bunk was a blind man. He told Xiao Yuan to call him "Cricket." He said, "I hear you've brought quite a few timepieces. I can keep time more accurately than any clock. Listen: tick tock, tick tock . . ."

He imitated a cricket's chirp with marvelous accuracy, amusing Xiao Yuan so much she laughed out loud.

"I learned from an old cricket at my family's hearth. As time went on, I turned into a timepiece. Joy can be found in this."

One of his long, thin hands kept groping at his chest, the hand showing his apprehension.

"Do you need help?" Xiao Yuan felt she had to ask.

He did not answer. She heard muffled drumbeats, as if from a small drum.

"This is my heart beating. I've always wanted to make someone hear my heartbeat, and now I've succeeded. I'm so glad, knowing that you heard."

Yet his expression was not glad. He seemed to be waiting for something, gloomily.

"The time is two-ten and twenty seconds," he said.

"Correct. She's coming over," Xiao Yuan said.

"Who?"

"That thing that has an appointment with you."

"Ah yes, she's coming!" He began to laugh. "What do you think of me as a timepiece?"

"You work too hard, Cricket! You belong at the hearth. If it were me, I would rather be one of those hermits or vagrants in the thick grass."

The color of the sky grew darker. The locomotive whistled. They had already passed Shenyang.

Xiao Yuan finished getting ready to sleep. She saw Cricket still sitting motionless. The young man on the upper bunk put his head over the edge to look below, clearing his throat with affectation. Xiao Yuan realized he must have been following her conversation with the blind man. She felt a little uncomfortable, but since Cricket sat there, very dignified, she also felt inferior.

She gently lay down and said, as if into the air, "I like to travel. Making a journey is the same as clinging to one place. If you settle down in your hometown, it feels instead as though you are drifting along."

"Xiao Yuan, Xiao Yuan, you must have such a big heart!" Cricket exclaimed sincerely.

She gradually fell asleep. In a hazy state she heard the sound of the small drum at even intervals accompanying the rustling sound, *sha sha,* of the rain. How pleasant! Then she heard a frightened scream.

It was the train attendant screaming because the passenger in the berth above Cricket had fallen, dead, to the floor. The blind man sat as motionless as before. He said, "He wanted me to help him free himself, but I could not. Oh Xiao Yuan, I really want to weep now!"

The traffic police and the doctor came. The body was carried away, spreading a sickening, putrid odor through the air.

Xiao Yuan lay back down. She wanted to continue tracking the sound of that small drum, but didn't hear it any more.

"There is a Lady of the Camellias in our hometown. Her performances have been enigmas to everyone so far," Xiao Yuan seemed to say to him, and seemed to say to herself. "Her type of performance is my favorite. I sit listening, my mind wandering. Then, afterward, for a week on end, her singing hovers in my brain. Her songs aren't about our past life, or about the emotional life of people today, but instead about the life we have never even imagined."

"Just like the life we are experiencing in this moment on the train, isn't it?" he said.

The lights were turned off, so Xiao Yuan couldn't see Cricket's face, but she felt he was smiling. A warm current flowed across her heart. She thought, What an incredible night! Tomorrow at dawn, however, he and she would each hurry off after their own tasks. There are some people who you know, without their having been in contact with you for very long, were already in your heart. Xiao Yuan liked to be in contact with strangers. She never made things out to be more shocking than they were.

"Are you always waiting?" Xiao Yuan asked him.

"No, I like to venture out on my own. People like me are always surrounded by all sorts of colors. I've never seen colors, naturally, except in my imagination."

"Will you give me your hand?"

"Yes."

She felt the sound of the small drumbeat on his wrist.

"I don't want to let go of you."

The train would reach the station in forty minutes. He said he was going to the bathroom and was gone.

Xiao Yuan only then noticed that he had no luggage.

It was raining in the city where she had arrived. The street scene was gray, dripping wet everywhere, the mist spreading through the cafés where a mass of heads bobbed to and fro endlessly. She quickly found the hotel where she had a reservation.

"Are you here on official business?" asked the elderly man signing her in at reception.

"I'm here looking for someone," she said.

"Ha, that's certainly a good reason to travel."

Finally she sat at a table. The room with its enormous windows put her in a sanguine mood. She placed the small desk clock Wei Bo had given her on the table. The hand with which she lifted the clock would not stop shaking. She pressed her hands over her ears and immediately heard the beating of a drum. The drumbeat came again and again, filling the room. What was happening? She stood up and concentrated. Ha, it turned out to be someone knocking! That person was knocking neither fast nor slow.

"Who are you looking for?" Xiao Yuan put her head out at the door.

"I'm looking for my older brother," the young man said, his head lowered. "He's been missing for five days. Do you have any clues about him? I'm sorry, I know you arrived on the #87 train, so I followed you. My brother is blind, he has difficulties outside. I've been looking all over for him, I feel dizzy. You don't mind my being here?"

"Please come inside, sit down, and explain slowly."

"No, if you have no clues, I'll go."

"Does your brother live with your family?"

"He left home a long time ago to live independently. He was nearby, though, so we could always see him. No one imagined he would leave his hometown and travel far away. Besides, he didn't take any luggage. Someone saw him living in someone else's home, in some small, remote county. Is that possible?"

"Don't worry too much. I think most people will like your brother. He's a remarkable man! I just fell in love with him, for example. Yes, fell in love!"

"Is it true, Ms.? Oh, you have eased my suffering! I love you, too! Let's shake hands."

He held Xiao Yuan's hand tight, his hand as strong as his brother's, but without the small drum pulse. Xiao Yuan followed him with her eyes as he left, stab after stab of pain in her heart.

She ran errands to several places across the city. Every place she went she would ask herself, Will I see Cricket? For those two days she seemed to have been traveling in a dream.

During the return journey on the train she finally gave way to despair. She lay there motionless, her thoughts frozen in place by a gigantic block of ice. In the middle of the night a man's voice said from the radio, "The time is two-ten and twenty seconds."

Xiao Yuan said to her husband Wei Bo, "I like the feeling of returning home in the middle of the night. Looking out of the taxi window, it seems as though the road is always obscured by fog, the streetlights constantly blinking. Every time I ask myself, Did I just get off the train? Is this the road that goes through my hometown? The taxi drivers are always from somewhere else, which adds to the sense of strangeness. Then, suddenly, you're in a familiar atmosphere."

Wei Bo nodded, smiling. He thought, Xiao Yuan really is very intelligent. What a shame, why did he no longer love her? Besides, she no longer loved him. He shared the feeling she spoke of—might it be what "home" meant? Their natures were similar; they were the kind of people who try to have every advantage in the world. Wei Bo sighed and wondered how things would end for people like him and Xiao Yuan. His thoughts went back and forth over the problem without his noticing that Xiao Yuan had already packed her luggage and was ready to leave.

"Are you going? I'll see you off."

"No, don't. I'm so afraid of people seeing me off. It's like saying goodbye forever. I'll be back soon."

This time Xiao Yuan was flying to the south.

A man with a beautiful white beard sat next to her on the plane.

The bearded old man was reading a medical book about massage. The book was full of drawings of human figures covered in acupuncture points.

Xiao Yuan likewise raised her book on medicinal herbs. Each read their own. The flight would last about two hours.

An hour after takeoff, the old man pulled an acupuncture needle out of the small bag he carried with him and stuck it into the acupoint between his thumb and first finger, the "tiger's jaw," and then left the needle there, saying in a satisfied way, "How beautiful!"

"Yes, the human body is beautiful," Xiao Yuan echoed.

"Perhaps we're in the same trade?" he asked her.

"No, I'm just fond of plants. These herbs are miraculous. Did they have a medicinal function before there were humans on earth? Did they treat the illnesses of dinosaurs, for example?"

"I often think of questions like this, too. I'm a massage therapist, I find the body's acupoints fascinating. Each species of animal has acupoints, but only the ones on the human body are little worlds unto themselves. When I was young I would feel bored with life, but, ever since going into this line of work, I'm enthusiastic about it. Look at this needle. Can you guess how my nerves respond?"

He pulled out the needle and let out a long breath with an expression on his face as if he had reached the Buddhist's paradise of bliss. Xiao Yuan envied him.

"The human body contains limitless energy."

When he said this he unexpectedly looked downcast. Xiao Yuan thought his subtext might be: No one dared to activate that energy.

"You must know Dr. Liu from Nest County?" Xiao Yuan raised her eyebrows as she spoke, trying as hard as she could to pretend not to care.

"Of course I know him. He belongs to our society for the study of folk medicine. Although I don't approve of his worldview. He's self-centered. I suppose you've experienced how charming he is?"

"Yes."

"He's enchanting, but callous. How else could he only care about himself?"

"What you say makes sense."

"There was a patient, a young woman, who died on account of him. Rumors flew to the heavens. Still, his medical practice has very good word of mouth. Patients even come from other provinces to see him."

"He belongs to his patients, so he can't belong to a woman."

"Maybe there's no alternative. I've always tried to understand him. He's so full of energy."

After getting off the plane Xiao Yuan and the white-bearded man hurried down the road, slipped into a hutong, and went inside a small bar. They both got very drunk.

"You'll tell him, won't you? I'm so ashamed! I want you to tell him how disgusting I look when I'm humiliated," Xiao Yuan shouted.

"That won't make any difference, young lady! Why would you want him to see you like this? Drinking is one of life's great pleasures. It can activate human energy. Drink up, in thanks to everyone who makes us have such complicated emotions!"

"Cheers!" Xiao Yuan said, then began to cry.

She couldn't remember exactly what happened at the small bar that day. Only an impression lingered in her brain: the old man's face stuck full of needles, the longest one inserted into his face and sticking out through the back of his head. It was very shocking. The old man seemed to be lecturing. A friend repeated into his face, "Is what you're doing worth it? Is it worth it? Is it?"

Later she was hurried outside. Someone gave her a stool and let her sit, weeping, at the side of the street. Crying sobered her up, but when she looked around she saw only the small hutong, and not the bar. She thought back to what the white-bearded man had said to her on the plane and was amazed at how she had just behaved. She wondered, Was this the energy inside her body?

Xiao Yuan walked for a long time before leaving the dark little hutong and reaching the main street.

She finally found the hotel where she had a reservation, a small five-story building with gray balconies.

A staff member dressed in black led her to a room on the third floor.

In the middle of the night she suddenly heard the blind man reporting the time. The sound was completely distinct. Her inner disturbance quieted. She placed the radio by her ear. Among the numerous pieces of news, to her surprise, the announcer reported on a story from Nest County with interviews about its silkworm industry. Xiao Yuan listened closely to the gentle narrative of the women who tended the mulberries as she relaxed and fell fast asleep. She woke up once, got out of bed, turned on the light, walked across to the wallpapered wall opposite, entered the wall, and went back to sleep standing inside it.

The next day Xiao Yuan ate at the hotel and then took the public bus to a middle school in connection with her work. On the bus she discovered she couldn't focus her thoughts. Also, she kept feeling as though there were someone in hiding about to attack her. Who could it be?

The school was plain and simple, without even a wall around it, the buildings scattered across a poor neighborhood. She was going to the school-run factory workshop to purchase teaching aids. The factory workshop was in the basement of a tall building.

The lights were on in the factory director's office. Xiao Yuan sat at the table, realizing she was trembling. The factory director had an equine face, his eyes and nose both resembling a horse's.

"You came by plane?" When he asked her his horse-eyes stared, dazed, at the lamp.

"Yes, I arrived yesterday."

"So you were on the same flight as Old Needle!" He clapped his hands.

"I sat next to him. How did you know?"

Her body suddenly erupted with fever, and she stopped shivering.

"Because you said you arrived yesterday! Old Needle, he constantly flies back and forth and very seldom lands. What was your impression of him?"

"I think . . . I think he's someone who can be trusted."

"That's right! That's the sort of person he is! If it weren't for him, our school factory would have failed a long time ago. He taught me how to avoid disaster."

The factory director brought samples to show Xiao Yuan. They quickly signed the contract.

The director wanted to take her out to eat. She followed him up the stairs. They had just exited at ground level when Xiao Yuan was knocked to the ground. As she was falling she thought, Luckily there's no cash in my bag.

When she regained consciousness it was already midday. Oddly, her purse was next to her, with nothing missing from it. Only her head hurt like it would explode. With an effort she stood up and limped toward the restaurant. The sun directly overhead scorched her, and dust flew upward from the road.

"Come in, come in!" the server said, inviting her to enter.

It was black inside. The horse-faced factory director sat in the darkness.

"You said you were going to the bathroom, but then you were gone a really long time," he said. "There are all kinds of criminal organizations around here. I was worried about you. If Old Needle were with you there would be no problems. How did you get separated from him?"

"I . . . I didn't want to, but I . . . I was drunk."

"I understand. You lack any willpower."

He ordered a tableful of dishes and buried his head in the food.

The meal was tasty, and Xiao Yuan enjoyed it, too, but her vague misgivings had not gone away. She stared at the factory director, hoping he would reveal something, but he focused on eating and drinking. His eyes darted around as if he didn't recognize Xiao Yuan.

"Xiao Yuan, oh, Xiao Yuan, you haven't fallen in love with me, have you?" he asked abruptly.

"No, I haven't. Director Xiao, you really know how to tell a joke!" Xiao Yuan actually blushed.

Annoyed, she thought, What am I supposed to make of this?

"Good, that's good! Don't be offended. I asked because this sort of thing happens frequently in the organization. Old Needle, Dr. Liu, and I belong to the same organization. Its members blanket the earth! People say members of our organization have a rare charm, although I don't know exactly what it is. It's so easy for me to end up having to apologize. I couldn't stand it if you fell in love with me and I didn't realize it until afterward."

"Then you know Dr. Liu well?"

"Ha, we've been friends for decades! I heard someone say you and he had a fling."

As the factory director spoke his horse face grew gentler, the long narrow eyes almost overflowing with tears. Still, Xiao Yuan could not catch his eye; he seemed not to see her the whole time. She wondered, What does he actually think of me?

"In those years Old Needle, Dr. Liu, and I went to pick medicinal herbs high up on a mountain, a truly tall mountain, its peak covered in snow. Dr. Liu was the only one who flew across the cliffs that day. Old Needle and I came back in a grim state. It was humiliating."

"Flew across the cliffs?"

"Oh, that's only a metaphor! We've never seen him again since then, even though we belong to the same organization. He has a unique ability that allows us to receive news about him. Sometimes he and a certain woman venture nearby, but in the end he's always on his own."

As the factory director talked, someone at the entrance gestured to Xiao Yuan in an anxious way. Xiao Yuan said "Excuse me" and ran to the door.

She fixed her eyes on the man, who was wearing a hat that covered his eyes, and turned out to be the principal of her school.

"Xiao Yuan, have you forgotten what you came here to do?" he asked in a serious tone.

"I came to sign a contract. This is . . ."

"Shhh, don't look in his direction. He's dangerous. Weren't you already knocked down once? Here's a plane ticket, for three-twenty p.m. Hurry, you need to catch the plane."

The principal, not letting her explain, pushed her out onto the street.

Confused, she returned to the hotel, picked up her suitcase, and rushed to catch the plane. She felt she had been wronged, without knowing why. She wanted to cry again.

On the return flight the cabin was almost completely empty. Xiao Yuan sat alone in the window seat watching the clouds sink below. She called to mind what had happened over the past few days, and then understood all at once: she was living in a circle, where everything she encountered was precisely what she had wished with all her heart would happen! The timepiece in her briefcase was reporting the time at this moment when she was several thousand meters in the air. Oh, it was him! It was him! How could it be him? Xiao Yuan came back to life. She closed her eyes and sat in her seat imagining the scene after she would get off the plane.

The plane touched down at four-thirty in the afternoon. Why was it as dark as a winter night? She checked her wristwatch by the airport's lights. It was twelve-thirty in the morning. Xiao Yuan felt that today's time had been a whole day of chaos. The taxi driver's face was familiar.

The taxi drove along the highway.

"I've driven you several times," he said.

"Oh, yes. Driving at night is very interesting. It seems like the whole world is asleep, and we are the only ones racing back and forth across the surface. Then lions appear, surprising us." Xiao Yuan sighed, lowered her head, and smiled to herself.

"Let me say, Ms., you're the happy kind of person. You have very wide contacts. You can use ideas from places like Africa and South America. I'm not wrong, am I?"

"Not at all. But I don't know whether I'm happy or not."

"You do know, it's just that you don't use the word 'happy.' You must recognize that feeling. Look, it's one o'clock at night, and you're storming back and forth across the earth, searching for lions. In my view, you're using every minute and second to enjoy life!"

He laughed out loud with his head thrown back. Xiao Yuan felt embarrassed.

"Has the Lady of the Camellias taken your taxi?" she asked, trying to redirect the topic.

"Of course, I've driven her quite a few times. She also has the habit of traveling at night. You and she are like the lesser and the greater sorceresses. One time in the taxi she tossed her head back and sang at the top of her voice. The taxi didn't hit any lions. It only ran over a number of wild ducks. I can't understand how there were so many ducks on the highway in the middle of the night."

"Her singing is beautiful."

"I can't understand it when I hear it. Still, I want her to keep singing, not to stop."

"I have the same exact feeling as you. Wait, where are you driving?"

"I don't know. You should orient us. Tell me which way to drive."

"Damn it, I can't make anything out . . . Hey, driver, is this the road through my hometown? When did we get off the highway?"

Sweat flowed down Xiao Yuan's forehead. She turned toward the rear windshield, keeping both eyes open. It was a six-lane boulevard with numerous cars, all driving fast, in front and behind them. Suddenly she laughed out loud, facing backward in the seat, and her nerves relaxed.

"I understand. You're enjoying life," she said in a quiet voice.

She heard the timepiece in her bag reporting the time again. How beautiful!

She took a long inhale of the cool nighttime air, yearning to hear that voice report once again, but he (or it) was silent.

"Ms., why do you doubt whether you are on your native soil? I never doubt this. We just scattered a flock of ducks in front of us. On nights like this there are all kinds of accidents. Look, you're already home."

Xiao Yuan sat for a while in the living room until she caught her breath. She asked Wei Bo, "What time is it now?"

"Six-twenty. I just ate. What happened to you? Your clocks?"

"Oh, they're all right there in my bag. I was just asking out of habit. I like traveling late at night, but it must bother you."

"No, it doesn't bother me at all. You don't need to be polite. Late at night, it's wonderful to hear the footsteps of someone dear to you in your dreams."

"Oh, Wei Bo, I love you."

"I love you, too, Xiao Yuan."

Xiao Yuan took the radio clock out of her bag and placed it on the table. She thought of how intense her life was, with one thing linked tightly to the next. If density were the standard of happiness, then the taxi driver had been right: she must be happy. Let alone that she also had Wei Bo and their two sons. Dr. Liu had the medicinal herbs that grew on the tall mountain and also his patients. He and she were cars on two different roads, accidentally colliding and then separating. Yet, that was what it meant to be happy.

She adjusted the knob and heard the music playing from inside. An elderly singer sang a folk tune, the voice remote and bold. She pressed the radio to her cheek, her fatigue immediately disappearing.

That night she got into bed very late because everything that had happened on her trip made her too excited to sleep. After turning off the light she saw an airy figure standing at the head of her bed. The shadowy human form kept bending over her. Xiao Yuan couldn't hear his voice, but, without her knowing how, his suggestive words repeated in her mind, "Everything is provided for, everything is provided . . ."

"Wei Bo! Wei Bo!" she shouted.

"Xiao Yuan, what's wrong?" Wei Bo asked drowsily from the next room.

"Have you been to the cemetery recently?"

"No. It's too early to think about that kind of thing. We're still young." He was now completely awake.

Xiao Yuan wrapped the blankets tight around her shoulders, once again feeling that she was happy. In the dark she remembered the performance of the Lady of the Camellias, sensing that she was suddenly in touch with her, with a connection that seemed like love. Could she fall in love with another woman? She thought the question over, not reaching a definite conclusion.

Outside the window was another moonless night of passion. Xiao Yuan heard people from the soap factory impatiently pushing aside the bushes, their secret whispers everywhere.

FIVE

The Antiques Appraiser

Mr. You from the antiques shop was fifty-four years old, but still a young man in the eyes of his acquaintances and friends. His skin was smooth and un-wrinkled. He had beautiful, slightly melancholy eyes.

In the past he had been the kind of handsome young man girls welcomed. At school the teachers doted on him. His personal life was hardly smooth sail-ing, but there were no life-or-death crises. His nature quietly settled into shape apart from anyone's notice. Now people believed him to be an antiques appraiser in reality as well as name. Almost all of the antiques in the city underwent his evaluation.

A stranger looking at Mr. You would have seen no trace of time's passage on that face—he looked too much, in fact, like someone a little over thirty. Only people who knew him well could discern the subtle signs on his face. Cuilan, for one, had recently seen his age with her own eyes.

She had run into Mr. You by chance. Disturbed by Wei Bo's problems, she was walking down the street aimlessly when, without knowing why, she stepped into the antiques shop. The lobby was filled with samples of bloodstones, callig-raphy and paintings by famous people, and porcelain utensils. The owner of the antiques shop came out to greet her and attentively sized her up, making her uncomfortable and a little angry. Then he said, "Ms., you've finally come. He is upstairs waiting for you."

"Do you mean Mr. You? Why would he be waiting for me?" she asked.

"You'll know when you go upstairs." He pointed to the staircase.

There was not a ray of light in the hallway upstairs. Cuilan hesitated. Which of the rooms was Mr. You's? A small animal, probably a cat, tugged at the leg of her pants.

"Come in." Mr. You's hoarse voice came from the right.

Cuilan pushed the door open and entered. He sat by the bed and seemed the whole time to be in a stupor. A bright incandescent bulb illuminated him from overhead. The flesh on his face hung loosely, forming two large bubbles under his eyelids. It was the face of an elderly man. Bewildered, Cuilan wondered, How does he make the skin on his face stretch taut? The room's furnishings were unusually plain, nothing beyond a wooden bed and a chair. Several pieces of his clothing had been tossed into a built-in closet, which stood half-open. Mr. You, usually so elegant, lived here!

He must have caught a cold. He coughed a few times, then strained to say, "There are no rivers that cannot be crossed, Cuilan. You understand this principle."

While speaking he also showed the ferocious smile she had seen before. It made her a little nervous.

"I am the guardian of the treasures stored underground. The treasures don't really need me to guard them. In the dark they stay in place in methodical order, secretly mocking me. Cuilan, you're an expert. What do you think of my condition now?"

"No, I'm not an expert. I work at a gauge and meter factory." Cuilan's mind strained as she spoke. That incandescent bulb irritated her. "I think you're a pessimist. You should go outside to play. You're very handsome, all the girls like you. There won't be rivers that you cannot cross. You're not like me, I'm such a mess. Recently I feel like I'm heading toward a dead end."

"See, we can share our sorrows with each other here. What's the weather like outside?"

"It's a sunny day. Put your clothes on and go downstairs. I'm leaving."

"Wait a minute! Look inside the closet for me. I'm too scared."

Cuilan walked over to the enormous closet and pulled the door all the way open. The scene before her eyes made her fall back two steps. An exceptionally pretty woman was lying underneath the clothing. She raised herself, revealing a bizarrely thin and scarred neck.

"I am the vagrant A Liang. I have an incurable illness," she said.

"Hello, A Liang. I find your face familiar." Cuilan looked attentively at her.

"I'm your cousin Niu Yiqing's neighbor. I had nowhere to stay until I found this place. I think it's safe here. Mr. You is very good."

"That's because I love you," Mr. You responded from off to the side.

"Cuilan, I have lost my hometown." A Liang, whose name meant "light," raised one palm into the light and gazed at it, murmuring. "You already know our hometown is no longer on the surface of the earth. Every day I sniffed here and there along the ground until I found the upstairs of Mr. You's building. I know this place is my home, even though my being here harms Mr. You."

"Nonsense, ridiculous." Mr. You stood, shaking his head vehemently.

Cuilan turned around to ask him, "Is there anything I can do to help?"

"You've already helped us, Ms.," he said.

"I don't understand."

"You've brought in fresh air from outside. This is exactly what we needed. People who live in antiques shops have trouble breathing because of the ghosts and spirits surrounding them."

Cuilan stared in shock at the flabbiness of the skin on his face. She thought the skin might fall off as she looked at it, revealing the skull inside. She averted her eyes, but that face would not release her and oppressed her more and more. At last her head grew dizzy. She cried out and sat down on the floor.

After a while she heard Mr. You talking quietly with A Liang.

"Whether or not to cross the river is your decision," he said.

"There are too many people. If you think we should cross the river, then let's cross. I won't leave you."

"We'll go across to that side, look around, and then leave. What do you think of this plan?"

"I've already seen my father. He swept all over with a broom. He probes every-where."

"If you don't want to see your family, we won't cross the river."

"Good, we won't cross the river. Someone outside is calling Cuilan."

It was the owner calling to Cuilan from the shop. She went out following the sound. He clutched her hand and pulled her down the stairs.

After Cuilan left, Mr. You's face began to transform. From the top of the fore-head, like a silkworm sloughing its skin, the face became smooth piece by piece. Finally, he regained his youthfulness, with the same appearance as when people outside saw him.

"The air in this room is poisonous," he said to A Liang. "What do you think of me now?"

"I can't see your face, only a ball of light."

The two of them went downstairs hand in hand to eat. They passed through the antiques shop and went into the restaurant across the street. The antiques shop's owner stood at the entrance staring at their backs. He saw Mr. You's body send out flashes of electric light.

Mr. You ordered several light dishes. They sat down and ate.

"When I was in the countryside, they said my life was worthless, that I would fall into a demons' den," A Liang said.

"They were not entirely wrong. You're not afraid, little one?"

"I'm excited. I like this kind of life."

A Liang's wan cheeks suddenly flushed with two red spots.

"That's good, that's good," Mr. You said, as if thinking of something, "but I'm not sure of living like this. I can't even say how many years I've lived."

"I'm not afraid. Why are you scared when night comes?"

"Because my heartbeat is too loud, deafening, louder than a drum in my ears. Especially while I wait for them to come. Haven't you heard it?"

"I haven't heard it. The night is so quiet, I don't hear anything at all. I'm worried about you. I want to help, but I can't hear anything, or see anything . . ."

"No one can help . . ."

He put down his chopsticks with an absentminded look on his face. He pointed to the bare wall opposite, wanting to say something, but saying nothing.

The owner of the restaurant came over and said to A Liang, as though there were nothing strange, "Mr. You has seen that river again. We should follow him, because his whole life has been difficult."

She simultaneously plucked a lily from the wall and gave it to Mr. You as though performing a magic trick. A Liang said, "Oh," and took some time recovering her composure.

Mr. You stuck the lily in the buttonhole of his suit and walked to the counter to pay the check.

"I want flowers, too," A Liang said, pointing to the blank wall.

"How many?"

"Two."

The owner reached out and plucked at the wall twice, but her hand remained empty.

"Thank you," A Liang said humbly.

"There is a strong negative energy in the antiques shop. He's been on guard for so many years, his destiny is almost consumed. Don't leave him, no matter what. Mr. You will walk to the dark end of the path he has started. He's that kind of person. We have watched him for twenty years from this side of the street. Look, he's waiting for you to go over."

A Liang drew her arm through Mr. You's, and they slowly walked down the street. Her full attention was on the lily in Mr. You's pocket, that fresh bloom. A Liang thought, Only Mr. You suits this type of flower. Her mind became brighter.

They walked a long way, reaching the road to the outskirts of the city. A Liang was confused by her own strength. An uncle of hers saw them and stopped, surprised, at the side of the road. He stayed there until they had walked far into the distance. He was her actual uncle, her father's brother. He remembered her having been mad for several years, but the A Liang he had just seen was like a dewy lotus flower. He suspected he had mistaken someone else for her.

"Listen, the production team's bell," A Liang said.

The two of them sat on a wooden bench beside the road. A Liang rested her head on Mr. You's shoulder.

"I understand now that the lily bloomed specially for you. We people from the countryside have a few secret routes mapped in our heads. I wandered through the alley off of Plum Street that day. All the alleyways in a place like that look exactly the same. Afterward a lamp lit somewhere inside of me, and I walked and walked until I reached your shop. You were looking at that vase with a magnifying glass when you turned around and saw me. You showed me upstairs, then went back down again to continue your work."

Mr. You said nothing. He knew this was love. He knew he was a fool! His ideals now made him seem like a hypocrite. Couldn't A Liang die at any time?

He drummed up the courage to say three words with an effort, "I'm not worthy."

A Liang gently stroked his back and continued, "The gutters in the village are also route maps. I looked back and forth until they were familiar, recorded fast in my mind. That man just now was my uncle. He enjoys moving back and forth through these ditches and pools more than anything else. I would sneak behind him and discovered the secret. I had gone to the city once before. There's actually no difference between the city and the countryside, or, if I had to say what difference there is, then it's that the city is even more lonesome than the country. Once the sky is dark, and I start to think of the antiques, I cannot feel my body around me. I don't call out to you. I know you are somewhere very, very far away."

He could finally speak. He said, "You are my beauty. I will carry on resisting, for you, for myself. Next time, shout to me. I will shout back to you."

They stood and turned home.

A swallow flew past. A Liang thought of her mother. Would she return to the village if her mother were still alive? For her this was a troubling question.

The sky was already dark when they got back to the antiques shop. Mr. You opened the door with a key. It was dark inside, too. The electricity was out, an everyday occurrence at the shop.

"They're already here. Go and hide," Mr. You said.

He pushed A Liang away and disappeared among the display cabinets.

A Liang's whole body turned cold. A firefly lit and then went dark inside of her. She groped her way to the wall, feeling along it to the stairwell. There was someone squatting on the stairs. It was the antiques shop's owner.

"After I got off work I came over to look around. There are three electricians repairing the circuits."

"Owner Zhu, have I brought more chaos into the store?" A Liang asked in a quiet voice.

"No, it's nothing. Besides, I'm not afraid of chaos. The three of them, I mean the electricians, are upset. The repairs are getting more difficult. It's the kind of damage that doesn't leave any traces behind. The shop is tottering, about to collapse. Mr. You always takes charge. Are you going upstairs? Go to the room and stay there. Mr. You cannot fail. You should believe in him."

A Liang felt her way to the door, but couldn't open it. She sat down in the hallway. She sensed, as usual, an eerie stillness. Even though Mr. You would share his woes with her after every incident, saying he was tired and out of breath, or close to a collapse from which he might never wake, A Liang did not hear anything. She had asked Mr. You about this, and he had said, "That is because you are at the center of the turmoil."

All of a sudden she felt wet plants on the wall, a large quantity of them, probably flowers. Oh, the entire surface of the wall was spread with roses.

"Hold on, hold on!" she said.

"I'm here . . . near you . . ." His voice was faint.

A Liang pressed her face into the roses, the thorns pricking her cheeks. She thought, "How good, I also have flowers that bloom for me. I'm not afraid of dying. The sensation of death must be good."

She thought again of the three anxious electricians, imagining them as figures clambering around the hall of the antiques shop like monkeys. Some person or wild animal swatted her from above. Rose petals fell onto her face. She stood, feeling happy.

"Who are you?" she murmured.

"I'm your cousin." To her surprise it was a woman. "I came to the city a long time ago and have been selling flowers this whole time."

"So it's Xiao Mei. Where is your flower shop?"

"It's a secret. Don't you have secrets, too? The air here is so fresh."

A Liang heard Xiao Mei's voice above her little by little moving further away. The door to the room was by her right hand. She gently pushed it open She knew Mr. You was sitting on the bed.

"Roses," she said.

"Yes, roses and evil spirits. I will resist until the last moment. I'm going down below. Goodbye."

The door gently shut. The room was not as dark because of the moonlight. A Liang recalled someone telling her that some of the flower shops in the city were actually moneylenders. Maybe A Mei was in the moneylending business. That would be very dangerous.

The incandescent bulb suddenly turned on, stabbing her eyes. A Liang felt an inarticulate fear. The door was locked tight, and the windows also shut. What was there for her to be afraid of? Still, she hid inside the closet.

When the sky was light Mr. You returned, holding a shattered bronze incense burner in his hand. He threw the incense burner onto the floor, lay face-up on the bed, and went to sleep.

A Liang had seen the incense burner clearly, but when she bent over to pick it up it had vanished. There was nothing on the floor. She started to laugh quietly, finding this amusing. She opened the door, stuck her head out, and saw that the hallway looked the same as usual. She yearned for those roses.

Inside one of the rooms, Mr. You went in a dream to Sea Line Drive. A blood-red sun was sinking as a crowd of people raced along. Mr. You also began to run, shouting, a stranger's name in his mouth. He thought once again that he had reached a critical juncture of life and death. Ahead was the sea. Should he dash into the water? He was not allowed much time to think, now the crowd was carrying him. Both of his feet left the ground. Growing excited, he could not keep from crying the name aloud, "Wu Dawei! Wu Dawei . . ." He saw the seawater surge toward him. That swaying duck egg yolk must be the sun.

For many years young Mr. You felt that he was developing a strong, wild nature. No one knew this tendency in him. People saw him as a cultured, careful, excessively particular, and slightly effeminate appraiser of antiques. His palms would often break out in heat, his fingertips trembled, and he had difficulty focusing. In these respects, his constitution did not suit his profession. His secret was in his teeth. He had a mouthful of sharp wolf fangs that Cuilan had observed unawares, much to her shock. This mouthful of teeth showed his passion.

In the past he and Long Sixiang, the worker from the cotton mill, had a well-matched physical relationship, but they eventually tired of each other. Where are there feasts that never end? From then on Mr. You confirmed to himself that he was not fit to start a family. Naturally he still pursued women. Then, beyond women, the whole of his remaining energy went to his specialized profession. In Mr. You's mind, his work took the form of several endless tunnels. He even thought that he was born to this work—to venture into the darkness of history, to merge into and remold those histories. For him the fascination of this work was no less than the attraction of women. As a result, he repeatedly suppressed his decadent side, laying the foundation of a universe in this dark world without sun or sky. His daytime work was merely surface; only his nighttime wandering was substantial. The owner of the antiques shop knew what was happening and was pleased with Mr. You's work. Only a few people in the city knew the secret: the antiques were all living things, mysterious and supernatural, that relied on the weaving together of a conspiracy to survive. Strangely, the young woman from the countryside, A Liang, seemed to understand this point innately.

Ever since Mr. You's attachment to antiques, his personal life divided into two parts. He was good at harmonizing his contradictions, so he never went down dead ends. On the contrary, there was always a way out: "dark willows, bright flowers, a village appears," as the poem goes. Reaching the age of fifty, he had convinced himself that he was more or less a failure when it came to women. Luckily he had made uninterrupted progress in his profession.

A customer told him a legend about a suit of armor inside the ancient city walls. The man had bolted into the shop during a rainstorm. When he came in he left the shiny green raincoat draped over his shoulders and dripped water carelessly everywhere. He stood in front of the display cabinets and forced Mr. You to hear him out. His voice was low and hoarse. The pale lamplight blurred the contours of his face, creating a disturbing effect. Mr. You thought to himself, Where did he come from?

"My father was in the same line of business as you," the man said abruptly.

"What?"

"He was a grave robber. He worked until he was seventy-three before retiring. A workaholic. He died recently. His final words to me were the story about the ancient city walls."

Mr. You saw the owner, who was in the shop, swaying back and forth, his face clouded with suspicion. He was secretly anxious for this person to leave.

"Did you want something for your collection?" he asked, leaning closer to the unwelcome guest.

"Your shop could not have the object I want. I want a golden suit of armor."

He looked at Mr. You calmly, even arrogantly, until the appraiser lowered his head.

"I will work with you. Where can we meet?" Mr. You said.

"At the mouth of the Little Moon River, the third willow tree, at one a.m."

He turned around and left in a hurry. There was a puddle of water where he had stood.

"Did you make an arrangement with him?" the agitated shop owner asked Mr. You.

"Yes, I agreed."

"You must honor your promise! I'm worried about you."

"There won't be any problems. At worst someone dies."

Regarding the events of that night, Mr. You could recall only the flock of pheasants wildly beating their wings. There was, essentially, no ancient city wall. Mr. You followed the man into a culvert, then they came out of the culvert and sat beneath a large bridge to rest. When the great oppressive, dark flock flew past them, Mr. You even thought the birds were eagles. The man just said, "Oh, shit," then disappeared. The assault of the pheasants was not itself frightening, but it left his whole body filthy. Their only way of attacking him was with the droppings that were like obscenities raining down. Before long he turned into "shit man." Even his eyes were pasted shut. "Help!" he shouted once, then, realizing how ridiculous it was, stopped shouting.

He felt in his pocket for a handkerchief, covered his face, and climbed onto the bridge, finally breaking away from those evil spirits. On the bridge the wind blew hard, cementing the bird droppings on his face, neck, and hands into a shell. He felt he was catching a cold. All of a sudden his epiphany—this was the golden suit of armor! A solution, in a certain sense, had been reached.

After showering he sat in the owner's office. The owner wanted him to try as hard as he could to recall the events of the night. He said any point of detail was valuable—was "historical truth."

"There's nothing else," Mr. You said, dejected. "The pheasants played the leading role. I couldn't tell how many birds there actually were. Their droppings were acidic. Is that man a relative of yours?"

"Ridiculous!" The manager was upset. "He crept out from underground, this robber baron. There's a scar on the left side of his neck. Did you really think he was related to me?"

"I'm sorry. I don't think he's a robber, though. He's polite. Although last night I didn't see his face once. When we were in the culvert, I thought I would pass out."

"It was a smokescreen. First remove your precautions, then launch the sudden attack."

"Actually, it wasn't an attack. I was just too nervous. Oh, those born to this world should broaden the path of their thoughts a little. Don't you agree?"

"At last you have some understanding. Keeping your promise is very important. Mr. You, could we say that I belong to your father's generation? Over so many years you haven't disappointed me. This incident should not either."

Mr. You stared at his boss, who now looked a little awkward. He didn't understand what the man was saying and only wanted to fall asleep. The whole time a stubborn question hovered at the border of his mind: was the shop owner a human or an ape, after all? Despite the random *hua hua* sound behind the owner's filing cabinet, despite the owner rapping on the desk sternly, saliva splashing in all directions, Mr. You's head drooped, and he fell asleep. This was the first time in all his years at the shop this had happened.

Afterward he apologized to the owner, who didn't think what had happened was unusual. He said that he sympathized with Mr. You. He knew the roaming during the night used up a person's vitality. Previously several members of the shop's staff had lost their lives this way. Mr. You's being able to return alive already made him proud. It was because of Mr. You that he truly felt the heroism of being the ruler of one's home.

"What do you mean, 'the ruler of one's home'?" Mr. You asked.

"You have become the staunch defender of this city. Didn't you know?"

"I didn't know, really, and I don't care about that."

"Whether you care about it or not, you are its defender. Could those streetlights, those chimneys, for example, do without someone to guard them? You guard them unawares."

The owner waved him away, clearly not believing Mr. You's ignorance of certain matters.

Mr. You's ignorance wasn't faked. Based on experience he judged all of this to have something to do with his "specialization," but he couldn't figure out what relation these strange nighttime events actually had to his profession. Sometimes he thought that if he had a clear sense of these events, they might become boring. The ancient city walls, a golden suit of armor, the Spring and Autumn Period . . . such alluring phrases!

Now the shop owner had a new name for him: staunch defender. It sounded awkward, but lofty. Which type of defender could he be? When he was confused, he would even get wrong which street he lived on, especially when he'd been drinking. The owner's words must have some basis. His not taking notice of the streetlights didn't mean the streetlights excluded him. Hadn't he collided with the lampposts a number of times? Hadn't his eyes been bewildered by the thick smoke seeping from the chimneys? The time his eyes had been mesmerized, and he was temporarily blind, someone had guided him by the hand onto the train heading north, so he took an unexpected trip in that direction. He had felt since early on that the owner had great wisdom, even though it was a kind of wisdom that terrified him. At first Mr. You had not wanted to be a night roamer. He was still interested in social contact and felt a sense of safety in the human crowd. Later on, without his noticing, he had changed. It seemed to be the fate of an antiques appraiser.

The night was the homeland he held dear, but there were also many enemies in the dark. He was already used to resisting, straight through to the point of mental and physical exhaustion. People in the city were familiar with the handsome sight of Mr. You's dark figure. If he walked down the street at daybreak, everyone who worked a morning shift saw him. They would pause to watch his receding back, saying, "It's him." After these two words, some object loosened in their minds. Mr. You was also already used to people taking an interest in him. Lately an idea would occur to him: perhaps these people, who appeared so kind, as if they were his friends and people from his hometown, were themselves the enemies he fought during the night.

There was nowhere he hadn't been. His figure often appeared at the black market square below the theater. When the Lady of the Camellias returned to her hometown to perform he went to hear her sing twice in one week. He also frequented the foreign currency trade markets that were kept out of sight in poor neighborhoods and did some business there. He went at least once a month to the teahouse by the docks where every sort of hero gathered. Yet for Mr. You these daytime activities didn't matter. Daytime was only a period of waiting. He might come across someone who fastened eyes on him, like the brave man who had charged into the antiques shop on the day of the rainstorm. Next Mr. You and that person would make an appointment—an agreement about nighttime activities.

He grew increasingly anxious because the day's time grew shorter and shorter. Had he heard those chimneys would be torn down? A number of times he felt the sky had not completely grown light before it darkened. No one arranged meetings with him. He could only sit on the steps at the entrance to the shop, craning his neck to look around.

In the prolonged time without meetings, Mr. You went through a spiritual crisis. He asked himself if he should desert his profession, leave this possessed city, and open a shop in the prosperous region to the east where his uncle lived. His uncle had described the excellent prospects there many times on the phone. He was old and frail and lived alone. He hoped that Mr. You would inherit his property. Mr. You couldn't make up his mind. A voice in his heart warned him, telling him some truth about his mission. His mission, so-called, was what the shop owner had mentioned about chimneys and streetlights.

Mr. You's emotional low soon passed. He was always good at adjusting his plan of action and finding alternative paths. He believed he could be sure of himself. The vagrant A Liang had, within a short time, revealed a new universe to him; he felt his entire body and mind bathed in her radiance. She even broadened his view of his profession. Because of A Liang, the overcast city was now saturated with points of light.

Nights were fuller than before. He and she had breakthroughs and took risks individually, but they cared about each other. Mr. You believed that their caring for each other was why he could better neutralize danger now. One day his friend Cuilan said to him, "Mr. You, you're radiating charm. Even I can't deny it! My hometown produces beautiful women, and A Liang is a beauty among beauties. You're very lucky!"

"Do you think she will die, Cuilan?"

"It's difficult to say. Doesn't everyone die? Why make so much out of something ordinary?"

"You're right, I'm too vulgar."

"Not everyone has the chance to be with a genuine beauty."

He resolved to take hold of every minute and second of life. One time, by a river, he gazed at the opposite bank and saw an outline about to bulge out—it was a golden shield, from an unknown dynasty, the decoration on its surface arcane and compact. "A Liang! A Liang!" he gently called. The black river water rose upward, little by little, turning into a mountain, obscuring the sky. A Liang was not nearby. He knew she was somewhere in the city. Then he heard an enormous noise, like the cascade of a waterfall. Behind him someone was speaking to him urgently, telling him to look at the bridge. The bridge stood there, its yellow lights connected into a line, with nothing different than in past days. He turned around and saw a small elderly man.

"I'm one of your customers," the man said. "I've only understood this truth for the past few years: those of us in this business can't rush operations. Look, it's two in the morning, still early."

"The bridge is fine," Mr. You said.

"Naturally. We are here, the bridge is here. Hasn't it been thirty years?"

"Let me calculate." The words escaped Mr. You's mouth.

Then he was silent again. What was he calculating? How could it be calculated?

"Don't rush, it's still early," the old man encouraged him. "Any forgotten incident can be remembered. After tonight, there will be tomorrow night. Just now I said thirty years, when in fact it's been nine hundred and twenty altogether. So don't rush. I live at 132 Sea Line Drive. You are welcome to visit as my guest."

He vanished among the structures. Mr. You turned around once more to face the bridge, which was still there, with a truck driving across. It appeared his status had been approved by certain people. There were always significant persons, insiders to his specialized trade, loitering nearby. Mr. You sensed that his profession had expanded into a borderless realm. This undertaking not only occupied his entire time, but also remolded his whole life.

Mr. You found 132 Sea Line Drive. It was a pachinko gambling parlor, not an apartment or an ordinary house. When he entered, the pachinko machines all had people in front of them, and the hall was bustling. The old man sat in front of the third machine, focusing all his attention on operating it. Once he saw Mr. You he laughed out loud until it sent bursts of cold through Mr. You's heart. Mr. You noticed that everyone else had turned off the machines, gotten to their feet, and were looking at him, many of them glowering.

"Thank you for honoring us with your presence late at night. You see, everyone is busy at their work. Talking here isn't convenient, let's go upstairs."

They passed through a narrow stairwell and corridor and went into a room. The room was too cramped to turn around, with the ceiling so low he could touch it. There were no lights inside. Rays from the large building opposite streamed at an angle into the room, misted and obscure. The room was not soundproof; Mr. You could hear the racket in the pachinko hall below. He sat on the chair the old man offered him, feeling his knee press against the other's knee if he moved it at all. He could smell the old man's stomach on his spraying breath. There was a cot beside him. Did the old man sleep there? He remembered that the old man had come to his antiques shop to purchase an expensive painting by a well-known artist, so he should have been fairly wealthy. Why would he live in such a birdcage?

The old man reached out and placed a hand on Mr. You's shoulder, saying to him, as if in confidence, "I don't usually turn on the lights. I like the secretive atmosphere. Sitting here, your thoughts can roam the entire city. What do you feel at this moment?"

Mr. You stared wide-eyed at the tiny window, that sole source of light.

"I'm a little cold." He thought it sounded like he was complaining.

"That is an ordinary reaction. I have a question for you: why did you break the electric circuits in your shop?"

Mr. You sensed the old man snickering to himself, so hard that his entire body shook.

"Which time do you mean?"

"March 27th, on the day of the big storm."

"You have an incredible memory! That time I wanted to manufacture an accident. It was probably because I couldn't stand being lonely. I plotted for a long time beforehand."

Mr. You narrated mechanically. He was thinking, Why would I confess?

"You're honest. Let's not talk about unhappy things. If you don't mind people in your same line of business, then you should come to my place here often. There's always a lively scene late at night. 132 Sea Line Drive is one of the symbols of this city. If I look at our pachinko hall from the end of the street, it's inspiring. The place is simmering with life."

"Do all of you belong to an organization?" Mr. You's lips and tongue felt dry as he spoke.

"No, this is a free trade port, people come and go as they please. Where are you going? Do you want a drink of water? Stop, it's dangerous outside!"

Mr. You had gone, acting on his own. He groped his way to the stairwell and walked down the narrow stairs. No one paid attention to him. They were all staring ahead at their pachinko screens.

He reached the street. At this moment the old man emerged in pursuit and, out of breath, caught hold of his sleeve. There was another man with him who grabbed Mr. You's other sleeve and hollered, "Boss, should I teach him a lesson?"

"No, don't! Let him go!"

The man unhappily loosed Mr. You's sleeve with a shove and muttered something before going back inside the hall. Mr. You turned around to take the measure of #132. How strange, the pachinko parlor had vanished, and the place where it had been was now a dark vacancy.

"This kind of place, oh, it only exists once you go inside," the old man said. He seemed to be laughing again.

Mr. You, not accepting this, walked back toward #132 and straight up to the gap. This time the old man did not follow him or move from his original spot.

Mr. You stood in the empty space between the two structures and heard the sound of a conversation coming from above.

"If you want it, it will be there, because it wants to play with you, too," the woman said.

"Lucky I came, or else it wouldn't be," the man said.

Mr. You considered a while, a ray of light penetrating his mind. His eyes searched for the old man, but he had also vanished. The entire area was still. Mr. You raised his head to look upstairs exactly as a light turned off in a window, probably the window from which the conversation had come. He believed in his heart that the old man was nearby because everything he could see suggested this. The old man had said his pachinko hall was a "free trade port," a fitting metaphor. Now Mr. You had entered the free port, which meant that tonight he was a free person. "What does it mean to be a free person?" Mr. You, without knowing what he was doing, spoke his question aloud.

"I am a free person! Come with me!" someone said behind him.

Mr. You turned his head and saw an electrician from the antiques shop. The electrician tugged on Mr. You's sleeve, turning him toward the empty space, his movements violent, like a drunk hassling him. After they crossed the empty space between the two buildings, Mr. You heard the call of a nightingale.

"Is that the public park up ahead?" Mr. You asked.

"No, that's the gallows. I want to die, we're going there."

"But I don't want to die."

"Then why did you come to the free trade port? That makes no sense!"

The electrician abruptly let go of Mr. You and pounced toward a clump of bushes in front of them. With a burst of crashing and rustling, the vegetation gradually hid his small, thin form until he could no longer be seen. He seemed unhappy with Mr. You. Mr. You remembered the electrician's humble and timid manner in the antiques shop. He'd never thought he could behave so violently.

Mr. You smelled the air of the wilderness. Could there be a wilderness in the city? There was no wilderness around him. Sea Line Drive was not far ahead—that road that had nothing to do with the sea. Under the streetlights, the thick, eye-catching growth of bushes looked like temporary scenery placed on a stage. Mr. You approached the bushes and gently called, "Xiao Wu! Xiao Wu!"

He couldn't see the electrician, but heard him answer in a lowered voice, "Don't shout, don't shout! You awful person, leave me alone! Now! I'll fail if you don't go, I have bad luck . . ."

Mr. You's face burned with shame as he left the bushes and turned onto the sidewalk of Sea Line Drive. Why was he ashamed at this moment? He didn't know the reason, but it might be an illusion, like many times before. He tried as hard as he could to cast off this feeling of embarrassment. He wanted to go home and rest. Just when he was about to turn at the intersection, the old man from the pachinko parlor reappeared.

"This entire zone is my territory. What do you think of it? Why do I call it 'my territory'? I see it as mine, so it is mine. I'm not the head of any criminal society. People like you and me appear every night. As time goes by our steps and the earth under our feet interact. Listen, *da da da!* You have your own territory. I'm right, aren't I? I know you see the entire city as yours. So do I."

Mr. You discovered that the old man in his leather shoes and windbreaker walked along with quite an air about him, like a political VIP: self-confident, arrogant, wildly ambitious.

"I invite you to visit our shop again," Mr. You said.

"Of course I will, we don't need an appointment," he confirmed.

The streetlights went out exactly as the sky started to turn light. The elderly man signaled with his hand and got into a taxi. Mr. You stood, dazed, in the same spot, unable to speak for some time.

"Mr. You, how could you get mixed up with this lowlife!" the antiques shop's owner said.

Mr. You wondered, Where had he come from? He appeared to have been hiding nearby.

"I'm free to get mixed up with anyone," Mr. You said stiffly.

"Oh, I understand. Of course, of course, I don't object . . ."

Mr. You couldn't work out what the shop owner understood and was too tired to think it over in detail. He was very sleepy. Why did he keep dozing off when the owner was talking to him?

At first he was walking along a familiar road, and the sky was light. He didn't know whether it was because he had been napping. He saw the sidewalk completely blocked by a thicket. There were even bushes in the traffic lanes. His boss chattered at his side: "Why would there be such thick bushes? Because too many people are not afraid to die!"

Mr. You, muddled with sleep, stooped over the thicket and then heard someone speaking.

"I'm not afraid of loneliness. Don't worry about me."

It was the electrician again. Mr. You straightened up, skirted the thicket, and hurried, tripping and stumbling, toward home.

"Fast or slow, the result is the same: days pass. Better to pass them in stability," the shop owner said.

Mr. You, his eyes hazy with sleep, returned step by step to the shop.

Once he entered the shop his head cleared, as if he had just woken up after sleeping his fill. The owner wasn't with him, and Mr. You didn't know where he'd gone. The door to the owner's office was open. Two men wearing black uniforms sat inside, one of them pointing at Mr. You and saying, "Look, he's back."

The two men turned out to be wearing police uniforms. As Mr. You moved toward them, they watched him sternly, not moving, saying nothing.

"Did something happen?" Mr. You couldn't help opening his mouth.

"Of course something happened. Don't you know all about it? It's related to the electrician's disappearance."

The fat one was speaking. He seemed impatient and full of malice.

"I knew about it. He wanted to go missing. No one could prevent him."

"We are not investigating that incident. It's not our jurisdiction. We are here to inquire into the matter of the vagrant woman. There is talk of abuse." He stared wide-eyed at Mr. You.

"That's impossible, we're lovers."

"Abuse can also take place between lovers. You're not taking advantage of her?"

The fat one rolled his eyes back a few times in frustration. Mr. You did not intend to talk.

"You must examine yourself. She's a real beauty, and with your face . . . ?"

He looked at Mr. You derisively. Then he stamped his foot and left, impatiently pushing his colleague along. Mr. You heard the police siren wail outside. He broke out in goosebumps.

He went back to the room upstairs and saw A Liang had returned. She lay in the closet eating something.

"What are you eating?"

"I'm eating a potato. The people in our village gave it to me. I want to make a trip back."

"There are many people here who care about you."

"Both of them are good people. I nearly fell in love with that thin one, although he's not as good as you are. Their work is noble, you do know that, and their concern is genuine."

"Yes, I know. They really showed concern for me. Maybe I need this concern. Why am I so uneasy? I'm constantly afraid of the cold. I should go to sleep for a bit."

He lay on the bed covered by the blanket, the fat officer's malicious face appearing before his eyes, keeping him from sleeping.

"A Liang, you can make a trip back tomorrow."

"No, I only want to go back, but I will stay here."

"Why?"

"Because of love, naturally. At night I gather with people from the village. There's a small night café, with Persian chrysanthemum everywhere and mice running back and forth across the floorboards. There are eight of us in all. We sing together, oh, all the nostalgic songs. Relationships in our village are poor. There's a girl who wants to push me into the well. She confessed to me last night, she described the plan to me in detail. I don't know why, but we both thought it was an excellent plan. You, did you fall asleep?"

"Hmm."

"Why do I like her plan? Because she came up with it for me. In the past no one cared about what happened to me, then suddenly I learned about the scheme. It turns out this girl has been paying attention to me, and all the time I didn't know it. I thought and thought about the twists and turns, the causes and effects, and it made me happy. When I was in the village I really wasn't very optimistic. I don't know why I was afraid of dying there. I wanted with all my heart to come to the city. In the countryside I was timid. When I was about to leave, the village was no longer on the surface of the earth. I sniffed back and forth all day, but couldn't find the entrance, and I rarely came across people from the village. Now, though, you see, I've met so many of the villagers all of a sudden. Do I run into my fellow villagers in the city because they moved here first? Someone said the secret tunnels underground shorten the distance. How could that be? I can't imagine. You, did you fall asleep?"

Mr. You really was asleep. A Liang had said so much all of a sudden that even she wondered at herself. She would have fainted if she had talked so much before. Now she was in good spirits, and not light-headed. Could her illness be better? Her hands were still as cold as ice. There was still a faint pain in the area of her heart.

She crawled out of the closet, put on her clothing, and tiptoed into the hallway. She saw the electrician standing there. His face was as white as paper, and he looked very feeble.

"A Liang, I love you."

"I know. Why are you still here? Didn't you go back to your hometown?"

"I deceived you. I didn't go back to my hometown, I went looking for death, but then I couldn't stand to die, so I came back."

"It's good that you've come back. This is what you should have done," A Liang said seriously.

"Then I'll go. I'll be back at work tomorrow."

"Good."

A Liang stood in the hallway for a while after the electrician left. When she raised her head, she saw roses again. The fragrance of the roses excited her. Her mind filled with images of the nighttime revels. At this moment she heard Mr. You speaking.

"He's a remarkable person. I am far inferior to him."

One night neither Mr. You nor A Liang went outside, but slept soundly in the room instead. Possibly the many nights of roaming had consumed their energy.

When A Liang woke with the first haze of dawn, she heard someone from the village singing a familiar folk song. The woman stood outside the door. A Liang prodded Mr. You, who said drowsily, "Go, go with her. There is a secret tunnel underground. I saw the tunnel, it's just at the end of the hallway. They always come up from there . . ."

A Liang pushed the door open and saw Xiao Lan, the girl who had wanted to push her into the well. She now produced an affectionate feeling in A Liang, who called her "little sister." She continued singing, her voice quite sweet. A Liang's tears flowed as she listened. Then Xiao Lan finished singing and watched A Liang without making a sound.

"Little sister, do you think I can still go back?"

"No, because the entrance to the village is sealed. Don't keep longing for things in the village. Give up this idea. Look how happy you are here."

A Liang drew her arm through Xiao Lan's. The two of them walked together to the far end of the hallway. A Liang looked and looked, without seeing any secret tunnels on the floor or the walls. She asked how she had gotten inside. Xiao Lan said, "I climbed in through the window, of course. The spider man helped me."

"Who is the spider man?"

"The store's electrician. He said he would help if it had anything to do with A Liang, because he is pursuing you."

"So you came to help me?"

"Yes. Didn't you say you were homesick?"

"My homesickness doesn't need help. I wanted to catch this disease. When I heard you singing, I thought, this is real pleasure. I caught this disease in order to enjoy myself, ha! That's why I say I don't need help, although I'm grateful to you. You are so good to me!"

Inside the room Mr. You heard their conversation and was deeply moved. He stood up and went through the door to greet them, but he saw that the girls had already gone downstairs. He glimpsed Xiao Lan in profile. She looked pretty and guileless, not at all like someone who had evil ideas. She ran here at first light to sing a folk song for A Liang; this was no ordinary friendship. What sort of affection was it? Mr. You thought he could enter their artistic realm, since he had been within it all along. This was why he and A Liang came together. Mr. You thought up to this point and felt that he understood something of Xiao Lan's scheme. Many years ago, hadn't his mother tossed him onto a country path?

The owner came up the stairs, unable to hold back his smile, and said, "Mr. You, it's a Daoist paradise here, all the women who come here are beautiful. If I were you, I would be endlessly grateful to heaven. Of course, you are also very charming."

"Someone is plotting to murder A Liang."

"Really? A Liang is the history of the village. Is someone trying to wipe out this history? Or using murder to push her from the darkness into broad daylight? This is a profound question. Let me think it over. I will personally consider her best interests in this situation. Did she climb out through the window?"

"Who?"

"Xiao Lan, I mean. She clambers up and down like a monkey!"

"She went downstairs with A Liang."

"She's very brave! If she runs into me, I'll turn her in at the police station. She knows that I've forbidden her to come here, but she still struts around the place. Mr. You, I really admire people like her."

Mr. You wondered, What is the owner here for? He stood there talking as if he had come to see the excitement, as if he were making a summation of what happened in front of him. It was obvious that he was deeply invested in what was going on among A Liang, Xiao Lan, and the electrician. Not long after A Liang took refuge here, she had become a public figure at the antiques shop, which went beyond what either she or Mr. You had anticipated. Mr. You felt irritated by this situation and was always trying to escape everyone's attention. The more he tried, the more everyone closed in around them, until even the electrician professed his love for A Liang. There was also the owner, who for some time had known these circumstances as well as he knew his own palm. He might be playing a game of cat and mouse with the young woman. At this thought, Mr. You's eyes swept the end of the hallway. He saw the mouth of the secret tunnel. The tunnel's entrance was gray and white in color, like a ball of floating fog, making what was inside the tunnel indistinct. Behind him, laughter came from the owner.

"Mr. You, can you be sure you are not mistaken?" His voice sounded flippant.

Mr. You walked toward the tunnel and was still far from the end of the hallway when the ball of vapor shrank into the wall. Mr. You touched the wall and felt a few plants with thorns.

"I want to move to the countryside, too, but the village has already moved to our walls!"

The owner's mocking voice made Mr. You's face turn slightly red. He leaned close to Mr. You, even breathing in his face, gnashing his teeth as he said, "That kind of passageway cuts our hearts into separate pieces. We go back and forth in contact with that place, and the days become very, very short . . ."

He abruptly turned around and hurried downstairs.

Mr. You recalled A Liang's manner toward the people in the store, thinking of how she was composed, calm, never agitated, as though the antiques shop was her home. This was a miracle, with her a girl from the countryside who had never been to the city. She seemed to be welcomed here. The people in the store put up no defenses and regarded her as belonging to the place. As to why they held this view, it was definitely not because of him. He realized this early on and resented it.

As he stood musing in the hallway, the sound of a fervently whispered dispute between the two young women came from the stairwell. Mr. You saw A Liang holding the Longquan celadon vase in both hands, her face red.

"This is authentic Longquan celadon," she said.

"Authentic? Today the meaning of authentic is forgery," Xiao Lan said, looking sideways at the vase.

"What do you mean? Are you saying the antiques shop sells forgeries?" A Liang's eyes glittered.

"Uh-huh. It's a good practice: the authentic goods are counterfeit. Even people in the village understood this principle. Also, someone entrusted me with bringing back one or two forgeries from your place here."

"I suppose you have an argument. Let me think. You is here. You! Can you show us how to authenticate this vase?"

Mr. You, full of interest, watched the two of them as he said, "A fantastic question to debate first thing in the morning. Xiao Lan has an argument: today's authentic articles are forgeries. Only people with courage dare to acknowledge it. I haven't heard this viewpoint for a long time. It is the truth. Apparently only people from the countryside have clear heads. Did you pick up this vase to admire it?"

"The shop owner let us play with it. He's made peace with Xiao Lan now, he says she's a good influence on the shop. I am truly happy, Xiao Lan is my support!"

The young women placed the vase on the windowsill at the farthest end of the hallway and then stood there talking.

Mr. You remembered he had not eaten breakfast, so he said goodbye to the two of them and went downstairs.

A feeling of annoyance rose from the bottom of his heart. He'd noticed a vicious light in the eyes of this girl. She made him nervous. Even though they had only met once, he could appreciate her power. He believed she had come to ruin his relationship with A Liang. Beautiful women with sharp faces were often mischievous. Mr. You couldn't guess what devilish plan his boss had in mind. The owner had always liked to laugh at him as a way of controlling him.

He hurriedly ate a piece of pastry at a breakfast shop and rushed back home.

He pushed open the door and saw at a glance A Liang and Xiao Lan sitting inside the closet, facing each other, having a heart-to-heart talk. Xiao Lan saw him come in and tapped the vase with a chopstick, saying, "Mr. You! Your work is so noble!"

Her sharp voice sounded like she was mocking him. Mr. You bent over toward her and asked, staring into her face, "In your opinion, does this vase signify nobility?"

"Of course. I can tell that it's dark and deep inside. Listen, doves' wings fluttering!"

She placed the mouth of the vase to her ear. A Liang also leaned closer to listen.

"We have vases like this in the countryside, too. We place them on the hearth to ward off evil. Although I have never seen such an ancient object before. I'm afraid to ask how many hundreds of years old it is," Xiao Lan said. "The vases we have there fit doves in them. The vase appears small when it's actually vast inside—vast to an extent we cannot imagine, so we need an appraiser of treasures like you to measure it. How could craftsmen make vases like this in ancient times? When I think about all of this, I feel your work is truly noble."

After hearing her speech, Mr. You's wariness toward her was dispelled. He once again sensed the influence of those secret tunnels on his life. Xiao Lan was the kind of person who could come and go through the tunnels making contact. She had so quickly understood his work.

Xiao Lan stepped out of the closet and said to Mr. You, "I still need to go to work today. I season the meat for the barbecue stand."

After she left, A Liang asked Mr. You, "What do you think of my new friend?"

"I think she has a lot of personality," Mr. You said.

"Yes. Also, she's a beautiful woman, the genuine article."

A Liang raised the vase close to Mr. You's ear. He immediately heard the cries of a great flock of birds. His eyes shimmered.

"I will put the vase back." Her voice seemed to come from a remote place.

The door silently shut. Mr. You's vision grew blurred.

When Mr. You started work at the antiques shop, the owner was forty years old, strong and in his prime. He sat with Mr. You in the downstairs office with this very Longquan celadon vase placed on the desk. The young Mr. You sat there listening to the owner introduce his new career. Gradually, he detected the enormous magnetic field around his boss. In the days that followed, he attempted many times to escape the owner's influence. He even played the trick of going missing, staying away for two months in a row. In the end, he discovered himself still in the owner's net. The owner's gloomy enthusiasm attracted him. From almost the first day, his cause became Mr. You's own cause.

On the surface, their shop on this street was cold and deserted, only occasionally patronized by customers. The antiques shop even looked a bit mysterious. Yet Mr. You knew there was surging nameless excitement inside. No matter whether the owner, or the employees, or the electricians, or those collectibles, the entirety contained some hidden object. In the late watches of the night he could hear a whistling in the shop, a sound that rose straight to the clouds and became one of the symbols of the city. Not long after he started at the shop he began to lose sleep. The owner mentioned, apparently by coincidence, that he also had insomnia. He told Mr. You it aggravated his headaches, which were sometimes so severe he drove his car headlong down the road. Mr. You didn't know how to drive, so instead he began to patrol every place in the city at night. In this way during the nights he gradually came to know the city's viscera. The deeper he went, the stronger his interest, and the more the owner's mental process amazed him. Several decades passed in astonishment while, to Mr. You's surprise, he never grew weary. He wondered about this hundreds of times without reaching an explanation. Does everyone live among age-old specters, only without knowing it? Still, many people were born knowing! A Liang, for instance, or Xiao Lan. These girls had profound psyches. They didn't need much thought to understand the antiques shop's enterprise, and they merged into this place at once.

"Mr. You, the chinaberry trees on the street are blooming." The shop owner appeared at the entrance.

"Didn't they bloom in spring? It's late autumn."

Mr. You looked at the owner, puzzled. The owner laughed and said, "These trees were planted over ten years ago and have their own timetable. The girls glow with youth. Our gloomy atmosphere can't suppress their exuberance. Just now I saw them run across the street like a gust of wind. Is A Liang actually ill?" he asked probingly, staring at Mr. You. However, he seemed to have no interest in the answer. He went back downstairs with a wave of his hand.

Mr. You began to straighten up the room. He placed the blankets on the shelves in the closet. He could smell the fragrance of chinaberry flower spreading from the blankets, the same smell as the girls' hair. Mr. You suddenly became the young man from decades earlier who was fond of women. He bent over to pick up the pink back cushion, and a tiny vase rolled out of it. This vase's form was the same in all aspects as the previous one, but it was not even a quarter of the size. Mr. You had never seen this tiny vase. Had Xiao Lan brought it from the countryside? He placed the vase under his nostrils and smelled firewood. The design on the vase seemed to pulse in front of his eyes. Mr. You's hands trembled. How beautiful!

He finished clearing the room and sat on the windowsill to rest, unable to calm himself for a long, long time. In the large building across the street a qigong master began to practice martial arts. He made shockwaves of air that reverberated through the huge glass window with a crashing sound. Two passersby on the sidewalk below came to an astonished stop to watch.

"Should we run? Should we run?"

"No, that's ridiculous! It's not from the earth, it's a person."

Mr. You distinctly heard them speaking. In the daytime he often heard customers in the shop say similar things and was used to hearing them. Maybe the questions each person faced were exactly the same. If the ground split open, whether or not to run? Through the glass window the figure of the qigong master became thinner and airier, then started to drift, finally merging into the blasts of air. Even though separated by a distance, Mr. You felt the impact from across the way. He got down from the windowsill and pulled the curtains shut.

He went into the main hall downstairs and saw the owner talking with a customer in lowered voices. It was the man who had come in during the rainstorm and said there was a golden suit of armor inside the ancient city walls. The owner beckoned Mr. You over with a hand.

"Mr. You! Didn't you make a tiny promise to this gentleman?"

Mr. You stood there silently, separated slightly from the two of them. He rolled his eyes in an effort to remember, but couldn't recall his promise. His legs were shaking, and at the same time he recognized the odor of bird droppings. Small animals stirred inside the cloth bag that lay next to the customer.

"Can you remind me?" Mr. You asked the owner.

As though hearing a command, the two men on the sofa got to their feet at the same time. The customer sped outside while the owner returned to his office. Through the glass door the customer could be seen getting into a taxi that drove away in a puff of smoke. Dejected, Mr. You walked into the office.

"His undertaking requires sensitivity, while you are too slow to react," the owner said.

"Yes. People like me can only stay behind to keep watch over the antiques shop. Could he be descended from warriors? That seems to me his type, even though he calls himself a grave robber's son."

"Grave robbers might be warriors. Identity is not crucial. For that kind of work, any identity will do. There's a powerful, headstrong flavor to it. When I was young, even I made an attempt, but in the end I failed in battle. You must walk the night road carrying your head in your hands, to show you are not afraid of losing it. You will know nothing of rest. There will be no roof above you when you sleep, and when you flee for your life you will have to jump into cesspools."

While the owner was speaking, Mr. You felt ashamed. He thought of that night of pheasants, remembering the sensation of his entire body covered with bird droppings. He asked himself why he couldn't get used to these things.

"Everyone has their own position." The owner heaved a sigh. "Mr. You, we haven't accumulated large amounts of capital, that plan has always been pushed into the future. I just sit here, those events appearing in my brain as if I were there in person."

The owner stood up and put both hands behind his back, his fat body sway-ing. He seemed to maintain a difficult balance. Mr. You thought, What is hap-pening inside his body?

He suddenly fell to the floor with a muffled thump. The corners of his mouth twitched.

Mr. You squatted down and put his hand close to the owner's nostrils.

"Don't . . ." His voice was as thin as gossamer. "We operate separately . . ."

Mr. You walked out of the office, gently shutting the door as he went. He saw the figure of the electrician going upstairs. Mr. You pursued him.

"Something happened to the owner," he said.

"What?" The electrician creased his thick eyebrows. "He's a good father, isn't he?"

"Aren't you afraid?"

"Afraid of what? Everything is sequential. Oh, so much beauty! Especially the omens that finally appeared yesterday. They were planned more than twenty years ago."

The electrician stopped, blocking the stairwell with a perverse look. Mr. You couldn't go upstairs and had to sit on the staircase. The electrician also sat down.

"Should we report this to the police?" Mr. You said lightly.

"We could report it, of course," the electrician put one hand on Mr. You's shoulder, "although that wouldn't be the owner's style. I know, help me carry him to the car."

He went outside, brought the car to the entrance, and the two of them carried the heavy body of the owner to the vehicle. While lifting him, Mr. You felt himself almost suffocating. How could the man be as heavy as a cow?

"Where are you taking him?"

"To the small square below the theater so he can breathe," the electrician said.

Mr. You returned to his room and lay down. He began to reflect on the time-table problem mentioned by his boss. Antiques had their own timetable. He could only capture the trend of developments from a few threads and traces. What trend did the owner's fainting show? Mr. You's glance shifted to the win-dowsill, and he stared at that miniature vase. In his line of sight, an astounding flow of communication took place. He said to himself, "This is the true country-side, A Liang's birthplace."

"Mr. You, I'm back," the electrician said at the entrance.

"Didn't you go to the little theater?"

"No. He woke up again."

"He's as changeable as the weather."

The electrician walked over to the window and picked up the vase, flicking its belly with his stubby fingers, putting the opening to his ear to listen. He furrowed his brow tight the whole time.

"Rumors are flying through the countryside," he said.

"What rumors?" Mr. You asked.

"I'm not too sure of the details. Just think, would A Liang and Xiao Lan have hidden here for no reason? The countryside is savage."

"Thank you."

"You think that you're attractive."

"It's a shortcoming of mine. Do you think there's nothing wrong with the owner?"

"Of course not. He already went back to his room. He and Xiao Lan seem to be having a fling."

The electrician sat on the windowsill, signaling with the vase in his hand to the people in the building opposite. Mr. You looked across in the same direction and saw the qigong master standing in front of the window with two petite women standing beside him. Mr. You was stupefied because they were A Liang and Xiao Lan.

"I'll kill him!" the electrician wailed.

He ran downstairs.

Mr. You saw the two girls tangled like snakes around the qigong master's body. He wanted to turn his eyes away, but couldn't. He gasped lightly, and his vision blurred.

After some moments the three of them fell down, although he couldn't tell whether it was because the electrician had burst into the room.

Mr. You lay back down, his vision fixed as before on the tiny vase. Outside the sky grew dark little by little, the tiny vase turned into a tiny shadow, then the window of the qigong master's home turned black as a cave. Mr. You sensed that he was going down into some secret tunnel. The exit ahead was extremely narrow. If he turned his body as flat as an African carp, he could swim through it. He was obviously not someone who would seek out death, he was too indecisive. He almost envied the electrician. In the forest on the road at night, the electrician had already demonstrated his belief. Had A Liang seen through Mr. You?

On the road below two children shouted as they ran along, "Mr. You! Mr. You!"

The owner silently reentered.

"Mr. You, my heart has recovered."

"We've been defeated, sir."

"Well, we are always defeated. It's our destiny."

They sat side by side on the bed like patients in a hospital. Mr. You was a little uneasy.

"Where do you come from?" Mr. You asked, then felt a hair-raising terror.

"In those years, one time when your father and I were gambling, he lost you to me. Still, that doesn't explain anything. Don't you agree?"

"Uh-huh. Past events have no meaning."

The owner was a little impatient and wouldn't sit for long. He stood up restlessly and left.

She came back in the middle of the night. She got into bed, her entire body boiling hot.

"A Liang, are you ill?"

She curled up, groaning in pain.

"I will join Xiao Lan in the old mansions in the south part of the city. Those mansions . . . How can you not have been to those mansions? They're fake buildings. The exterior looks fine, but push it lightly with your hand—it's the work of termites."

"A Liang, let's go to the hospital."

"No, I won't go. My time is almost here. This is happiness. Xiao Lan is there waiting for me, and so is the qigong teacher. This event has become quite easy. How can there be buildings like that on earth? You push it toward the south, and one kind of structure appears; you push it toward the north, and another emerges. Termites are remarkable, even the qigong teacher can't compare with them. Xiao Lan and I will each go into our own mansion, never again to wake . . ."

"I've treated you unfairly, A Liang."

"Have you really? I can't set my mind at rest about you. Tomorrow when the sun falls behind the mountains I will set off on my way. Once the sky is dark I can enter the mansion."

From behind her Mr. You gently embraced her. It was like embracing a specter. Then his hand touched a hard object. It was another small vase, a pair to the one on the windowsill, that A Liang had placed near her heart. "There are many vases in this building," Mr. You mumbled.

"I summoned all of them. After I leave, they will stay with you for a while, to keep you from feeling lonely. We all have vases like this on the hearth over there."

She was silent for a short while. Her breathing became even. Her suffering seemed to have passed.

Mr. You heard a faint steam whistle far off in the distance, a sound he associated with a certain frosty dawn and the cold wind on a country path.

SIX

The Doctor's Worldview

There had been a libertine period in Dr. Liu's youth. Even in those days, though, he hadn't lost his reason. He was difficult to please, so he soon tired of that lifestyle. He built up another way of life, one that appeared on the surface to revolve around his medical profession, while in practice it had much more expansive prospects. He had become a serious and self-satisfied loner. This is not to say he would "not be disturbed with a woman in his lap," as the saying goes, nor that he followed conventions, as seen from his affair with Xiao Yuan. Still, his special life had been established. His modest clinic in Nest County was a miniature landscape where people came to him for relief from their physical and spiritual suffering. Some ten or more years earlier he had many times been in so much pain himself that he had not wanted to live.

He wore his white lab coat from dawn to dusk almost daily, even when he went to dig for medicinal herbs in the mountains, where the branches often tripped him. The people of Nest County held him in high esteem out of an appreciation for this respect for professional appearances. Beyond his contact with patients, he also had a few mysterious connections with the world outside of Nest County. At least twice a year several strangers would come to see him. On arriving they would stay over in a hotel near the clinic and then go with Dr. Liu into the mountains on foot. They left after two days. Someone had asked Dr. Liu about them, and he said they were colleagues who brought him medical supplies. A busybody who had followed them said they weren't up to anything interesting. All they did was diligently climb the mountain in silence. After reaching the peak, they sat on boulders staring into the distance. Maybe they were watching that hawk? Then they went back down the mountain. The busybody said, "It's rare to see people this boring!" In the eyes of the residents, though, Dr. Liu's talk was full of wit.

Dr. Liu's medical skills were ordinary and, while he excelled at treating pain, he never promised his patients anything. This medical ethic was actually why the people of Nest County preferred seeing him to going to the larger hospital. "What use is the hospital? Our illnesses are incurable. Not being in pain is enough." All of them spoke this way. They thought being treated by Dr. Liu was both inexpensive and effective. Dr. Liu was trained in Western medicine, but his research for some time had been in traditional herbal medicine. He had always felt that there was an undeveloped new world within herbal medicine, a world that grew alongside the human body, with reciprocal, invisible connections between them. The herbal decoctions he made had proved popular.

What was traditional Chinese medicine, according to Dr. Liu? Clearly not just the medicine, but instead the deeper meaning it held. At night he often reached out, grasping randomly at the air until he touched downy plants. They seemed to grow on a wall that had numerous caves hollowed into it. To learn the characteristics of the medicinal herbs, he sometimes spent the night in the mountains, sleeping in the thick grass with an ear pressed to the ground. Sometimes, he heard the *aidicha*, which grows "low to the ground," tremble. He became excited, believing it was secreting a substance with anti-inflammatory properties.

"Dr. Liu, please give me stronger medicine. I want to get rid of the ache in my bones," an elderly patient said.

"You must have patience. Taking herbal medicine is like transplanting the plants inside of you. You have to let them take root in your body. This is painful, too. Let the latter pain eliminate the former pain."

"Dr. Liu, I haven't even taken the medicine yet, but your description puts me at ease."

The old man stared wide-eyed into midair, as if he were actually watching the mystical herbs grow. He thought, Dr. Liu's herbs grow for me; my illness is their soil. He discovered the seeds of all kinds of plants strewn across the doctor's white lab coat. The seeds were just then sticking their heads out to explore.

In Dr. Liu's dark world, humans and plants grew entwined together. The dense plants, especially their roots and seeds, could at times suffocate people. When this happens, humans must take flight. Yet humans cannot truly fly away, so they hang suspended in the air close to the surface of the earth, their bodies sprinkled with seeds, gratified and suffering at the same time, wanting to fly even higher while trying to descend to the ground.

Long ago Dr. Liu had heard vaguely about the world's great interconnectedness. The first group who came to Nest County in the spring of that year had three people altogether, all wearing black gowns strewn with rare and unusual seeds. They only stayed for one day before leaving. Dr. Liu felt waves of emotion watching the three shadows as they went. The connections were formed in that visit, both the person-to-person connections and the connections among the plants. He thought of how this kind of interconnectedness took place every minute and every second, similar to the working of the wind. He had stood at the entrance to the clinic to welcome them, the three who entered silently with lowered heads. Outside the wind blew with the sound of countless children crying. Many children cried in Dr. Liu's mind, too. They came and went; that is to say, they connected Dr. Liu's Nest County and the world.

"In Suzhou they're starting to plant medicinal herbs in the parks, but I don't see the point."

"Plants used for medicine are always better grown in the wild. The earth knows which ones she should produce."

"The vast majority of rare varietals disappear before people discover them."

"No matter how the world develops, interconnection is always necessary."

"We should say that before humankind there were medicinal herbs, in preparation for humankind's appearance."

The comments above were made by the three dressed in black. Their words brightened and expanded Dr. Liu's inner being. From that day he began to identify messages from distant places. The day spent with them on Nest Mountain, he had scanned the distance with them, mountain after mountain extending straight to the horizon. Returning home that same night, he paged through a book on medicine, and to his surprise several types of unfamiliar plants appeared in his mind. He worked out their growing habits and area of distribution all at once. He named an herb with thin leaves "stubble" and spent the entire night poring over the plants from his imagination.

Beyond traditional herbal medicine, Dr. Liu was full of interest in acupuncture. When Old Man Yu came to his clinic with his head stuck full of needles he looked frightful. He strode in, head held high, with two younger men following.

They sat up in the clinic in earnest conversation deep into the night. Old Man Yu said he had discovered Dr. Liu while researching acupuncture needles. How else could there be this mutual interaction between him in the big city and Dr. Liu in this remote little county? He believed needles entering the body were sounding the universe. No need to fear the divide of mountains and rivers—the distance would vanish in an instant. Many years of practice led him to believe this more and more deeply. His assistants showed Dr. Liu a very long needle, as long as a person is tall. Seeing the needle Dr. Liu was suddenly so moved that hot tears filled his eyes and some tight knot in his heart was loosened.

They returned to their hotel late at night to rest. Dr. Liu went upstairs to sleep in an overstimulated state of mind. He soon entered a dream, but woke from it a while later. He heard someone calling him from the examination room downstairs. The corridor was unlit, so he had to feel his way down. Strangely, his feet were not stepping on the ceramic tiles of the floor, but on a jumble of grass. The air overflowed with the scent of wild grass.

"Dr. Liu, don't walk all over. Sit down here." He heard Old Man Yu. "Take off your left shoe. I'm going to put a needle in the *yongquan* acupoint."

Dr. Liu took off his shoe and felt his foot held by large, rough hands. Time passed, then a numbing electric current charged from the sole of his foot straight to his forehead. He almost fainted.

"I'm going to leave the needle inside your body. You can move around as usual. It won't stop you."

Dr. Liu couldn't get any words out. He thought he was sitting in the mountains, blades of grass pricking his cheeks, grass everywhere. The dark shadow in front of him was Old Man Yu, his head lowered as he busied himself with something.

"Old Man Yu, can you explain how you discovered me?"

The vibration of Dr. Liu's voice caused waves of numb pain throughout his body. He could hardly stand it. Unable to hold himself up, he fell to the floor. He heard Yu's droning voice.

"I found you near the *zusanli* acupoint, below the knee. Are you listening? Oh, the *zusanli!* A region as vast as an entire province!"

As he continued speaking, his voice little by little moved further away.

When Dr. Liu waved his hand the motion unexpectedly turned on a fluorescent light. He stood up, looking with bewilderment at his own examination room. His left foot was still slightly numb, but he could already walk. He raised the desk lamp to illuminate the sole of his foot, where he saw a dark red scab at the *yongquan* acupoint. He touched it with his hand, but felt no pain.

It was two-thirty at night, and probably about two hours since he had entered Old Man Yu's kingdom of needles. The event was unthinkable. "If he jabs the needle into your left foot, he must be to your right," Dr. Liu said, inexplicably, to himself. He tried as hard as he could to recall what had just happened, before he finally remembered what Yu had said about the *zusanli* acupoint. He had said this point on the lower leg was as vast as an entire province. There must be a reason for his words. Just now when the needle entered from the *yongquan* point, hadn't it produced the momentary hallucination of being at the North Pole? Dr. Liu sensed that this Old Man Yu hadn't come from some big city; he must have come from "inside," just like the three people in black gowns. He spoke of a large city to the south in order to conceal the fact that he came from "inside." What kind of place was "inside"? Dr. Liu didn't know. Maybe it had something to do with medicinal herbs of the same type as *qingmuxiang*.

Dr. Liu heard a rustling sound inside his medicine cabinet. There were probably worms, many worms, crawling inside. The herbs were collected just after drying and held the fresh clear scent of the sun. Oh, he could picture the worms' enthusiasm! They could get in through any hole and were parasitic on the plants. Dr. Liu thought of the small worms inside the *danggui*, the "returning home" root, and the calm look the worms had—the expression that meant they came from "inside." Every time he saw the *danggui* worms, he seemed to hear their knowing whispers, "I am the *danggui*, the *danggui* is me."

As he went upstairs the small light in the stairwell turned on suddenly. A few insects flew circles in the lamplight, coiling into beautiful patterns. Dr. Liu's legs went soft, and he sat down on the stairs.

"Liu, Dr. Liu! I'm dying of pain!"

Someone outside beat on the door and roared.

Dr. Liu opened the door and saw the janitor. He had fallen to the floor and curled into a ball.

Dr. Liu gave him an herbal medicine to drink, watching as he revived by degrees. He thought the janitor, too, had the expression of someone in the know. He helped the man into a reclining chair.

"I want to go for a walk inside the ancient city walls, otherwise I cannot close my eyes in death," he said.

"What you say makes sense."

The man's hands twitched. Dr. Liu grasped one hand and held it tight. He felt himself merging into a single body with the janitor, the same way the *danggui* worm felt toward the *danggui*.

"You won't die for the moment," he said to the janitor.

"I won't? But I hate living."

"Your son-in-law is coming to your house to celebrate your birthday."

Dr. Liu watched him without changing expression. The rigid hand relaxed as the color of life returned to his cheeks. Then intense pain attacked him again.

"It will get better," Dr. Liu said.

After another moment, he let go of the man's hand. The janitor stood.

"You never make mistakes. I admire you, Liu."

The janitor slowly walked out of the examination room, his figure disappearing into the early morning haze.

Dr. Liu exhaled a long, long breath. Twenty years earlier he and the janitor had enjoyed a drink together at a small bar. The janitor performed the feat of swallowing nails for him. Then he said to Dr. Liu, "There's an iron deposit in my stomach." From then on the doctor had been continuously studying his peculiar physique. The speed of the janitor's decline surprised him. The distinctive body that took nourishment from minerals suddenly had some kind of blockage, and the man atrophied day by day before his eyes. Recalling this, Dr. Liu remembered the needle inside his foot. The slight warmth in the sole gave him a comfortable, unobstructed feeling. It might be similar to how the iron ore upheld the janitor's body. Dr. Liu cleaned the examination room in a cheerful mood and placed the steam disinfector on the gas stove. Even though he had not slept that night, his spirits glowed, the way they always did.

Women occupied an important place in Dr. Liu's life, but that place had changed in the past few years. This is not to say Dr. Liu lost the capacity to love women, but rather that his interest in relations between the sexes had cooled, and he was somewhat resigned to his fate. In sexual relationships he could now always see the ending from the start, which was an extreme disadvantage for a man making love. A certain cold indifference slunk inside him like a poisonous snake. He felt too aware of his own life. He was afraid that the outcome would never be good, regardless of who the woman was, for a man like him who on opening his eyes saw the world in three dimensions, both the front and reverse sides in panorama. He had not planned to be a lifelong bachelor, but he understood his own nature too well. He'd considered marriage from all angles, without having started a family yet.

There was a beautiful patient whose rheumatic pain Dr. Liu treated with herbal medicine, as a result of which she fell deeply in love with him. Her name was lovely, she was called Danniang, and she had narrow phoenix eyes.

"We should have children and live like ordinary people," Danniang said to him upstairs above the examining room. "You could devote a portion of your time to a family."

Dr. Liu thought she was right, yet for some reason his spine ran cold. What sort of husband would he be? What sort of father? He was unsure of himself when faced with Danniang, passionate, beautiful, but oppressive. Late at night he imagined countless scenes of family life, experimentally inserting himself into the situations, and then every time expelled in disgrace. His conclusion was that Danniang would make a mess of his life.

Danniang lived in a nearby city. She always took the train to see him at first light and then back to her city the following afternoon. One morning when she arrived at the clinic she saw the entrance shut and a closed-for-business notice pasted on the door. Dr. Liu had written on the sign that he would be away for a week. The suitcase in Danniang's hand tumbled to the ground. She seemed to be thunderstruck. They had spoken on the phone only that morning.

"Miss, do you need to catch the train?" a white-bearded man asked, plucking at her sleeve.

"Yes, I'll catch the train. There's still the last one scheduled."

She was not resigned. Late that night she dialed the doctor's cell phone.

Dr. Liu's voice was thin and weak, as if he were standing out in a field in the wind. The phone kept cutting out.

"Danniang, I'm in the countryside. It's dark here, raining . . . I can't take the ferry across today, I'll have to splash through the stream . . . I know you didn't wait for me, that was the right thing to do. Are you asking what I think of myself? I'm a coward. I really am sorry."

Danniang hung up the phone in the dark, understanding in her heart that this was parting forever. The passageway was already blocked. From today onward she would draw closer to her lover from another direction, an approach that was the same as abiding separation. At first she questioned herself: what had gone wrong? Later she gradually understood she was destined to walk on Dr. Liu's road her entire life. Her romance with him was the point of departure. Dr. Liu would not see her again, but he had brought her onto this path with no way back, altering her life entirely. As for her feelings, she believed all of this suited her. She remembered the time when she was young that she'd used the *bawang* or "hegemon" herb for divination. Oh, she had great expectations then! Why did she no longer expect anything for herself?

Dr. Liu hadn't gone to the countryside. He was in the rooms above the clinic. He had watched Danniang's departing figure from far away, sensing his heart at that exact moment slowly transforming into a fossil. He thought about how using medicinal herbs to cure this woman's illness had been to sweep her up into his world. He didn't know whether this was good or bad for her; it was what had happened. The *qingmuxiang* in the mountain cave appeared in his mind again. How had those lovely, isolated little grasses evolved into the form they took today? What factors in the environment corresponded to their mystical efficacy? Receiving Danniang's call in the night had made him actually hallucinate, so that he seemed to be in the wilderness splashing across a stream. That hopeless despair was like an abyss. Yet being at the abyss calmed him down, while some facet of his nature began to show itself.

After lying upstairs for four days (not for a week), he resumed seeing outpatients and went back to being the humorous and witty doctor who could relieve their suffering. He also made house visits to several of his older patients and, in bringing them comfort, felt himself inwardly fulfilled.

"We and you are members of a secret organization."

This was what an elderly man with a tumor said as he squeezed the doctor's hand.

"I will add some of the herbs from Nest Mountain," Dr. Liu said.

"You're completely right. We belong to an organization. When I wake up in pain in the middle of the night, I see my compatriots hiding among the medicinal plants. There are many of them, one here, one there, scattered to the edges of the sky and sea. Liu, knowing you, I can die without regrets. I have learned the right treatment for my illness from you, and these five years have been fulfilling. Thank you."

A bird flew out from its hiding place and alighted on Dr. Liu's shoulder. It had yellow and white feathers, a brown beak, and eyes that were a little like Danniang's.

"Liu, this bird flew out of the mountains and now it treats my home as its own. It comes and goes as it will. You see how strange this is."

"I don't think it's strange. Do you talk with it?"

"I am always talking with it. At night, in those isolated, helpless moments, it brings me endless comfort. It has a family, I can see that in its eyes."

"You've become its kin."

While they were speaking the bird flew away, leaving the smell of its body, a pleasant odor, in the air.

"Liu, I have everything. I can see anything, even though I lie here unable to travel. It hasn't rained in so long that I was worried about those *dijin* plants 'decorating the ground.' Last night the rain came, and they were overjoyed!"

Tears shone in the eyes of the elderly man with a tumor. Dr. Liu saw the shadow of a mountain sweep across his face.

The doctor's state of mind was oddly carefree when he left. Hadn't he seen Danniang again? He no longer believed his life lacked something. Very few people had continual new wonders to make their lives fulfilling the way he and this elderly man did.

There was nowhere Danniang was not. Only a few days later he saw those beautiful eyes again in the face of a girl.

She had contracted roundworms, so he'd expelled them. Her mother brought her for a follow-up visit.

"Doctor," the girl said suddenly, "you don't need to kill them all. Leave a few, let them stay in my stomach. They aren't hurting me."

"She's so beautiful! You have such a pretty girl!" Dr. Liu said to her mother.

As the girl left she sang a strange nursery rhyme that seemed to be about a lizard's happy life. She repeated, "The lizard's eyes, the lizard's eyes . . ." Her expression was so solemn, as though she were looking into the eyes of the lizard. Dr. Liu wanted to say that the eyes of the lizard really were the most beautiful eyes in the natural world, even more beautiful than Danniang's eyes.

Watching the little girl skip away, Dr. Liu felt that his life was turning into a legend. Everything was to his heart's content, and wonderful! The patients understood him; they colluded with him in his undertaking. Is there greater happiness for people on this earth? Thinking this way, he even felt that Danniang was heaven's gift of joy to him. There was joy, even though there was pain.

At dusk Dr. Liu stood on the street at the door of the clinic. He wanted to take the pulse of this small county town. He sensed the many messages mingled with the southeast wind, information that, although chaotic, seemed to be drifting to form a certain shape. At this moment a three-wheeled cart pulled up to the door.

"Liu, are you waiting for me?" The janitor took off his straw hat to greet him.

"Did that bird come along?"

"Of course it came. Five birds altogether in that nest under the eaves. My leg is much better. As for the ancient city walls, I've already found a map."

"I wish you good luck."

Dr. Liu went back into the clinic and shut the main door. His mental process became animated. That morning he'd received a magazine called *Trends in Medicine* in the mail from a friend in the big city with news on its cover that made him secretly excited. Naturally, it was nothing real and factual, only a kind of forecast, an observation and analysis at a deep level. Dr. Liu held the magazine under the lamp to read a few lines, closed his eyes, and in his mind that indecipherable map appeared. Although he did not understand, he scouted a location with his thoughts, intoxicated by this game. For a moment, he even heard the roar of lions. "Oh . . . oh!" he quietly marveled, a cryptic smile appearing on his face.

When winter approached Dr. Liu went to a county in the central part of the province. The trip was not in connection to his professional work, but rather to satisfy his curiosity. The folk medicine society in that county ran a magazine about qigong to which he had submitted a manuscript. The magazine was well-known and appeared to be backed by a financial consortium. The editorial department was enormous.

Dr. Liu's train arrived at noon. He found a small hotel to stay in, ate lunch, and then went to the magazine's offices. He had a premonition that he would meet an old friend—one of his visitors—there.

The magazine's offices were in a secluded little alley. There was a very small sign on the peeling paint of the wooden door, on which was written: OFFICES OF EXPLORING THE MYSTERIES OF QIGONG. The wooden door was shut tight. Dr. Liu watched it for a while, but there was no sound of movement inside. He rapped on the door, then finally pushed it open. Inside there was still no sound or movement. He had definitely noted down that the offices would be open today. All he could do for now was return, discouraged, to the hotel.

"Hu Gua! Cucumber!" someone behind him bellowed.

Dr. Liu turned around to look. A short man was waving to someone else who was walking over from the end of the alley. The man called "Cucumber" was nearing old age, wore ragged garments, and had a dark face.

"Are you looking for Hu Gua? Here he is. He's the head of the magazine," the short man said.

Straightaway Dr. Liu remembered that the magazine's director really was named Hu.

Director Hu nodded toward Dr. Liu, pulled out a key, and opened the wooden door. He made a sign for the doctor to enter with him. They passed through a tiny courtyard, abundant with flowers and grass left to grow, a scene of untamed charm and still pleasantly green even though it was almost winter.

The editorial department was a two-story building in the old style of gray bricks, with numerous rooms, and the doors of every room downstairs were wide open. Dr. Liu didn't see a single person inside the rooms. The director's office was at the end of the hallway, its door open, too. The two men entered the spacious office together.

"Please sit down," Director Hu said.

Dr. Liu sat in the uncomfortable chair.

There was an enormous writing desk in the center of the room with newspapers, magazines, correspondence, and manuscripts piled carelessly on top. At the exact center of the desk, near the lamp, sat a grave little monkey. The little monkey stared straight at Dr. Liu, watching him until he became uneasy.

"Don't pay attention, I've spoiled it," Director Hu said, smiling. "Your article is excellent, full of theoretical initiative."

"Thank you. I'm incredibly honored that you read my article personally."

"Ha ha! If I didn't read it, who would?"

"Excuse me, I didn't know. I thought you would have turned it over to the editors who work for you."

"I have no editors," Director Hu said without changing expression.

"I don't understand."

"I really have no editors. This is a one-person magazine."

"How embarrassing! Have I offended you, Director Hu?"

"No, you haven't offended me. I'm really very happy you've come to visit the magazine. I know, you don't believe I can run the magazine alone, but this is a fact. I have a part-time artistic designer and no one else. I do all the other tasks, from proofreading and layout to sending the magazine to the printer. I can see from your expression that you're a little disappointed. You probably thought there was a large group of people here. There really isn't, as arranged by heaven above. You're inside the organization, you ought to know that loneliness is our fate."

"It's hard to imagine." Dr. Liu stood out of respect and shook hands with the director.

The monkey jumped up and ripped a hole in the doctor's white lab coat.

"Oh, it's jealous. Let go, quick!"

Dr. Liu sat down, his emotions surging.

"I don't feel lonely, though. Our people are everywhere in the world, many even abroad. I don't see myself as one person. Now that I have a magazine, I am a group of people, and, counting the readers all over the world, I become a crowd. Ha ha!"

He flipped at random through the pile of letters on the desk and pulled out a large envelope.

"Aha, here it is! This is an organization from Guangxi. They meet regularly to discuss my magazine and are always making proposals or recommending plans for improvement. The suggestions are vital and on the mark—it's very exciting. In my imagination, the organization had a large membership. Then one day they came, like you, to see me in person. I was shocked to discover the readers from Guangxi were only one person. He was an elderly man who lived alone on social assistance. He saved up his food rations to subscribe to the magazine, which he called 'spiritual nourishment.' Liu, now you understand, our enterprise has nothing to do with the number of people. Yes, the problem of the soul has nothing to do with the number of people. I chatted all through the night with the reader from Guangxi. That night the globe rotated between us. Wind from off the Atlantic Ocean blew in our faces."

When Director Hu put the letter down the little monkey snatched it away, ripped it to pieces, and swept the torn scraps off the table with its leg.

"Look!" Director Hu began to smile. "It's always jealous. The reader from Guangxi really knows how to write a letter—the style as powerful as riding a horse across the sky, the logic rigorous and precise. A pity you can't read it!"

Director Hu suggested he and the doctor go sit beside the well behind his office because the air in the editorial department was stifling. Dr. Liu noticed that when they left the monkey stayed on the writing desk.

"Am I right in thinking that Director Hu must have many local sympathizers?" Dr. Liu could not help asking.

"Yes, I have many sympathetic friends," the director frankly acknowledged, "two thousand subscribers in the county town and its surrounding area alone. They don't discuss the magazine's problems with me like the reader from Guangxi, of course. They support me because of their good opinion of me. Before running the magazine, I was an excellent cobbler, and many of them sought me out to repair their shoes. They remember my former profession and respect me for it. They're pleased to see an ordinary person dance with words and play with ink. That's exactly what they say, 'dance with words and play with ink.' People in this county have a lot of curiosity. Ha ha!"

As they talked they came to the well. It was extremely deep, and Dr. Liu hastily shrank back, feeling dizzy at one glance. He even felt an ominous air rising from the bottom of the well.

They each sat on one side of the rectangular platform beside the well. Director Hu said the air was much better here. He had headaches year-round, so he was very sensitive to the air. He asked whether Dr. Liu had noticed his advertisements around the county town. As he was speaking, he took out a small ad about the size of a cigarette case from the bulging pocket of his jacket and handed it to the doctor, saying it was a gift. A black arrow, and nothing else, was drawn on the colorful scrap of paper. Director Hu said the artistic designer had created it.

"I put out ads every day because I worry the magazine will be forgotten. I post them everywhere, from this county town to the countryside. One time I went on a business trip to the grasslands of Mongolia, where I actually saw this same ad on an electricity pole. I went closer to look and, no mistake, it was my ad. My friends must have posted it there. This is called 'having people close to you everywhere.' For more than twenty years my magazine has maintained a steady subscription rate. It makes me proud."

"Allow me to ask: how many subscribers are there? There must be many of them?"

"Oh, enough. Two thousand and twenty-five subscriptions in all. That is, two thousand here in this county, and twenty-five in the rest of the world—including yours."

Dr. Liu noted that when he said these two numbers his face was covered with smiles. Director Hu was clearly very pleased. He went on to tell Dr. Liu that he had two readers in Mongolia, Chinese living abroad. Dr. Liu waited with respect for him to tell the story of these two readers. Suddenly something went wrong in the editorial department. Dr. Liu heard a window shatter and smash to the ground. A disturbance came from inside the room.

Director Hu jumped up and ran into the building with Dr. Liu following behind. At the door the director abruptly turned around and made a decisive gesture, saying, "Go straight back to the hotel! Whatever you do, don't stay here! You can come again tomorrow, but today, I'm very sorry, I can't meet with you."

He went into the editorial department and bolted the door from the inside. After some time he let out an awful shriek, three heart-rending screams in all. Then everything was quiet.

Dr. Liu, devastated, left the editorial department.

He had just left the magazine's offices when the short man caught up to him from behind.

He had a dark, weathered face with cunning small eyes that blinked continuously. Dr. Liu noticed he had the large hands of someone who did manual labor. The man said, gasping for breath, "What did Hu Gua tell you? That old fox, I want to be his assistant and dredge up some editorial work, but he never gives me a direct answer! He only cares about his own interests, and takes all the advantages in the world for himself!"

Dr. Liu, watching him sideways, asked, "Do you hate him?"

"Hate him?" The man was stupefied for a moment. "No, you're mistaken, Doctor! Who could hate Hu Gua? He's the pride of our county town! Look at you, you came from far away to see him. Why else would anyone come here? Every year two or three groups come to visit Hu Gua. You should know he used to be my neighbor. It was my father who taught him the craft of shoe repair. He shouldn't forget to be grateful."

The man's small eyes blinked even more severely, as if he were faced with a complex and difficult question.

"Will you go back to see Hu Gua tomorrow? Mention my problem to him, Doctor! I implore you! My departed father implores you!" he said earnestly.

"Do you like Hu Gua's magazine?"

"What are you talking about? I don't understand much of the profound theory, but it's spiritual support! We ordinary people who work for a living need a bit of spiritual sustenance. Are you willing to help? Think about it, someone like me would be reliable. I understand Hu Gua's entire project. Before, when he studied my father's trade, he and I were like brothers."

Warmth flooded Dr. Liu's heart as these simple words returned him to his youth, but he had reached the hotel, so he paused, shook the short man's hand, and said, "No, I can't help you. You've made an excellent impression on me, though. I am very happy."

"Ha, I am also happy to speak with you! Goodbye!"

Dr. Liu ate dinner in the small hotel where he was staying, then went out, with vague misgivings, and strolled down the sidewalk. This county town looked no different from the several other county towns he had visited around the country: not antiquated, but not fashionable either. The buildings were placed chaotically and made of cheap materials. Shops and stores, private residences, entertainment centers, social organizations, all mixed together into one, without any sense of order. There were numerous cars on the street, pedestrians, and idlers. Dr. Liu looked all over without seeing any sights that interested him. He pondered what connection Director Hu and his magazine might have to this county town. He didn't sense there was any relationship between the two. However, could what he saw be only an outer image, and this ordinary and banal surface, unmoved by any tides, be precisely what concealed an exciting, unimaginable connection underneath?

A child rolling a hoop down the sidewalk rushed straight toward Dr. Liu, who hastily ducked away. Then a second child rolled another iron hoop over. Dr. Liu escaped to the entryway of a building, where he stood until one of the windows opened and someone leaned out, shouting, "Who are you looking for?"

Dr. Liu suddenly understood that the county town did not welcome idle strangers.

"I'm just passing through. I'm going to the offices of *Exploring the Mysteries of Qigong*!" he shouted back.

"It's not open in the evening," the person advised before shutting the window.

Dr. Liu looked left and right to make sure there was no one on the sidewalk at the moment and walked quickly toward the hotel. He rushed back inside as though taking refuge.

"Someone's waiting for you in your room," the manager smiled, squinting.

"Who?"

"Your friend. We recognized him, so we let him in."

Dr. Liu saw the short man in his room.

"I came to tell you Hu Gua has been badly injured and won't be able to see you. He sent me to offer his regrets. He recommends that you head back early."

"Oh, how upsetting! Was he seriously hurt? Where?"

"He hurt his left eye. It might have to be removed."

"Oh no! I'll go see him at the hospital."

"Whatever you do, don't disturb him. He asked me to tell you not to. Don't worry, he's optimistic. I think he's even pleased. He told me that the physical wound cut through his mental difficulties. We all have problems on our minds, so we know what that means. Don't you agree?"

"Hmm."

"Dr. Liu, what's your impression of our county town?"

"I sense an atmosphere of freedom here," Dr. Liu spouted.

"Exactly!" He clapped his hands in enthusiasm. "What did you just say? Right, freedom! Our town is very free. Think about it: a town with nothing eye-catching has the offices of a magazine known all across the country. How rare is something like that? All of this is connected to my elderly father, who was a good judge of character. He was so perceptive. I can't measure up to him."

He stood to say goodbye to Dr. Liu. He suddenly noticed the hole torn out of Dr. Liu's lab coat.

"Is this the work of the Monkey King? I see, you really are lucky!"

"How long has the monkey been in Director Hu's editorial department?"

"It has been there the whole time, ever since the magazine had an office. It has never left; it's at the root of Hu Gua's life. Hu Gua's transformation into a man of heroic ambition is all due to the Monkey King being there. Hu Gua once told me that when he drinks he doesn't know whether he is the Monkey King or Director Hu."

"Did it attack you?"

"No, it's not interested in me. People like me aren't high enough quality."

At this moment Dr. Liu felt himself nearing that enormous, profound mystery of qigong, but soon he was pushed away again. His mind became an obscure expanse.

"I forgot to tell you that my surname is Zhu. I'm going now. Goodbye."

He left, leaving a mystery behind.

After showering and getting ready for bed, Dr. Liu realized that his room was unusual. It was large but only had a single window very high and also very small. Once he turned off the light, the room was pitch black. The night here was particularly quiet, a real nothingness. At first Dr. Liu thought he would feel nothing if he went to sleep, but he was wrong. Exhausted, he couldn't rest; the nothingness became a tangible abyss. Now if he shifted slightly on the bed he felt the gut-wrenching fear that he was slipping down . . . "Aaah!" he finally shouted.

All the lights in the room turned on automatically, but it stayed as frighteningly quiet as before.

Dr. Liu went over to open the door leading to the hallway. Nothing could be seen outside. He felt something scurry past his leg and into the room. It was the Monkey King, a terrified expression in its eyes. It jumped onto the bed and worked its way under the blankets. Dr. Liu's heart overflowed with pity, and he had a premonition something significant had happened. He thought it over and, deciding to finish what he had started, got into bed to get some sleep.

When he got inside the blankets, the trembling Monkey King snuggled onto his chest with a rustling sound. In the dark it made a curious crying noise, so that warm tears welled in Dr. Liu's eyes. Strangely, in his excitement he was soon tired, and felt happy at the instant of falling asleep.

When he woke the sky was already light. The Monkey King was not on the bed. He examined every corner of the room and bathroom without seeing it. He stood there, vaguely disappointed. He wanted to go back to the magazine offices to look around, but gave up the idea because of Director Hu's warning. He turned around and saw the short man named Zhu standing in front of him again, his manner neither modest nor overbearing.

"I worried you would be looking for me, so I hurried over at dawn," he said.

"I was planning to go looking for you. Tell me, what happened to the Monkey King?"

"The Monkey King? Ha, it's back on good terms with Hu Gua already. That's how it always is with him and the monkey, fighting like enemies destined to be together. The truth is, Hu Gua told me to come. He asked me to watch you get on the train. He doesn't want you to stay here, that's what he said."

"How is his eye?"

"It's inflamed and will have to be removed."

"If I go to the station, are you planning to come with me?"

"Of course. It's my duty."

After Dr. Liu took his seat in the train compartment, the short man named Zhu clasped his hand.

"Doctor, I assure you, you've left Hu Gua, and me, with kind memories. In our lives after today, when we're at work, we will often think of you, and speak of you . . . Oh, how wonderful! For instance, I will say to Hu Gua, 'That year the doctor came whose lab coat was torn by the Monkey King . . . ,' then Hu Gua, the one-eyed hero, will understand and take it right to heart."

He raised his voice to the point that the travelers around them pricked up their ears. Dr. Liu was incredibly touched.

"Then goodbye, Mr. Zhu! If needed, I can send Director Hu herbal medicines."

"You shouldn't, it won't do any good. Hu Gua will be angry. You don't know him at all. Only I understand him, I know he will bear the burden alone. He has secret resources."

He stepped off the train. Dr. Liu's eyes followed the short silhouette as it disappeared on the platform, and he suddenly thought that he had seen Zhu somewhere before. He remembered: hadn't he been the one, that year on Nest Mountain, who had crossed back and forth across the precipice of the cliff like a madman and showed an astonishing skill at jumping? He had disguised himself so well! This meant that, many years before, Dr. Liu had already been in indirect contact with the magazine offices, only he had not known it at the time. He repeated to himself, "Director Hu, Director Hu, where will the winds you stir up blow from tonight?"

The passenger on the upper bunk looked over and said earnestly, "Are you coming back from the shrines to the revolution, Doctor?"

"Yes. How did you know?"

"I could tell from hearing your conversation. Places like that have become very quiet today, but so beautiful, and such a high realm. I am coming from there, too. I go once every two years. I don't go in, I just look around from far away. This satisfies me. In fact you and I were staying at the same hotel, but you didn't notice. The dusk here surpasses paradise."

The train departed. Dr. Liu fixed his eyes on the high and low scattered houses through the window, his thoughts at a complete halt. After a while, the county town vanished into the haze.

He returned home in the early morning. From far away he saw the man with a tumor, Old Man Lin, looking around at the entrance to his clinic. The elderly man's color looked good, and both of his eyes gleamed. Was it the reflection of a dying light? Dr. Liu opened the door, and they walked together into the dispensary. He put down his luggage and began to clean.

"Dr. Liu, yesterday the bird brought its family—one son, one daughter. We communicated the whole night. I was too happy, so happy that part of my body started to hurt. I thought my time would come soon, but I couldn't put my mind at rest. What if I died, and someone shut my windows so it couldn't come in with its children? I thought it over, and I have to trouble you with this responsibility. I can't rely on anyone else. Will you promise me? I have no children, so when I die I want to leave the house to it and its children. Do you think that will be possible, Dr. Liu?"

The doctor gave it a thought, and then a serious answer, "I think that will be possible."

"Wonderful! Your spirit shines even more after your journey. I suppose you must have met him."

"Who?" Dr. Liu was surprised. "Who are you talking about?"

"I'm talking about 'him.' You went to his place there, of course. When I was young I went, too. He is an ideal in a dream. Now I have even more faith in you."

He took a few medicines for pain relief and left. As Dr. Liu disinfected he recalled the marvel the old man had spoken of and connected it to his own mysterious chance meeting the day before. An unclear tableau appeared again in his mind, the few people inside it trudging along under cover of large trees.

The next day when it was time to close, Dr. Liu, concerned about Old Man Lin with his tumor, walked to the lane where the old man lived with his medicine case on his back. The closer he came to the house, the more strained the doctor felt, but he did not know why.

Oh, the two-story wooden building no longer existed. The site was empty, nothing remained. Dr. Liu's legs went weak. He sat down on the ground, his heart full of sorrow. How could this have happened? Was there a conspiracy? A taxi stopped beside him, its horn blaring. The driver, Lao Gu, got out.

"Dr. Liu," he said, "why are you sitting on the ground? You shouldn't mourn too much. Old Man Lin died in the mountains, and I saw him off at the end. Shortly before his death he decided to have me bring someone to help him demolish the house. As his distant relative, I had to do what he requested. He was confused at his age, naturally. He said he didn't want to leave any trace of himself on the earth, since he had poisonous hatred in his heart, but his act made a lasting memory for all of us. He died in the mountains without making a sound. There were some birds calling in the distance, but none that came near. I think he'd thought it all out. I dragged him to the crematorium, then he was put in that little urn. In this empty space where his home stood there will be a new house built right away. The people from the housing management office have already been to see the site. Everyone praises him. Dr. Liu, get in the car. I'll take you back."

Dr. Liu sat in the back seat listening to Lao Gu babble on, this man of many words.

"I think there was nothing missing in his life, and then death has its meaning. I asked him why he was going into the mountains. He answered that he always thought of himself as a bird that has to die in the mountains. So once he reached the mountains he was very peaceful. In the night the fog left his hair and face wet. He said, 'Fly, fly . . .'"

A number of people stood at the entrance to the clinic, all of them discussing

Old Man Lin, and all showing their envy in their tone of voice. When Dr. Liu got out of the car they surrounded him.

"What kind of medicine did you give him? I want to die with dignity, too."

"You must treat all with the same benevolence, Dr. Liu!"

"You do the most of any doctor to put our minds at ease . . ."

The supporting crowd carried the doctor into the clinic.

SEVEN

Wei Bo in Prison

Wei Bo would be sentenced to serve three months. After the judgment was pronounced, his wife Xiao Yuan came to visit him once.

Wei Bo saw that on the other side of the dividing window Xiao Yuan shone with health and was looking much younger than usual. She seemed immersed in some fine emotion. Wei Bo was happy for her.

"Wei Bo, three months will pass in the blink of an eye," Xiao Yuan said.

She winked at Wei Bo, because the guard was next to her.

Wei Bo nodded his head. He understood what Xiao Yuan meant. They were encouraging each other.

Xiao Yuan didn't like to be sentimental. She believed that since Wei Bo had chosen to go to prison, he had chosen the life he wanted.

Wei Bo's job was hauling sand. Every day after breakfast he went with the other prisoners to the riverside, where they moved sand with carrying poles from boats to trucks. For the first few days Wei Bo thought he had been sent to hell, since he had not done manual labor for a long time and was nearing fifty.

The third night, after he had endured the day's punishing labor with clenched teeth and lay on the prison cell bunk, a warm current of joy unexpectedly surged through him. He covered his head with the blanket and focused on listening to his own heartbeat. He imagined the situation of his lover Cuilan. At some remote place outside, Cuilan, fine-figured, like a peahen, was loitering among tall trees. She sometimes stopped to press her delightful face onto the surface of the tree trunks. Wei Bo could not guess the meaning of her actions, because he had never seen her behave like this before.

The urge to sleep crept up on him, but the burning ache in his shoulders wouldn't let him. He was grateful for this pain, because it kept his mental process active, producing more of these fine associations in his mind.

His encounter with Cuilan had not been purely accidental, of course. Lying in the prison cell, Wei Bo felt keenly aware: this woman was his life's lucky star. He said to himself, "Wei Bo, good fortune is your path." Ever since he had gone to Cuilan's hometown, he thought constantly of that bleak village as being connected to his own ancestral home. These two places were separated by distance, of course, and the scenery was completely different, but both gave him the sense of "hometown." The hometown in his memory had the look of these two places. He had only gone to visit Cuilan's family home because of what Mr. You had said: "Ms. Cuilan's background is extraordinary. You should know that her family comes from Camphor Tree Village!"

Wei Bo didn't understand and asked in return, "What is there to Camphor Tree Village?"

Mr. You repeated, as if it weighed on his mind, "It's hard to explain everything at once. It's hard to explain!"

So Wei Bo went to Camphor Tree Village.

His feelings toward Camphor Tree Village were the same as Mr. You's: "It's hard to explain everything at once." It was at Camphor Tree Village that his attitude toward Cuilan changed. This alteration was itself very strange, and he didn't know why it had to be this way. The decisive factor, without doubt, was his choice to go to prison. That is to say, he went to prison because his attitude toward Cuilan had changed.

With a fine happy feeling, Wei Bo thought things over until late at night when he was comfortable enough to sleep. For six days in a row he paid no attention to the other three prisoners in the cell. His mood seemed unusually elated because of the physical hardship. Starting the third day, when night came, events from before with Cuilan came into view one by one, as in a movie. Even though he and Cuilan were no longer in intimate contact, roaming through these imaginations brought Wei Bo a kind of spiritual satisfaction, unlike in the past. So now he looked forward every day to those three hours at night lying on the bunk before falling asleep. He thought the choice to go to prison had been the correct one.

This was the night of the seventh day. He finished listening to the correctional lecture, showered, and was about to lie down. Someone behind him spoke. It was the cross-eyed man who slept by the door.

"Wei Bo, you have a disgusting disease, you blackguard—you deserve execution. How dare you look down on the rest of us! I've been watching you for days. You disappoint me."

"Oh, excuse me, I didn't realize. You know my nickname, too. I didn't expect that. Why are you in? For how long?" Wei Bo said humbly with a smile.

"You have no shame, asking such a hypocritical question. You should ask yourself this question! Why are you in? I'm in for the same reason. Prison is a good place for education. I learned that lesson too late, or I wouldn't be in this state now. You can call me Lao Zhang."

Wei Bo thought, What a mess. He's going to flush away the night's happiness.

"Wei Bo, I want to talk with you about your case. You don't object?"

"Thank you for your concern, but I don't want to talk. I have trouble sleeping, so I shouldn't talk at night."

"Is that true?" Lao Zhang moved closer, watching him with a strange expression in his eyes.

He bumped against Wei Bo, who saw the small, sharp knife in his hand.

"No, Lao Zhang. What I meant is that I don't want to lie. There's a bad atmosphere in prison."

"Who said there's a bad atmosphere in prison?" Lao Zhang's voice became menacing.

"That's not what I meant. I mean the windows in the cells are so small the air is filthy."

"You damned liar!" Lao Zhang laughed, securing the knife in his pocket.

He clapped Wei Bo on the shoulder, motioning him to sit on the bunk, then announced, "Now that you're in, according to the custom of the prison cell, you have to open the doors of your heart to us. You must make your case public."

Wei Bo only then noticed that the two other men had been craning their necks to watch him for some time. He was embarrassed, but also stimulated.

"I'm in prison because I was in love with my mistress Niu Cuilan. I discovered that to love her well I needed to put a distance between us. If not, we would always be tangled up with horrible, messy problems. So one day I committed a crime on purpose, and this is why I went to jail."

"Good!" The three men commended Wei Bo in unison.

"I've told it all. So, Lao Zhang, what crime did you commit?"

"I didn't commit a crime. My life forced me to charge into the jail holding a handgun. I didn't shoot. My thoughts were dark. My wife and I couldn't manage to live with each other. So I thought the only thing I could do was to go to prison.

All right, they took away my gun and let me inside. From then I've known that people can accomplish whatever they set out to do."

When Lao Zhang spoke these words, his eyes became very kind, even slightly blurry. He changed into a completely different person, almost like an intellectual. Next he said, "My thoughts really were dark. I didn't take my wife very seriously, but then I discovered she had found a lover. Every time I saw her with that man I wanted to murder him. When I had this impulse, I was afraid for my life. My whole body shook. I thought it would be better to kill myself than someone else. I raised my knife, but every time it made me faint. I came to understand I couldn't kill myself. Going to prison seemed the only way. So that's how the attack on the prison happened. The people there asked me politely to come inside. My wife came to visit when the time came. I asked myself whether I still loved her, and the answer was that I did not. Even though she loved me and wanted to wait for me. Hearing her say she loved me produced a deep sympathy for her. Before I rarely felt sympathy toward anyone. I couldn't let her wait for me. I was a demon, I might kill someone, and the more afraid I was the more I wanted to murder. So I decided to stay in here. Every time my sentence is almost finished, I commit a crime and receive an increased sentence. I've stayed for nine years and will continue. It's all because of my wife's good influence. Aaah," Lao Zhang sighed, drawing out the sound.

"Wei Bo, I admire you after hearing your case. You never thought of killing your lover?"

The three men surrounded him, staring into his eyes with intense expressions.

"No. I wouldn't dare murder someone or even kill myself. I faint at the sight of blood."

"So that's it," the three men said in unison, looking at each other and laughing.

"I'm Lao Lu," the man with a crew cut said. "Wei Bo, what is your opinion of Lao Zhang's case?"

"For the moment I have none. I think he has a sharp temper. I admire his intelligence. Not everyone can pull off charging the prison with a gun. A sad sack like me can only get a three-month sentence. As for his case, maybe it's the same as mine. Only the parties involved understand the subtleties."

"Good, Wei Bo!" The men cheered and started to applaud.

They alarmed the guard, who entered with a gloomy look, put Wei Bo in handcuffs, signaled for him to leave the cell, and kicked him in the rear. Wei Bo heard the other prisoners furtively laughing behind his back.

The guard brought Wei Bo to the stairwell and shackled both of his hands to the iron banister.

He left with a stream of curses. Wei Bo's body was in a tortuous position, and he could not pine for his lover Cuilan. Soon his hands grew numb. The bones all over his body hurt as if insects were biting them. It was more painful than the first two days hauling sand. About two hours of suffering passed. He tried to faint, but his consciousness was insistent. He could even hear the low voices talking in his prison cell. Those three were clearly not asleep and seemed to be discussing him. Why? Why were they making a spectacle of him and subjecting him to this torture? Hadn't he "opened the doors of his heart" to them? Wei Bo couldn't understand what had taken place that night. His mind was in chaos. He started to sweat, slowly soaking the prison uniform, which stuck cold to his back.

Gradually he entered a state of frenzy, mixed up with an idea, which was: let these damned handcuffs cut off both his hands, he would rather not have hands than die on the stairs in this shameful pose! Half dazed, he took a deep breath, then pulled violently on both arms . . .

He felt his hands missing, but he had gained his freedom. He went upstairs and charged into the feebly lit prison cell. He thought his appearance plastered in blood would terrify the three men.

When his gaze fell onto his hands, though, he saw that they were there, with the handcuffs still on his wrists. The cuffs were fake, it turned out, and the guard had been making an empty show of power to frighten him!

"Good!" they started to yell again.

All three men sat up in their bunks, watching Wei Bo intently.

"What are you going to do?" Lao Lu, the man with a crew cut, was shaking.

"I want to kill someone."

"Hurry up and go to sleep, you still have two hours," Lao Zhang's voice came from by the door.

He immediately shut the door and turned off the light.

Wei Bo lay down on his bunk, too. Even though the handcuffs were still on his wrists, he went right into a dream once he closed his eyes. He slept deeply.

The next day the guard prodded him awake with a baton. The other three men had gone, not waking Wei Bo on purpose.

The guard took off the handcuffs and roared, "Hurry up and get to the riverside!"

"But I haven't had breakfast," Wei Bo said.

"How dare you talk back, damn it!"

As he said this, he struck random blows at Wei Bo with the baton. Wei Bo covered his head with his arms and ran through the door.

He ran to the riverside, taking a place in the work team hauling sand.

At first he was all right. At one point Lao Zhang walked up to him and said,

"I saw your lover. She came to visit, but you weren't out of bed yet. What a perfect beauty!"

"You exaggerate. Did she say anything?"

"I heard her saying nice things about the prison to the administrators, and also that she regretted not being able to come here herself!"

Wei Bo pondered the information Lao Zhang had given him. Rolling the news back and forth in his mind, he was surprised to feel himself closer to Cuilan. She really was a good woman, she had understood his feelings from the start. Why was he so foolish? He thought again of how he hadn't been able to see her because he craved sleep, making her waste the trip. It was disgraceful. He didn't know why Cuilan had fallen in love with him.

After hauling seven or eight loads of sand, Wei Bo was so hungry he struggled to stand, then fell down. He curled up and closed his eyes. Someone stuffed a drinking straw into his mouth. He heard someone next to him ask, "Is it cholera?"

After he drank the beverage he forced his eyes open to discover everyone was far, far away, except for one person. It was Lao Lu, the man with a crew cut from his prison cell. He was holding a gun!

"I'm carrying out my orders," he said. "You have cholera. You're not allowed to move around. Stay there and don't move."

"All right, I won't move. Do I have cholera? Why don't I have diarrhea?"

"You'll have diarrhea, don't worry! Strange things do happen under heaven!"

Lao Lu had started to holler, but there was not a single person around, and no one heard him shout.

"Lao Lu, I don't feel well. Tell me about your case," Wei Bo entreated.

"Don't come any closer. I'm afraid you're contagious! If you come closer I'll shoot, I really will."

Wei Bo had to let the idea go and stay sitting on the sandy ground. He saw the unfinished bottle of orange drink on the ground and a sausage link tossed down next to it. Flies circled the sausage. Wei Bo, suddenly bold, snatched the sausage and stuffed it into his mouth, finishing in two or three bites. Then he drank the rest of the juice. Now his hands stopped trembling, and his head was also much clearer.

"Look how greedy you are," Lao Lu's voice reached him.

"I have cholera. It's dying, nothing more. What do I have to be afraid of?"

"As long as we're sitting here bored, I'll tell you about my case."

Lao Lu, apparently touched by Wei Bo's behavior, sat closer to him. While he was talking he even tugged at Wei Bo's sleeve and tossed the handgun to the ground.

"Listen, Wei Bo. I . . . I went to prison because I was impatient with life. Recently I keep asking myself, If everyone has bad times in their lives, why am I the only one who's always impatient? If I were more patient, I would go to work every day and make a living to support a family, like the majority of people. Of course, I'm not saying there's anything wrong with going to prison. I've stayed here many years, and there's been nothing bad about it. I'm trying to say that there's nothing wrong with being outside, that it's possible to stay there. Why did I feel like I couldn't stay there another day? These past few days I've often wondered—could I still live outside? I think I've thought of a way that I could get out and live. Still, I think the inside is great, too. Doesn't Lao Zhang, who's so smart, live with me? Wei Bo, do you have any opinions?"

"Well, you still haven't told me what your case was about."

"I already told you. You weren't listening hard enough."

Lao Lu looked unhappy, but couldn't help continuing.

"I was tired of living, and couldn't decide whether to change. It made me anxious to the point of madness. I rushed around everywhere, until I rushed in here. Now it looks like my rampage came to the right place, don't you think? Since then my experience has widened so much because of this clever guy Lao Zhang. To say what's in my heart, I also don't want to leave because the authorities have started to put me to use. Look, they issued me this handgun, it's a real gun. Is this ordinary trust?"

He abruptly raised the gun and shot twice into the sky.

Wei Bo's face turned as white as paper. All the blood in his body seemed to congeal.

"Don't, don't! I'll do what you say!" he stammered.

"Look, you're afraid of dying again. 'It is easier for the mountains and rivers to move than for human nature to change!' Now stand up, turn around, and let me shoot. I hate seeing the faces of the condemned."

Wei Bo glanced toward heaven, where an enormous hawk flew in the blue sky. He did not know where it was flying; it seemed to have paused there on that spot. He slowly stood, turned around, and suddenly broke into a frenzied run. He ran for his life, unable to stop, until he was almost suffocating. In his madness he saw someone's face, then a black object, before he fell ignobly to the ground.

The face was still Lao Lu's, and the black object was Lao Lu's long outer coat, which he had thrown over Wei Bo, pinning him to the ground. Wei Bo recalled, ashamed not to have noticed, that Lao Lu had been wearing this long black overcoat, the kind the police wear in winter, the whole time.

"Where am I?" Wei Bo foolishly asked.

"You ran in a big circle. You're plenty strong. Quick, get up. The canteen is there up ahead, everyone's waiting for you to eat."

"I don't have cholera?"

"Cholera my ass, you ran faster than a dog! If you don't hurry I'll shoot again!"

Wei Bo had hauled sand for more than ten days. He'd gradually adjusted to the way of life and was even somewhat pleased with himself. He felt he was still capable. He'd gotten to know Lao Zhang and Lao Lu, while only Xiao Yan, with his odd look, never had a heart-to-heart with him. Xiao Yan didn't seem to enjoy talking with anyone. However, when he looked at Wei Bo, Wei Bo thought Xiao Yan had many things to say to him. When Wei Bo opened his mouth, Xiao Yan would walk away with an indifferent air. He thought Xiao Yan was the most difficult to communicate with of his three cellmates.

One day a levee burst, and Lao Zhang and Lao Lu were ordered to join the rescue efforts. Without saying why, the authorities let Wei Bo and Xiao Yan rest in their cell for the day. Wei Bo thought that they probably did not trust the two of them. Were they worried he and Xiao Yan would escape when they got to the levee? He felt insulted, since he wouldn't run away when what he was worried about was being released from prison after his three-month sentence. The issue of his sentence bothered him whenever he happened to think of it. Hauling sand had not only tempered his body; he was also sleeping much better. Wei Bo recalled all of a sudden that he'd come up with a way to go to prison because he suffered from insomnia. He was so weak-willed.

Xiao Yan lay on the bunk the entire morning not saying a word. Wei Bo lay on his own bunk, taking advantage of this hard-won rest to imagine scenes of himself with Cuilan. He felt content and relaxed. Why had he never had these fine sensations outside of prison? Wei Bo often looked sideways at Xiao Yan on the opposite bunk. Xiao Yan had his hands pillowed behind his head and appeared calm, the ill-tempered expression on his face the past several days gone. Wei Bo estimated him to be no older than thirty-two, a young man in his best years. Yet he was a little haggard, and his health seemed poor.

Wei Bo came back after lunch to discover that Xiao Yan was missing. According to the rules this meant he had to report to the guards. The cellblock door opened with one push. He went to the guard room and saw Guard Yang, the one who had handcuffed him, on duty again. Wei Bo's report seemed to shock him.

"How was his emotional state?" Guard Yang asked.

"The same as usual."

"You idiot. Since he was planning to escape, of course he would pretend to be the same as usual. Head on back to the cell. You should reflect on what you've done!"

He pulled a green whistle out of his pocket and blew an eardrum-piercing screech. Wei Bo ducked into his cell covering his ears.

Before long he heard a disturbance outside. A large detachment of troops ran past below the window. People were shooting guns into the sky, intermixed with the shrill, sad sound of women weeping. What was happening? Wei Bo was too unsettled to just sit there. He was worried about Xiao Yan. After all, they had lived in the same room for more than ten days.

Wei Bo drummed up the courage to open the door and go into the hallway, where he saw that several prisoners had come out of the cells next to and opposite his. They were debating something, but they shut their mouths when they saw Wei Bo.

"What happened?" Wei Bo asked.

"A search party for an escaped prisoner. This chance is once in a lifetime. Let's go outside and watch the excitement!"

As he spoke the man raced out with some of the others.

Wei Bo, unable to control his curiosity, ran outside.

The landscape outside had changed profoundly. Once the figures of the other prisoners disappeared there was no one on the exercise grounds in front of the building. It was quiet in all directions, as if nothing had taken place. Wei Bo was shocked, remembering what had just happened. Why had Guard Yang left the door unlocked and let the prisoners run loose? Wasn't this a serious neglect of his duty? What would happen next if they took the chance to escape? Wei Bo decided to return and stay in the cell to avoid catastrophe.

As he entered the cell someone scurried out from a hiding place and struck him so hard he saw stars. Oh, it was Guard Yang! Wei Bo was filled with regret.

"I'm finished." Guard Yang, exhausted in body and spirit, sat down on the ground.

"Did he escape?" Wei Bo asked.

"How could he escape? Of course he couldn't. But we can't find him . . . Don't ask me questions. Let me think through the details." His voice became a whisper.

Abruptly he raised his voice and asked Wei Bo seriously, "Tell me the truth. Did you see the diamond ring?"

"What diamond ring? I don't understand."

"He has an expensive diamond ring that he carries at all times. I heard the details of his case, so I know he has it ready for his girlfriend. An uncommon obsession! I'm the only one who knows his secret, so I've helped him keep it safe. Damn it! How could I share classified information with a criminal like you? Listen, I have to find him, even if he dug hundreds of feet deep."

Yang seemed to recover his strength all at once as he stood and returned in a fury to the guard room.

The cell doors were all opened wide, the rooms inside empty. Wei Bo thought there was no need to behave and stay inside the cell, but to avoid getting into trouble he didn't want to go far. So he walked back and forth along the corridor, sometimes going to the entrance to watch. Outside all was quiet, straight through to nightfall. As for Yang, he stayed in the guard room immersed in silent meditation, pain occasionally showing on his face. Diagonally across the corridor Wei Bo saw that look and wondered, Did Yang think he had let Xiao Yan down? Did he think Xiao Yan's feelings for his girlfriend outweighed his crime? What an improbable guard.

With no one keeping watch, Wei Bo swaggered to the canteen, ate, and returned.

This time the pale-faced Guard Yang already stood at the entrance to the cell-block.

"Will you go with me?" he asked.

Wei Bo burst out, "Do you mean to catch Xiao Yan?"

"Uh-huh."

One in front of the other, they crossed the exercise grounds at a quick pace and went down into the gray office building's basement.

"They're in the storage room two levels underground," Guard Yang said in the darkness.

They entered the storage room, where the lights were on, but no people. Yang bent over and searched the ground for a long time. Finally, he found the diamond ring. He put it on his middle finger and said, bashfully, "I haven't married yet. Days in the prison are so depressing, I'm not in the right state of mind."

Wei Bo asked Guard Yang where Xiao Yan was. He answered, "Where else could he be? He's in the cell, of course. We're late. He was just here with his girlfriend."

Wei Bo was surprised at Yang's assurance. How did he understand Xiao Yan so well?

"So his girlfriend went to the cell, too?"

"Of course not. Didn't you see me pick up the ring? They took care of their physical needs, then they fought, and the young woman ran off. Number 13 (that means Xiao Yan) can only stay in love with her while he's in prison. I'll take the ring and give it back to him as soon as possible, so he doesn't lose faith in life."

"You don't seem to like working as a guard."

"That's nonsense. You're a criminal, how can you judge me? I have my own interests."

They left the basement. As they crossed the exercise grounds, it was still quiet in all directions. Guard Yang left Wei Bo, saying he was going to report to the warden, and telling him to return to the cell.

When Wei Bo entered the cell he saw all three of his cellmates had returned. That odd expression was back on Xiao Yan's face.

"Xiao Yan, I just went looking for you with Guard Yang. He picked up your ring," Wei Bo said.

"Traitors!" Xiao Yan raved in fury, "Both traitors!"

He covered his face with his hands and began to weep.

Lao Zhang and Lao Lu pulled Wei Bo over to one side, Lao Zhang cursing at him in lowered tones, "What kind of trick are you up to? Why are you pressuring him, do you want him dead? He has no road ahead of him, and you're still pressuring him. I didn't realize you were so ruthless. I hope you die! Who asked you to come here and ruin things? Huh?"

Confused, Wei Bo couldn't understand what he had done wrong. He thought that maybe Guard Yang shouldn't have picked up the ring. Maybe Xiao Yan had hoped to forget the ring forever? Thinking about Guard Yang's sequence of activities, Wei Bo sensed how Xiao Yan's love terrified people. What kind of love was it, after all?

Wei Bo had insomnia again. The incident with Xiao Yan upset him so much that he felt his life growing darker. He'd believed that when he went to prison his emotions would be calmer, but that seemed to be a mistake. Now Wei Bo could see no way out. Would Xiao Yan really walk this dead-end road? Wei Bo tossed back and forth in bed, more unable to sleep the more anxious he became. Later, just as he was about to enter a dream, the whistle blew. He had to get out of bed.

The next day Guard Yang ordered Wei Bo to go with Lao Zhang and Lao Lu to help with the rescue efforts. Wei Bo saw Xiao Yan sitting on his bunk. He seemed to be trembling.

The three men joined in carrying sandbags. Wei Bo had not slept, so his legs were weak, and his whole body oozed cold sweat. He calculated how soon he would collapse. As expected, he fell to the ground before the third round of sandbags reached the levee. He thought, "I'm disgraceful." Then he fainted.

When he came to, he found himself lying underneath the bridge pier. He heard Lao Zhang's voice.

"What's wrong with you? You give up at nothing, you rotten egg!"

"How long was I sleeping here?"

"You slept from morning to afternoon! If I hadn't hidden you, they would have taken you for torture on the tiger bench."

"I deserve to die! How is Xiao Yan? Isn't he more hopeless than I am?"

"He's not hopeless, he just pretends as a way of getting ahead. This morning I received an internal report saying he would be employed. That is, his sentence is almost over, so he'll be kept on as a guard! Isn't that the way to earn leisure, with just a single effort? Why's he the only one with such good luck, Wei Bo? Is it because he's a risk-taker? Huh? An honest person like me doesn't go to extremes, so they don't hire me. I'm forced to dig through my mind for ways to add to my sentence. It's so unfair! Wei Bo, what's your opinion?"

"I respect you very much, Lao Zhang."

"What use is respect? My goal is always out of reach. You must have seen how I'm suspended in midair. She came back again and gave me an ultimatum— I have to get out of prison by the end of the year or else she'll hurt herself. Her threat is making me fall to pieces."

Lao Zhang gazed at a distant chimney where a flock of birds wound in circles, now high, now low. Wei Bo thought, Lao Zhang's thoughts are also flying.

"Have you thought of going back to your hometown?" Wei Bo spoke his mind out loud.

Lao Zhang laughed, clapped Wei Bo on the shoulder, and said, "You blackguard, all the way through! You'd carve out my organs and let them roast in the sun! I won't lie to you, I have been searching for my hometown since I was fifteen. No one told me where it was, I only had a few vague clues to follow. Years passed with little result. Straight up until . . . up until I went to jail, when there started to be a turn for the better. In between there were a few unpleasant, cruel details, but I don't want to think about them. In short, I struggled my way through. I fought with a prisoner on the work site, and we smashed heads together. I stumbled to the creek to wash, thinking I was seriously injured. Just at that instant, I saw the outline of my hometown in the clear water. It was the shape of our prison today. The buildings had an ancient, simple style, not broken-down like our prison. How did I know it was my hometown? Because my parents and my grandfather were sitting at the entrance smoking tobacco! The image of my hometown lasted at least ten seconds before vanishing little by little. My parents died early from physical and mental illnesses, which was another reason I've had to search for my ancestral home. I searched, and found my hometown is a prison. Was this why I charged inside with a gun?"

Wei Bo sensed that Lao Zhang was impatient talking about the details of what had happened, as if his thoughts were steeped in a different mood—an atmosphere of fright and longing. Wei Bo was unsettled and, with his strength returning, wanted to go back to the cell for a good rest. However, Lao Zhang kept pressing down on his shoulders, not letting him move, so Wei Bo guessed there were still things behind the scenes Lao Zhang wanted to reveal to him.

"Only one person in the entire prison knows what goes on behind the scenes: the warden. He's eighty-five, but I know they won't let him retire. There are some photographs from the past at his house. I saw my parents in a sepia picture. They stood looking surprised at the entrance to their home—which is the building made of gray bricks and tiles over there on the exercise grounds, the public bathroom now. The warden told me my father had buried some object in the prison. He wouldn't tell me where it was buried. These past years I've searched in all the corners, and even dug three feet deep. That added three years to my sentence."

"Can you take me to the warden's house?" Wei Bo asked.

"No, I can't. He only has enlightened prisoners visit him. He belongs to that generation. An old-fashioned worldview. I was in prison five years before he was willing to see me. How could he see you? He has asthma and becomes weak when he falls ill. One time when he was ill I went to take care of him at home, and he told me that he'd supplied the gun I held when I stormed the prison. After I heard him say this I started to remember that it had been a young man with a shaved head who provoked me to charge the prison. This made clear to me that for nine years I'd been walking on the right path. Don't you agree, Wei Bo? Ha, sharing all these complaints with you makes me feel much better. Do you want to go eat? Do you need to lean on me? It looks like you've recovered, you can go on back."

Lao Zhang went up the large bridge, running until no shadow was left behind. Wei Bo returned to the prison.

After eating he went to his cell. Xiao Yan was the only person inside.

"I heard you've had good luck," Wei Bo said.

"Your news is out of date. Someone's replaced me. The authorities say I'm weak-willed and need additional training. They pointed to the incident with the ring. It looks like I'll still have to endure my girlfriend."

That odd expression appeared on Xiao Yan's face again when he spoke. Wei Bo now understood that it was a look of agony. Wei Bo asked, "Will she visit in the near future?"

"Uh-huh. When she comes, the guards let her move around freely, then she finds me and terrifies me. Last time, I'd given up and thrown away the ring, but you guys wouldn't let me go free. It was my own fault, too, of course. I can't resist her."

"She must be a beautiful woman."

"She's a devil-woman, a vampire bat. I can't pass the trial."

175

While the two men were talking Guard Yang appeared at the doorway. Xiao Yan immediately lowered his head and started to shiver. Unable to stand, he turned to his bunk and sat down. He lifted the pillow with a trembling hand, and Wei Bo saw the ring. A thin smile appeared on Guard Yang's face as he made a sign beckoning Wei Bo to him.

Wei Bo and Guard Yang went to the guard room. Yang silently smoked two cigarettes in a row.

"You called me in, did you want my help?" Wei Bo asked.

"Don't sleep too heavily at night. This is the assignment I'm giving you. There was already a murder in the cells when I neglected my duty. Humiliating!"

"I don't think he'll do anything."

"Do you dare to guarantee it? You don't understand him just because you're older than he is." Yang rolled his eyes toward the ceiling, as if his thoughts were floating overhead. "Watching the life disappear was horrible, I haven't slept well since . . . My work doesn't allow for the slightest mistake. How are you? Does Cuilan understand your situation?"

"I think she understands, she has a great capacity . . . Still, I may have miscalculated, because the last time she left without waiting for me. I'm not sure about her at all."

"It would be strange to be sure of her!" Guard Yang suddenly raised his voice in excitement. "If you were, you wouldn't have come to the prison and be hauling sand. This world revolves on strict rules!"

Yang tossed his cigarette butt to the ground and stamped it out, having made up his mind about something.

"Wei Bo, go back to the cell, and don't sleep too deeply. Isn't there a proverb that says 'lovers always end in marriage'? I want to have full confidence in its being right."

In the corridor Wei Bo recalled that Guard Yang had called him "Wei Bo" instead of "Number 85." Strange and incomprehensible! He had also called Wei Bo's girlfriend "Cuilan," as though naming an old friend.

Inside the cell the three other men had already lain down and turned off the light. Wei Bo entered softly and went to bed. He could tell that none of them had gone to sleep. They were all waiting for something to happen. Wei Bo had gotten used to this atmosphere and even looked forward to something happening. He still fell asleep in this state of anticipation and slept deeply. Guard Yang's urging had been no use.

Morning. The four of them were woken at the same time by the whistle blast. The river water had not receded, so they had to continue carrying the sandbags. Wei Bo saw how energetic his three prison friends looked, while he could not lift his spirits. He kept wondering why Cuilan had come to visit, but not waited to see him. Had someone said something bad about him to her?

At noon when their box lunches arrived at the work site they ate standing. Xiao Yan walked over, vigorous and red-faced, his dissipated air swept away. He said, "Wei Bo, this heavy labor is addicting! I will be reformed and compete for a guard assignment."

Wei Bo scanned for Lao Zhang and soon found him. He was embracing a fat woman prisoner as they walked toward the bridge piers. Lao Lu, holding a food box and full of smiles, was passing by and followed Wei Bo's gaze.

"Ha ha! They're choosing the right time for their crime! It doesn't matter, this kind of thing is only a tempest in a teapot here! Lao Zhang can handle himself better than anyone else I know. He has a personal relationship with the warden. Wei Bo, now do you know what 'rushing to the rescue' is? Rescue means romance!"

"Why is Lao Zhang the only one who gets to have romance?" Wei Bo asked.

"True . . ." Lao Lu drew out the word, "because it falls to him. Don't you think Lao Zhang is destined for romantic encounters? You're really slow."

He shoved Wei Bo, letting him see the handle of a gun in his pocket. He came close and said quietly, "If Xiao Yan causes trouble at night, I'll shoot him dead."

Wei Bo glanced at Xiao Yan in fear, recalling the assignment Guard Yang had given him last night. Xiao Yan glanced sideways at Lao Lu. He saw the pistol, but seemed not to care. He put down the lunch box he was holding, walked over, and embraced Lao Lu, shouting, "Why do we always wait for our destiny? What do you have to say? Fortune comes and goes, but we wait as stubbornly as those bridge piers. Soon the floodwaters will drown them!"

Lao Lu shoved away Xiao Yan's arms in disgust, jumped back, pulled out the handgun, and fired once.

Xiao Yan clapped admiringly, saying to Wei Bo, "See, he's so brave! A violent person like him shouldn't stay in prison!"

"Then what sort of people should stay in prison?" Wei Bo asked.

"People like us, more dead than alive, always indecisive. We ought to stay here. I think Lao Lu stays here more for us than for himself."

Wei Bo furrowed his brow and considered a moment, then said, "What you say makes sense. Are you really not afraid of him?"

"I hope he will free me, but he refuses. Once you're in prison, don't expect to be released. See how well Lao Zhang adapts to the environment."

Wei Bo opened his mouth in surprise, but no words came out.

At this moment the fat guard Liu came over and summoned Wei Bo to the visiting room, saying the authorities had arranged a special visit for him—out of humanitarianism.

"Hurry and change your clothes, Niu Cuilan is waiting for you."

"I don't need to change, I have no other clothing."

Wei Bo reflected that just about everyone here knew Cuilan. How was this possible?

The visiting room was empty. Guard Liu ordered Wei Bo to wait and walked away.

Bored, Wei Bo sized up the little room. There was only a wooden chair. It had no windows. Surprisingly, an oil painting hung on the opposite wall, the picture of a person, but also like a wild animal. Wei Bo glanced at it a few times and began to feel uneasy, so he hastily averted his eyes. The door was open, and a tall guard walked back and forth in the corridor outside. Wei Bo stayed seated at first, until he discovered the guard looking at him with astonishment as he passed, so he stood back up, embarrassed. He didn't want to look at the painting or at the guard, so he faced the blank wall to the left. He stood there so long his legs started to ache. He shifted the chair so its back was toward the door and sat back down. Even with his back to the door he still sensed the guard's line of sight falling on his back, making him restless. Someone was speaking. It was the guard, who had paused at the door to chat with someone else.

"How was the harvest this year?"

"Awful. Still, there was a large crop of soybeans. It's not like you can harvest whatever you want."

Wei Bo turned the chair around. A look of surprise appeared on both faces at the same time.

Wei Bo saw Cuilan's Fourth Uncle, the man from the countryside.

"Oh, here you are!" Fourth Uncle laughed, showing yellowed teeth. "Cuilan sent me in her place. She wants me to bring her news about you. If you're thinner, for example, or whether your morale is good."

"Where's Cuilan?" Wei Bo felt his heart skipping.

"Everywhere, and nowhere. Even I have to depend on luck if I want to see her these days. I ran into her at the door of the opera house when she was coming out with an older woman. I was so surprised my legs shook. The two women were like ghosts!"

"Was it the Lady of the Camellias?"

"Yes, exactly, the Lady of the Camellias. Then Cuilan asked me to visit for her . . . Wei Bo, how could you change this way? It's not at all what Cuilan expected!"

"How did Cuilan think I would be?"

"I can't tell you, just that it's not the same. It was all good things she said. You really do look like you're declining, and you haven't shaved for a long time. How could you let yourself go like this?"

"He doesn't look that bad," the guard interrupted. "Your expectations for him are too high. In prison, high expectations are strictly forbidden."

"What this man says makes sense," Fourth Uncle nodded. "In my view, you're thin, but not too thin. It's just that the integrity in your face is gone, and your eyes are abnormal. How did that happen? Before coming here I ran into Xiao He, Cuilan's ex-boyfriend. He and Cuilan are back in close touch recently. They're not a couple, of course, Cuilan contacted him to ask for his help. Your going to prison meant a lot of difficulty for her. She couldn't bear it without anyone to ask for help. Don't you agree?"

"I think all people have troubles on their minds. How is Cuilan doing?" Wei Bo lowered his eyes.

"Her life is wonderful! She's more optimistic than before, and very active around the city. Her relatives all say she's a 'late-blooming rose.' Thanks to Wei Bo's good influence!"

"Fourth Uncle, do you still live in the country?"

"No, I moved to the city. I think my niece needs me. Look, aren't I coming to visit you for her? She's a busy person now, off doing good deeds everywhere."

"Doing good deeds?" Wei Bo was startled.

"She listens to people's complaints. Anyone she knows who has love problems comes looking for her. She stopped going to work a while ago, she's too busy. One young man fell in love with her when she was listening to his complaints. Wei Bo is fortunate to have such a remarkable girlfriend."

The news Fourth Uncle brought was a great shock to Wei Bo.

Unable to sleep that night, he tossed back and forth on the bed. The noise infuriated Lao Lu.

Lao Lu pulled out the handgun, aimed at Wei Bo, and fired. Wei Bo's calf stung, and he shouted, "Aah . . . aah . . ." in despair.

"If you shout again, I'll kill you! You will die quietly, and we will bury you."

Wei Bo covered his injured calf with the blanket and lay there not making a sound. What was happening? He was still conscious, and, aside from his calf, the other parts of his body seemed to be fine. In the dark he worked up the courage to feel the injured leg with his hand. It was all right. To his surprise there was no blood flowing, and it was not so painful, only stinging.

Xiao Yan quietly came over holding a flashlight. The beam shone on the wound, illuminating the bullet, which was completely embedded in the flesh. Aside from that tiny hole, the surrounding skin was clean. This sight gave Wei Bo an unreal sensation, and he felt nauseated.

"It won't hold you back. It will be better when you get used to it," Xiao Yan said in a small voice.

Wei Bo recalled the violent sound of the gunshot and couldn't understand, for all his pondering, what was happening.

Later the three men all began snoring. Only Wei Bo was too overwrought to sleep. What stimulant was in that bullet? What kind of prison had he entered? He was more and more able to adapt to its atmosphere, but he still believed himself an outsider. He thought of the people around him one by one: Xiao Yan, Lao Lu, Lao Zhang, Guard Yang, the guard at the door of the visiting room . . . There was no doubt, they had assimilated to the prison atmosphere. They all had a few bizarre ideas and unusual experiences, just as Wei Bo had bizarre ideas and unusual experiences. Why couldn't he assimilate? His slow responses worried him. He recalled what it had been like to cross through the rooms of his ancestral home. He had once found a box of firecrackers in a display cabinet and planned to go back for it after he ate. By the time he finished and went back to look, he could not find the room. He had been anxious in the same way then.

He tried to sink into the land of dreams, counting to help himself sleep, and was about to succeed.

The shrill whistles seemed to pierce his eardrums. Even his head bounced. He had to get out of bed with everyone else. It was another new day.

EIGHT

Officer Xiao He's
One-Sided Love

At thirty-six the policeman Xiao He had some time ago married and had a
son, but, no matter what, he could not forget his first love. The object of his first
love was Niu Cuilan, the woman who worked at the gauge and meter factory.

In Xiao He's memory, Cuilan was the most beautiful woman he had ever
met, lovely from her appearance to her inner self. Yet in the brief time the two of
them had been together, he had never told Cuilan this—he was young and shy,
and tended by nature toward contortions. His romance with Cuilan was like a
dream, one from which she soon woke, while he would be tangled up with it for
the rest of his life. He wouldn't try to entangle her, of course. He could never do
anything she wouldn't like. Everything he did was part of a game to make her
happy. For example, he once sent Cuilan five yuan with a note enclosed saying
the money was a gift for her birthday. After Cuilan received this small sum she
was so happy she sent him a brutal letter full of invective that ordered him to deposit twenty thousand yuan in her bank account to serve as the "fee for her lost
youth." She also threatened to send men from the underworld to beat him. The
letter was delivered by a mutual good friend. Later Xiao He showed her reply to
Wei Bo. He wanted for the relationship between Wei Bo and Cuilan both to last
and to be severed, a conflicting mentality that caused his strange behavior. Xiao
He had never been able to make his true intentions clear.

For many years, whenever he had free time, he concerned himself with Cuilan's movements, wanting in this way to keep an indirect link to her. He often reflected that it was good luck that he lived in the same city as Cuilan. They seldom saw each other after their separation, because Xiao He made a point of avoiding her, but on drizzly spring days he sometimes had the sudden urge to go for a walk on the street where the gauge and meter factory stood, hoping to meet the lover of his dreams. Naturally this meeting never happened.

Xiao He was excited to learn, unintentionally, about the romance between Cuilan and Wei Bo, the man who worked at the soap factory. He thought of ways to approach Wei Bo. The love in his heart transformed into a strange sense of duty that controlled his brain with irresistible force, leading to his inexplicably bad performance in front of Wei Bo. After meeting Wei Bo he had a nervous breakdown. For an entire week he lay on his bed dreaming strange dreams, revolving the details of the party at his friend's house in his mind. After a week he finally awakened to the true meaning of his strange behavior: he had done a noble deed. As to how his showing of Cuilan's letter to his rival had been noble, he was probably the only one who understood. Xiao He didn't mind that.

In the depths of Xiao He's inner being, that dream of first love was symbolized by Pear Mountain. So many years had passed while he had not returned there, other than in dreams. He and Cuilan had never climbed the high mountain of scattered stones, only examined it from below. Over the years Xiao He slowly became conscious that he'd chosen the trip to Pear Mountain as a memento of his breakup with Cuilan because the frightening mountain wasteland was so like his inner being. Can it be that people only approach the abyss of the inner self from a state of passion? As to what that desolate mountain meant, Xiao He, as before, knew only the half of it. He was a persistent man who couldn't forget he had once drawn near Pear Mountain.

At first he believed the tranquility of family life would wear away a certain part of his inner being. For the first few years of marriage his temperament did develop in that way. He rediscovered, though, that the "certain part" remained the same, like the rude prediction his mother had made about him: "Dogs can't change that they eat shit."

Should he promote the romance between Wei Bo and Cuilan? The answer to this question was for Xiao He as profound as Pear Mountain. All of his actions were the acting out of an emotional impulse he could not control, a passion lying between what was moral and what was evil that compelled him to hover between Cuilan and Wei Bo. His job as a policeman had made him comparatively sensitive to evil.

Xiao He had not expected Wei Bo's sudden imprisonment. He soon worked out the character of this move (he knew Wei Bo had gone to prison on purpose). This turn of events only aggravated Xiao He's inhibited fervor. He wasn't sure what he would do, but he felt at every moment that he would do something. He never divulged what was on his mind. Even his good friend Yuan Hei could only guess at Xiao He's thoughts based on observation. This kind of solitary passion made Xiao He's ideas turn extraordinary. Recently, he'd often battled with fear of himself.

After Wei Bo went to prison, Xiao He and Cuilan met a number of times. He noted that Cuilan was now calmer. It seemed as though she had already made up her mind. Xiao He could see that Cuilan's love for Wei Bo was true. She had never loved him that way. He said to himself, "My love for Cuilan is as deep as Cuilan's love for Wei Bo." He took pride in this.

"When the police surrounded us I was talking with Wei Bo about the Lady of the Camellias. We were in the park, where the fragrance of the blossoms on the tall osmanthus tree floated in the air. Delicate white mushrooms spotted the grassy ground. Wei Bo stood up, shook the grass seeds from his clothes, and said, looking at the tree, 'I'm going. Take good care of yourself.'"

Xiao He could recite the dialogue above from memory. Cuilan recited it every time they saw each other. While she spoke, Xiao He listened with envy, and when she finished he would think back on his Pear Mountain and its desolate rocks. He knew no osmanthus tree would grow on Pear Mountain. Although at the time Cuilan had not been unmoved.

"I think," he said to her, "you shouldn't stop sending him news about your life outside. Prison can change a person."

"Oh, Xiao He! My life would be such a mess without your friendship."

"Let your life be a mess. It's what Wei Bo hoped would happen."

"Are you positive?"

"I'm sure."

On the way home Xiao He thought with confusion of those words he had said to Cuilan. Cuilan relied so much on his judgment now. Or might she only be pretending to rely on him, to make a good impression so that he would keep running after her? Xiao He lacked confidence. He'd said those words based only on an obscure premonition. He'd said, "Prison can change a person." He felt Cuilan had immediately understood and took this to heart. Was that because she was trying to change herself?

Fourth Uncle's visit to the prison in Cuilan's place was a scheme Xiao He and Cuilan planned together. At first Xiao He came up with this ruse out of malice toward Wei Bo. When he and Cuilan sat in a teahouse plotting, the expression of deep, direct affection on Cuilan's face moved him. His feelings were chaotic;

his thoughts lost their logical sequence. As a result, there was a shift so that the scheme of the prison visit became Cuilan's one-person conspiracy. She had a flash of inspiration, the good idea of making a fool of Wei Bo.

"This all is due to love. Don't you think so?" she said.

"I'm too ashamed, Cuilan."

"You don't need to be ashamed. Aren't we learning how to live?"

"You're right, I am learning, too."

The two of them looked at each other for several seconds, then began to laugh in comprehension. Xiao He couldn't help exclaiming, inwardly, Life is so beautiful. What had he done to merit this reward?

"Your way of thinking always enlightens me," she said with sincerity. "I feel that you understand everything. You can cope with anything you meet."

"Actually, you are the one who understands everything, Cuilan."

Xiao He saw himself, a different self, in the expression in Cuilan's eyes. This same situation had taken place years ago, when he was so young! He'd believed himself a diseased tree rotten from the roots up, but, because Cuilan was there, his rottenness brought good luck instead of holding him back. Just now, for instance, hadn't his rotten plan turned all at once into a noble idea? Fourth Uncle really was the most suitable choice. A specter who had emerged from a graveyard in Cuilan's hometown was the best person to relay Cuilan's love.

Cuilan had unburdened him of the vague, heavy weight on his heart when he'd arrived at the teahouse. Now that the true situation was out in the daylight, he was a little dejected, but even more carefree. Everything turned out to be so simple.

"Xiao He, where did you come from?" Yuan Hei asked him with suffering on his face.

"From the teahouse. I was meeting an old friend."

"I don't have any old friends. My life is painful."

"Aren't I your old friend? You're so stupid!"

"I guess I am. Let's go have a drink."

As Xiao He drank with Yuan Hei, melancholy rose in his mind again.

Across the dim bar a man and a woman sat with their backs to them appearing to weep. Xiao He and Yuan Hei recognized their own inescapable sadness.

"Should we cry?" Yuan Hei said gently, his face dark.

"I can't cry."

The drinks arrived, and they silently emptied their cups. Each drank two glasses.

Xiao He's nerves relaxed by degrees. He watched the movements of the couple opposite. They were absorbed in kissing.

"Yuan Hei, Yuan Hei, please answer my question: is the tall camphor tree behind the detention center still there? You have to tell me the truth."

"It's still there, I just saw it yesterday. I am telling the truth."

"Good. Year after year it's still there. Am I worrying too much, Yuan Hei? I left home in the morning and went to the police stand to direct traffic, but unfamiliar images kept appearing in my mind. For example, a baby crawling among the vehicles at the far end of the road."

"There are always incidents like these. The tree was still there at two o'clock yesterday afternoon."

"Thank you, Yuan Hei. Let's shake hands. I'm so unsure of myself."

Yuan Hei felt Xiao He's hand was ice cold.

"I've only been talking about myself. How is she?" Xiao He said, his eyes showing his gloom.

"She is further and further away from me. I'll have to train as a long-distance runner."

"You can do it, I have no doubts. She's a perfect beauty. Drink up."

"Really? Really?" Yuan Hei asked, grabbing Xiao He's arm.

"Of course it's true. Last time at the overpass bridge, after you and she broke up, I saw her standing on the bridge from far away. She watched you walk away for a long, long time. On her part, even your separation was on account of love."

"Xiao He, your vision is so sharp! Why can't I reflect this way?"

"My problem is in a different area. I'll be washing vegetables in the kitchen, for example, when I'm suddenly confused. I ask myself: will the lamppost downstairs, and that green wrought-iron mailbox across from it, still be in their places at three in the morning? Everything that happens is bizarre!"

While Xiao He said these words in a loud voice, the sweethearts opposite separated and were now facing them, not moving their eyes from Xiao He.

"Are you going to resolve our doubts, Officer?" the young man said. "You were speaking of our heartsickness. Once you described that state, we were sure of it. Thank you!"

He and the petite girl came over and shook hands with Xiao He, both looking into his eyes as if searching for something in them. Then the two of them left.

"Xiao He, look at the welcome you receive!" Yuan Hei said.

"This young couple has lost confidence in their hearts," the son of the bar owner said.

The bar owner's son, who was a little over forty, worked in another province and was back on vacation. He'd been sitting at a table against the window this whole time. He gazed at Xiao He in appreciation.

Yuan Hei braced himself, two small stars appearing in his eyes. He said with excitement, "Xiao He, it's so good that you said this! I've always admired your unexpected ideas. Come on, drink up!"

"Would these two guests wish to go on the river at night?" the son of the bar owner asked.

"What a good suggestion!" they answered in unison.

They had just finished this sentence when the sky outside turned black. A wild gust of wind blew into the bar, unnerving Xiao He and Yuan Hei.

The owner's son stood at the door hailing a taxi. The three of them squeezed inside.

"Relax, it's a very reliable fishing boat, not one of the pleasure boats in the park. It's a practical toy, used to make a living. Who ever heard of a fishing boat overturning in the river? It's never happened. I'll steer, you two can row up in the front. The police officer isn't anxious about those bridge piers, is he? We'll get a clear look at them! This bit of wind doesn't count for anything, as long as you concentrate . . ."

In the taxi the owner's son continued talking. The other two men were baffled but eager.

The taxi flew along and then slammed to a hard stop by the river. The wind on the river was strong, so strong they could hardly stay on their feet. In the obscure rays of light Xiao He saw Yuan Hei covering his ears with both hands, with a look of startled fear. A dark shadow was moving toward them. The shadow pressed closer to the bar owner's son and asked, "Are there three people?"

"Three."

"Have you made up your minds?"

"Uh-huh."

The fisherman walked over and pulled up the anchor. They jumped onto the deck.

Without their knowing how it happened, the fishing boat soon reached the middle of the river. Xiao He and Yuan Hei were both rowing for the first time. The bar owner's son directed them from the stern while he steered. They rowed wildly, panic surging through them.

"Yuan Hei . . . Yuan Hei . . ." The voice of the owner's son seemed to come from the remote wilderness.

"Xiao He, are we going to wreck?" Yuan Hei screamed.

Xiao He didn't answer because the violent turbulence jolted him sharply again and again. He was so nervous he could hardly breathe. The sense of unreality from earlier in the bar disappeared without leaving a trace.

Waves struck, and water flowed into the boat. Yuan Hei's shoes were damp. The thought flashed across his mind: Am I done for? He was not at all prepared.

The boat spun in circles in the middle of the river. The water leaking in was increasingly serious. Xiao He and Yuan Hei couldn't see the bar owner's son, although he should have still been steering. On this kind of night almost nothing could be seen on the river. In a frenzy Yuan Hei shouted until his voice was hoarse, "Xiao He, one, two, three! One, two, three!"

He didn't know how long he kept shouting before the fishing boat suddenly balanced. The two of them taught themselves how to row the boat. Their feet were in the water, and they both shivered. Strange, for all their effort, why weren't their bodies warmer? Xiao He saw the enormous dark shadow of the bridge pier. He reached out a hand to touch it, feeling the suggestion of warmth on the rough cement, reminding him of the pit stoves in winter in his hometown.

"I don't want to die!" Yuan Hei's voice sounded like he was crying. "I want to keep seeing her! Xiao He, can you hear me?"

"I can hear you, Yuan Hei! What's all this about dying? We've passed the bridge pier. I just touched it, it's really there! Who would have thought so, on a night like this?"

The wind lessened. They rowed with good rhythm, the fishing boat's advance gradually becoming a straight line. Yet they could not see the shore or any other sign. They could only believe the oars in their hands, as well as the steersman at the stern. "Row, row, the sky will always grow light," Xiao He told himself.

"Xiao He, if we collide with a motorized sailboat, we'll end up in the river."

"Shhh, don't waste your energy. At times like this we have to be robots devoted to the task at hand. When we get back I will commit to memory: 'In the middle of the night at the center of the river, all objects remained in place.' Yuan Hei, don't you think we've lived good enough lives? Ha!"

"Yes, good enough," Yuan Hei answered in a lowered voice.

"When we get to shore, let's go back to the bar for a drink."

To fight the urge to sleep, they chatted as well as they could while rowing. Yuan Hei talked about his mature lover, the prison guard; Xiao He talked about his Pear Mountain; they also talked of the city's customs in earlier times. Even though his arms ached as though they might break off, Xiao He's mental process was abnormally active. All of a sudden he returned to that earlier time. It was when the zebra crossings on the city's paved roads were still made of ceramic chips pieced together. There was a roasted snacks shop that sold five-spice peanuts behind the factory where Cuilan worked. Xiao He would buy a bag of shelled peanuts every time he arranged to meet Cuilan.

"Xiao He, quick, look, isn't that a mountain? I see . . ."

Before Yuan Hei's words were finished the fishing boat struck against some object, making a huge noise.

The boat turned out to be leaning against the bank. The city in early morning light appeared before their eyes. They both felt that the city was unfamiliar, with landscapes they had never seen before.

At the same time the two men remembered the bar owner's son, the one who had proposed this activity. A look toward the stern, which was empty. Not a trace of him there. Yuan Hei jumped into the rear compartment of the fishing boat.

"He's making fools of us," Yuan Hei fumed. "He's a good swimmer so he went back home ahead of us. What a lowlife! The flooding's bad in the back. The boatman will be furious. Quick, run!"

They threw the anchor carelessly onto the shore and left at a quick pace.

Yuan Hei said he was so cheerful he had to go for a drink at the bar.

"Xiao He, in the future I will become someone like you," he pledged.

They returned to an atmosphere they knew well. Oh, those cars, the pedestrians rushing to the morning shift, the middle-school students poring through the steamed bun stands, the vendors selling soy milk at the side of the street, all let them feel the breath of life against their faces. Even though their bodies were damp and dripping, waves of warmth gushed through both men's hearts.

The bar owner's son sat with a squinting smile in the same place as before. He called in a loud voice to his father, "Two rounds of rice wine! Pig's hearts, peanuts!"

Yuan Hei smiled coldly, raising his glass with both hands as he toasted Xiao He.

Xiao He finished the drink with him, then walked over to the owner's son, lifting his glass and saying, "Mr. Huang, let me raise a toast to you!"

This made Yuan Hei smile, too, his eyebrows raised.

"Cheers, drink up! You are the warriors of today's society. You both make astonishing choices. You remind me of when I used to work at a wild animal refuge. I enjoyed spending an evening, a terrific night, up on a mountain with a wild boar. Your choices in life are amazing!"

Yuan Hei mused, How does he know what choices Xiao He and I made?

Xiao He and Cuilan's secret meeting place was a basement coffee shop. Inside there were five round tables, every table with a black velvet screen blocking it.

"Xiao He, I'm done for," Cuilan said as she sat down.

She stared at her coffee cup, eyes glazed, her lips trembling.

"Don't worry. Tell me about it."

"He said to Fourth Uncle, 'Now that you've come, old man, why should I be indecisive? I will wear through the floor of the prison!' I never imagined that things would turn out this way."

"That things would turn out what way? It's all normal. Wei Bo is encouraging himself."

"But I keep thinking he's had a change of heart."

"It's better that you have this feeling. The two of you will last as long as heaven and earth endure."

Cuilan raised her head and saw a hideous face appear on the surface of the black velvet.

"Oh!" she cried out in surprise.

It turned out to be the server bringing their small dishes. His uniform was made of the same black velvet as the screen. He suddenly smiled, revealing two fangs.

"It's not very safe outside on drizzly days like this. What would the two of you like to order?"

Everything in front of Cuilan's eyes was blurred, but she heard what the server said.

"I want a fang. Are you ruthless enough to knock one out and give it to us?" Xiao He said.

Cuilan heard his voice. The back of her hand felt the touch of a furry claw.

"Go away! Go away!" Cuilan cried with all her strength. She couldn't see the young man clearly.

"Shouting will make it better," Xiao He said calmly. "I live next to the peanut fields now. There are so many wild hares, I hear them running when I'm in bed asleep. The moonlight's beautiful. Wei Bo is inside, in a pretty good state of mind, and he's a smart guy. He has many people delivering messages for him. That young man just now was one of them."

Cuilan opened her eyes with an effort and said feebly, "There are people hiding behind the screens. Why are they hiding?"

"Out of natural instincts. Some people just like to play hide-and-seek."

"Oh, how frightening!"

"Cuilan, I'll see you back. You don't need to care about what other people think. Or we could go to the theater?"

"No, I'll go by myself! I'll go now, you stay a while."

She left.

The server walked out from behind the screen and said to Xiao He with a troubled face, "She's gone. It's not safe outside, listen to the sirens . . ."

"Don't worry about her. She's very independent, not at all the way she appears on the surface. This is a great place, very original decorations. Who's the owner?"

"I'll go get her."

The owner, a full-figured woman, appeared.

"Your girlfriend is beautiful," she said sincerely. "Our Xiao Zheng is enchanted by her."

"Her boyfriend is in prison," Xiao He said.

"I guessed that the last time you came. That boyfriend is staying where he should be. I'm happy you haven't gone there. But you look so hollow! Why?"

"Because her boyfriend is in prison. I reach out a hand and can't touch my own head . . . Do you think he should stay there?" Xiao He tugged at his ears.

"This is an astonishing story, and also a satisfying one. It looks like Xiao Zheng has no chance. Xiao Zheng!"

"My opportunity is gone. I will withdraw to live as a recluse." Xiao Zheng made a funny face.

The owner had Xiao He follow her into another room to see something there.

A red lamp made the gloomy room look frightening.

The owner stared into Xiao He's eyes, asking one word at a time, "Do you actually want to help him, or do you want to kill him?"

"I want both," Xiao He said, averting his face.

"You're honest, Xiao He. I would say to you: you're a good man. Go listen to the Lady of the Camellias sing. That will help you decide soon."

Xiao He didn't go to the theater. He followed along the riverside, the voice of the Lady of the Camellias hovering around his ears. He thought, The owner of the coffee shop is so good at understanding what people are thinking. She had allowed him to immerse himself in beautiful imaginings. People in this city had originally been by themselves, completely alone, until the voice of the Lady of the Camellias produced a response among them. How could a city like this one, apparently cold and detached, hold a Lady of the Camellias as passionate as fire? Xiao He sat down on a stone bench beside the river, the wind from the river brushing across his face.

"You wrecked the deck of my boat," the fisherman said, standing in front of him.

"I'm sorry. Can I pay you for the damage?" Xiao He lowered his head in shame.

"There's no need for repayment. I was happy to save a person's life."

"Thank you."

The fisherman walked down to the river, where he lived on the boat. His boat, steady at berth, was like a tamed whale.

NINE

Sentimental Education

A Si and Yuan Hei were sitting on the stone bench by the river where Xiao He had sat. They appeared a well-matched couple, but they had been separated for many years.

"A Si, it's so strange how I've never seen you when we live in the same city. I thought you were hiding at the bottom of the river like a mermaid."

"Maybe it's because I live at night and don't go out much during the day."

"Your life sounds lively. Who is your boyfriend now? Can you tell me?"

"Of course I can. He's an opium dealer whose life is in constant turmoil. I don't know whether he really loves me. He may love his smuggler's life more."

"A Si is so beautiful. How could he not love you?"

"He could. That's exactly what makes him attractive."

"I understand."

"You're wiser than before. It's a woman who's changed you. What is she like? She must be charming. Yuan Hei has such good luck."

"She's very charming, but she's always trying to get rid of me. It's given me a nervous breakdown."

"Independent women are the most beautiful. You men agree on that."

"A Si understands what being human means."

A fisherman, the one Yuan Hei and Xiao He had met that night, walked toward them. Yuan Hei said to A Si, "Look, the judge of our fates has arrived."

The fisherman only glanced at the two of them before turning around and going down to board his boat at the riverbed.

"That's not a real fishing boat, it's a reformed pirate ship," A Si said.

"How do you know?"

"I recognized that old man. For more than ten years he's been watching by the river. He's very brave and rich in experience. He used to pilot sea vessels. Yuan Hei, I have to go. I see one of my former customers at the corner waiting for me. He's waved to me three times."

"Oh no, A Si! We have to separate when we've just met. Where can I find you later on?"

"As you will. Either at the Camellia Apartments or the hot spring spa. I'm usually at one or the other."

Wind blew from the river. She was like a butterfly in the wind.

Yuan Hei, with lowered head and a lost air, walked toward the fisherman's boat. He crossed the gangplank and went into the cabin. The boatman sat in the dark interior rubbing hemp between his hands to make a rope.

"Has she gone? This young woman is reliable. How could you let her go?"

"You've got it wrong. I broke up with her ten years ago."

"You're a fool."

"You're right. Now I'm caught up in another foolish problem."

"Then you've become more intelligent."

"Uncle, tell me what you think: why are women the way they are?"

"Don't ask this kind of question. If you're tired then lie down, there's a blanket here."

Yuan Hei lay down. Once he lay down he couldn't keep his eyes open. He continued to feel the swaying motion of the boat.

He didn't know how much time passed, but he was not dreaming. He heard the elderly man lighting a kerosene lamp. Later he also heard the man talking to a woman who was outside the boat. His voice was unusually pleasant and sounded like a bass singer's rising and falling from sentence to sentence. Yuan Hei tried to hear the woman's voice, but couldn't catch anything except for a few incomplete words. He decided to conquer this urge to sleep and sat up suddenly. He saw the man carrying dinner to the small table. He hurried over to help.

"Uncle, I just heard a woman speaking."

"It was A Si. A Si met with some trouble. I think she will be able to deal with it."

"Is she your lover?"

"A Si is like my daughter."

The kerosene lamp illuminated the fish, hot peppers, and vegetables on the small table. Yuan Hei had a drink with the old man, Gu Dabo or Uncle Gu. He saw their two shadows swaying along in the cabin with the water currents, rocking back and forth. Gu was a good talker, but his narration was so illusory Yuan Hei felt slightly irritated.

Uncle Gu had met A Si nearby. She had fallen down the embankment, scraping her hands and face. She refused to go to the hospital, so Gu invited her onto his boat, and she immediately agreed. She lay in the cabin for two days with a fever. She was cut and bruised from chasing the opium dealer, who had cast her away. He'd boarded a steamer and left without looking back.

"Gu, I love you."

As A Si spoke she clutched the hand he had bandaged for her.

"A Si, you should believe in yourself."

"I already believe in myself. I want to live with you."

They lived together on the boat for a month.

One day they sold all the fish and returned to the boat. Gu stared at the rays from the setting sun pulsing on the floor of the boat, recognizing certain familiar objects in the light. Then he said to A Si, "A Si, he's come back."

"Impossible!"

"You'll have to leave. I promised my nephew he could stay in the cabin for a few days. He's a young worker who comes here on his vacation."

A Si made a scene crying. After she finished she refused to listen to him, jumping onshore and running away by herself.

A smile appeared in the many folds of Uncle Gu's face when he had told the story up to this point. He downed another glass of liquor.

"Ah!" he sighed. "Tell me, Yuan Hei, if we changed places, could you stand to give up the life I have today?"

"I couldn't, of course not." Yuan Hei fidgeted uneasily. "You live like an immortal. Every time I see your boat moored here, my heart leaps. Why can't I think through problems the way you do? You're right, I am a fool."

"That's because you don't believe in yourself. Now you'll be confident, won't you?"

"Yes. Cheers!"

"Cheers. Tomorrow I'm going to Dongting Lake. I'll be back in five days."

"Do you ever take time off?"

"One or two days at most. I like my work."

Yuan Hei climbed onto the embankment in the dark. He wanted to get another close look at Uncle Gu's boat, but it was already indistinct. There might have been a fog rising on the river. The boats became blurred contours, like wild animals lying on the riverbank, the points of light like the eyes of the beasts.

When he walked down the embankment he discovered the streetlights were not lit. A man walking head-on toward Yuan Hei ran into him, caught hold of his arm, and said, "There's a pachinko hall at 132 Sea Line Drive. Go try your luck."

The man spoke in a rush, then he let go of Yuan Hei and walked away.

The pachinko hall was humming. Yuan Hei sat in front of a machine where a fantastic beast, its gaping bloodied mouth grinning at him, appeared on the screen. After ten minutes passed, his screen still showed the monster. The machine would not obey his control.

Yuan Hei stood up and went further inside. He was in a narrow corridor with machines on both sides, a focused gambler in front of each one. He walked and walked, surprised that the room did not end. He didn't know where it led. The old man who had spoken to him out on the street walked over to him.

"What do you think of this humble establishment?" He patted Yuan Hei's shoulder.

"Is it the largest pachinko hall in the world?"

"It is. On nights like this, buffeted by the storm . . . Do you want to continue your tour? This is a 'free port,' all who come can visit as much as they want. Look, a good friend of yours is here."

The elderly man edged sideways past Yuan Hei, who saw A Si coming toward him.

"Yuan Hei, my luck is awful, but now it's changing because I've run into you. Sensational — Yuan Hei at the free port!"

"A Si, I've lived in the city for so long without knowing there was a pachinko hall here."

"That's because you hadn't reached the time when you pay attention to this type of place. When the time comes, it appears."

"I seem to be stepping onto a floating bridge."

"You're not used to the atmosphere here yet. Let's go out for a cup of coffee."

A Si's voice fell, and Yuan Hei saw a door.

As they walked through the glass door together, Yuan Hei distinctly heard a popping sound, like an enormous bubble bursting. He asked A Si what was making the noise. She answered that it was free matter in the air.

"Did you notice the manager's eyes? His left eye is fake, it's a miniature video camera. Oh, he really is a kind, dear person! Running a pachinko hall like this one is so difficult, since the thing's always hiding itself, moving from one place to another, east to west, as if it were nowhere on the globe. Who could succeed at this? Once I entered the hall, my wounds healed. I felt so embarrassed."

After A Si said these words, the gloom in Yuan Hei's heart lessened, too.

"Who deserves to have freedom?" A Si softly questioned the darkness.

"Today I learned many things," Yuan Hei said from the heart.

They tried to find a coffee shop, but it was already late at night, and all of the shops had closed.

"A Si, let's go back to the free port. I think I'm brave enough now."

"Are you positive?"

"I am."

"You're so cute, Yuan Hei. The free port isn't the kind of place you can just go to because you want to go there. We came outside, so it no longer exists. Don't you think this is an intelligent trap? Before, when I was at the cotton mill, I had no idea this pachinko hall existed. After I lived on Gu's boat for a while I knew. Once you enter, unless you exit right away, you won't be certain about anything. You kept walking further and further inside. What did you see? Yuan Hei, what did you see?"

"I saw A Si," Yuan Hei said with an entranced look.

A Si laughed out loud.

"Then what you're saying is, if I come back tomorrow night, I won't find the pachinko hall? But it's clearly there, next to the shantytown."

"If you don't believe it, you can try yourself. These matters are dangerous. Goodbye, Yuan Hei. I will see you again in the near future, because we are looking for the same thing."

She turned into a small hutong beside them. At first Yuan Hei tried to follow her out of curiosity, but, before he got too far, a man built like a pylon appeared under the feeble streetlight. He promptly knocked Yuan Hei to the ground. As his head struck the ground, he heard the blaring sound of a suona horn.

Yuan Hei lost consciousness, then regained it. He sat up to see the man still in front of him.

"Do you want to go back to the pachinko hall?" the giant asked.

"Yes."

"That blow was to knock the crazy idea out of you!" he raised his voice.

"Did I break the rules?"

"Trying to die on purpose will not succeed."

He made a frightening, cold smile and walked into the depths of the hutong.

After these experiences, Yuan Hei felt exhausted and wanted to go back home for a good sleep.

He had just returned home when the phone started to ring. It was his lover, the prison guard Feixia, a widow with two daughters.

"Yuan Hei, I haven't been in a good mood recently. You can't come to my house. Find another way out."

"Feixia, thank you for calling. But I . . . have no other way out."

"Then you need to look for one. Look in places like the ancient city walls."

"I understand."

Yuan Hei put down the phone. He didn't understand anything. His slowness to react annoyed him. The ancient city walls? Legends said there was a stretch of the old wall within the city, but he did not know anyone who had seen it. Yuan Hei thought that Feixia might have posed him a serious question. Did she want him to go looking for his soul?

Feeling empty, Yuan Hei lay down on the bed, his desire to sleep completely gone. He saw through the windows that the sky was light outside.

The day became more and more like torture. Feixia was not happy with him. She thought he had no opinions of his own and wasn't the right companion for her. Yuan Hei agreed that he had no opinions about the things that happened to him. The previous night at the pachinko hall, for example, A Si had been steadier than him. Naturally, this was related to his never having been somewhere like that before. Feixia seemed to want him to go more often to places like the ancient city walls and the pachinko hall and find within them a real man's self-confidence. He had been alive for more than three decades without knowing the truth about these places around the city. He hadn't even gone to them before. How was this possible?

Yuan Hei slowly smoothed the path of his thoughts. He thought that A Si was someone who understood the unknown background. Meeting her twice that day had been no accident. Maybe she had been moving around him all along. Hadn't she said they were trying to solve the same problem? In that case, he ought to go find A Si. Finding A Si was finding a "way out." He decided to go to the Camellia Apartments (what a beautiful name!). He had to wait until night because A Si had said that she lived at night.

Yuan Hei didn't end up entering the Camellia Apartments because just as he reached the entrance he received a call from A Si. She said, "Yuan Hei, don't come. My lover's back, I can't visit with you now!"

How strange. How did A Si know he was at the entrance to the apartment complex? It appeared her problem was already solved. Yuan Hei all at once gained confidence. If A Si's problem could be solved, his problem should be possible to solve. Yuan Hei fixed his eyes on the flickering, interlaced lights along the road, and a way out, blurred and vague, seemed to emerge from them. He heard his heart beating in step with his feet, again and again with increasing force. He said to himself, "Yuan Hei will not give up, Yuan Hei still has potential." His heart filled with gratitude toward A Si. It was her, and Xiao He, who had drawn him into the place he should have gone to sooner. Now he was filled with yearning for that unknown world, a longing rooted in the body, just like his longing for Feixia. He felt the youth that had been gone too early return to him.

After deciding what to do, Yuan Hei walked in the direction of the riverside. He hadn't gone very far before the manager of the pachinko hall appeared. To Yuan Hei's surprise he was carrying an emergency lantern that swayed back and forth with a piercing white light.

"Think about it, how many people are wandering through the city on a dark night like this?" he asked Yuan Hei.

"Many, probably," Yuan Hei was vaguely roused, "some who have already succeeded."

"What sort of success? Moving the free port into their homes?" His tone was mocking.

"I can't be certain. Are you here to meet me, a stray cat?"

"Yes. Tonight you must turn to the left, into the rooms beneath the opera house."

The elderly man turned off the lantern. He was hidden in the darkness.

Yuan Hei crossed the street and headed back. On the deserted sidewalk a dark shadow dashed into his arms.

"Yuan Hei, Yuan Hei!" she gasped.

To his surprise it was Feixia. Her strong body was burning to the touch. Yuan Hei held her close, and the two shared a long kiss. Yuan Hei felt like his body would explode.

"Yuan Hei, this isn't me. It's my stand-in!"

She violently struggled apart from him and ran away. Yuan Hei didn't even know in which direction she had run because he hadn't seen her figure, or even heard her footsteps.

When Yuan Hei arrived at the opera house, the manager of the pachinko hall was already waiting there, raising the emergency lantern high.

A side door to the theater was open. Yuan Hei entered following the old man. On the stairs down to the basement, the man insisted, "The people in this room are all my customers. You won't run into anyone you know. You can let your nerves relax. Look, they're creating an air of enthusiasm."

He opened a door and pushed Yuan Hei into a room. It was a large room, unlit.

Someone held Yuan Hei tight around his waist, making him sit down with her on a wooden bench. From the voice it must be a girl. The old man put out the emergency lantern. Nothing could be seen.

"When I saw you come in with the manager, I thought to myself, Yuan Hei turns out to be a handsome young man! I thought you were over forty, middle-aged." The girl's voice was like singing.

"I'm thirty-two. Did the manager mention me to you?"

"No. It was A Si who told me. You and I can sympathize; we have the same disease. Please hold my hand. Hold it a bit tighter, even tighter. I'm not afraid of the pain."

Yuan Hei felt the hard callouses that covered the girl's palm, like the hand of someone who did hard manual labor.

"I'm a bench worker, I make dies. Use more strength, if you don't I won't feel my own existence. Good, good, thank you. My lover fell into the planer. The other workers all said he was playing inside the machinery, but I saw him being flattened with my own eyes. I'm called Chan, the 'cricket,' a name for a short life."

"Did all the people in this room come here because of sentimental problems?"

"The people? No, you and I are the only ones in the room. The voices you hear are coming from outside, or they might be hallucinations. I often used to hallucinate sounds."

"My lover is fine, though. I just saw her," Yuan Hei said unhappily.

"Oh, I'm sorry, I didn't mean to curse your lover. We sit here to talk about love."

"Good," Yuan Hei said reluctantly.

"You're not pleased? This opportunity was hard to come by."

"No, I'm pleased. Anyway, I have nothing to do now, and my heart is empty."

Chan released his hand and stood. Yuan Hei heard she was crying.

She cried for a good long time. Yuan Hei honestly couldn't stand it, so he opened his mouth and asked her, "Did you come here to find a way out, too? The manager of the pachinko hall brought me here. I have doubts about him. Could it be a trick?"

"No! No!" Chan stopped crying immediately and stamped her foot.

"You cried so much it bothered me, so I was trying to distract you," Yuan Hei laughed.

Someone was coming. They both heard this person enter the room. The person did not speak, just squatted in the corner to the right of them. After a while, the person struck a wooden match—he raised the match, then tossed it away.

Yuan Hei with difficulty could see it was a man.

Chan came closer to Yuan Hei and said in a quiet voice, "He is my lover."

The man in the corner squatted a while, stood up, and went out.

"Have you and he separated?" Yuan Hei asked.

"Separated? There is no way of parting from him. I just told you, he has already died once. This is the most hopeless kind of person—you cannot decide whether in the end to treat him as dead or alive. That's why I was crying. He's been nearby all along. This is the underground fortress of freedom. Did the pachinko hall manager tell you? As long as you keep the manager in sight, your thoughts will become reality. Now I can't feel my right foot. Hold my hand tight again, good! Thank you!"

"Why didn't you go over to him?" Yuan Hei also asked.

"I'm not sure of myself. Besides, I don't know whether he's about to die suddenly."

"The fortress of freedom doesn't give you confidence?"

"Of course I have confidence!" She raised her voice abruptly. "Why else would I stay here?"

Yuan Hei felt an object stab his hand, making him shout at the piercing pain. He flung away Chan's hand and jumped to his feet. Blood was flowing from his palm.

"I need to wrap the cut," he said feebly as he moved in the direction of the door.

"Stop! I promise you, nothing will happen to you."

"Why would you hide a razor blade in your hand?"

"I didn't do it on purpose, it's who I am. You don't know yet, all the people who come to the free port have that part of their personalities. You won't die, I can bind the cut for you with this piece of cloth."

Yuan Hei didn't know where she had gotten the cloth. Maybe she'd carried it with her. They busied with it a moment. Yuan Hei saw the silhouette of the man from before reappear by the door.

"Let's go over to him," Yuan Hei said in a quiet voice.

Chan clutched Yuan Hei's injured hand tight, not letting him stir. The strange thing was that, when she held him this way, his wound didn't hurt as much. Yuan Hei thought that the man and Chan were holding onto each other without letting go, while he was squeezed in between them. He should leave. "I'm going," he whispered to the girl.

Yet he could not struggle away from her. She was incredibly strong.

"What play is being performed here?" The voice of the pachinko hall's manager came from behind Yuan Hei.

Once the manager spoke, that man at the doorway could no longer be seen. Chan's hand let go of Yuan Hei.

A stream of white light suddenly stabbed their eyes. It was the manager's emergency lantern. In the lamplight Yuan Hei saw the expression of fear on Chan's even-featured face. She fled from the room. Even the sound of her footsteps could not be heard.

"These two are old customers at the free port. Let me think, it's been about eight years. They came separately to live in my hall at night. Sometimes they would meet each other here, but soon avoided each other again. I have to go take care of other customers. You stay here."

He turned off the emergency lantern and hurried out.

Now Yuan Hei was left alone inside the empty room. He thought, The manager must have his reasons for telling me to stay here. Besides, if he went back now, his heart would still feel pain. Better to see how things turned out here. At this moment he especially wanted to see Chan and her lover again. What kind of love was there for a man who had died inside the planer and came back to life? Distressed, Yuan Hei paced the empty room. There were points of light, although he did not know from where. His hand touched the wall, which was a bit damp. He took a deep breath, and the air had a bitter taste. Was it left behind by the couple?

Someone in the corridor moved toward his room. Yuan Hei, unable to control himself, went to meet this person at the doorway.

"Did she leave? If she's gone, I'll come inside. I'm worn out, I want to sleep for a bit on this bench. There's a bench on that side, too, where you can sit down to rest."

It was Chan's lover. Yuan Hei thought the man seemed wide awake.

"Are you and she playing hide-and-seek?" he asked.

"It's always like this between her and me. My background isn't good. She can't accept me. I was abandoned as an infant, thrown into a sweet potato cellar, and she can't forget this stain on my birth. She can hardly be blamed. A child thrown into a cellar right after being born must be repulsive."

"I envy both of you. Look, I really am here alone. My lover has never come out looking for me late at night, never once."

"Impossible. Even if she hasn't come here, she must know you're here. I would guess she was the one who told you to come to this kind of place."

"How did you know?" Yuan Hei was surprised.

"Well, this is the free port. The people who come here are all those, are all those . . . Oh, I've forgotten the word. It's so quiet . . ."

He started to snore. He slept soundly and must have been exhausted.

Yuan Hei's fervor rose to a pitch. He went into the corridor.

He fumbled along the hall, reaching the stairwell. A pachinko machine was placed above the staircase, the screen glowing, and a strange animal with its bloody mouth inside, laughing ferociously. The sound shook the entire basement. Yuan Hei's legs went weak, and he almost fell onto the stairs.

He climbed upstairs instead. By the time he stood in front of the machine, the beast had retreated into one corner of the screen and made no sound. The manager of the pachinko hall came out from behind the machine. He asked Yuan Hei, "Want a try at gambling?"

"I don't gamble, I have other methods," Yuan Hei said.

The manager turned off the machine and moved closer to Yuan Hei, saying softly, "Listen carefully."

To start, Yuan Hei did not hear anything. Afterward, faintly, the Lady of the Camellias' voice, which he knew well, came from overhead, the sound increasingly distinct. What was she singing though? Her voice had never been hair-raising and spine-chilling in this way. Yuan Hei sensed she was not performing onstage, but rather inside an enormous, emptied building. Although he had never heard this aria, he recognized how excellent the actress's performance was. He stood in the darkness unable to stop the flow of tears. Through his tears he decided on a plan.

The Lady of the Camellias finished singing. Heavy silence fell over the underground room. The manager was nowhere to be seen.

Yuan Hei felt his way to the door, arriving at the small square outside. He suddenly felt stifled in his chest. He couldn't breathe smoothly, only gasp with his mouth open like a fish out of water. What was happening? He undid his collar, straining to inhale. He glimpsed in passing several evening stars in the narrow sky and saw the thick, hanging layer of clouds descending, as though trying to tell him something. He had a sudden desire to return inside the free port. He staggered like someone having an asthma attack back to the door. It had already been locked from inside. He kicked against the door, the effort making him feel even worse. He grabbed at the front of his shirt with both hands, thinking he was finished.

He struggled this way for half an hour in the same place, as his eyes little by little went dark, until at last all was black.

When Yuan Hei woke he saw himself lying on his own bed. Feixia sat beside the desk. She hadn't turned on the light. The moonlight shone in from outside. Her face was completely white, like a Japanese geisha.

"The power of the free port is astonishing! People coming out lose the ability to breathe for a short time. Now I start to remember. I experienced happiness in there. Feixia, how did I get back home? Did you carry me on your back? How much trouble for you!"

"I did carry you. You were ill, skinny monkey. I tell you, I am not Feixia. I am her body double. Now I'm going, goodbye!"

She gently shut the door.

Yuan Hei crawled out of bed and boiled himself some noodles. He would still have to go to work the next morning.

He finished eating, cleaned the kitchen, and went to shower, before finally going back to his room.

He saw Feixia's glasses case lying on the table. Why did she keep declaring she was a body double? What would it feel like to be someone who believed she was her own stand-in? He opened the glasses case. There were no glasses, and instead a furry animal tail, the cut very neat, with traces of blood still on the surface. A note written by Feixia was pressed underneath the tail:

She fled. The night was dark, so chances were everywhere.

Yuan Hei remembered that Feixia had told him there was a nameless species of small animal, many of them, inside the ancient city walls. They had lived between the layers of the enormous wall for generations. He placed the tail under his nose and immediately smelled a delicate scent, like muskmelon.

Yuan Hei placed the tail in a pot of narcissi on the windowsill. He thought, Maybe this tail can still grow on its own? Maybe the "free port" is the ancient city wall Feixia mentioned?

TEN

In Nest County

Not long after Wei Bo went to prison, his wife Xiao Yuan disappeared from the city.

This was a premeditated act. Xiao Yuan made a major decision for the first time in her life. She wanted to become a different person through a change of environment. Not even the spirits and ghosts knew that she had found a place as a geography teacher at Nest County's middle school. She packed her belongings and moved. She wasn't worried in the slightest, since Wei Bo and their two sons no longer needed her.

Xiao Yuan didn't have much confidence about her future career. She was the type of person who first took a step and then looked ahead before taking the next one. She liked this little county town set against the mountain and near the water, and the place's simple customs intoxicated her. There were also the students, who soon grew fond of their pretty middle-aged teacher. Every day when class ended a crowd of them gathered around to see her to her residence on campus. She felt this job was much more meaningful than her previous one. She'd never imagined the standards of the students in this little town would be so high. The main thing was the children's abundant knowledge of plants and animals. They were also filled with curiosity about foreign lands, their natural environments and their peoples' customs.

The students' preparation for every class astonished Xiao Yuan. Her geography class more often than not turned into a general discussion, each student contributing the interesting parts of what they knew to everyone in the classroom. Even though discipline was a bit of a mess, every student reached a certain level of achievement.

At first Xiao Yuan believed her students would be longing for the chance to travel the world, that being the usual reason for students to like a geography class. This view was transformed one day when two of her students came over to her campus apartment to play. The two girls belonged to a group of students fascinated by botany. Xiao Yuan had been to their homes, single-story houses with back gardens full of strange and wonderful flowers and plants. The two families had both placed large wooden racks in their gardens with wide-mouthed glass bottles arranged on shelves, the bottles filled with sandy soil and a few lush herbs and other plants growing inside. The girl called Little Rose told Xiao Yuan that the reason for growing plants in glass bottles was to observe the activities of their roots. When Little Rose was questioned about her opinion of travel, she answered, "Teacher, every day I can come to the garden to travel. There's a little world right here. At night, after the lights are out, I listen carefully. My bed is close to the large glass bottles, and the sandy earth is loose inside them. I hear the root hairs of the phoenix-tail fern growing downward, making a noise, zi zi. Plants have no feet. The bottles are their world, so this is how they travel."

"I understand, Little Rose. In fact, you are my teacher. Then how do these gardenias, the Cape jasmine, travel?"

"The gardenias," Little Green, the other girl, interrupted, "the gardenias travel the world with their scent. I went on a trip to the provincial capital, where I stayed in a tall, closed-off building, but every night I smelled them. Whoever grows Cape jasmine will be entangled with it for a lifetime. There's also the medicinal plant aidicha, an anti-inflammatory. No matter where I am, if I have inflammation, I remember the aidicha. I concentrate my thoughts on the bodies of these plants, then the inflammation goes away. You must have noticed I planted a large patch in the garden."

The confessions of these two girls stirred Xiao Yuan's mind for a long time afterward. She thought of the timepieces she had brought on her travels in the past, feeling that her activities had been fairly naive. In comparison, the living plants the girls tended were genuine timepieces! If she hadn't come to Nest County, she would never have known this secret. What kind of place was this county town, both open to the world and sealed off from it? Xiao Yuan felt gratified to have the remaining half of her life to understand Nest County gradually. In the days to come she would discover one after another of those timepieces at her side. Xiao Yuan smiled at herself in the mirror, these first omens already indicating that her relocation was a success. In this county town encircled by large mountains she slept with such tranquility at night! Here she truly had the sensation of "home," which she had not felt in so many years.

"Teacher Yuan, if I let someone take a mouse that I raised to Honduras, could it live there?"

The speaker was the shy classmate Lü, a small, short boy. They were coming out of the dining hall.

"I don't really know." Xiao Yuan thought and then said, "Ask the mouse, it should be able to tell you."

"Thank you, teacher."

As Lü hurried away, Xiao Yuan noticed that he ran like an adorable pet mouse. He lived in a dilapidated single-story house at the tail end of the street. Xiao Yuan knew about the small animal paradise inside. One time while she sat on his family's roomy wooden bench, a glossy cockroach had staggered its bold way onto the leg of her pants.

Xiao Yuan was intoxicated by the children's world and rejoiced in her good fortune. One night she even slept in Little Rose's bedroom, while Little Rose slept on a temporary camp bed. That night Little Rose suddenly got out of bed.

"Little Rose, where are you going?" Xiao Yuan asked with surprise, sitting up on the bed.

Little Rose didn't answer her. Murmuring something to herself, she opened the door onto the garden. Xiao Yuan put on her shoes and followed. She worried the girl was sleepwalking. There was no moon that night, but Little Rose was familiar with the way and seemed to have feline eyes. She took a small iron rake from the wooden shed, removed a glass bottle from the wooden rack, placed it in a burlap sack, and then left, shouldering the bag.

"Teacher, don't follow me. I'm going to Nest Mountain. My phoenix-tail fern doesn't want to stay here."

"I'm concerned about letting you go by yourself. Anyway, tomorrow is a day off. I want to go with you there to have a look around."

"But it will be unhappy."

"Who?"

"Little Phoenix, my fern."

Xiao Yuan could only go back inside the house. She was anxious for the girl and furious at herself for not insisting on going with her. She kept her eyes open watching the darkness, not daring to move around, afraid to wake Little Rose's parents with any noise. She thought that, if something happened to Little Rose, she wanted to die with her. Oh, she had wasted so many years and was still so thoughtless. She had yielded right away, just because her student brought up a little fern's wishes. She lived by unusual principles.

Xiao Yuan's apprehension lasted straight through to the morning. With the first light in the sky Little Rose returned. Under the lamplight she glowed with youth, aside from her face being dirty.

"On this trip . . ." Little Rose said half of a sentence but was too excited to continue.

Xiao Yuan hugged her scrawny student tight, almost weeping.

"I'm going, Little Rose. I won't spend the night in your home again. Don't think you can persuade me."

Xiao Yuan's initial reason for coming to work in Nest County was, naturally, Dr. Liu. This was a turning point in Xiao Yuan's life, where she altered the plans she had made before. She had believed she was parting from Dr. Liu forever, yet, as the time lengthened, her thoughts underwent a transformation. She said to herself, "Why not take the road back? Maybe the right path for me is to retrace my steps!" She could return to Nest County, and she would do even better than in the past. She went through a few circuitous personal connections to contact Nest County Number 2 Middle School, then secretly set up a home here. She hadn't sought out Dr. Liu with any urgency. She meant to let him discover her. Besides, she didn't know whether he had a companion now, so a bit of prudence seemed right.

The little city stimulated her more than she had imagined it would. Everything was novel, and almost every day unexpected things happened to excite her. Daily she went to class and left class, made visits to her students' homes, sat at rest periods, and in the early morning drank soy milk under the cooling arbor by the side of the street. In doing all of these things she felt like a completely different person, one without a past, someone young without psychological burdens, even though she had passed the age of forty years ago. She confirmed in this way that, even if she never resumed contact with Dr. Liu, Nest County was still the right place to come, to this town dilapidated on the outside, with facilities falling out-of-date, while storing boundless vitality within. If she hadn't settled down here, she would never have known this one of its secrets. There was a perpetual calm here, not the calm of a stagnant pool, but rather a calm formed by regular waves of enthusiasm.

In Xiao Yuan's eyes, the middle-aged male teachers at County Number 2 Middle School were individually charming, deep and reserved in temperament, the type she preferred. Though they all dressed like farmers (probably from lack of money), they had a certain focus to which men from the city where Xiao Yuan had lived could not compare. She eventually learned that a few of the teachers were bachelors and predicted she would probably form a special connection with one of them. She wasn't sure why this hadn't taken place. Looking into the reasons, the most likely cause was that her thoughts were with Dr. Liu. Within the month she had gone a number of times to watch the street where he had opened a clinic, each time halting far off and watching the white door. Each time, nothing gained. As if on purpose to frustrate her, no one entered that door or came out of it. This was, however, the precise result for which Xiao Yuan hoped.

Dusk here was so melancholy. If Xiao Yuan stood at dusk on the gray stone steps at the entrance to her home, watching in the distance that silent Nest Mountain, she always wanted to shed tears. To restrain her emotions, she, like her students, dug up a piece of ground behind the building and scattered some brightly colored seeds. Little Green had given her the seeds, and, when she asked what species they were, Little Green tilted her head back and looked upward, saying, "I don't know, Teacher. Here you plant things, but don't hold out hope, it's no use. You toss them into the soil and forget as soon as possible. We all do this. I used to think that seeds would grow into the plants they were harvested from, but it's not that way at all. You can wait and see."

These seeds had been scattered more than two months without a stir.

Little Green shook her head helplessly and said, "Maybe the soil's not right, and they've died."

Oh, but the students' flower gardens were abundant! Flowers, grasses, and trees would simply pour into their rooms. Climbing wisteria covered the walls, piling up on the roofs. There must be some arcane mystery at work here, one Xiao Yuan could not fathom. Perhaps it was a sign that she had not yet blended into this place.

The people from the county town rarely went outside of it, as satisfied with themselves as they were. Xiao Yuan always felt a bit ashamed in front of them. She thought there would be a turn for the better with time. She said to her mother on the phone, "This place touches my soul. I've never been so passionate about life . . . No, don't come, you'll be disappointed. There's nothing to see here. Everything is hidden here, too hidden, dull . . . I'm talking about the surface appearance. Oh, it's not like the county towns in our country, it's like a village in a foreign country. I'm happy here, please believe what I'm saying. Goodbye."

She hung up the phone, her heart surging. It was a familiar emotion she had been steeped in ever since coming to Nest County. The mood was like when she was little and had picked up an injured baby sparrow and taken care of it. It affected the soul and disturbed one's dreams.

After Xiao Yuan phoned her mother, her emotions rose and fell in waves.

Yesterday she'd decided to visit the mathematics teacher at her school. She had spoken to him, and he had agreed, although his expression had not changed. His surname was the Zhong that meant "clock," and he was a bachelor who lived on the outskirts of town instead of on the campus. He told her the location of his house and said that it was made of earth.

"Walk to the third ancient peach tree, and you'll see it," Zhong said.

"Why don't you live at the school?"

"Because I keep bees."

Nest County was not so very large. Xiao Yuan soon found the three peach trees.

The earthen house was very low. She thought that Zhong, with his tall frame, would have to bow his head to enter.

Zhong sat in the doorway drinking tea, holding a dictionary level in his hands. Seeing Xiao Yuan, he placed the dictionary on the bench and walked toward her. He said the inside of the house was crude and plain, so it was better to sit outside to have a pleasant chat.

Xiao Yuan craned her neck, aiming her eyes at the interior, but it was too dark to see anything. She sat down on the small lawn chair Zhong had arranged for her. Zhong went to make tea. As anticipated, he lowered his head to go inside.

"Teacher Zhong, where do you keep your beehives?"

"Oh, the beehives. Here or there, it doesn't matter," he said ambiguously.

Xiao Yuan noted how extremely bright his eyes were. Few people from her city had eyes like these. Was it because he lived year-round in a place with fresh air?

Zhong guided Xiao Yuan in a large circuit around his earthen house. Wild trees and wormwood half as tall as a person, numerous wildflowers, and butterflies fluttering in a dance appeared before her eyes, although she did not see honeybees or beehives. Zhong probably did not keep them near the entrance to the house. Oh, those butterflies. So many species—and how gorgeous their colors were!

When they went back to sit under the eaves, Xiao Yuan voiced the question on her mind: "There's no village here, no work unit. How is this house here?"

"Oh, you want to know that. This house made of earth was my parents'."

Zhong went inside to brew the tea. Xiao Yuan took the chance to follow him inside.

Her eyes took a while to adjust to the dark interior. Zhong's home was extremely tidy, even simple. A few pieces of old furniture arranged neatly in the two rooms in front and behind, a mosquito net hanging on a wide wooden rack, a semiconductor radio placed on a bookshelf. Xiao Yuan noticed that these were real earthen walls, diffusing a cool, dark air. The kitchen was constructed in a cubby in the back with a gas range. Zhong was brewing Xiao Yuan another of the same tea made up of various small flowers.

The flower tea was soon brewed. Xiao Yuan carried it on a tray to the tea table outside.

"Teacher Zhong, you're truly happy!" Xiao Yuan said.

"You've realized this so soon?" His bright eyes stared fixedly, a bit absently, into the distance.

"If I didn't already have someone in mind, I'd want to marry you!"

"Ha ha! You're encouraging me!" he finally laughed.

"What is the beekeeping for?"

"To tell the truth, there are no honeybees here. I don't know why, when there are so many flowers. If it were spring, there would be several times as many as you see now. I won't attract honeybees that belong to other places here. It would be immoral. The result is that I sit at home imagining the original honeybees that should have arrived but tarry into the future. I also keep a journal about what I imagine. You see how ridiculous I am. I already have a thick book on honeybees. Let's talk about you, Teacher Yuan. Do you use a diary to record the things missing from your life?"

"Me?" Xiao Yuan uneasily shifted her gaze away from his face. "I don't keep a diary, but I have many timepieces. When I traveled for work . . . I don't need those timepieces any more, they are out of order here. Oh, Nest County is a remarkable place! Though you must think yourselves very ordinary? About things like keeping a journal on honeybees, for instance?"

"You're right, I'm an ordinary person."

"Did you grow up in this house?"

"Yes. When my parents were here, our family was very welcoming. We didn't have many guests, but the family had good connections. My parents bought this building from a farmer and chose a place with hardly any habitation because they often needed to be alone. You see, I inherited their disposition. But Teacher Yuan, I'm truly happy that you came today!"

"What do you usually do during the holidays?" Xiao Yuan asked.

"Me? My hobby is listening to the radio in the middle of the night while the honeybees are buzzing, *weng weng*. At that kind of time, you can sense yourself genuinely connected into one body with the entire world. This radio functions particularly well. It gets stations from every part of the world. I listen and listen, sometimes straight through to daylight."

"I heard you were solving a world mystery in mathematics."

"That's a game of mine, it brings me joy."

Through the branches and leaves of a large jujube tree, Xiao Yuan saw the sun precisely as it lowered bit by bit. The surroundings became surpassingly still, even the butterflies were not flying. She felt the vivid enchantment of this realm and was silent. Zhong also did not speak. Xiao Yuan thought that he might be solving that difficult problem at this very moment. She saw his lucid gaze misting over. She couldn't bear to disturb him.

The scent of the flowers came in onslaughts as Xiao Yuan sat in the lawn chair and seemed to remember many events from the distant past. There was a shadow crossing back and forth across the grid of her thoughts. Surging pleasure rose from the bottom of her heart. She didn't know how much time passed before the sudden sound of Zhong's words.

"Friendship is glorious!"

He was watching her, full of smiles.

"I love you, Teacher Zhong, but I have to go."

"I love you, too. Let me send you on your way."

Zhong saw Xiao Yuan to the ancient peach trees, then she went to the station alone. After walking ten or twenty steps she looked back out of curiosity. Zhong was not visible. How strange, the area all around was deserted. He couldn't have gone underground, could he? She didn't want to investigate more deeply. That would ruin her mood, this moment when she sighed with emotion.

Returning to the school, she went to eat in the dining hall. The sky was already dark when she emerged. She ran into the student Lü again.

"Why are you so flustered, where are you going?" she asked the boy.

"I came to look for my friends at the dining hall. The mouse extermination campaign is about to start. I have to ask people to take away the eight mice I have at home. There are still five with nowhere to go!"

"Did you find your friends?"

"No. They weren't eating here."

The adorable figure slunk away along the base of the wall like a giant mouse.

Xiao Yuan prepared her lessons at home for a while, but couldn't put her mind to it—what had happened today was too exciting. She paced outside, seeing the few light purple clouds in the sky, recalling the short time she had spent with Dr. Liu in this town. This was the first time she called that event to mind since she came here, because she'd been busy straight through, without enough time to take in all of the fresh realities. To tell the truth, even though during that day she spent in Nest County with Dr. Liu they had taken a turn around town and climbed Nest Mountain, she hadn't paid much attention to anything. In her impressions it was an ordinary county town, rustic and backward. Why did she keep thinking of this place after she went back? It can be seen that people's superficial impressions are not reliable. At the time, some things, of which she had not been explicitly aware, must have entered her consciousness. Naturally those things might be related to Dr. Liu, but they could not all be related to him. She'd made up her mind to go to Nest County almost in an instant, then taken action.

"Student Lü, are you still looking for your friends?" Xiao Yuan asked in a loud voice.

"No, no . . . I'm not!"

The boy fled as he spoke. He probably hadn't expected Xiao Yuan to be concealed in the shadow of the banana tree.

"Slow down, don't go. I want to ask you a question!"

"What question?" He approached Xiao Yuan.

"Why do the seeds I scatter never sprout?"

"This is normal. You should forget. It's up to the plants, only they can decide. We decide things for ourselves, they decide things for themselves. In some ways, we and the plants, we and the animals, belong to a big family. I can't explain this all, teacher. You'll know when you stay here longer. It's the kind of thing outsiders usually ask us."

Lü, anxious to make arrangements for his mice, hurried away.

Xiao Yuan considered Lü's words carefully, along with what Teacher Zhong had said about the honeybees. A few indistinct objects appeared in her mind. What they actually were still awaited definition. After she reached her building, she sat by the piece of land she had dug up and meditated. She thought that what Lü had said was right. It was unreasonable of her to look forward to the seeds growing. That anticipation had a peremptory element to it. The moon shone on the soil, whose furrows seemed to store ancient objects in indescribable forms. Xiao Yuan squatted down to look, though she still only saw the soil. Should she keep a journal about these nameless, these unborn plants?

Late at night, Xiao Yuan woke. She went outside again.

Her student Lü appeared again, like a nocturnal little animal.

"Student Lü, why aren't you asleep?"

"I was sending away another little mouse, but I still have four."

"Are you waiting for someone?"

"I think some friends will pass through here. I heard there was someone hurrying this way."

The smell of sweat spread from the boy's collar. Xiao Yuan imagined his whole day of toil. She reached out a hand to stroke his round, round head, but he clearly did not notice her. All of a sudden he heard some signal, jumped up, and ran far away.

Xiao Yuan felt that ever since she came to Nest County she had been completely cut off from the former life in which she had existed. The natural environment and customs of the two places really were not in any aspect much alike. Xiao Yuan had been to many places around the country and was not the type of person to get a big shock out of small surprises, but Nest County made her continually, inwardly startled. She had taught before, but never felt the enormous potential that these students possessed. Her position in relation to the students was inverted. She had become the real student.

One day in the classroom she lectured the students on the tectonics and topography of the Gobi Desert. She discovered not even a few of them were listening to her. They were all absentminded, and some had their heads together whispering. What was happening? Wasn't the Gobi Desert in Xinjiang the most beautiful place in the motherland? Or were they interested at this moment in something else? She stopped and sat down angrily on the lecture platform.

"May I report to Teacher," Little Green stood and said, "there is a bit of an issue. That is, the whole class has prepared this lesson for a long time. Most of our classmates have written long, long notes on it."

"What do your notes say?"

"They are about the Gobi Desert, naturally. We discuss this topic almost every day, searching for materials to dig into and to add to what the others learn, to the point of nervous exhaustion. Now the Gobi Desert is like a playground next door."

"So that's what it is. Who would like to read a bit from their notes then?"

Not one student answered. The classroom was a space of stillness and also awkwardness. Little Green stood.

"Teacher, no one wants to read. These notes are written to read by yourself. You can't read them aloud, no one would understand what they heard. When we write them even our families stay away."

"Yes, you can't read them aloud. They will be misunderstood," Lü said, standing shyly.

"What do you discuss then?" Xiao Yuan asked.

"All of the discussions use a method of allusion," Little Green answered with utter seriousness. "We talk about the weather, about playing chess, about matters of national importance, when in fact our topic is the Gobi Desert. Teacher, do you understand?"

Xiao Yuan's mind was in chaos. She shook her head. Her body felt like it was floating.

That day Xiao Yuan returned to her campus apartment hanging her head with a dejected air. Thinking back, her instructional method must have been a failure for some time at the County Number 2 Middle School, only she hadn't noticed. Despite this, she still admired the students: they were remarkable! How could she enter the world of her students' psyches? She didn't go to dinner; she couldn't eat.

Someone passed in front of her window. It was Zhong.

"Teacher Zhong!" she cried.

She knew he was going home. He always left the school late.

"Oh, Teacher Yuan!" His bright eyes paused on her face. "You didn't go to the dining hall to eat. What's on your mind?"

"My students, they . . . aren't happy with me," Xiao Yuan stammered.

Zhong laughed, saying, "There can't be anything wrong. They dote on you, I promise! I've listened to your classes! Can you go with me now? I'd like to take you somewhere, it's not far from here."

She followed him, turning several corners until they came to where the city met the outskirts. There was a row of single-story houses and a pond. They circled the pond, coming to a place where three ancient pines stood. The three large trees reached into the sky, a stone table and wooden chairs underneath. The classmates Lü and Lin from Xiao Yuan's class lay on the wooden chairs not making a sound, their eyes fixed on the light dimming in the sky. The boys were completely unaware of their teachers watching them. Zhong made a sign, and Xiao Yuan followed him away.

"Let me see you home," he said. "In the classroom your energy is too focused. You should allow your students to be absentminded. Here's a method you can try in your teaching—join a collective absentmindedness. Just think, it would be excellent communication! I'm not at all worried about you. Your students love you. Haven't I listened to your classes? Go get some good sleep. Everything is normal. Look, the flowers in your garden have opened. This is a good omen. See you tomorrow!"

He left. Xiao Yuan stood in the same spot, shocked, not able to comprehend: how did he know the flowers in her garden had opened?

She circled around behind the building. Oh! So many tulips. They had flowered directly, without passing through the budding stage, and in the last rays of the setting sun they were beautiful enough to make one's heart ache. The spectacle had been conjured like a magic trick. She thought a moment and was certain it had been ten days since she had looked at her back garden. Tulips couldn't mature and flower in ten days, could they? Maybe this was the particular time of Nest County. The time of the psyche does not need eyes. No wonder Zhong had seen the flowers.

Xiao Yuan, harboring thankfulness, squatted beside the tulips, thinking that this was how her students had repaid her. Even if she couldn't improve their minds, she surely loved them, and they made constant discoveries together. The tulips gently nodded in the evening breeze. Through the flowers Xiao Yuan saw an obscure world. She no longer had the extravagant dream of entering the students' world right away. She could wait. As long as she persisted . . . Zhong was right, no use worrying. Everything would be fine. She had just begun!

As soon as she stood up she felt hungry. She decided to go have wontons.

"Teacher Yuan, there's been someone asking about you!" The woman who ran the wonton shop was full of smiles.

"Who was it?"

"The man who saved my child—Dr. Liu."

"Oh, does he know I'm here?"

"He played a major part in your work transfer. I heard him talking about it with the school principal here in my shop. Dr. Liu said your expertise would be given full rein here. Didn't you know?"

"I really didn't."

"Such a good doctor! So lonely!" The woman who ran the shop winked at Xiao Yuan.

Xiao Yuan's face burned feverishly, which it rarely did. She opened her mouth, but no words came out.

She walked through the peaceful lane, thinking that her meeting with him was approaching. She didn't know why she wasn't excited, only calm, as she experienced the significance of this event. She felt strangely toward her own composure. She couldn't have become someone from Nest County in three short months, could she? However, before—but nothing could be more normal! If she hadn't come here, where else could she have gone? It was possible that she had been moving in this direction for over forty years and had finally arrived here. If not Dr. Liu, someone else might have connected with her. She recalled her chance meeting with the doctor, but everything was vague—the setting changed to nighttime, people's faces streaked with shadows. Of the one passionate night upstairs in the small building she had almost no substantive memories, other than the thick smell of the dried herbal medicines. Xiao Yuan wondered whether that feeling would be more real if the central role were changed to Teacher Zhong. She began to hesitate: did she want to see Dr. Liu or not? She consoled herself by saying it was impossible for them not to meet, living in the same small county town.

"Teacher Yuan!" someone in the dark called to her.

The woman from the wonton shop had caught up to her.

"He's my child's benefactor," she said, gasping for breath.

"Thank you for telling me. I believe he's that sort of person."

"Thank you, too." The woman moved into the shadows and disappeared from sight.

Xiao Yuan went back home. She turned on the light and saw with one glance that the narcissus on the windowsill had bloomed, three blossoms altogether, like three girls. Little Green had given it to her. Little Green really was a thoughtful child.

When she finally turned off the light and lay down, she discovered she could prepare her lessons in the dark. Her mental process became active. In the classroom of her imagination, the communication that had never taken place before finally did . . . Afterward she fell deeply asleep. She entered the bed of a great river, and walked, and walked. A voice kept asking her, "To the right or to the left? Have you made up your mind yet?"

She had already made up her mind. She felt herself enter her students' world, but the currents were rapid. Oh, she could hardly stand. Was there a strong wind on the river's surface? The voice answered her, "It's always like this here. To the right or to the left?" She could not keep her footing, nor could she fall.

After finishing his last house call, Dr. Liu walked into a restaurant called the Broken Bridge. He was a regular customer.

He sat looking comfortably at the painting on the facing wall. It was a yellow cat in a picture frame, a melancholy look in its eyes. Perhaps it was overfamiliar, and that was why it so often appeared in Dr. Liu's mind. He'd been waiting for an opportunity ever since the time he'd gone to the wonton shop and chatted with the woman who ran it. He couldn't rush into looking for Xiao Yuan, but he knew his chance was close. He had truly come to understand only after Xiao Yuan took the teaching position at Nest County Number 2 Middle School that the person he loved was her, not Danniang. The reasons for this were unclear to him; he simply felt that only with Xiao Yuan could he envision a kind of family life. In this way he both resembled and differed from her. His extinguished passion revived. He was eager to try. He even thought of establishing a new model of family with her, one of half-independence.

Dr. Liu's eyes gleamed, excitement flooding into his heart. To his surprise he heard the yellow cat in the picture frame screech. What was happening? He stood up and stepped closer to the cat.

"Dr. Liu works so hard. The weather's good for crops this year," a woman said from behind him.

She deftly arranged peanuts, a pot of green tea, and a cold celery dish.

"How many cats do you keep in the shop?" Dr. Liu asked her.

"Three. The black female is about to give birth."

"It's cozy here." Dr. Liu laughed to relax his nervous tension.

He ate his meal cheerfully. The pregnant cat lay on his leather shoes, conveying the warmth peculiar to small creatures through his body. It moved him, and made his thoughts wander in succession to faraway places. His thoughts of Xiao Yuan grew stronger in the cat's aura. They were like two people in an alley in the dark of night walking toward each other, relying wholly on the sound of footsteps to judge their relative positions . . .

When he left the restaurant, he saw Lao Gu standing by his taxi raising a hand in greeting.

"Dr. Liu, have you run into a problem in your life?" Lao Gu said in a loud voice. "I'd like to have a hand in solving it."

"Ha ha, Driver Gu, how did you know?"

"Your problem is written on your face. The answer is inside my taxi. Get in the car."

Dr. Liu sat in the front passenger seat. He saw a scrawny, dark-faced boy in the back seat. The boy held a pet mouse in his hands, its two round eyes flitting around.

"But Lao Gu, I need to go back to the clinic. Someone is waiting for me there. Besides, I'm still carrying my medicine kit."

"It doesn't matter. We won't be going far. Have you guessed who this boy is?"

"I would guess he's a student at County Number 2 Middle School."

Dr. Liu turned his head and smiled at the boy.

The car stopped by the roadside not far from the train station. Two tall young Uyghurs were waiting there. One of the young men held a wooden crate in his hand. The boy in the taxi jumped out and handed the mouse to him. The young man carefully shut the crate. The three of them walked into the train station.

"The boy who was in the taxi is your girlfriend's student," Lao Gu said. "The town is going to have a mice extermination campaign, so he's been like an ant in a hot pan, working day and night to find a way out for his pets."

"How do you know my girlfriend?"

"Why wouldn't I know her? Didn't you ride in my taxi the last time she came to Nest County? She's really a beauty. She must like it here. Look, he's crying. He doesn't want to give up his pet."

The boy squatted at the side of the road, covering his face with both hands.

Dr. Liu was severely shaken, so when Lao Gu said to him, "We're here," he got out of the taxi as if in a dream. He pulled out his key to open the door of the clinic, and the key fell to the ground. Episodes from the past were in his eyes as his memories revived.

Old Needle was sitting in the patients' waiting room. How had he gotten in?

"Ha ha, Dr. Liu! I came in yesterday, but you didn't notice me," Old Needle said, immensely pleased with himself. "Why didn't you bring the beauty back?"

"Master Yu, who are you talking about?"

"I mean Teacher Yuan. She and I had adventures at altitude."

"Aha, that's who. I . . . I am a little scared."

"Scared of what? Isn't she a person from 'inside'?"

Old Man Yu lifted his simple cloth bundle and stood, telling Dr. Liu he was traveling on foot to a neighboring county. Dr. Liu cautioned him that the sky was already dark, but he answered that when the sky was growing dark was the best time, and that he was only happy taking the night road.

He went out whistling. Dr. Liu fixed his eyes on Yu's receding back, the dreamlike sensation returning.

He returned to the waiting room where Old Needle had just been, recalling their talk in an unsettled state of mind. Suddenly he heard a cuckoo's call. On the windowsill there was a cuckoo clock, obviously left by the old man on purpose. Could Xiao Yuan have given it to Old Needle? How were he, Yu, and Xiao Yuan, three people from different places, connected by invisible threads? Maybe, as Old Needle had said, Xiao Yuan had been a person from the "inside" all along. Maybe she hadn't known this before. There were many people who didn't dig into these questions early on, the way he had, and who began to wake to their realization in the second half of life.

Dr. Liu put the timepiece carefully away in a filing cabinet. His whole body quivered.

Without turning on the light, he sat in the dark examination room continuing to tremble.

He didn't know how long passed before the cuckoo clock in the filing cabinet began to chime again. He shook more severely. Was he catching cold? He felt in the dark for a medicine bottle and took an aspirin. Another while passed, then he slowly calmed down. He thought of the little boy transferring his mice, and the boy's suffering. More important, the boy was Xiao Yuan's student! "Xiao Yuan, Xiao Yuan," Dr. Liu repeated, sinking with pain.

Someone was cautiously knocking at the door.

The door was unlocked. The person pushed it open and entered. It was the driver Gu.

Dr. Liu turned on the light as he said, "Driver Gu, you came at the right time! I want to ask you a question: why can't I have a family life?"

Gu smiled, slowly lit a cigarette, and inhaled.

"It's because of love," he said with a perplexed look, "but now you will have the chance to start a family, also because of love."

"Are you positive?"

"I'm sure. Last time I could tell that she might become a woman from Nest County."

"I'm blind compared to you."

"Lovers are always this way. In my youth . . . Quick, go look for her. Those students from the middle school are gathering at the three pines. I sense that she is hurrying there right now."

Dr. Liu rushed along an alley of broken streetlights. The night was utterly quiet. He could hear his own footsteps distinctly, but no one else's. Xiao Yuan was obviously not coming over from the opposite end. He walked out of the long alley and saw the row of single-story houses, and a pond past the houses. As he rounded the pond, someone scurried past him at an angle and went on ahead. It might have been the boy from the taxi.

Dr. Liu breathed a little more rapidly. He was sweating.

Under the three pines were hung two lanterns, and seven children altogether stood underneath the trees. Dr. Liu stopped and took cover in a dark place. A girl's clear voice sounded.

"Tonight Teacher Yuan will lead me on a survey of the Gobi Desert. She said it was a reward for my contributions to her flower bed!"

Dr. Liu looked out through the spaces between the banana leaves. The seven children were already out of sight. The place where the lamps had hung was now pitch black, with only the pond to the side reflecting light.

He couldn't make up his mind whether or not to leave. He heard a noise. A little girl wearing light colors was following along the pond. A beam of light shot out from one of the nearby houses, and Dr. Liu recognized the girl who came to the clinic frequently to have worms expelled. Every time her mother brought her. Wasn't it dangerous for her to walk alone in a place like this late at night? Did she live nearby? Dr. Liu moved forward to meet her, saying kindly, "Little Pearl, where are you going?"

"I'm going home. Do you want to walk me there? Then follow behind me," she said in a loud, bright voice.

Little Pearl walked very quickly. She must have feline eyes, the dark didn't frighten her at all. Dr. Liu stumbled along behind, having to concentrate to keep up.

They passed through the banana trees and entered an even denser little grove of firs. There was almost no path under their feet. Dr. Liu didn't know this part of the outskirts of town very well. He wondered, Is the little thing really going home? He asked her, "Is your home in the forest?"

"No. My home is still up ahead."

"Have the roundworms been troubling you?"

"They never trouble me, they behave. My mother makes trouble at home. I want to run away."

Dr. Liu worked his way, with difficulty, out of a large patch of fir trees. The needles stabbed at his face until he bled. Little Pearl paused. They stood at the opening of a vast wasteland, scattered with clumps of wild grass, and not a building in sight.

"Little Pearl, why would you come here to play?" Dr. Liu said.

"It's a good place, and there are foxes. Besides, my mother is nearby. I clap my hands, and out she comes. Whenever I can't stay in the house, I come here."

"I'll take you back home," Dr. Liu said, apprehensive.

"No! No!" she stamped her feet and shouted.

All of a sudden she ran, flying along, disappearing into a growth of wormwood.

Dr. Liu followed, thinking he couldn't leave the girl in this desolate place. Now he could hear no sound of her. She must be in that clump of wormwood.

When Dr. Liu crouched down, all sorts of noises were released from inside the earth, such complex, disordered sounds. He even heard the noise the earthworms made, and the sound of raindrops seeping into the soil, although no rain fell from the sky. Before he had always thought his paradise cave was on Nest Mountain; now it appeared there was a far more restless movement underneath the ground than on the mountain. Why was this? Maybe because the earth, the little animals, and these plants were too close to humankind? They needed a harmonized relationship with humanity. It made things very hard for them. In that secret cave on the mountain, if he hadn't gone spying, how many generations would those *qingmuxiang* have continued on? There was something underneath working its way out right next to the wormwood where he had a foothold.

The body of a mouse not much smaller than a cat dug its way out of the muddy ground. Dr. Liu now noticed the growing light in all directions from the moon. The small thing had dark gray fur and was not the least afraid of the doctor. He even saw the flash in the mouse's eyes. The eyes were extraordinary.

The troubling noises all around were still severe, like a forewarning of a violent change about to take place. Was this why the mouse had escaped?

"Little Pearl! Little Pearl!" Dr. Liu quietly, impatiently called.

At once he felt the bizarreness of his own voice mingled with the racket all around him, the din of discordance coming from another world. It made him fall silent, ashamed.

The mouse watched him, plainly studying him. Dr. Liu suddenly understood that it was here with Little Pearl, and that this was the safest place for her. He was the only intruder. A girl's voice sounded, the one he had heard earlier.

"Our teacher can't sleep. She walks back and forth in the wild country. I'll watch her so she doesn't feel alone. She hasn't gotten used to the way we live."

All of the din quieted down when she opened her mouth. Dr. Liu couldn't see the girl, only hear her speak. Based on the voice, she ought to be to the right, behind the clump of wormwood.

"What's your name?" Dr. Liu shouted toward her, making his hands into a trumpet.

"I'm called Little Green. I know you, doctor, but I won't tell. There are fifteen of us in the wilderness, sixteen adding our teacher. We're holding a conference on the topic of Tectonic Landforms of the Gobi Desert. I can't keep talking, I have to go make a speech . . . Teacher Yuan! Teacher Yuan . . ."

Her voice was further and further away. Dr. Liu did all he could to follow, but he couldn't keep up with her. He felt he would simply go insane. At last he stopped walking. The racket started all around again, each kind of underground animal making noise, but he didn't see a single person. He said to himself, "Apparently this is Teacher Yuan's geography class." Respect for her rose from the bottom of his heart. She must have so much energy to hold a class conference somewhere like this! Also, her students loved her. Dr. Liu all at once sensed an unknown world appearing in front of him. This world belonged to Xiao Yuan. He knew so little of it. Hadn't he seen nothing? Xiao Yuan and her students must have seen him this whole time!

"Xiao Yuan!" he couldn't help shouting. Immediately sweat bathed him, and his hair stood on end.

"Shhh, don't make a sound." It was a boy's voice. He was in a growth of grass to the left. "Now that you're here, you have to keep quiet. I don't know who you are. It doesn't matter who you are. You can't just go yelling all over. This is our geography class. Our teacher is explaining tectonic landforms. Tectonic landforms! Do you understand?"

Dr. Liu didn't understand, but he heard distinctly the little animals underground digging with more vigor—the sounds each species of animal made were not each alike. Some dug almost to the surface, making the wormwood tremble madly under the moonlight, in a ghastly manner.

"You'd better leave. You haven't had training, so you hear our class, but don't understand it," the boy said.

Dr. Liu's heart went cold. He realized that even Little Pearl didn't need his concern. Events were taking place that he couldn't understand. He had come here looking for Xiao Yuan, but what had he found?

Dr. Liu didn't want to leave, because Xiao Yuan was here. The troubling noise all around intensified. What was that voice? He finally thought of running, to run in a different direction. Why couldn't he be as nimble as Little Pearl? He made an effort, not exactly running. Even walking was difficult. Objects kept tripping him, if not stones then small animals. His head was covered in sweat. He was going in circles around his starting point. Meanwhile that voice pressed closer and closer, a voice extremely hard to understand, a sound like a naked signal. Dr. Liu seemed both to understand and not to understand what he heard, although he determined that the voice was coming from underground. He abandoned his flight and went to sit down on the ground, but he sat on a head. The person shouted in pain, crying out, "I am your patient Old Man Lin!"

Dr. Liu's mind flooded with warmth—at long last, meeting someone he knew. He felt for the man's head, but only touched a stone. He shifted the stone next to his feet, calming himself down. He let himself sit more comfortably, assuming an attitude of letting the waves roll over him. He remembered that for some time now he'd been continually picturing the scene of his reunion with Xiao Yuan. Not long ago he had still believed he was the one to help Xiao Yuan come to Nest County, because he had gone to see the principal of County Number 2 Middle School, who was a patient of his. He'd happened by accident to hear someone mention that Xiao Yuan wanted to come to Nest County even before going to see the principal. Who knew, might he not have "happened by accident to hear someone mention"? Was Xiao Yuan controlling everything instead? He didn't know the person who gave him the information very well, only that he was also a teacher. Now that Old Needle said Xiao Yuan was "a person from 'inside,'" he wasn't sure about her at all. He had known much earlier that there were many people in this world you could spend a lifetime trying to understand, and not understand them very deeply. Old Needle was this type, for example, and now add Xiao Yuan. But this didn't affect her charm for him. The more he was unsure about her, the more he was attracted to her. What was her geography class doing at its conference, on a night like this, on this clamorous wasteland? The saying "close meeting, at daggers drawn" appeared in his brain. This site was where flora and fauna met close, daggers drawn, with the inhabitants of the land. Dr. Liu finally understood the meaning of the special rumbling noise underground. Tears overflowed his eyes as he thought of how he had been together with Xiao Yuan all along. The incident on the train to the capital was an overture. Starting from that one moment Dr. Liu had entered an enormous enigma within an enigma. He insisted on believing that the essential mystery appeared as a curve.

"Your eyes! Your eyes!" Little Pearl shrieked.

She had been nearby the whole time, but Dr. Liu had not seen her. He wondered why she was warning him to pay attention to his eyes. He still remembered the song the little girl had sung about a lizard's eyes. He blinked his eyes and looked toward the sky. His vision blurred. His eyeballs might be covered by a layer of membrane. By this point he was convinced: he would not see anything clearly on a night like this.

They were all here, only not on the same level as him. They were underground discussing the topography of the Gobi Desert among the racket made by the plants and animals. It must be a marvelous event. Could the train to the capital have been heading toward a tunnel leading to the earth's core? Small wonder Xiao Yuan brought so many timepieces. Yet now they were in Nest County . . . Dr. Liu had never pursued a woman this way. Hadn't he been ashen and cold not long before? What was happening to him?

He rubbed his eyes and saw the clumps of grass still violently sway from the animal activity at their roots. The extraordinary rumbling continued. Dr. Liu felt he could face it. He stroked the surface of the earth with his right hand, feeling it was warm. He longed to hear her voice! Her voice must have been transformed. They were together, but could not hear each other.

Even though he wasn't drowsy, he lay down on the ground and fell asleep.

When he woke up it was already morning. He saw Lao Gu's taxi driving toward him.

"This is right," Lao Gu said, "this is as it should be. Quick, get in the car."

Dr. Liu, a little distressed, got in the car.

"Are you learning how to love again?" Lao Gu asked him.

"Yes. I hope I will be brave. Lao Gu, where are you driving? I need to go back now. I have a lot of things to do today."

The car drove straight into the wasteland.

Dr. Liu saw a few people walking toward them from the west, slowly coming into focus. Wasn't that boy Xiao Yuan's student who was sending away his pet mice? He looked like he had a heavy burden on his mind. Dr. Liu's heart skipped violently. He had seen her. He put his head out the window and waved to her. He told Lao Gu to stop the car, but he seemed not to have heard and drove ahead. Xiao Yuan had also seen him. Why was the look on her face so wooden? She looked exhausted, her face lined. She seemed about to wave, but only raised her arm halfway and then lowered it. There was only that instant before they drove away from her. Dr. Liu twisted around to look through the rear window. He saw only the students. Xiao Yuan was not among them.

"Lao Gu, I want to get out of the car."

"It's too late, she's not there." The suggestion of a smile floated on Lao Gu's face.

"How is that possible?"

"Things are always this way. Aren't you getting used to it?"

Dr. Liu fell silent. In fact, he had been undecided about whether to get out of the car. He'd felt at that instant that Xiao Yuan was so remote she seemed to be from another world. Was this even the Xiao Yuan he knew? As for the original Xiao Yuan, how much did he understand? Those timepieces appeared before his eyes. He almost wanted to cry, but got himself under control.

"How lovely! You're home," Lao Gu said.

Dr. Liu returned to his ordinary, busy life. He preferred this kind of life.

He helped Little Pearl again by expelling the roundworms. Her mother said to him, "Dr. Liu, I have a question: didn't you and Little Pearl have an affinity in a former life? It's like she's going home when she comes here."

"Shhh, don't say that. Your daughter has much greater ambitions, you wait and see."

Little Pearl's dark, shining eyes glared at Dr. Liu, who suddenly remembered the secret between them. Her small face now stared in accusation, and the doctor lowered his eyes in confusion. He told himself that this child was his guide, perhaps also the contact person. She wouldn't reveal what had happened that night to outsiders. He wanted to return to the wasteland, but realized vaguely that these events could only happen by chance, not be sought after. He consoled himself with the thought that, as long as Little Pearl was his patient, his connection with that side wouldn't be broken.

He watched the mother and daughter leaving, a few ancient images rushing into his mind.

"Dr. Liu, I want to make full arrangements for my final days. What do you recommend?"

The one speaking was Old Man He, who worked in reception at the large tax bureau building. He looked at Dr. Liu with profound significance. Not like he was seeking advice, but like he was testing him.

"I think that if you take each thing you do to be the last thing you will do in this life, you will do your best. Does that count as full arrangements? I am not sure about this."

"Your suggestion has value, especially taking it as a doctor's recommendation. Ha ha!"

As Old Man He left he shook hands with Dr. Liu, who once again repeated, "I really am not sure about this."

The doctor's thoughts flew to another place. He hated his own flippancy.

The janitor was sweeping. All of the patients had gone. Already it was dusk, although there was still light outside. Dr. Liu preferred this time of day, when the surrounding air seemed to hint that something or other would happen to excite him. Naturally, most times nothing happened, but those eaves he was looking at had such kind expressions! The period of the buildings was not so old, the quality of the brick walls was only average, but, to Dr. Liu, they wore a special expression. Weren't these the real buildings in the eyes of a person from Nest County? Dr. Liu thought again of Old Man He's words, and said aloud, without knowing or being aware, "After all, I am a little sure."

Xiao Yuan couldn't bear to look back on the night in the wasteland. At the beginning, all had been so splendid. The geography class was beyond anything she could have imagined before. Then suddenly it happened. Underneath the starry sky she and her students dug into the deep strata, in that darkness made a turn surveying, and then dug out, back to the surface. This was only a metaphor, but the conference proceeded that way. Everyone was excited, all of them responded to the earth under their feet, Xiao Yuan even felt the cruel sunlight of the Gobi Desert gradually shifting along her back. In the noise and racket of the wilderness, the young people made their speeches in unison, their voices rising and falling like waves, while Xiao Yuan heard each one's voice.

Xiao Yuan couldn't see her students, but she knew they were all around her. She hoped the conference would continue. She held her breath nervously and lectured on passing strange subjects. The materials didn't belong to her prepared lessons, were no more than her imaginings, her improvised elaboration. When she opened her mouth to speak, the surroundings abruptly fell quiet. Even the old cricket by her feet stopped chirping. In the atmosphere that seemed to have lasted as long as heaven and earth there only remained her one voice. She was a little frightened, but strove to act calm and kept speaking until she finally finished. Three students ran out from behind the clumps of grass to hug her. She smelled the sour odor of sweat on them. With a boom, the clamor and racket started again, as those little animals clawed, scratched, dug, single-minded, pushing their way to the surface of the earth to see what there was.

At daybreak she saw Dr. Liu. The man putting his head out the window of the taxi really was him. He looked like he had aged. Why was he so calm? He raised his hand to wave, but only lifted his arm halfway and then lowered it, as if he couldn't make up his mind whether to greet her. His cold, cold eyes froze her heart! The car whooshed away, without the slightest hesitation. It was like a knife cutting into her stomach; she bent over at the waist.

She didn't know how long passed before she came around. She felt the strangeness of unexpectedly standing alone in the wasteland. Soon she identified the path. Wasn't it the one she and Teacher Zhong had taken? That meant his home was nearby. The flowers alongside the path were even more luxuriant than the last time she had come, especially the chrysanthemums.

"Oh, you're here. Today's off to a good start!" he said.

"Don't I look awful, all covered in dirt?"

"No, not at all. Why would you think that? You look extremely well, full of spirit—you gained what it was you wanted. In Nest County, there is nothing that cannot be sought."

"Your saying that gives me strength. You always give people strength. I should fall in love with someone like you."

"Please believe what I say—you're in the best condition now."

He brought out a chair and made her sit down, then carried out flower tea.

"Did they all come at night?" he asked, watching her eyes.

"They all came. You were right, they love their teacher. The communication was indescribable. I don't think I deserve this happiness."

"Of course you deserve it." Zhong laughed. "Though I think something must be on your mind. Just now I said in Nest County there was nothing that cannot be sought. Another part follows: as long as you are careful to learn from experience," he added.

"Do you mean I've already succeeded?"

"Just about."

Xiao Yuan all at once felt enlightened. She thought, Zhong's mind is like crystal. The flower tea brought on a very slight melancholy and homesickness. Oh, the sky was so blue. She remembered Wei Bo, her sons, and her former colleagues who were so far away. Was the Lady of the Camellias still performing onstage?

"Teacher Zhong, your flower tea has magical effects."

"Probably because I always take care in making it."

"Do you think I shouldn't give up?"

"You can't. How could you give up, Xiao Yuan?" He smiled, changing the direction of his gaze to the azure sky.

"Thank you, Zhong."

"Let me see you on your way. Such a peaceful morning!"

Xiao Yuan talked, looking at Zhong in appreciation. She had just been through landslides and the ground cleaving, to be suddenly back at a beautiful, sheltered little bay. Zhong had just said she was full of spirit, and at this moment she really did have that sensation. Weren't these wild plants beside the road all telling them the pain and joy of growing?

"Will the beekeeping soon become part of the plans?" Xiao Yuan asked.

"Yes, I will be busy soon. A friend who keeps bees is moving here. My friend will be here in about a week."

"Hard to say it's a coincidence?" Xiao Yuan asked, startled.

"Of course not. In Nest County, your thoughts turn into reality. It's the same for me."

Xiao Yuan noted how there were many more species of wildflowers, lush to excess, as if they were snatching the time to bloom in competition. She had never seen so many wildflowers. A thick layer of petals covered the path. She couldn't bear to step on them.

On the main road, Xiao Yuan turned her head around and saw Teacher Zhong's perplexed look as he stood beneath a flowering tree, a large flock of wild doves flying over him.

Xiao Yuan's steps became very light. Because it was so early, there was not a single person around. When she thought of herself meeting someone like Zhong on a morning like this, thankfulness filled her heart.

She returned home and saw her student Lü sitting on the stone steps at the entrance. He hung his head in solitary worry, not noticing she was back.

"Student Lü, what are you thinking about?"

"I want to help you, Teacher. I sat with him in a taxi. He was uneasy, he had a black hole in his mind. Last night I saw him again in the wasteland."

"How do you plan to help me?"

"Maybe I can't help. I only came to tell you that I think he was looking for you but couldn't find you."

"Thank you. I'm touched."

After Lü left, Xiao Yuan shut the door. She planned to shower and have a good sleep.

Before she went to sleep she pulled the curtains shut and turned off her cell phone.

She woke up anyway and with one look saw someone standing in the dusky dark. How had he gotten in?

Before Xiao Yuan had time to think he came over to the bed.

Oh, how wonderful, even better than she had pictured.

"Tell me, how did you get in?"

"How hard could it be? There are tunnels everywhere in the wilderness."

"Can you live with me here? Not now, but one day?"

"I don't know. I'm always afraid of something. Last night I was blocked from your world. I still have to make an effort, I haven't finished preparing."

"You should make the effort. My students gave me a few new flower varieties and planted them under the window. These flowers, oh, they only bloom when people aren't paying attention. I only began to notice flowers after I came to Nest County. Are any of your patients flower farmers?"

"Almost all of them are," Dr. Liu said excitedly as he got dressed. "Xiao Yuan, I can't bear to leave. But that's nothing, after all we're in the same county town. Now I can get up every morning thinking the sky sparkles like crystal, because Xiao Yuan's home is just to the south—cross two streets, walk a little further, and I will be here!"

He silently disappeared the same way he had entered.

Xiao Yuan stared at that door, laughed merrily, and fell back asleep.

She slept straight through to nightfall before waking.

Her students quietly called to her from outside the door, "Teacher Yuan! Teacher Yuan!"

Without her realizing it, the single-story building where Xiao Yuan lived was surrounded by blossoms. The species the students had given her and planted below her window was a type of climbing vine. After a few heavy rains the vines rapidly climbed up onto the eaves, where they opened enormous golden trumpet flowers, every bloom so large it was unreal, as large as a soup bowl. This type of flower had only a light fragrance that reminded Xiao Yuan of her youth.

"Little Green, what is this flower you and the others gave me?" Xiao Yuan asked.

"I don't know. These flowers are so much fun. Teacher, when you go away will you miss them?"

"Oh, I hadn't thought of this question."

"They're flourishing so well I could see them poking their heads out from far away. Something must be about to happen. Something good. I congratulate you in advance, Teacher."

"What will happen?"

"I don't know."

For a good while after Little Green left, Xiao Yuan stared at the new inhabitants of the roof. From the start she had thought she had seen these flowers someplace. Aha, she remembered: it was in the sanatorium in the capital, that time she went to visit the Lady of the Camellias. She had seen this same trumpet flower winding around the trunks of those diseased trees. At that time, she felt the way these two species of plants twined together was unbalanced. She had never imagined she would meet these flowers again in Nest County. The look in her eyes was a little distracted as she recalled how agitated she had been in that period, how she'd been unsure of herself. The Lady of the Camellias' singing must have awoken a will inside her. Listening then, why had that song seemed so bizarre, so piercing? The sanatorium was a difficult place to understand. That scene of cold, abnormal psychology where even people's faces were ashen. The bleak, estranged look of the garden, although when a person was within it, it was possible to feel something absorbing, relentlessly, all of one's attention. People have no way out other than surrender.

The unexpected finding of this same species of flowering plant in her memory inspired her. Well, this was the good event Little Green had pointed her toward. She danced with joy at her reunion with these flowers. From the beginning, the Lady of the Camellias had been singing to encourage her, but Xiao Yuan hadn't matured enough to understand the song that entered deep into the soul. There was enough time for everything. Didn't she comprehend now? The phone rang inside the building.

"Xiao Yuan, have the flowers all opened?" It was Dr. Liu.

"How did you . . . how did you know?" her voice choked.

"I planted them."

"So that's how. Even the spirits and ghosts don't see what you do. Then do you know what flower this is? Hello, did you hear what I said?"

"I don't know. Here these things can't be known beforehand. Goodbye, Xiao Yuan."

"Goodbye."

Looking out the window, she could see Nest Mountain. This building seemed to be specially prepared for Xiao Yuan. In the mountains, Dr. Liu had let her observe those lonesome medicinal herbs—qingmuxiang, aidicha, the plant with seven leaves and one flower. The herbs grew in concealed mountain caves, giving one a sense of distant past ages. Dr. Liu wouldn't let her stay long because, he said, the herbs would be frightened. Now the mountain was still that mountain, and Xiao Yuan wanted to communicate with it, but her mind felt empty. She imagined, her eyes shining with rapt radiance, Dr. Liu lying on the grass in his white lab coat during the night.

Her state of mind was like the clouds opening or the fog dispersing. She cheerfully went out onto the street.

In Xiao Yuan's eyes the county town always had an unchanging expression, almost as if it were shy. These casually placed two- and three-story buildings, with a number of single-story houses, all chaotically gathered together. She knew the best games were in the back gardens. On nights when she couldn't sleep, she'd lost her way three times in the town, each time finding herself standing in someone's back garden, not knowing how she had charged into it. The gardens were very enchanting and occupied broad spaces, the trees and flowers unusually lush, green vines climbing all the way up to the roofs and piling back down. Xiao Yuan stood underneath the trees and heard each and every quiet whisper, avidly, almost bursting. All this time the fronts of these houses looked like nothing special. The doors were always open, sometimes people came out of them. Xiao Yuan felt that the residents' faces were familiar, only she couldn't say what their names were. They all called her Teacher Yuan. Some of the families might have had children who were her students.

"Teacher Yuan, come have a sit at my house!" a white-bearded man said kindly.

Xiao Yuan saw with a jolt the fervent light in the elderly man's eyes and went inside.

It was a single-story house, a room in the front and in the back. The old man was a widower, but the house was tidied and neat. When Xiao Yuan asked his name, he waved a hand and said, "I won't tell you. It's too much for you to remember, I'm not important."

He let Xiao Yuan sit in his beautiful back garden, carrying out to her curiously flavored peppermint tea. Three kittens rushed out of the house, coiling around the tea table chasing one another.

Xiao Yuan plucked a grape from a handy vine and put it in her mouth, asking, "Are you a retired flower farmer?"

"Naturally. The majority of people here are. Did Dr. Liu tell you? No, you don't need to answer. Recently, Dr. Liu made final arrangements for me. I have about two months to live."

"Can you tell me about your arrangements?"

"Of course. It's my favorite thing to talk about. I want to die out of doors, in the place where you're sitting, where you can see Nest Mountain through the grape leaves. It might rain, naturally, so I'll ask people to come put up a tall plastic awning for me. It will be a good place even if there's rain."

"Very good, extremely beautiful," Xiao Yuan couldn't help echoing him.

"Dr. Liu will come by every day, placing the medicine where I can reach it."

"He surely will."

"Teacher Yuan, your students often come to help in my flower beds. You see how well my days pass. Nest County's goodness can't be seen from outside."

"Yes, it would be foolish to leave," Xiao Yuan said from her heart.

The pretty mother cat appeared by the violet hibiscus. The three white kittens rushed over to their mother.

"After I die, they will go to Student Lü's house," he said, smiling.

"Student Lü's house is an animal paradise," Xiao Yuan said warmly, "and he's sent all his little mice away, so your kittens won't clash with them."

"I can't bear to leave. But what's to be done? This day was always coming. Look, Dr. Liu gave me a cell phone. He wants me to call him if I'm lonely at night. He also said that if he gets the call when he's on the mountain, he'll give me a detailed account of Nest Mountain at nighttime. I put the cell phone by my pillow when I sleep, though I haven't called Dr. Liu yet. I only have to feel for the cell phone to hear the sound Nest Mountain is making. You should know that great mountains always make sounds late at night. Teacher Yuan, in my view, you're a happy person."

"You're too right!"

They talked about some other things, such as Nest County's geography. The old man said more, while Xiao Yuan said less. The neighbors came in and put a large bowl of red jujube cake on the tea table, then left right away. Xiao Yuan ate the cake, which made her feel tipsy. She said to herself, "I haven't had a drink."

As she was leaving the elderly man's house she passed through a dusky corridor. An object like a wing swept across her face, panicking her. The man said behind her, "Don't worry, Teacher Yuan. It's my aunt paying you her respects."

Xiao Yuan returned home and sat down to prepare her lessons.

Her mind was so transparent, she could see through anything! She finished her work without the slightest effort. It was not late at night, but she heard the sound Nest Mountain made—indistinct and low, its tone a touch frightening, but also alluring. Could the jujube filling in the cake cause hallucinations? These people of Nest County, they enjoyed their lives so much! Xiao Yuan's ears perked up to receive the messages Nest Mountain was sending her. She thought again of the city she had lived in for more than forty years, thought of the times she had spent with her sons. These memories were vague, only the Lady of the Camellias' singing was clear. How had she come from the city to here over these few decades? Why did she have the sensation now of a path growing wider and wider?

Xiao Yuan glimpsed in the mirror that she had a patch of red dots on her face. She leaned closer to look and looked again, starting to be alarmed. She remembered what had happened in the corridor of the white-bearded man's home, as well as what he had said. Had a dead person left these marks on her face? Had what touched her been the woman's feathery hand? She thought the aunt must have brought her good fortune because she felt filled with wisdom. The thought set her mind at ease. The old man's back garden was so vital and thriving! Would it be sad or joyous to die in that atmosphere? Xiao Yuan didn't entirely understand her neighbors in Nest County. She was very deeply drawn to them, precisely as she had been drawn to Dr. Liu. Perhaps she had been moving in this direction for years, until she finally arrived. She was in her essence a person of Nest County, only in the past she hadn't known.

Lü ran by her doorway. He was always in such a hurry, so absorbed with living every minute. It must mean living with such intensity! In her heart she envied this boy, but also felt she couldn't endure living as he did. She was afraid she would faint constantly. He had gone to the white-bearded man's home, there, under the grape arbor, where the finest thing in the world was happening.

"The best thing would be to put up a transparent, colorless awning," Xiao Yuan said out loud, "the kind with a peaked top, so the rain will run down the side. Drip, drip. Drip drip. It will be possible to hear the voice of the mountain."

"Teacher Yuan, don't worry. We've made arrangements."

It was Little Green speaking, standing behind her.

"Ha, I was talking to myself. How did you know everything?"

"It's our custom here. We place great importance on every person dying with dignity. Of course, not everyone's requirements are the same. We do as much as we can to help each other."

Xiao Yuan and Little Green stood hand in hand in front of the building. On the roof the golden, bowl-sized trumpet flowers still bloomed, lively, noisy, as if competing to win, or not to lose, at blowing their horns into the blue sky.

"Teacher Yuan, did we plant these flowers' seeds for you, or did that doctor? I've seen him busy at your door."

"Maybe both. What do you think?"

"Yes, that makes sense. Teacher Yuan, the day after tomorrow I'm leaving on a journey. I came to say goodbye. I'm going with the man I love to the west, to a border county town."

"Oh, you have a husband! Congratulations!" Xiao Yuan jumped in surprise.

"We haven't married yet. I like his county town. Walking down the streets you can see real wolves, the stately kind. They live together with the people."

"Will you bring a few seeds for plants?"

"No, there are many varieties of plants there. Besides, if plants truly want to move, they always have their ways."

Xiao Yuan hugged Little Green tight. She was too fond of her and didn't want her to go.

Overwhelmed with heartsickness, she watched Little Green's figure leaving. There was some gladness in the feeling—at her student heading out for a new life full of confidence. At this instant the narcissus on her windowsill opened seven blooms, forming a little circle. They were dancing in a ring. Xiao Yuan's heart brightened. She felt Dr. Liu would definitely come tonight. He would first go to the home of the white-bearded man, then come to her here. She saw the face in the mirror become beautiful. All people, all events were encouraging her and Dr. Liu. Was that the custom here? Up to now she had been independent and thought for herself. She'd never been through this kind of love. A voice was speaking from the bottom of her heart, she could not fail. In a place like this, failure wouldn't be allowed. She'd observed with attention, and her conclusion was that every inhabitant of Nest County was successful. This unremarkable town simmered with life force!

Next door the teacher Xiao Zhu was returning home. She had also seen Little Green.

"I'm not at all worried about Little Green," she said to Xiao Yuan. "Two years ago she spent the night in the caves of Nest Mountain with a South China tiger. She's more mature than other children of the same age. Really, she's a precocious girl! We all thought she should stay at the school as a teacher, but she has greater ambitions and long-term goals."

Xiao Yuan, a look of loss appearing on her face, recalled Little Green's warm and considerate nature.

Teacher Zhu comforted her by saying, "Even though she's gone away there, we'll get news from her often."

"Really?" Xiao Yuan asked.

"Of course, this is her hometown."

"I understand."

Xiao Yuan returned inside to sweep and clean because she guessed that Dr. Liu would come at night.

She dusted all the furniture, even wiping the windowpanes crystal bright. As she worked, elated, a scene like a shot in a film suddenly flashed through her mind. That first time she and Dr. Liu met, on the train. She got up from the bunk. It was early morning. Dr. Liu was still sound asleep across from her. She lowered her head and saw his black leather shoes placed close next to her travel shoes. Afterward she'd forgotten this happening because they'd started their passionate affair. Whereas, now, she'd completely forgotten what happened in their affair and remembered only this detail distinctly. It truly was a whole life decided by one look. Why hadn't she known at the time? She knew that she lacked Little Green's great courage, but she had come here anyway. She had returned home, this was also her hometown. It was unimaginable that she had gone so long before coming here, and that she had only recognized the true face of her hometown the second time she came. What else had happened in her life, in its darkness?

Dr. Liu gave Lao Zhu medicine and kept him company chatting for a while about recent events, such as the mouse extermination campaign, then he stood up and said goodbye. He looked at his watch. It was one-twenty at night.

Out on the street there was a trash collection truck driving past. Dr. Liu saw ahead of him a white silhouette beside a mailbox. It was her. He seemed to remember having agreed to meet, but had they?

"Forty-seven years of waiting doesn't count as too long?" Xiao Yuan's voice was teasing.

"For me it was forty-nine. Look at this mailbox. When I went to elementary school it was here. Nest County has an old saying: all things remain until the last moment."

"I'd like to take you sometime soon to have a look around where I grew up. The main thing will be going to hear the Lady of the Camellias' opera. She doesn't have too much time left. Will you agree to go?"

"I want to go very much, because it was the Lady of the Camellias who guided Xiao Yuan. I'm so grateful to her. I think the insomniacs who come and go on the streets of your city late at night must have talked about us long, long ago."

"It's quite possible. We're here. Look, the flowers you planted! They're silent at this time of day because there are too many things they want to say."

"When I scattered the seeds I never expected them to grow so big. I thought the blooms would be tiny little stars the size of a fingernail!"

"Should I shut the curtains?"

"Leave the windows open. Nest Mountain won't be silent, it's active at night."

"Your idea is the same as mine. Even from so far away, the Lady of the Camellias' singing might float in through the window. I'm a little homesick."

ELEVEN

Brave A Si

The day Gu Dabo, or Uncle Gu, returned from Dongting Lake, he saw the tiny figure of Miss Si running toward his fishing boat. He hastily hung his laundry in the sun to dry and stepped off the boat to meet her. In this moment his heart was filled with joy because A Si was his joy. During his days at the lake, she had kept him company at every moment, so that he had never felt apart from her.

"A Si, I brought back white lotus root and salmon from my trip. Will you come aboard for a drink?"

"Yes," A Si said briefly.

Gu could see her bellyful of worries from her face.

They busied themselves in the cabin. A Si thought to herself that this place was more like home than her apartment. He knew how to pass the time! Slowly she entered his realm, tossing her troubles to the back of her mind. With a drink of liquor in her stomach, she had that same delusion again: she must belong to this fishing boat.

"I took a small boat onto the lake. When my boat reached the place, that great fish lay in the reeds, not moving because that was its territory. I hesitated a moment, it had so much presence. I was the fisherman who'd come to take its life. I stabbed with my harpoon, straining, letting the little boat follow the fish's twists and turns until it was exhausted. Sometimes this job disgusts me. Still, on the whole it's not bad. Especially early in the morning."

"Wouldn't you lose touch with your trade more each day if you didn't kill the fish? And wouldn't your soul dry up more every day?" A Si said in a soft voice, as though she were dreaming.

"I don't know. A Si must have already found the solution. Cheers. This isn't that fish, I ate it on the way back. You see, this work of slaughter is my lifelong passion. I'm incurable."

"It's not only slaughter. There's also friendship, and love, and the pleasure of labor. Gu Dabo, won't you reconsider my proposal?"

"No, I won't reconsider. A Si, you were talking madness. An old man like me with debts of blood piled up, I can only walk to the dark end of the path I've started. Have some more fish soup."

"This time I've gotten into big trouble. The city won't forgive me."

"How is that possible? A Si is the city's Camellia Queen. You're only tired."

They climbed the embankment, then stood there chilled by the wind. A Si held Gu Dabo tight around the waist, but couldn't shake off the sensation of being suspended in midair.

There were no cars or people out on Sea Line Drive, a strange deathly quiet shrouding the road. Just the day before A Si and the opium dealer had fooled around at the "free port" most of the night. They had passed back and forth through the crowd, not doing anything because they couldn't decide what to do. Later the opium dealer lost patience, said he had a piece of business to discuss, and left her at the entrance. He drove away, while A Si remained at the hall. She felt the ill will toward her rising like a wave inside and, slightly panicked, decided to leave.

"Was that your friend?" someone asked her. "I think he looks like a wanted criminal."

Numerous people tried to trip her up, and she fell down twice, striking her forehead against the machines. Then someone pushed her violently from behind, shoving her onto the road. Once she reached the road she could relax. She called to mind the nightmarish half month she'd spent with the opium dealer, and all at once experienced a sense of safety. Safe, although as hopeless and hollow as death. Later she arrived at Gu Dabo's boat.

"Gu Dabo, how would it be if I belonged to you alone?"

"In that case, this city would have one less Queen of the Flowers, and you will turn into a dried lemon."

They held each other tight, and slowly A Si felt her feet touch the ground. At the same time, they saw a white coffin-shaped truck stop at the side of the road.

"He's waiting for you, A Si."

"Goodbye, Gu."

A Si got into the coffin-like truck and sat behind the opium dealer.

"Who was that?" the opium dealer asked her.

"He's my father."

"I don't think so. He's a handsome guy."

A Si giggled. The opium dealer's expression grew gentler.

The vehicle stopped at the entrance to a narrow alley. A Si protested in a loud voice, "Go to the Camellia Apartments! Why aren't we going to the Camellia Apartments?"

The opium dealer pulled the door open and got out first. A Si had to follow him into the alley.

The alley, both of its sides closed in by walls, seemed to be empty. They hadn't gone very far when the opium dealer abruptly stopped, turned around, and steered A Si to the right so that they entered a home at the same time. Since the building had no windows, she couldn't see anything. She knew it would be one of his frightening friends. She repented too late.

"You're here? Just as well you've come," the hoary man said, his voice dry.

"She can't go down into the sewer, so she'll have to keep watch at the entrance and move some small things around," the opium dealer said.

A Si heard the tone of flattery in his voice with an involuntary shiver of disgust.

"So delicate!" The other man's laugh was earsplitting.

The opium dealer grabbed A Si's right hand hard as the three of them left through a back door.

Night had fallen suddenly outside. She even saw a few stars.

She was all but hauled along by the opium dealer. He and the other man walked too fast for her. She felt as if they were in the wilds, even though they seemed to be walking through a place crowded with buildings. Her tiny brain couldn't take in the environment around them. She was nervous, while also feeling wronged. In her mind she complained to her lover: why couldn't you think of something a bit more fun to do? What are these thieves' tricks for? Oh, she could hardly catch her breath! They suddenly reached their destination.

An ill wind blew out of the opening of an enormous pipe. A Si wore thin clothes, so her whole body rustled with shivers. The two men were out of sight in the blink of an eye, leaving only her standing there. With the faint light from the sky, A Si looked over the surroundings. She saw a very tall embankment and heard the sound of the river flowing. There were some people quarrelling inside the sewer pipes. It seemed to be a man and a woman. They started to fight. The woman, apparently injured, screamed in terror. A Si wanted to leave, but there was nowhere to go because of the almost impossibly steep half-circle slope of slippery cement that faced her. There were no other outlets. How had she fallen into this trap? She couldn't have come out of the sewer, could she? Their voices came nearer and nearer. The woman's groans of pain were distinct. Oh, they were out of the pipe.

"Look, the opium dealer's woman is here on watch like a dog," the man said to the woman. "This is love—one side willing to pay out and get nothing in return."

"She's trash. She'll be beaten to death sooner or later," the woman replied with venom.

"What about you? What kind of trash are you? Oh, you poisonous bat!"

The man suddenly fell to the ground next to the pipe. A Si saw the flash of a knife. The woman had done it.

"Hey, you!" she said to A Si, "He won't get up for a while, help me watch him. I have to go do my job."

"I want to go with you!" A Si said.

"Don't talk nonsense," the woman reproached her. "How can you enter without a travel pass? Are you out of your mind? Unbelievable!"

She angrily vanished inside the pipe. At first her footsteps were audible, then there was no sound at all. A Si was very afraid. The man regained consciousness.

"A Si, let's have a go," he said, "Such a lovely night!"

"Aren't you injured? Your arm's still bleeding. You could die!"

A Si grudgingly took off her clothing. The strange thing was that once she did her body burst out in warmth. She had thought she was waiting here for the opium dealer, but this guy was the one who arrived. While their two bodies were entwined, A Si felt much better than when she'd arrived here. Even the chill wind blowing from the pipe changed into a summery draft. Afterward they both stood up and put on their clothes.

"I don't like you at all," A Si said. "It's always like this now. Can you lead me out or not? I'll go mad here."

"Sure I can, it's my duty. I must lead you out of this dead end. It's really wrong of you, coming to a place like this without a travel pass. It's suicidal. Is the opium dealer trying to kill you?"

He, like the opium dealer, grabbed A Si's right hand tight. They went together into the noxious fumes of the pipe.

Even with the stench that spread through the darkness, A Si could smell the odor of the man's body, the fresh fragrance of honeysuckle out of keeping with his roughness.

"Why does he want you dead?" he asked again.

"He doesn't." A Si hesitated in answering.

"People often die where you were waiting. After a year they turn into mummies. Does he collect specimens as a hobby?"

"Maybe. I want to ask you: I have no travel pass, so what should I do if I'm inspected?"

"What else can you do? Run for your life and look to fate. In our little organization, people looking for death come here and then get captured."

"What organization do you belong to?"

"The same one as the opium dealer. He got a travel pass recently."

The walking became difficult. A Si's legs were submerged halfway up her calves in the sewage. She sensed imminent disaster. Thinking of the disgraceful exit that was approaching, she couldn't catch her breath. The man quickly released her hand. She swept the air a few times, without striking his body. After that she heard his steps splashing in the water moving far away into the distance. A Si made an effort to follow but couldn't catch up with him. She also couldn't be sure whether she was hurrying ahead or going to the side. It seemed that no matter which direction she went in she never struck against the walls of the pipe, while it was always the same filthy water and sludge under her feet.

A Si slowed her pace. She thought, There will have to be an end eventually. That man just now had said it was up to her to fight for her travel pass, and when she got it she could return home with no difficulty. She was thinking this when something bit her left ankle. After some time passed, she felt with her hand and discovered her leg already swelling. She muttered, "I won't get a travel pass." If a poisonous snake had bitten her, she wouldn't walk out of this place. She didn't want to die here in the foul fumes, but she walked slower and slower. She remembered what had happened that morning, remembered the fine time she had spent with Gu Dabo. Gu said she was the city's Camellia Queen. Was she really so beautiful in his eyes? Even the opium dealer had said Gu Dabo was a handsome guy . . . He had an unusual beauty about him. A Si's destiny was poor. She couldn't be a fisherwoman, she could only be one of the city's night walkers, like those insomniacs. Now she felt cold. Was she dying? No, she was still on her feet, staggering. For so many years she had pursued the same thing. Had she found it now, or not? A Si heard herself laugh. How strange, she ought not to laugh. She couldn't stop, though, and hearing the sound of her own laughter she saw that workshop at the cotton mill. Outside the workshop there was the well-lit cement road, both sides lined with lovely tall scholartrees. How had she gone from that place to here? She made an effort to think. Then her stomach started to burn with fever. It seemed she would not die. Why had no one given her a travel pass? Was she undeserving? Oh, her body really was feverish, but the injury to her leg was not fatal. She could grit her teeth and walk out of this place. If they could leave, so could she! When the opium dealer had said she could only "keep watch at the entrance and move some small things around," maybe he'd been goading her.

A Si didn't remember herself fainting. When she came to, she heard the opium dealer, A Yuan, the "yuan" for "rescue," inquire from above the stretcher on which she was lying, "Why not give her a travel pass?"

"Because . . ." the man walking in front answered.

A Si wanted to hear what he would say, but she fainted again.

When she woke up again she was already back at home. A Yuan sat on the balcony. His back in silhouette looked so solitary. He was groaning.

"A Yuan!" A Si called him.

"You're awake, wonderful. I was just thinking, there can be no one in this world who loves me more than A Si. What's wrong with me? You fell into the filthy water, up to your neck in the slime, but you still clutched in your hand the bag of money and valuables I'd given you . . . and there was that scorpion, it almost took your life. Oh, A Si, a piece of rotten wood like me should be split by lightning!"

"Don't blame yourself for being the way you are, A Yuan. What 'money and valuables' are you talking about? Why don't I remember anything about them? There was a sewer tunnel, is that right?"

"Don't try to think about it! You received the highest level of travel pass. From now on you can go wherever you want. All of the secret venues will be open to you."

Her leg was still bandaged, but she could get out of bed. A Yuan supported her out onto the balcony, where they sat side by side in rattan chairs. A Yuan held up a perfume bottle to her eyes.

"What's this?"

"The red scorpion. When we found you, it wouldn't leave you, so I brought it with me. For you, as a memento. Don't you think it's beautiful?"

"Extremely beautiful. How did you revive me?"

"Our type of people always carry some medicine on us. The red scorpion has another name, 'seven steps and fall.' It's your fate not to die. The scorpion fell in love with A Si."

A Si stared at the little animal, a feeling of affection for it rising from the bottom of her heart.

"Is this my travel pass?"

"Yes, it is. Don't you think it looks like one?"

"A Yuan, when you leave, put it back in the sewer."

The Camellia Apartments were always enveloped in a strange stillness. In front of them, a dark red setting sun hung in the murky sky. Yet the time was precisely noon. A Si asked A Yuan what time it was. He answered twelve o'clock. He didn't think it was unusual.

"How is the sun setting behind the mountains . . ." A Si murmured.

"This has happened a few times at the Camellia Apartments, but you didn't know because you always sleep during the day. In my opinion, A Si is lucky to live here. Do you see that person dancing around in the flower garden? Is he a friend?"

"That's my neighbor, the Informant. He's cheerful when I come back after being away. Let's go in, I'm worried he'll report you to the police."

A Si went back to bed. A Yuan said he had urgent business and left carrying the scorpion.

It finally occurred to her to check the status of her injury. The inflammation around her ankle had gone down. There was no visible wound, but if she looked carefully she could distinguish a pale red dot. Maybe she hadn't actually been bitten by the scorpion. She plainly remembered her leg swelling when she was inside the sewer tunnel, although it might have swollen for other reasons. A Yuan had made it seem real when he'd shown her the red scorpion . . . the little animal was a precious work of nature to be sure. Where had he gotten it? He was always finding the most beautiful objects. A Si submitted to his judgments.

She got out of bed, showered and washed her hair, and changed into comfortable clothes. Then she took a stack of food from the refrigerator and started to eat. A Yuan had prepared it all. He was such a considerate lover!

After A Si finished eating she decided to create a distance between herself and A Yuan. She didn't want to repeat that frightening, nauseating experience. She said to herself, "A Si is no longer young, A Si wants a few years of easy living, A Si—"

The Informant stood at the doorway, a pained expression on his face.

"Miss Si, did I just hear you say you wanted a rest? This is not like you. You're such an important figure in our apartment complex. You have duties, you cannot follow your heart and do whatever you want!"

As he spoke his voice grew louder and louder and he gesticulated with both hands. A Si watched him with astonishment, full of suspicion. She hesitated a moment before slowly saying, "Excuse me, why did you report me that year and call the police in to arrest me?"

"You still don't know?" His expression immediately changed, showing his interest in this question.

"Miss Si, oh, Miss Si, are you really so foolish, or just pretending to be? When you were sent to the police station to be educated, it was to raise your status at our apartment complex! Look at me, month after month, year in and year out watching your home to help you, conscientious at my work, and what is it for? If you think I have selfish motives, then you're wrong. I told you long ago, nothing will affect your status at the Camellia Apartments."

He placed a bunch of wilted yellow chrysanthemums on A Si's windowsill. A Si felt that the wrinkled suit and cheap necktie he wore were a kind of disguise. This elderly man was no ordinary person. Perhaps a long time ago, when A Si was still a little girl, there had been some connection between her and him. She thought the look in his eyes hinted at such a relationship. He turned back around and said, "People in this world always have some responsibility. Miss Si should make demands on herself."

A Si found his words comical, but instead of laughing she remembered some melancholy event from the past. After he left the apartment, she couldn't stop trying to recall what had happened. She remembered the water on the lake, the west wind, the wild ducks, and a disappearing motorized sailboat. She couldn't, however, remember who had been with her at the time. Regardless, it wasn't the opium dealer, or Gu Dabo, because she was still a young child. Could she have been with the Informant? What duty did she have?

In the winter A Si went back to the spinning mill. The factory had gone bankrupt long before. There was no one inside, and the doors of the workshops were all locked. There was an evergreen tree close to a window. A Si climbed the tree, gradually worked the wood-framed window open, and reached one leg over to sit on the wide windowsill. The workshop had been emptied of its machines. The concrete floor had been pried up in places and was covered in bumps and depressions. She discovered a coarse coir rope wound around an iron stake next to her. The rope hung all the way to the floor.

Now she stood in the junked workshop she had known so well. She glanced toward the back of the workshop and saw a high loft built at the far end. She cautiously walked toward it.

The loft was very high because this old-fashioned style of spinning workshop was itself very tall. The stairs were makeshift and looked dangerous. Who could live in a place like this? Someone was speaking overhead.

"I'm the old receptionist, Hong Sheng. Miss Si, do you want to come up?"

A Si drummed up the nerve to step onto the fragile stairs and slowly climbed. When she'd almost reached the loft, the old receptionist lifted her in.

"Thank you. I'm so embarrassed," A Si said, her face red.

In the loft there was only a narrow metal-frame bed, a small desk, and two chairs. A Si saw several picture frames with yellowed photographs inside arranged on the desk. She picked them up and looked closer, recognizing her very young self in a crowd of people.

"Uncle Hong, what work do you do here?"

"I lost my job. I built this loft to live in myself. I want to record the history of the cotton mill. Did you know this factory has a hundred-and-fifty-year history?" A Si watched his face with its tree-bark skin while she shook her head.

"I've written almost up to your generation. You, and Long Sixiang, Jin Zhu, Xiao Yan . . . I gave you the name 'lovebirds.' You are the lovebirds who flew away from this hell. Even though I've grown old, I'm excited every time I hear news about Miss Si. You are the pride of the cotton mill workers."

He pulled a large notebook out of the desk drawer, paged through it for a few seconds, then shut it again with a thwack. The path of his thoughts seemed to be broken off, as he started in again from a different point.

"The manager of the hot spring spa also came from the cotton mill. Miss Si probably didn't know? He's very good at disguises! Think about it, you and your sisters found work there one after another. Could it be a coincidence? This is a classic episode in the history of the factory."

She was not sure when the bats came flying into the building. They were terribly frightening as they wound in circles through the workshop, striking against the walls and making ear-splitting sounds. A Si's hands nervously clenched into fists.

"Miss Si, you belong to the earliest group to jump into the sea of business. I've already recorded some of your deeds. The spinning mill will vanish from this earth, but history cannot disappear. This hellish workshop cultivated outstanding women like you. It's truly a human miracle. You lovebird, now you fly higher and higher. You will not fall so easily, will you?"

The old receptionist sat by the desk as he talked. A Si saw the wrinkles of his elderly face shrinking severely, like a silkworm shedding its skin. Gradually even his eyes, nose, ears, and mouth all shriveled into a heap, a wrinkled pile like a false mask about to be removed. He was still talking, but she could not see his mouth. A bat ferociously swooped at him, struck his bald head, and was out of sight again. The elderly man bent over the desktop and started to snore. A Si wanted to see whether or not his face had shed its skin, but his hands covered it in a death grip, so that she could not see. A bat collided with A Si's face, leaving half of it numb and tingling. She thought for a moment before deciding to leave.

When she was halfway down the stairs, she heard the elderly man above call, "Miss Si, don't let yourself relax!"

She was about to climb the coir rope up to the window when the door to the workshop suddenly opened.

Four men wearing helmets and dark glasses and dressed in protective gear appeared at the door. One of them started to scream in terror, pointing at A Si: "That's a poisonous bat! Look at this woman, what's wrong with her? Could she be immune, like the old monster Hong Sheng?"

The men stopped paying attention to A Si. They charged at the loft stairs, smashing at them randomly with the metal rods they were holding. With a rumbling sound the loft came collapsing down.

A Si saw the wooden planks scattered across the floor but not the old man. Was he buried underneath?

The four men stood there, apparently baffled by the scene before their eyes. The shortest one saw A Si still standing at the doorway and demanded, "Were you and this person trying to reverse the verdict of history?"

A Si didn't answer, because she honestly didn't know.

Another man said, grinding his teeth, "Huh, even if he's hiding in hell I'll catch him. He actually dares to construct historical incidents! Look at these rotten boards."

They rummaged among the planks with the metal rods without discovering anything. A Si found it so funny she had to run outside with a hand muffling her mouth.

The sunlight outside was dazzling. The grayish cement path had aged, but those large, tall scholartrees along its sides were still as lovely. A Si had turned back to glance a few times at the workshop in which her youth was buried, this time with surprise because the workshop's roof was torn loose. It had just been in place! She sensed this site concealed danger, that she must leave right away. She started to run.

She'd finally reached the main factory entrance and was trying to rest, when someone caught her. It turned out to be A Yuan. His body reeked. He said he'd just come out of the sewer.

"See you tonight at one-thirty, at the free port!"

He shoved her away, got into a car alone, and drove off.

A Si took a final look at the cotton mill and felt empty. She remembered what Hong Sheng had said and understood what he meant in speaking the word "history." Wasn't history an event that repeated unforgettably in the mind? Those four men in protective gear appeared to be giving someone a warning. Who was supposed to see the warning? A Si's spine ran cold, she felt the threat was for her. Her history, in disarray, that she couldn't endure to look back on, that sometimes troubled her in the middle of the night, that she dreamed she could live over again. If the factory's history truly had been demolished, like the loft, her history had also disappeared, and that was for the better.

A Si walked down the street, oblivious to everything, feeling how alone she was. She thought of the metaphor "a leaflike little boat in the wild wind and vicious waves." This was her view of her own life. Why had A Yuan never taken away her loneliness, only made it worse?

She knew she was covered in dirt and dust, yet she didn't want to go home. Let the people she knew see her true face. She had no use for disguises, and disguises were no use anyway, so many people could see through them, including Gu Dabo.

She went into a café and ordered a large cup of coffee. The café was in a decadent style. A sixties-era record player played clanging revolutionary songs. The room was dark, with none of the lamps turned on, and the sole ray of light came from the ceiling where there were several missing tiles. Large rats ran back and forth along the roof beams.

The customers all seemed to be overwrought. Even though they spoke in lowered voices, they sometimes made cries of fear. A Si was not used to these young people, but she was genuinely tired and had to sit there enduring the torment of their voices. Three people at one table almost broke out in a fight, but they controlled themselves and sat back down. What day was it today? A Si struggled to answer.

Someone rushed toward her like a gust of wind, grabbed her by the shoulder, and shook her.

"It really is A Si!" Long Sixiang said with excitement. "You've been missing for so long. We couldn't find you anywhere! Lao Yong and I are going to get married. Had you heard?"

"Congratulations! When is the wedding?"

At her question, Long Sixiang immediately looked depressed.

"Soon. He and I both think it should be soon, only we haven't decided on a specific date. A Si, do you think I should get married? Or is taking my time like this better?"

"I can't say for sure. With this kind of event, who can say for sure?"

"It really is you, A Si! Are you going to the free port tonight? I'm going. I just heard someone here say the free port will vanish tonight. You and I can watch the scene."

"Sixiang, are you still at the hot springs?" A Si had to ask her.

"Yes, A Si! I don't think I'll ever leave in my whole life!"

Long Sixiang placed her coffee on the table, covered her face, and started to cry.

A Si patiently waited for her to finish weeping. Long Sixiang did not cry for very long.

"I've met a very gentle guy who would make a good husband!" Long Sixiang seemed abruptly to remember her good fortune. Her eyes shone with radiance. "He comes almost every week. Once I blundered and almost accepted his marriage proposal, then later I woke up and realized I should ask myself: why would I get married? I couldn't find a reason, so I blew him off after that. This man can't measure up to Lao Yong, naturally, it's just that he's more suitable to marry. A Si, I have to go, I can't stand the atmosphere in this café. It reeks of corpses."

She rushed out, again like a gust of wind.

A Si murmured to herself, "Sixiang really is a lovely woman." She wondered, For Sixiang, what was history?

A tall server walked over, leaned close to her ear, and said lightly, "Is Miss Si planning to go to the free port?"

"How did you know?" A Si was surprised.

"All the customers here go to the free port," the girl answered calmly. "Look outside, the sky will be dark as quick as you can say 'dark.' Our owner doesn't allow turning on the lights. Come with me."

She led A Si as they circled around the tables in the dusky light. A Si noticed there was no one left, the only sound their footsteps.

"Did someone die here?" A Si asked, remembering Long Sixiang's words.

"Many," the server vaguely replied.

The server's hand became like a pair of pliers, only letting go when A Si shouted in pain. As she released A Si, her silhouette turned to the side and was invisible in an instant.

A Si stood in the dimness, for a time not able to tell where she was. After a moment she saw the riverbank and a fishing boat. There was a lamp in the cabin. Gu Dabo's figure stood at the prow.

However, she couldn't reach the riverbank in front of her. The more she tried, the further she was from the boat.

As a thunderstorm splashed down, A Si took cover from the rain in the doorway of a paper warehouse. Inside the warehouse giant rolls of newsprint piled up all the way to the ceiling. There was a narrow walkway among these wares lit by a small lamp. A Si saw a number of people gathered in the aisle, their bodies dripping wet. They all looked terrified.

"Did he gain his release?" one person said. "How frightening!"

A Si thought to herself that she didn't want liberation. She yearned to be tied up tight in ropes so that she could never go too far. Had she gained her release, though? The people were all watching her, eagerly, as if asking her something. Clearly these people who looked like soaking wet chickens hadn't been liberated. A Si discovered a man who looked like A Yuan in the crowd. She stood on tiptoe trying to see if it was him, but the people pressed and jostled back and forth, so that she couldn't get a clear look. Someone patted her on the shoulder and said, "If you want the view from on high, you can climb onto the rolls of paper."

A Si lowered her head. Even supposing she found A Yuan, would it signify anything? She didn't belong to their group. She would always be isolated and left in the dark.

Outside there were explosions of thunder, then lightning ignited the giant pile of wastepaper at the doorway. A huge fire sealed off the door, expelling thick billows of smoke into the room. Everyone started coughing, A Si was also coughing. Suffocating, she tried to rush out, but these people would not let her go. They said through their coughs, "Hold on a little, it will get better. Such heavy rain, the fire will get smaller. Have you forgotten what you came here to do? Think it over carefully."

The fire didn't get smaller, nor did it grow. Everyone was waiting, waiting for what? Two people pulled at the front of A Si's clothing, not letting her leave. Suddenly a light shone in A Si's mind, and she shouted, "This is the free port!"

Following her shout, a dazzling ball of flame landed on the paper rolls inside the building. Within a few minutes the entire warehouse was burning. A Si had already dashed outside, in spite of everything that was happening. She sat in a flower garden in the middle of the road, the heavy rain washing over her. From there she witnessed a number of people buried in the sea of fire. Had A Yuan been in there?

The warehouse continued to belch dark smoke but had not collapsed. The fire put itself out. A Si heard someone next to her complaining that she shouldn't have been shouting and upsetting everyone. "Who doesn't know that it's the free port? What use was reminding everyone?" he said indignantly.

"There's a body! There's a body . . ." people at the entrance to the warehouse were shouting.

A Si's heart palpitated, thumping as she tore toward the warehouse.

Inside there were choking ashes everywhere, making it hard to breathe. The paper tubes hadn't been completely burned, and the fire was extinguished. Seven or eight people surrounded a corpse burned to charcoal. One of them callously turned the body over with a metal rod. A Si identified him as one of the men who had destroyed the loft in the factory. When the corpse was flipped over, a small glass bottle clattered as it rolled out and straight to A Si's feet. She picked the bottle up and saw the red scorpion inside waving its tail, enraged.

A Si became at this moment abnormally calm, so much so that she even surprised herself. It was like there was a heavy snow falling in her mind. It was the extreme of somberness. She pulled out her cell phone, giving both Long Sixiang and Mr. You a call. She told them there'd been an accident and asked them to come to the paper warehouse right away.

She leaned over and pressed a kiss onto the charcoal lips. She felt the skin of that mouth sticking to her own. Looking again at the corpse's lips, the mouth had become a black hole. She secured the glass bottle and stood, then walked out of the warehouse without turning her head. The thunderstorm pelted her body painfully, but she didn't notice. Many people holding umbrellas were chasing her. They called, "A Si! A Si . . ."

A Si found the sewer tunnel by intuition. Her smooth success made her involuntarily think of the issue of the travel pass. She kept going straight inside, where it wasn't so dark after all because of thin rays of light scattered everywhere. She thought every place there resembled where she had fainted.

She stopped, bent over at the waist, and twisted the lid off the bottle to let the scorpion climb out on its own. At first the little animal wouldn't move and seemed to be considering. A Si slowly, gently tapped the bottle with a fingernail and called it with a few endearing names. Then she placed the bottle on a piece of broken brick and did a Xinjiang dance in the sewage, quietly humming a Uyghur song. When she finished the dance she turned around to look, and the lovely scorpion was already gone. A Si sighed and put the bottle in her pocket.

When she returned to the street, she saw the disk of the red sun rising in the east. Was it another new day? What was happening?

"We've already had him cremated," Long Sixiang said to her, "as he'd directed me and Mr. You. He said not to linger a moment. Look, A Si, this is him."

Long Sixiang handed her a tiny celadon urn.

"Sixiang, thank you. Why is he only this little bit?"

"Yes, I thought it was strange, too, so I asked the workers. It must be that there's just a little because he exhausted himself. He really was a handsome guy."

A Si received the ceramic jar and examined it again and again while making strange moans.

"Is something wrong, A Si?" Long Sixiang asked with concern.

"He was so handsome . . ." A Si said.

"He was extremely handsome. He must have stood up in the incinerator . . . otherwise how could he have become just this little bit of ashes? The workers said nothing like this had happened for years." Long Sixiang was lost in reveries.

"Did they really say so?"

"They really did."

Long Sixiang, not reassured about A Si, took her all the way to her home in the Camellia Apartments. On the road she also made a call specially to Jin Zhu. They hadn't been at A Si's home long when Jin Zhu arrived by taxi.

A Si, not wanting to immerse her good friends in her grief, drummed up her spirits and narrated her adventure at the factory workshop.

"I'd heard Uncle Hong was writing the history of the cotton mill," Long Sixiang said. "I had thought history was those trivial things. For example, manufacturing development, professional business, product sales, that type. I never imagined he'd write our deeds into the history, I really would die of shame. A Si, was that book of history truly destroyed? Was he really martyred? Could he have escaped?"

"With the size of the workshop, I could see it all clearly. He had no place to run. He and his notebooks must be finished. He couldn't defeat those evil men and their sticks."

The three women all fell silent. Then abruptly their different mouths said the same words, "It turns out this is also history. Fortunately it's been destroyed!"

Jin Zhu also added, "Only the notebook was destroyed. I just saw Uncle Hong. He was quite calm. He said that since he can't record history again, he will create history. I didn't know what he was talking about, but now I do."

"We will create history, too!" A Si said with excitement. "I'll make some salmon for you to eat."

The three women blew into the kitchen like gusts of wind and started to busy themselves.

At times A Si would pause in a daze. Long Sixiang would exchange a glance with Jin Zhu and say in a loud voice, "Jin Zhu, listen. I want to die as happy as the opium dealer. Tell me, do you think my wish could be fulfilled? I'm not certain."

"I'm not, either. It depends on each person's fate. How can we make demands?"

A Si snickered, saying, "You don't need to put on a performance. I'll understand eventually."

All three drank plenty of liquor while they ate. They placed the urn filled with ashes on the dining table and toasted to it again and again.

"Jin Zhu, I heard you recently married?" A Si asked, in a distracted state of mind.

"Yes. I found happiness. We've all found happiness, haven't we?"

"Cheers, to the happiness of the three of us!" Long Sixiang said.

"Cheers!" they exclaimed in unison.

Their hands shook so hard that liquor spilled all over the place. A beacon shone in each of their hearts.

The Informant entered without knocking on the door. With a grave look on his face he walked over to the dining table, turned the celadon urn toward him, and bowed deeply three times.

"Are you A Si's friend? I think you've changed," Long Sixiang said.

"The gentleman inside this jar was well admired," he said.

His appearance became dignified, like a general. He rapidly turned around and left.

"A Si, later on you can consider this gentleman," Long Sixiang said.

"He's still a mystery to me. I also have other men to consider."

"A Si should seek out new happiness," Jin Zhu said.

"Look, my happiness is here!"

A Si pointed with her chopsticks at the salmon's bones inside the large soup tureen. They saw its skeleton eaten bare of flesh moving around in the soup. It swam in three circles, then paused at the bottom of the tureen and remained still. The three women looked at each other in shock.

"This is a kind of happiness you can practically feel. A Yuan had nothing to do with it. When you were with A Yuan, you couldn't feel happiness, only misery. But I still want to hang myself on his tree. Why?" As A Si said these words she thought of her mother, and her eyes fixed their gaze at a certain point in the air.

"Because it's in all of our natures to go a bit mad!" Long Sixiang sighed.

She then stood up abruptly, saying she wasn't feeling well and wanted to go back to rest.

After she left, Jin Zhu told A Si that Lao Yong had found another young lover. He kept pressuring Long Sixiang to marry him, but she'd decided never to marry. Jin Zhu worried about her, sensing vaguely that a turning point, for the worse and not the better, had arrived in Long Sixiang's life.

"In that sealed box of a workshop, Sixiang and I vowed to pursue our own happiness," she said.

Jin Zhu believed herself to have the best life among the three women, so she felt she had more responsibility to care for her two sisters. Their freedom today had not been easily won!

"Jin Zhu, don't be too pessimistic. From what I've observed, Sixiang is the kind of person who's always sure of herself. Just think, she died once before. In a difficult situation, would she sit and wait to be killed?" A Si said.

"You see and think clearly. I might be worrying too much."

A sorrowful look spread across Jin Zhu's face. She made a final toast toward the opium dealer's ashes and took her leave. A Si saw her to the main entrance.

Jin Zhu got into a taxi. When A Si turned around again she saw the Informant.

"If you want to meet your lover, you still can," he said.

"Where can I go to see him?" A Si's voice trembled.

"132 Sea Line Drive, the innermost machine at the free port, at two in the morning."

"Thank you."

A Si returned home and watched the tiny urn of ashes, grief overcoming her without her realizing it. She was not willing to cry, although she didn't know why not. She tried as hard as possible to remember the circumstances under which she had met A Yuan at the entrance to the cotton mill. All at once she remembered the cruel expression on his face. What was the meaning of that expression? She'd been worried on his behalf then, afraid he would end up involved in a murder. It turned out his cruelty was directed at himself. That strange accident of the fire, everything about it was obscure, shrouded by something, while another hair-raising, bone-chilling event was also pressing closer. A Si had stood in the midst of those people without fear. She was always like this, unafraid when placed in danger.

If she had known in advance about A Yuan's death scheme, would she still have blithely gone to the free port? The very words brought back the fact that she hadn't known it was the free port at first. She only now recalled that before the accident she had met Long Sixiang, who'd said she was also going to the free port. A Si had clean forgotten this incident. It stood to reason that Long Sixiang would have gone to the paper warehouse. Maybe she had stood there with A Yuan. Maybe she had actually witnessed A Yuan lose his life in the fire and not lent a hand to rescue him. Why hadn't she mentioned anything about where she'd been when the accident happened? A Si pondered Long Sixiang's attitude, feeling that she had behaved too calmly. She had probably known all about A Yuan's scheme. The human heart is unfathomable. All of those people had known A Yuan's plans, other than A Si! Had A Yuan done this so she could go on living undisturbed? A Si had to think so. It also tallied with the facts. Hadn't Jin Zhu just said she ought to seek new happiness?

A Si couldn't sit still at home, so she went back out onto the street. It was already afternoon. The city appeared listless, as if nothing had taken place. She walked at random, arriving back at the café without realizing it.

She saw that tall server again. The server kept a straight face, as though she didn't remember A Si.

A short, fat girl with a dejected look brought her coffee.

The record player was playing a song from the thirties, the sound intermittent. Most likely the record was damaged. A Si noticed she was the only customer in the entire shop.

"A Si, try a taste. It's this year's new bayberry," the girl said in a soft voice.

"How do you know my name?"

"Everyone is telling the story of that accident. We don't have any ill will, though. Please believe me."

Her expression revealed her painful grief. She seemed about to cry. A Si thought to herself that she didn't seem to be putting on a performance. Just as she thought this, she heard the girl speaking again.

"I loved that criminal A Yuan, too. He often came to our shop. This place is a kingdom of love. Just think, how could I not fall in love with him in this atmosphere? I don't resent your being with him, A Si, I only want to help you. There's a woman here who can act as a go-between for you—she always comes and goes at will between the two sides."

"Who are you talking about?" A Si asked.

"The one to the right side, there, the tall one."

A Si saw that patch of sky on the damaged ceiling rapidly darkening again until it was almost as black as the middle of the night. In the café the record player stalled, sound no longer issuing from it. The short, fat girl raised a small candle, the tiny shoots of flame fluttering. Her hair was loose, a bit like the female ghosts in the old plays.

Deep at the far end of the café appeared a spot of light. It was the tall woman also raising a candle. She was slowly moving toward the two of them.

"Silver, don't be pessimistic! Don't lose hope!" the short, fat girl suddenly said to the tall one.

The tall girl was stupefied a moment and seemed about to turn back, but she kept coming toward them. A Si thought, She's so young, maybe she hasn't even finished high school.

"I am that history," she said to A Si, a thread of a bitter smile on her face.

"What history?" A Si asked her.

"The history of the cotton mill. Don't believe my outer appearance, I am thirty-five years old. I also used to be at the cotton mill. One day I suddenly thought and saw clearly, and I became history. Isn't history thinking and seeing clearly? Don't the two of you agree?" She stuck the candle to the table. No one answered her question.

A Si noticed that the short girl was already nowhere to be seen. The café was extremely dark and gloomy.

"Silver, you've left your suffering behind, how wonderful," A Si said.

"A Si, feel my arm," she said in a quiet voice.

A Si reached out a hand. What she touched was not her, but a few plants with thorns instead.

Silver blew out the candle with a puff, reached out a hand, and pulled A Si toward the depths of the darkness.

A Si saw up ahead what seemed to be a vast open expanse. At least three people holding candles stood there, with wide distances between them.

"What are they doing?" A Si asked.

"They're sentries. You should be familiar with them."

"Then why don't I recognize them?"

"Because you have forgotten. Let's go ask this one."

They approached a short sentry. Silver greeted him.

"Anything brought in today?"

"No. We are truly empty! Silver, who did you bring?"

"A former beauty. Stand guard well then, don't be half-hearted."

Silver, pulling A Si by the hand, walked away from the sentry.

"Silver, why did you say I was a 'former beauty'?"

"Because you are history. Isn't that right?"

A Si thought and thought, without understanding what this meant. She turned her head to look at the three sentries, but the candles in their hands had been extinguished, so that she couldn't see anything.

"These three are also history," Silver said. "Be careful of what's under your feet, A Si. I love you, I don't want you to fall. We are going to the free port."

"Every time I go there the way is different," A Si said, excited. "Are you going there to look for someone, Silver?"

"Yes. I'm going to find my fiancé. We separated ten years ago. He was conservative, he didn't approve of my profession."

"Do you mean as a server in a café?"

"No, the same profession as you. I prefer to follow my heart and do as I please."

"Oh! I feel I've become Silver's reflection. Did you also leave the cotton mill long ago and jump into the sea of business? Let me hold your hand, I can't see anything."

This time she really did take hold of Silver's hand. She heard the sound of flowing water underfoot. There were a few couples in the water fervently debating something.

"Are we crossing a bridge?" A Si asked.

"You've guessed right. Do you see that spot of light to the left? That is the free port."

A Si looked to the left, but only saw a stretch of blackness.

"Why are these people standing in the river? I sense they are unwell."

"They don't have our good fortune, they haven't become history yet. It takes suffering and waiting."

One couple started to weep. The sound of crying made A Si a bit nervous.

They crossed the bridge and stepped onto a concrete floor. Silver suddenly pushed away A Si and shouted, "Run to the left!"

Then she ran away.

Afraid, A Si stretched both arms out in front of her, moving ahead like a sleep-walker. She walked for a time this way before actually finding that faint point of light. It was a small green dot, like a firefly, that would escape attention if you weren't looking for it. Excited, A Si sped up her pace.

She collided with someone's body. She heard that person say, "I am the sentry here. I could force you back, but now I'm so curious that I've changed my mind and decided to let you pass."

"Thank you for letting me pass."

Then she stood at the entrance. Above the door was the little green lamp. The manager smiled, squinting at her, and beckoned with a hand.

"I haven't come here in a long time," A Si said uneasily.

"It doesn't make a difference. People only think of places like this at moments of peril."

He seemed to be standing there specifically to welcome A Si. She followed him into the building, her mind agitated the whole way, her eyes opened wide and looking in all directions.

It was still the pachinko hall familiar to A Si. Those machines still lined both sides of the narrow passageway in two long rows. The lights in the room were not turned on, probably to create an atmosphere. The pictures on the screens were garish and grotesque. The manager walked quite quickly at first and then came to an abrupt stop. He patted the shoulder of someone on the right. The man paused the game with a cramped movement. The manager turned his head and said to A Si, "This machine is the one A Yuan often used. He deposited many things inside."

The manager also urged the young man, "Pachinko Ball, this is A Yuan's girl-friend. You should treat her well."

He finished speaking and walked further inside. The young man dragged over a high stool and let A Si squeeze in beside him in front of the machine.

"A Si, don't you know how to operate the machine? I'll help you. Look, this is A Yuan. He was seriously injured, but he didn't want to be rescued. He was a strange person . . ."

Pachinko Ball enthusiastically explained the images on the screen to A Si, as if he were personally in their realm. Yet the things he described were not on the screen. It showed only an expanse of yellow sand. In the middle of the sand stood a crude wooden cabin, and on the roof of the cabin perched a magpie. This image did not move. A Si looked at the image until she was tired of it, while he was still full of enthusiasm for the story he was telling. When he reached exciting points he also knocked A Si with his elbow.

"A Yuan didn't bleed, not one drop of blood flowed. Look at this big scorpion, his treasured pet! The scorpion couldn't tolerate the scorching temperature. It tried with all its might to crawl out of the bottle. A Yuan had arrived at the moment of his death, but he was comforting it! The Sahara, the Sahara!"

"Don't tell me A Yuan died in the Sahara Desert?"

"Why would I deceive you, A Si? I made the arrangements after his death myself. The bone ashes remained in the desert. I brought back the scorpion. He insisted I give it to you."

"The scorpion? Ridiculous!"

"Should we go pick it up right now? You don't want to watch his video any more?"

"But I haven't seen anything!"

"That's because you aren't willing to see. If you would only use a tiny bit of effort you would see. There, look at the right side corner, A Yuan is hiding there. He's speaking, he says: 'Woman, oh, woman . . .' He's talking about you. Do you see or not? This is the scorpion, he's holding it in his hands at his chest."

A Si dutifully watched the screen but saw only the yellow sand, the wooden cabin, and that unmoving magpie. She clenched her fists with impatience and sighed. At this exact moment the manager came over.

"A Si, A Si!" he yelled as he ran. All of the people rose partway from their seats on seeing him. "Quick, come with me. A Yuan's possessions are being delivered!"

The lights turned on as A Si ran, following the manager through the narrow corridor to the depths of the pachinko hall.

A Si felt she had run for a long time. The two of them finally reached a galvanized metal door that reflected the light intensely. The manager went to push the door. Just as his hand touched it, the door made a maddening metallic screech. A Si covered her ears with both hands, her face ghostly pale. The door finally, slowly opened, and in front of her that white mini-truck appeared. A large part of the front had been burned, and the windows had all been deformed by the heat.

"It was driven back from the desert. The motor's still fine."

A Si surveyed the garage, discovering a river in front of it. Outside the sky was already fully light. There were many people washing clothes at the riverside.

"I want to keep this truck." The manager's voice became oddly morose. "I haven't slept well in a few days. If I shut my eyes, A Yuan's deeds appear in my mind. He walked a brave person's road. I'm an ordinary businessperson, I don't dare look danger straight in the face. Even so, the city still needs someone like me. Doesn't it?"

"Of course it needs you," A Si said gently. "Your free port shaped A Yuan's nature."

"A Si, A Si, do you really think so? You don't know how much it cheers me up to hear these words!"

"Of course it's true. When A Yuan and I had no home to return to, this place was our home."

"Oh, I'm relieved, so relieved! A Si, someone on that wooden bridge is waving to you."

A Si stroked the body of the white mini-truck attentively. She also opened the door and had a look inside the vehicle. She continuously said in her heart, "Goodbye, goodbye . . ."

"I have to go. I'll come back before long."

"Come, do come, A Si. Nothing in the world is easier than coming to the free port. As soon as you have the impulse, just one step and you'll arrive."

A Si walked out of the garage. A gust of wind blew from the river. She smelled the familiar fishy odor of the water.

She hadn't walked far before she saw the wooden bridge, but it was empty. A Si stood there, unable to decide whether to go onto the bridge or turn around and go home.

Silver emerged beside the post of a streetlight, her appearance completely altered. She no longer looked like a high school student, but instead looked her full thirty-five years. She slowly moved closer to A Si, her expression firm.

"A Si, I won't call you my older sister. I am older than you, and the experiences I've been through have been bitterer than yours. Just now on the bridge, I was certain the matter had been settled—thanks to the free port's manager, it was he who gave me strength. I walked to the end of the bridge, the deep water under my feet. There was a couple whispering in the water. All of a sudden I heard my boyfriend's voice by my ear. I understood, he was still wandering this world, he was loitering like me. So I could not jump down into the water. He didn't go to the free port tonight. In fact, I had foreseen that I wouldn't meet him, but I still ran there. I am always this way. What I mean is, that patch of sky in my mind is always dark. Once dark, dark to the end. Still, I adapted soon enough and play all kinds of little games in the darkness as black as a winter night. These games bring out my interest in life. A Si, A Si, what am I saying?"

"You are saying your history, Silver. I am listening," A Si said gently.

"When I emerged, his smiling face filled my entire mind, and I saw a white dove. I thought that if I went in from the right side, I would find him. The reason he and I scattered and lost each other was because I had forgotten something. If I entered from the right side, maybe I would remember what it was. I ran inside. No one noticed me. I searched the entire pachinko hall, turning the men's faces toward me so I could see them. I was spit on and cursed, and so ashamed I wanted to die. The manager assisted this insane woman. He suggested I go search around the wooden bridge outside. Then I ran out onto the bridge, and came back down from the bridge again. You see I am mad."

"You are truly happy, Silver!" A Si said from the heart.

"You mean that my boyfriend and I have met?"

"This is what I mean."

Silver fell silent. She squeezed A Si's hand tight to show her gratitude. Without realizing it, they had reached the entrance to the hot spring spa. Silver told A Si many things about her life. They were steeped in the same mood, both sentimental and yearning. Silver said that the spa was also where her free life had started. She'd been in the earliest group to come here.

The entrance to the hot springs was quiet, with not a person there. A Si wanted very much for Silver to go inside with her, to let her revisit the old places. She also planned to introduce her to Long Sixiang.

"No, A Si," Silver said firmly. "We'll go to the theater. Let's go now!"

"To listen to the Lady of the Camellias? I heard she's been ill recently."

Silver pulled A Si across the street. They boarded a public bus.

There was no one on the bus other than the driver. He was wearing sunglasses and had a rough look.

"We want to go to the theater," Silver said, standing upright by the door of the bus.

"I know, you're going to the underground rooms. That place is enough to wear down a person's will."

He violently started the bus, and then stopped it just as sharply. A Si and Silver both fell down. Then he proceeded ahead as if nothing had happened. He drove for a stretch, before saying in a loud voice, without turning his head, "I go to the whorehouses, too. The woman I have my heart set on lives in those basement rooms."

A Si thought the driver was amusing. She asked him, "Do either of us suit your liking?"

"No, I already have a beloved! I grew up listening to the Lady of the Camellias."

"Outstanding. We're going there today to find the Lady of the Camellias."

"Hmm."

None of them spoke until A Si and Silver got off the bus.

A Si followed Silver up the stairs of the fire escape all the way to the top story, then, from a little side door, onto the terrace at the roof level. Seeing the terrace deserted, A Si said in a small voice, "There's no safety barrier."

"It's convenient not to have a barrier. So many people have jumped from here!" Silver responded loudly.

She invited A Si to sit on the edge of the terrace, putting both of her own feet out into the air. A Si, still feeling afraid, leaned her body back as much as possible. Silver was not a bit scared. She swayed, humming a tune. A Si listened carefully. It turned out to be the Lady of the Camellias singing, and Silver humming along with her. Her body swung, accompanying the rhythm of the singing voice. A Si's whole body broke out in goosebumps. She kept thinking that once the singing stopped, Silver would drop down, so she silently prayed for the singing not to end.

Listening, A Si realized that the singing was not coming up from inside the building, but rather down from the sky above. The Lady of the Camellias couldn't be singing while sitting in a hot-air balloon, could she? Someone spoke behind them: "She's truly beautiful. No matter which part, she is so beautiful in all of them."

"Naturally. She is our city's Camellia Queen."

When A Si realized that the person speaking behind her was Gu Dabo, she hastily turned around and stood up. She ran a few steps toward the fisherman and then stopped, turning her head to look back. Silver was already gone from where she had been.

"Silver!" she wailed in grief.

Gu patted her shoulder, repeating, "Don't worry, never mind. I saw her walk away, she went downstairs."

"Really?"

"I swear."

"Who were you talking with just now?"

"I wasn't talking."

"Then it was your heart speaking. I love you, Gu."

"I love you, too, A Si. Let's go down. We'll go to my boat. My nephew's here, he's a really handsome young guy."

"I don't love handsome young guys. I love old fishermen."

"Then come with me."

When they returned to the boat it was dusk again. Someone in the nearby single-story houses was playing a sorrowful melody on the erhu. A Si listened, her tears flowing.

The nephew was on the boat hurrying back and forth making dinner. Later he finally sat down across from A Si. He was built like an athlete, a fencer.

"His name is Xigou, the Grayhound. Such a lovable name!" Gu Dabo said.

They clinked their glasses together. The nephew was not at all timid, liberally embracing A Si and feeding her with his chopsticks as though he were her lover.

"A Si, you are Grayhound's first love. He already knows you well."

"I know, Gu. He knows about me from you."

When the meal was halfway finished, A Si wanted to go out in the river wind. The nephew walked with her out of the cabin, and they stood holding each other at the prow. A Si heard couples speaking in the water. She looked up, her head back, thinking of the Lady of the Camellias' singing. She sensed the fervor in the river water rising like a tide, so she asked the nephew if he wanted to go into the river with her. The nephew had just said "yes" when she pierced the water. He dove right in after her. Gu Dabo came out of the cabin and stood musing.

A Si couldn't swim. She drifted with the waves and currents, her mouth open, the nephew at her side supporting her, holding her head above the surface of the water. This was when the Lady of the Camellias' singing descended from the sky.

"Who are you?" A Si murmured.

"I am A Yuan. I was waiting all through dinner, but you didn't recognize me."

"Your transformation is too great. Didn't you abandon me for the netherworld? Now you've also turned into Gu's nephew. What else can you turn into?"

"How could I abandon A Si? A Si is the ideal I pursue. As for Uncle Gu, I was always his nephew. He was the one who raised me. Listen to this aria, such hopeless despair! For all the despair, 'when the cart reaches the mountain, there must be a road ahead . . .'"

He boosted A Si suddenly upward. She was on the deck of the fishing boat.

"Gu Dabo, how many times can one person die?" A Si asked.

"That depends on the person's potential. If the potential is great, countless times. A Si, here's some clothing, go change in the cabin."

"Has he gone?"

"Yes. You will run into him again."

"Is he actually your nephew or is he A Yuan?"

"Both. Isn't this for the better?"

A Si changed into dry clothing, came out of the cabin, and held Gu Dabo close.

"I only love you alone."

"Nonsense, nonsense. A Si is the proud Camellia Queen. How could she shrink back? Listen to that old woman, she's going mad. So lovably insane! When we were young we were all mad for her. A Si, do you want to see her? From here, count to the seventh fishing boat, and she's there."

They went aboard that fishing boat and entered the cabin, where they saw an elderly woman wearing heavy makeup. She sat by herself before a small square table with an oil lamp on it. That face was like a mask, even the eyes did not move. She made a gesture for A Si and Gu Dabo to sit down.

"Your singing nurtured several generations of us," Gu said courteously.

Passion surged through A Si's mind. She couldn't hold her tongue.

"It's like bringing the dead back to life . . . Yes, just now I had that sensation! I lay underwater and kept sinking down toward that dark, round object, when suddenly I heard a summons. It was like an electric shock, my whole body twitched. No, not an electric shock, I haven't described it the right way. I am trying to say that your singing gave me life. Thank you."

"This is my last struggle." The Lady of the Camellias smiled, revealing crude false teeth.

"I saw you in the sanatorium in the capital. You were as beautiful as an immortal. At the places where you had walked, flower petals littered the ground. I feel like this happened not so long ago." Gu Dabo's eyes misted over as he spoke.

"Thank you both. You are speaking of another person. That was the former Lady of the Camellias. For these ten years, the Lady of the Camellias has been in decline. Although she continues to struggle."

"You have astonishing energy. We adore you, madam," A Si said. "You are beauty, we believe it in our hearts." She also turned to Gu Dabo and said, "You don't know how inspired I am! I've conquered my enemies."

As they parted from the elderly woman, A Si held her hands tight in both of her own, moved to the point that her voice trembled.

"You are a miracle, madam! You must promise me to keep living forever."

"I promise you, Miss A Si."

A Si and Gu Dabo walked along the dim levee. A Si turned back and saw the oil lamp in the Lady of the Camellias' cabin already extinguished.

"A Si, you should also promise me."

"Promise you what?"

"What the Lady of the Camellias just promised."

"I promise you. I will always love you."

From that dark cabin came singing. At first it was chilling, then by degrees it grew livelier. The moon rose clear to the middle of the sky, scattering its silvery light toward the earth.

"A Si, you were right. She is a miracle. Who do you think that is?"

A Si saw a crookbacked elderly man walk toward the fishing boat. He ignited the lighter in his hand and raised it high, marking out a circle. He was making a signal.

"Who else could it be? The Lady of the Camellias' lover, of course."

The elderly man received no response the whole time he stood there.

"The two of them are separated by a Pacific Ocean," Gu Dabo said.

"Such a beautiful affair!" A Si said.

"A Si, we will part. Someone is waiting for you at home. Goodbye."

"Goodbye."

A Si had just come down the embankment when she saw the free port's manager. He rolled down the window of his car and waved to her, shouting, "A Yuan's truck will charge out of the free port tonight!"

The white car swayed a moment and was gone from sight.

Someone put an arm around A Si's shoulder. The fragrance of roses floated in the air. It was Silver.

"Silver, I was so worried about you!"

"I am a champion tested by long trials. I come to invite you, A Si. Come to the café later. When you reach it, then you will reach the free port. There are a few other entrances, naturally, but none as direct!"

Silver clapped A Si briskly on the shoulder, turned, and walked toward a store off to the side. Her tall, lean shadow disappeared at the door in the blink of an eye. It was a shop that sold smuggled cigarettes.

A Si felt curious, so she went up to the shop's display window and tried to peer inside. She saw again the things she had seen before at the free port—on a large screen, an expanse of yellow sand, the same wooden cabin in the middle of the sand, and the magpie perched on top. The door of the cabin slowly opened. A Si's mouth opened in anticipation, and her body wouldn't stop shaking. Yet there was nothing.

"Silver! Silver!" she cried.

A young girl's head emerged from the door. She said mildly, "Don't shout. Quiet now, that's better. Do you want to come in and sit down?"

A Si walked over and the girl dragged her into the building.

A Si remembered that there had been a business here before, a room arrayed with all different styles of hats and shoes. Now the shop room was empty. There were only a few large computer screens flickering in the darkness. The young woman said to A Si, "Your friend is here, too."

A Si saw a woman sitting motionless on the sofa.

"Hello. I am Wei Bo's girlfriend, my name is Cuilan. Please sit down."

The young woman pressed A Si into a seat on the long sofa and walked away.

"I know you are A Si, Wei Bo's former girlfriend. I've always wanted to meet you."

"Wei Bo is a very good man, but I'm not worthy of him. Even though I can't see very well what you look like, I know you're a beautiful woman, Cuilan. Seeing you, there is much less pain in my heart."

A Si held Cuilan's hand. She felt the strength that this woman's composure brought her.

"Wei Bo is the kind of man—he puts you at ease, he is impossible to forget, but then he rejects you entirely. Isn't that right?"

"You're very right!" A Si answered. "That's because he fell in love with you. The love between us was only like siblings, so he never rejected me."

"Tell me about your lover, A Si."

"My lover—he decided to torment me after he dies. He's the best lover in the world, of course, the kind who loves to the end, without holding anything back. He's in the Sahara Desert for now."

"I just saw a short video about him. It was very beautiful. I thought, now that he won't be returning, now that he is determined to love in this fashion, A Si should drum up the courage to start her new life over. This is the hope of the warrior. What do you say?"

"Exactly. I've just been searching for the entrance to a new life. Cuilan, Cuilan, Wei Bo truly has good fortune. He's still in prison, isn't he?"

"He's in prison enjoying his good fortune. He doesn't mistreat himself! He sent someone to speak with me, to tell me not to wait for him because he doesn't plan to get out of prison. A Si, while I was sitting here waiting for you, I wanted to say to you: let's each start new lives. How can people like us not have our own lives? As for Wei Bo and A Yuan, be done with them. All that belongs to the past, the sooner forgotten the better. Do you agree?"

"Cuilan, you're right! I admire you so much. Look, I can hold my head high again! Now I'll go to Gu Dabo's and tell him this good news. Will you go with me?"

"I will wait here for my new lover. He's hurrying here from the capital. A Si, go quickly. Go try your luck!"

Early in the morning A Si hurried to the riverside. She had slept well the previous night and felt the vigor of her body restored. At daybreak she had seen in a dream a well in the middle of the desert. The well had a narrow mouth and was too deep for her to see the bottom. She used her hands to ladle the water, but could never drink. Every time her hands neared her lips, the water flowed away. At last she bent over the burning ground, lengthening her neck to lap the water like a dog. She lapped for a long time before gradually quenching her thirst. As she drank the water, A Yuan kept saying in her ear, "A Si, A Si, what are you doing?"

The fishing boat looked a bit different. Oh, there was a gold pennant stuck to the prow and waving in the wind! Bubbling with enthusiasm, A Si went aboard. However, she saw an unknown man coming out of the cabin.

"Are you here looking for him? He's transferred the fishing boat to me. Please have a seat. I'm his good friend, a friend in the same line of work for over twenty years."

A Si saw a tuft of hair like a cockscomb standing upright on the man's head, and he had triangular eyes. He didn't look vicious and was even a bit comical. He would be about forty.

"My Gu Dabo always has fantastic plans!" A Si sighed. "Do you know where he went?"

"Where else could he go? Naturally, he went to sea. I'm called Liusha, or Shifting Sand. I know you are called A Si. Let's shake hands. His friend is my friend. You truly deserve to be called the city's Camellia Queen."

His hands were as rough as files; however, they were warm.

"Would you like to drink a little red wine?"

"Yes."

"A toast to our acquaintance!"

"Cheers! I think I've fallen in love with you." A Si's face was red with excitement. "We aren't just meeting now. I've seen you many times inside the free port. For many years I've wanted to speak with you. Your expression looked like you also wanted to speak with me. Why didn't we open our mouths? Liusha, why do you think that is?"

"For me, it was because you had A Yuan, and he was the one you loved."

"Ha, it was probably because of your noble bearing that I didn't change my affections."

"But A Yuan has only been dead for two days."

"It looks like I'm an incurable fallen woman."

"Gu Dabo was right, you are worthy to be called the Camellia Queen."

"I want to walk with you along the riverbank."

A Si held Liusha tight around the waist, the same way she had embraced Gu Dabo. In the haze a steamer was starting on its journey. The sound of the steam whistle made tears flow down her face. Liusha watched her as if he had his own thoughts. He caressed her shoulders, saying gently, "Cry, just cry. Our warrior must be content."

"You're wrong, I am crying for Gu Dabo. You don't know how much I love him. Of all people, he is the one I love the most . . . Now he's gone, the love between us has also become a thing of the past. They've left one after another, and now you've come. I love you, I won't let go of you."

Liusha did not make a sound. He felt all words were superfluous. Episodes from the past were in his eyes. How many years had it been? Eight years? Ten years? Whenever he returned from sea he went to the free port and sat in that corner waiting for A Si to appear. A Si was the sun in his heart. He didn't dare look straight at her; his heart revolved around her. In the free port smoke wound upward, the people drifted like shadows, entirely insubstantial. Only A Si was different. Rays of light radiated all around her . . . Not once had he failed to feel astonished, from the bottom of his heart: how could the earth hold such a miracle? The miracle now became reality. Why did his heart shiver, instead of feeling happy? Was he too nervous?

"Liusha, do you want to go to the Camellia Apartments?"

"I can't resist. I've secretly kept watch in the flower garden below your building, during a lonely winter, on the dull days when I was on leave."

When they came to the front of the building, just as A Si expected, the Informant stood at the iron gate to the apartment units holding a bouquet of roses in his hands.

"Miss Si, congratulations! He's a dignified young man!" he said.

"A fifty-year-old young man," Liusha corrected him.

The Informant followed them upstairs, entered the room, and then placed the flowers in A Si's vase. His eyes for the first time betrayed his heartsickness. A wisp of gray and white hair hung loose over his forehead.

"Miss Si, I will disappear from the apartment complex. After today you will have better guards to defend you."

"You are my good news, uncle!"

They held each other, then the elderly man walked out without turning back.

The two rattan chairs were still out on the balcony. Liusha understood with a look the things that had happened here.

"I'll go make you something to eat, A Si. I brought the best champagne."

He went into the kitchen as he spoke, and A Si followed him. With the *hua hua* sound of the running water, A Si's heart began singing like a little bird.

The phone in the living room rang.

"Is it Sixiang? What? Going to Iceland? Lao Yong's going with you? Wonderful! Give him my best . . . Don't know whether you'll come back? How can you be so pessimistic? Listen to me: it's no use being this way! You'll be fine . . . Promise me! What?"

"They've decided to ensnare each other to death," A Si said, in low spirits.

"No, they won't, A Si. I've seen this many times. In the end there must always be a way out: 'dark willows, bright flowers, a village appears.' Just believe me." As he spoke his triangular eyes were full of laughter.

"Yes, I believe you," A Si said, standing on tiptoe to kiss him.

Can Xue, pseudonym of Deng Xiaohua, is the author of many novels, volumes of literary criticism and philosophy, and short works of fiction. Formerly a tailor, she began writing fiction in 1983. *Love in the New Millennium* is her ninth book to appear in English. Her novel *The Last Lover* (Yale University Press, 2014) won the Best Translated Book Award for Fiction and was named a Book of the Year by the *Independent*. She lived in Changsha, Hunan province, in the south of China until 2001 and now lives in Beijing, where she writes every day (even during festivals) and jogs every day, too.

Annelise Finegan Wasmoen, an editor and literary translator, is Academic Director and Clinical Assistant Professor of Translation at the NYU School of Professional Studies. She is also a Ph.D. candidate in comparative literature at Washington University in St. Louis. Her translations from Chinese include novels, plays, and short stories by prominent contemporary and historical authors, including Can Xue's *The Last Lover*.

Eileen Myles is a poet, novelist, and art journalist living in New York City and Marfa, Texas. *Afterglow (a dog memoir)* was published by Grove in September 2017 and *Evolution* (poems) is out in fall 2018.